W9-BLA-670

WOMEN
OF
MYSTERY
III

WOMEN OF MYSTERY III

Stories from *Ellery Queen's Mystery Magazine*
and *Alfred Hitchcock's Mystery Magazine*

EDITED BY KATHLEEN HALLIGAN

CARROLL & GRAF PUBLISHERS, INC.
NEW YORK, NY

Collection copyright © 1998 by Dell Magazines

Introduction copyright © 1998 by Kathleen Halligan

All rights reserved

First Carroll & Graf edition 1998

Carroll & Graf Publishers, Inc.
19 West 21 Street
New York, NY 10010

Library of Congress Cataloging-in-Publication Data is available
ISBN: 0-7867-0570-1

We are grateful to the following for permission to reprint their copyrighted material:

"A Fine Set of Teeth" by Jan Burke, copyright © 1998 by Jan Burke, reprinted by permission of the author; "The Maggody Files: Spiced Rhubarb" by Joan Hess, copyright © 1991 by Davis Publications, Inc., reprinted by permission of the author; "The Man Kali Visited" by Janice Law, copyright © 1995 by Janice Law, reprinted by permission of the author; "The Roots of Death" by Margaret Maron, copyright © 1969 by Margaret Maron, reprinted by permission of the author; "Scars" by Kristine Kathryn Rusch, copyright © 1995 by Kristine Kathryn Rusch, reprinted by permission of the author; "Death in Small Doses" by B.K. Stevens, copyright © 1994 by B.K. Stevens, reprinted by permission of the author; all stories previously appeared in ALFRED HITCHCOCK'S MYSTERY MAGAZINE, published by Dell Magazines a division of Crosstown Publications.

"Secondhand Rose" by Joyce Christmas, copyright © 1993 by Joyce Christmas, reprinted by permission of The Evan Marshall Agency; "Once Upon A Time" by Amanda Cross, copyright © 1987 by Amanda Cross, reprinted by permission of Ellen Levine Literary Agency, Inc.; "Justina" by Dorothy Salisbury Davis, copyright © 1989 by Dorothy Salisbury Davis, reprinted by permission of McIntosh & Otis, Inc.; "The Bottle Dungeon" by Antonia Fraser, copyright © 1992 by Antonia Fraser, reprinted by permission of Curtis Brown Ltd.; "Accommodation Vacant" by Celia Fremlin, copyright © 1993 by Celia Fremlin, reprinted by permission of Gregory & Radice Author's Agents; "The Last, Best Chance" by Suzanne Jones, copyright © 1996 by Suzanne Jones, reprinted by permission of the author; "Caribbean Clues" by Patricia McGerr, copyright © 1984 by Patricia McGerr, reprinted by permission of Curtis Brown Ltd.; "The Last Open File" by Marcia Muller, copyright © 1997 by Marcia Muller, reprinted by permission of the author; "Solitary Journey" by Shizuko Natsuki, copyright © 1994 by Shizuko Natsuki, reprinted by permission of Woodbell Co., Ltd.; "Sic Transit Gloria" by Barbara Paul, copyright © 1997 by Barbara Paul, reprinted by permission of the author; "Unacceptable Levels" by Ruth Rendell, copyright © 1994 by Kingsmarkham Enterprises, reprinted by permission of Sterling Lord Literistic; "Fair and Square" by Margaret Yorke, copyright © 1982 by Margaret Yorke, reprinted by permission of Curtis Brown, Ltd.; all stories previously appeared in ELLERY QUEEN'S MYSTERY MAGAZINE, published by Dell Magazines a division of Crosstown Publications.

"Skin Deep" by Sara Paretsky, copyright © 1986 by Sara Paretsky, reprinted by permission of Dominick Abel Literary Agency, Inc.

Special thanks to Cynthia Manson for creating the *Women of Mystery* series, which I now have the privilege of continuing.

Thanks are also due to Cathleen Jordan and Janet Hutchings for their editorial suggestions.

Last, but certainly not least, thanks to Herman Graf for believing in this project.

CONTENTS

INTRODUCTION

Carrying on in the tradition of *Women of Mystery I* and *II*, we have once again turned to the pages of *Ellery Queen's Mystery Magazine* and *Alfred Hitchcock Mystery Magazine* to mine their vast archives for stories of mystery and suspense featuring strong female protagonists. Whether they are solving a crime as a private eye or detective or masterminding a crime, they are all women of mystery.

The stories in this collection reflect a unique feminine point of view. The characters run the gamut from familiar series characters and amateur sleuths to average women who find themselves in extraordinary circumstances. The thread that runs through all of these stories is that the main characters are all strong, independent women from all walks of life—journalists, police detectives, private eyes, amateur sleuths, housewives. Some stumble upon crimes, others are paid to track down criminals. Their stories have a feminine sensibility, address issues that are relevant to women, and at the same time are compelling and thought-provoking.

We have gathered together a hodgepodge of female sleuths from various mystery genres in this collection; from the hard-boiled private eyes of Marcia Muller, Sara Paretsky, and Barbara Paul to the cozy amateur sleuths of Amanda Cross, Dorothy Salisbury Davis, and Antonia Fraser.

Mystery fans may be acquainted with such familiar series characters as Marcia Muller's Sharon McCone, who feels compelled to close her "Last Open File" before leaving the All Souls Legal Cooperative for her new detective agency; Sara Paretsky's V. I. Warshawski, who travels to an exclusive beauty parlor in the Windy City at the behest of her pal Sal to solve a crime her sister is accused of committing; and Barbara Paul's Detective Gloria Sanchez, who investigates the tragic death of three young children.

On the cozy side, Antonia Fraser's Jemina Shore, a TV investigative journalist, spends New Year's at a Scottish castle where a member of the house party is murdered; Patricia McGerr's Selena Mead, government agent, uses her keen deductive skills to solve yet another curious puzzle; and Amanda Cross's Kate Fansler, amateur sleuth and professor of Victorian literature, is asked to shed light on the tangled mystery surrounding a friend's origin.

Some authors offer insight into working relationships among family member's. B. K. Stevens plays on family dynamics when dutiful Iphigenia gives up a fiancee and career in law enforcement to form an agency with her mother, Professor Woodhouse. Joan Hess introduces us to Arly Bee, chief of police in Maggody and her strong-willed mother, Ruby Bee, who strong-arms her daughter into investigating the mysterious disappearance of a local woman.

In addition to this impressive lineup are authors whose stories provide insight into the feminine psyche. Motivations of jealousy, guilt, and revenge are explored in stories by Ruth Rendell, Shizuko Natsuki, Kristin Kathryn Rusch, and Suzanne Jones.

Once again travel down the mysterious corridors and dimly lit alleys where our women of mystery are on the beat.

Turn the page and enjoy the journey!

—Kathleen Halligan

WOMEN
OF
MYSTERY
III

THE LAST OPEN FILE

by Marcia Muller

First Case

The big Victorian slumped between its neighbors on a steeply sloping side street in San Francisco's Bernal Heights district: tall, shabby, and strangely welcoming in spite of its sagging roofline and blistered chocolate paint. I got out of my battered red MG and studied the house for a moment, then cut across the weedy triangular park that bisected Coso Street and climbed the front steps. A line of pigeons roosted on the peak above the door; I glanced warily at them before slipping under and obeying a hand-lettered sign that told me to "Walk Right In!"

It seemed an unnecessary risk to leave one's door open in this low-rent area, but when I entered I came face-to-face with a man sitting at a desk. He had fine features and a goatee, and was dressed in the flannel-shirt-and-Levi's uniform of the predominantly gay Castro district; although his dark eyes were mild and friendly, he was scrutinizing me very carefully. I presented my business card—one of the thousand I'd had printed on credit at my friends Daphne and Charlie's shop—and his expression became less guarded. "You're Sharon McCone, Hank's detective friend!" he exclaimed.

I nodded, although I didn't feel much like a detective anymore. For the past few years I'd worked under the license of one of the city's large investigative firms; the day I'd received my own ticket from the state Department of Consumer Affairs, my boss had

1

fired me for insubordination. At first I'd seen it as an opportunity to strike out on my own, but operating out of my studio apartment on Guerrero Street was far from an ideal situation; jobs were few, I was about to run out of cards, and my rent was due next Thursday. Yesterday I'd run into Hank Zahn, a former housemate from my college days at U.C. Berkeley. He'd asked me to stop by his law firm for a talk.

I'd hoped the talk would be about a job, but from the looks of this place I doubted it.

The man at the desk seemed to be waiting for more of a response. Inanely I said, "Yes," to reinforce the nod.

He got up and stuck out his hand. "Ted Smalley—secretary, janitor, and—occasionally—court jester. Welcome to All Souls Legal Cooperative."

I clasped his slender fingers, liking his smile.

"Hank's in conference with a client right now," Ted went on. "Why don't you make yourself comfortable in the parlor." He motioned to his right, at a big blue room with a fireplace and a butt-sprung maroon sofa and chair. "I'll tell him you're here."

I went in there, noting an old-fashioned upright piano and a profusion of books and games on the coffee table. A tall schefflera grew in the window bay; its pot was a pink toilet. I sat on the couch and immediately a coil of spring prodded my rump. Moving over, I glared at where it pushed through the upholstery.

Make myself comfortable, indeed!

Ted Smalley had disappeared down the long central hall off the foyer. I looked around some more, wondering what the hell Hank was doing in such a place.

Hank Zahn was a Stanford grad and had been at the top of his law-school class at Berkeley's Boalt Hall. When I'd last seen him he was packing his belongings prior to turning over his room in the brown-shingled house we'd shared on Durant Street to yet another of an ongoing chain of tenants that stretched back into the early sixties and for all I knew continued unbroken to this very day. At the time, he was being courted by several prestigious law firms, as he'd joked that the salaries and benefits they offered were enough to make him sell out to the establishment. But Hank was a self-styled leftist and social reformer, a Vietnam vet weaned from the military on Berkeley's radical politics; selling out wasn't within his realm of possibility. I could envision him as a public defender or an ACLU lawyer or a loner in private practice, but what was this cooperative business?

As I waited in the parlor, though, I had to admit the place had the same feel as the house we'd shared in Berkeley: laid-back and homey, brimming with companionship, humming with energy and purpose. Several people came and went, nodding pleasantly to me but appearing focused and intense. I'd come away from the Berkeley house craving solitude as strongly as when I'd left my parents rambling, sibling-crowded place in San Diego. Not so with Hank, apparently.

Voices in the hallway now. Hank's and Ted Smalley's. Hank hurried into the parlor, holding out his hands to me. A tall, lean man, so loose-jointed that his limbs seemed linked by paper clips, he had a wiry Brillo pad of brown hair and thick horn-rimmed glasses that magnified the intelligence in his eyes; in the type of cords and sweaters that he'd always favored, he looked more the college teaching assistant than the attorney. He clasped my hands, pulled me to my feet, and hugged me. "I see you've already done battle with the couch," he said, gesturing at the protruding spring.

"Where did you get that thing—the city dump?"

"Actually, somebody left it and the matching chair and hassock on the sidewalk on Sixteenth Street. I recognized a bargain and recycled them."

"And the piano?"

"Ted's find. Garage sale. The same with the schefflera."

"Well, you guys are nothing if not resourceful. You want to tell me about this place?"

"In a minute." He steered me to the hallway. "Wait till you see the kitchen."

It was at the rear of the house: a huge room equipped with ancient appliances and glass-fronted cupboards; dishes cluttered the drainboard of the sink, a stick of butter melted on its wrapper on the counter, and a long red phone cord snaked across the floor and disappeared under a round oak table by a window that gave a panoramic view of downtown. A book titled *White Trash Cooking* lay broken-spined on a chair. Hank motioned for me to sit, fetched coffee, and pulled up a chair opposite me.

"Great, isn't it?" he said.

"Sure."

"You're probably wondering what's going on here."

I nodded.

"All Souls Legal Cooperative works like a medical plan. People who can't afford the bloated fees many of my colleagues charge buy a membership, its cost based on a scale according to their incomes. The membership gives them access to counsel and legal services all the way from small claims to the U.S. Supreme Court. Legal services plans're the coming thing, an outgrowth of the poverty law movement."

"How many people're involved?"

"Seventeen, right now."

"You making any money?"

"Does it look like we are? No. But we sure are having fun. Most of us live on the premises—offices double as sleeping quarters, and there're some bedrooms on the second floor—and that offsets the paltry salaries. We pool expenses, barter services such as cooking and taking out the trash. There're parties and potlucks and poker games. Right now a Monopoly tournament's the big thing."

"Just like on Durant."

"Uh-huh. You remember Anne-Marie Altman?"

"Of course." She'd been an off-and-on resident at Durant, and a classmate of Hank's.

"Well, she's our tax attorney, and one of the people who helped me found the co-op."

"Why, Hank?"

"Why a co-op? Because it's the most concrete way I can make a difference in a world that doesn't give a rat's ass about the little people. I learned at Berkeley that bombs and bricks aren't going to do a damned thing for society; maybe practicing law the way it was meant to be practiced will."

He looked idealistic and earnest and—in spite of the years he had on me—very young. I said, "I hope so, Hank."

He must have sensed my doubt and felt a twinge of his own, because for a moment his gaze muddied. Then he said briskly, "So, how's business?"

I made a rueful face, glancing down at my ratty sweater and faded jeans. The heels on my leather boots were worn down, and the last time it had rained, water leaked through the right sole. "Bad," I admitted.

"Thinking of looking for permanent employment?"

"With my references?" I snorted. " 'Doesn't take direction well, nonresponsive to authority figures, inflexible, and overly independent. Can be pushy, severe, and dominant.' That was my last review before the agency canned me. Forget it."

"Jesus, that could describe any one of us at All Souls."

"Maybe it's a generational flaw."

"Maybe, but it's us. You want a job here?"

"Do I want . . . *what?*"

"We're looking for a staff investigator."

"Since when?"

He grinned. "Since yesterday, when I ran into you in front of City Hall and started thinking about all the nonlegal work we've been heaping on our paralegals."

"Such as?"

"Nothing all that exciting, I'm afraid. Filing documents; tracking down witnesses; interviewing same; locating people, and serving subpoenas. Pretty dull work, when you get right down to it, but the after-hours company is good. We're all easygoing; we'd leave you alone to do your work in your own way."

"Salary?"

"Low. Benefits, practically nil."

"I couldn't live in; I've kind of OD'd on the communal stuff."

"We couldn't accommodate you, anyway. The only available space is a converted closet under the stairs—which, incidentally, would be your office. I might be able to raise the salary a little to help with your rent."

"What about expenses? My car—"

"Is a hunk of junk. But we'll pay mileage. Besides . . ." He paused, eyes dancing wickedly.

I remembered that look, from just before he'd raked in the pot at many a Durant Street poker game. "What?"

"I can offer you a first case that'll intrigue the hell out of you."

A steady job, bosses who would leave me alone, a first case that would intrigue the hell out of me. What more was I looking for?

"You've got yourself an investigator," I told him.

Hank's client, Marnie Morrison, was one of those soft, round young women who always remind me of puppy dogs—clingy and smiley and eager to please. A thinly veiled anxiety in her big blue eyes and the way most of her statements turned up as if she were asking a question told me that the puppy had been mistreated and wasn't too sure she wouldn't be mistreated again. She sat across from me at the round table and related her story—crossing and recrossing her blue-jeaned legs, twisting a curl of fluffy blond hair around her finger, glancing up at Hank for approval. Her mannerisms were so distracting that it took me a few minutes to realize I'd read about her in the paper.

"His name, it was Jon Howard. I met him on the sorority ski trip to Mammoth over spring break. In the bar at the lodge where we were staying? He was there by himself and he looked nice and my roommate Terry, she kind of pushed me into going over and talking. He was kind of sweet? So we had some drinks and made a date to ski together the next day and after that we were together all the time."

"Jon was staying at the lodge?"

"No, this motel down the road. I thought it was kind of funny, since he told me he was a financier and sole owner of this company with holdings all over Europe and South America. I mean, the motel was cheap? But he said it was quieter there and he didn't like big crowds of people, he was a very private person. We spent a lot of time there because I was rooming with Terry at the lodge, and we did things like get takeout and drink wine?" Marnie glanced at Hank. He nodded encouragingly.

"Anyway, we fell in love. And I decided not to go back to USC after break. We came to San Francisco because it's our favorite city. And Jon was finalizing a big business deal, and after that we were going to get married." The hurt-puppy look became more pronounced. "Of course, we didn't."

"Back up a minute, if you would," I said. "What did you and Jon talk about while . . . you were falling in love?"

"Our childhoods? Mine was good—I mean, my parents are nice and we've always had enough money. But Jon's? It was awful. They were poor and he always had to work and he never finished high school. But he was self-taught and he'd built this company with all these holdings up from nothing."

"What kind of company?"

Frown lines appeared between her eyebrows. "Well, a financial company, you know? It owned . . . well, all kinds of stuff overseas?"

"Okay," I said, "you arrived here in the city when?"

"Two months ago."

"And did what?"

"Checked into the St. Francis. We registered under my last name—Mr. and Mrs. Jon Morrison?"

"Why?"

"Because of Jon's business deal. He'd made some enemies, and he was afraid they'd get to him before he could wrap it up. Besides, the credit card we were using was in my name." Her mouth drooped. "The American Express card my father gave me when I went to college. I . . . guess that was the real reason?"

"So you registered at the St. Francis and . . . ?"

"Jon was on the phone a lot on account of his business deal? I got my hair done and shopped. Then he hired a limo and a driver and we started looking at houses. As soon as the deal was finalized and his money was wire-transferred from Europe we were going to buy one. We found the perfect place on Vallejo Street in Pacific Heights, only it needed a lot of remodeling, we wanted to put in an indoor pool and a tennis court? So Jon wrote a postdated deposit check and hired a contractor and a decorator and then we went shopping for artwork because Jon said it was a good investment. We bought some nice paintings at a gallery on Sutter Street and they were holding them for us until the check cleared."

"What then?"

"There were the cars? We ordered a Mercedes for me and a Porsche for Jon. And we looked at yachts and airplanes, but he decided we'd better wait on those."

"And Jon wrote postdated checks for the cars?"

Marnie nodded.

"And the rest went on your American Express card?"

"Uh-huh."

"How much did you charge?"

She bit her lip and glanced at Hank. "The hotel bill was ten thousand dollars. The limo and the driver were over five. And there was a lot of other stuff? A lot." She looked down at her hands.

I met Hank's eyes. He shrugged, as if to say, "I told you she was naive."

"What did your parents have to say about the credit-card charges?" I asked.

"They paid them, at least that's what the police said. Or else I'd be in jail now?"

"Have you spoken with your parents?"

She whispered something, still looking down.

"I'm sorry, I didn't catch that."

"I said, I can't face them."

"And what about Jon?" I recalled the conclusion of Marnie's tale from the newspaper account I'd read, but I wanted to hear her version.

"A week ago? They came to our hotel room—the real-estate agent and the decorator and the salesman from the gallery. The checks Jon wrote? They'd all bounced, and they wanted him to make good on them. Only Jon wasn't there. I thought he'd gone downstairs for breakfast while I was in the shower, but he wasn't anyplace in the hotel, he'd packed his things and gone. All that was left was a pink carnation on my pillow."

It was difficult to feel sorry for her; she had, after all, refused to recognize the blatant signs of a con job. But when she raised her head and I saw the tears slipping over her round cheeks, I could feel her pain. "So what do you want me to do, Marnie?"

"Find him."

"Aren't the police trying to do that?"

She shook her head. "Since the checks were postdated they were only like . . . promises to pay? The police say it's a civil matter, and all but one of the people Jon wrote them to have decided not to press charges. The decorator had already spent a lot of money out of pocket ordering fabric and stuff, so she hired a detective to trace Jon, but he's disappeared."

I thought for a moment. "Okay, Marnie, suppose I do locate Jon Howard. What then?"

"I'll go to him and get the money to pay my parents back. Then I can face them again."

"It doesn't sound as if he has any money."

"He must." To my astonished look she added, "All of this has been a terrible mistake. Maybe he ran away because his business rivals were after him? Maybe the big deal he was working on fell through and he was ashamed to tell me? When you find him, he'll explain everything."

"You sound as though you still believe in him."

"I do. I always will. I love him."

"She's got to be insane!" I said to Hank. Marnie Morrison had just left for the cheap residential hotel that was all she could afford on her temporary office worker's wages.

"No, she's naive and doesn't want to believe the great love of her life was a con artist. I figure meeting up with Jon Howard in his true incarnation'll cure her of that."

"Then you actually want me to find him?"

"Yeah. I'd like to get a look at him, find out what makes a guy like that tick."

As a matter of fact, so would I.

* * *

The recession-hungry merchants who had been taken in by the supposedly rich young couple were now engaged in various forms of face-saving.

Dealer Henry Richards of the Avant Gallery on Sutter Street: "Mr. Morrison was *very* knowledgeable about art. He asked all the right questions. He knew which paintings would appreciate and which would not. Had he followed through on the purchase, he would have had the beginnings of a top-flight collection. He may not have been rich, but I could tell he was well educated, and there's no concealing good breeding."

Realtor Deborah Lakein of Bay Properties: "From the moment I set eyes on the Morrisons I knew something was wrong. At first I thought it was simply the silk-purse-out-of-sow's-ear effect: too much money, too little breeding. But they seemed serious and were very enthusiastic about the property—it's a gem, asking price one million three. In this market one doesn't pass up the opportunity to make such a sale. Of course, his deposit check was postdated like the others he wrote all over town, and when I finally put it through it was returned for insufficient funds. The same was true of the checks to the contractor and decorator and landscaper I recommended. Oh, I'm in hot water with them, I am!"

Salesman Donald Neditch of European Motors on Van Ness Avenue's auto row: "Well, our customers come in all varieties, if you know what I mean. You don't have to be a blueblood to drive one of these babies. All you need is the cash or the credit. The two of them were well dressed—casually but expensively—and they arrived in a limo. I could tell they hadn't had money for very long, though. He asked a lot of questions, but they were the kind you'd ask if you were buying a pre-owned model. About used cars, he was knowledgeable enough to sell them, but I'd bet the Mercedes for his wife was the first new car he ever looked at."

Claire Wallis, clerk in the billing office at the St. Francis Hotel: "No one questioned their charges because American Express was honoring them. There was a lot of room service, a lot of champagne and fine wines. Fresh flowers every day for the three weeks they stayed here. Generous tips added to each check, too. The personnel who had dealings with them tell me she was young and sweet; he was more rough at the edges, as you'd expect a self-made man to be, but very polite. Security had no complaints about loud partying, so I assume they were as well behaved in private as in public."

Wallis referred me to an inspector in the Fraud division of the SFPD who had taken a list of calls made from the "Morrisons'" suite and had them checked out by the department before it became apparent that no criminal statutes had been violated. The copy of the list the inspector provided me showed that Jon Howard had called car dealerships from San Rafael to Walnut Creek; a yacht broker in Sausalito; aircraft dealers near SFO and Oakland Airport. The numbers for the real-estate agency and art gallery appeared frequently, as did those of contractor, decorator, and landscaper. Restaurants, theater-ticket agencies, beauty shops, and a tanning salon figured prominently. There were no calls to Marnie Morrison's parents, or to anyone who might have been a personal friend.

By now I realized that Jon Howard had covered his tracks very well. I had no photograph of him, no description beyond the one Marnie provided, and that was highly romanticized at best. I didn't even know if he had used his real name. I made my way down the list of places he'd called, though, visiting the yacht broker ("He didn't know shit about boats."), the aircraft sales agencies ("I told him he'd better take flying lessons first, but he just laughed and said he had a pilot on call."), and all the auto dealerships—including Ben Rudolph Chevrolet in Walnut Creek where Howard had called nearly every day but no one had any recollection of either him or Marnie. Finally I reached Lou Petrocelli, driver for Golden West Limousine Service.

"Sure, I got to know him pretty well, driving him around for almost three weeks," Petrocelli told me. "He was . . . well, down-home, like a lot of the rock stars I've driven. When she came along he'd get in back with her and they'd hit the bar, watch some TV. When he was alone he'd hop up front and talk my ear off. Money, it was always money. Was this house in Pacific

Heights a good investment? Did I think they oughta buy a van for the help to use for running errands? Which restaurants did the 'in' people eat at? Should he get season tickets for the opera? I thought it was funny, a guy who was supposed to be so rich and smart asking *me* for advice. He struck me as very insecure. But hell, I liked the guy. He was kind of wide-eyed and innocent in his way, and American Express was honoring the charges."

I asked Petrocelli to look over the list of establishments to which Howard had made phone calls. He confirmed he'd driven the couple to most of them, with the exception of the yacht brokers and the car dealership in Walnut Creek. They had traveled as far afield as the Napa Valley for wine tasting, and Marnie had insisted he share their hotel-catered picnic lunch. No, they'd never met with friends; Petrocelli didn't think they'd known anyone in the city except the merchants with whom they had dealings.

Around the time I reached the bottom of the list, other cases began to claim my attention. I'd been ensconced long enough in the cubbyhole under the stairs that All Souls's attorneys believed I was there to stay and began heaping my desk with tasks. They ranged from filing documents with the recorder's office to serving subpoenas to interviewing a member of the San Francisco Mime Troupe about an accident he'd witnessed—no simple matter, since his replies to my questions were in pantomime. I made some effort on the Morrison case when I could, but Marnie had stopped calling for reports. The last time I spoke with her she sounded so demoralized that three days later I stopped in at her hotel to see how she was doing; her room was empty, and the manager told me she'd checked out. Checked out in the company of a handsome young man driving an old Honda.

Jon Howard?

When I reported this latest development to Hank, he didn't seem surprised. "I had a call earlier," he said. "Some guy looking for Marnie. I was with a client, so Ted gave him her number."

"Then it probably was Howard. But how'd he know to call you?"

Hank shrugged. "You've been asking around about him, leaving your card. He could've talked to the limo driver, the real-estate broker—anybody."

"And of course she went away with him."

"She said she still loved him."

"I wonder if he plans to pull the same scam in some other city."

"Doubtful; he doesn't have her American Express card to bank roll it."

"What d'you suppose will happen to her?"

Hank shook his head. "Let's hope her dreams come true—whatever they might be."

A year later I added a follow-up note to the Marnie Morrison file: Her parents, whom Hank had contacted following her disappearance, reported that they'd begun receiving periodic money orders for a hundred dollars apiece, mailed from various Bay Area cities. They were convinced they came from Marnie, in repayment of the credit-card charges. Since they'd long before paid the bill, they wanted to give Hank a message to pass on to their daughter, should she contact him.

The message was that they loved her, she was forgiven and always welcome at home. Hank never was able to tell her.

A couple of years after that I appended a newspaper clipping to the file: The Morrisons had been killed in a fire that swept the southern California canyon where their home was located. The article rehashed the bizarre scam their daughter and her boyfriend had perpetrated and mentioned the money orders. A further odd footnote to the story ran awhile later: The money orders were now arriving at the office of the executor of the Morrisons' estate, earmarked "for my parents' favorite charity."

When I saw this last item, I was intrigued and wished I could take the time to locate Marnie. But in those early days at All Souls my caseload was heavy, and soon I was caught up in other equally intriguing matters. The Morrison case still nagged at me, though; it was my first—and last—open file.

My years at All Souls slipped by with a speed that amazed me—when I had time to think about it. On the whole, they were good years.

I closed casefiles both large and small, and even got my picture in the papers. I made lifetime friends: Anne-Marie Altman, who later would become Hank's wife; Ted Smalley, who rose from part-time secretary to operations manager; Rae Kelleher, whom I hired as my assistant when the co-op finally became solvent. Along with a fluctuating cast of partners and staff members, we organized parties and potlucks and poker games, or just sat at the big round table in the kitchen sharing triumphs and sorrows.

My personal life changed: I went from a tiny Mission district studio apartment to my very own house. I fell in and out of love, and each man turned out to be more significant than the previous. I lost one cherished cat but acquired two others. And I fell in love with flying and became a pilot.

But there were also bad times. I was forced to shoot two men, almost killed a third, and had to learn to live with the memories. It put a distance between myself and some of my colleagues—one that could never be bridged. The situations and people I encountered turned me cynical and much less willing to accept anything at face value. And I became increasingly concerned about the violent tendencies I'd discovered within myself. But by then I'd met a man who understood, because he'd been there and felt the same impulses. He sustained me through the more difficult times, does to this day.

When the All Souls partners tried to rein me in to a desk job, I knew it was the beginning of the end. I established my own agency while retaining my offices in the big Bernal Heights Victorian, but the co-op soon plunged into a spiral of acrimony and dissension, and I realized it was time to move on. Happily, Hank and Anne Marie decided to establish their own law firm and join me at my new location on a renovated waterfront pier; and we were able to take Ted and Rae along too.

The All Souls years were at an end. But not before I took a final look at my last open file . . .

File Closed

The movers had come for my office furniture. All that remained was for me to haul a few cartons to McCone Investigations' nearly new van. I hefted one and carried it down to the foyer of All Souls' big Victorian, then made three round trips for the others. Before I went downstairs for the last time I let my gaze wander around the front room that for years had been my home away from home. Empty, it looked battle-scarred and shabby: the wallpaper was peeling; the ceiling paint had blistered; the hardwood floors were scraped; there were gouges in the mantel of the non-working fire place.

A far cry from the new offices on the waterfront, I thought, but still I'd miss this room. Would miss sitting in my swivel chair in the window bay and contemplating the sagging rooflines of the Outer Mission district or the weedy triangular park below. Would miss pacing the faded Oriental carpet while talking on the phone. But most of all I would miss the familiar day-to-day sounds of the co-op that had assured me that I was among friends.

Only in the end friends here had been damned few. Now none were left. Time to say goodbye. Time to move on to McCone Investigations' new offices on one of the piers off the Embarcadero, next to the equally new offices of Altman & Zahn, Attorneys-at-Law.

I took the last carton downstairs.

Ted's old desk still stood in the foyer, but without his personal possessions—particularly the coffee mug shaped like Gertrude Stein's head and the campy lamp fashioned from a mesh-stockinged mannequin's leg—it was a slate wiped clean of the years he'd presided there. Already he'd be arranging those treasures down at the pier. I set the box with the others and, both out of curiosity and nostalgia, went along the hall to the converted closet under the stairs that had been my first office.

Rae Kelleher, its recent occupant, had already taken her belongings to McCone Investigations. With relief I saw she'd left the ratty old armchair. For a moment I stood in the door looking at each familiar crack in the walls; then I stepped inside and ran my hand over the chair's back where stuffing sprouted. How many hours had I sat there, honing my fledgling investigator's skills?

A cardboard box tucked under the angle of the staircase caught my eye. I peered at it, wondering why Rae had left it behind, and saw lettering in her hand: "McCone Files." Early ones, they must be. I'd probably neglected to remove them from the cabinet when I transferred my things upstairs. I pulled the box toward me, sat down in the armchair, and lifted the lid. A dry, dusty odor wafted up. On the files' tabs I saw names: Albritton, DiCesare, Kaufmann, Morrison, Smith, Snelling, Whelan, and many more. Some I recognized immediately, others were only vaguely familiar, and about the rest I hadn't a clue. I scanned them, remembering—

Morrison! That damned case! It was the only file I hadn't been able to close in all my years at All Souls.

I pulled it from the box and flipped through. Interesting case. Marnie Morrison, the naive young woman with Daddy's American Express card. Jon Howard, the "financier" who had used her to help him scam half the merchants in San Francisco. And Hank in turn had used the case's promise to lure me into taking the job here.

But I hadn't been able to solve it.

Could I solve it now?

Well, maybe. I was a far better investigator than when I'd operated out of this tiny office. The hundreds of hours spent honing my skills had paid off; so had my life experiences, good and bad. I picked up on facts that I might not have noticed back then, could interpret them more easily, had learned to trust my gut-level instincts, no matter how far-fetched they might seem.

I turned my attention to the file.

Well, *there* was one thing right off—the daily phone calls to the car dealership in Walnut Creek. When I'd driven out there and talked with its manager, neither he nor his salesmen could remember the memorable young couple.

I took a pen from my purse, made a note of the dealership's name, address, and phone number then read on.

And *there* was something else—the conversation I'd had with the salesman at European Motors here in the city. My recent experience with buying a "preowned" van for the agency put a new light on his comments.

My office phone had been disconnected the day before, and the remaining partners would frown on me placing toll calls on All Souls' line. Quickly I hauled the file box out to where my other cartons sat, threw on my jacket, and headed downhill to the Remedy Lounge on Mission Street.

The Remedy had long been a favorite watering hole for the old-timers at All Souls. Brian, the owner, extended us all sorts of courtesies—excluding table service for anyone but Rae, who reminded him of his dead sister, and including running tabs and letting us use his office phone. When I got there the place was empty and the big Irishman was watching his favorite soap opera on the TV mounted above the bar.

"Sure," he said in answer to my request, "use the phone all you want. Yours is turned off already?"

"Right. It's moving day."

Brian's fleshy face grew melancholy. He picked up a rag and began wiping down the already polished surface of the bar. "Guess I won't be seeing much of you guys anymore."

"Why not? The bar's on a direct line between the new offices and the Safeway where we all shop."

He shrugged. "People always say stuff like that, but in the end they drift away."

"We'll prove you wrong," I told him, even though I suspected he was right.

"We'll see." He pressed the button that unlocked the door to his office.

At his desk I opened my notebook and dialed the number of Ben Rudolph Chevrolet in Walnut Creek. I reached their used-car department. The salesman's answer to my first question confirmed what I already suspected. His supervisor, who had worked there since the late seventies, was out to lunch, he told me, but would be back around two.

Five minutes later I was in the van and on my way to the East Bay.

Walnut Creek is a suburb of San Francisco, but a city in its own right, sprawling in a broad valley in the shadow of Mount Diablo. When I'd traveled there on the Morrison case more than a decade earlier, it still had a small-town flavor: few trendy shops and restaurants in the downtown district; only one office building over two stories; tracts and shopping centers, yes, but also semi-rural neighborhoods where the residents still kept horses and chickens. Now it was a hub of commerce, with tall buildings whose tinted and smoked glass glowed in the afternoon sun. There was a new cultural center, a restaurant on nearly every corner, and the tracts went on forever.

Ben Rudolph Chevrolet occupied the same location on North Main Street, although its neighbors squeezed more tightly against it. As I parked in the customer lot I wondered why years ago I had neglected to call the phone number on the list the SFPD had supplied me. If I'd phoned ahead rather than just driven out here, I'd have discovered that the dealership maintained separate lines for its new and used-car departments. And I'd have known that Jon Howard's daily calls weren't made because he was hot on the trail of a snappy new Corvette.

I went directly to the manager of the used-car department, a ruddy-faced, prosperous-looking man named Dave Swenson. Yes, he confirmed, he'd worked there since seventy-eight. "Only way to survive in this business is you stick with one dealership, dig in, create your own clientele."

"I'm looking for someone who might've been a salesman here in the late seventies and early eighties." I showed him my ID. "Handsome man, dark hair and moustache, late twenties. Good build, below average height. His name may have been Jon Howard."

"No, it wasn't."

"I'm sorry?"

"I know the fella you're talking about, but you got it backward. His name was Howard John."

Howard John—simple transposition. The salesman at European Motors had told me he knew enough about used cars to sell them, and he'd been correct. "John's not working here anymore?"

"Hell, no. He was fired over a dozen years ago. I don't recall exactly when." Swenson tapped his temple. "Sorry, the old memory's going."

"But you remembered him right off."

"Well, he was that kind of guy. A real screw-up, always talking big and never doing anything about it, but you couldn't help liking him."

"Talking big, how?"

"Ah, the usual. He was studying nights, gonna get his MBA, set up some financial company, be somebody. He'd have a big house in the city, a limo, boats and planes, hobnob with all the right people—you know. All smoke and no fire Howie was, but you had to hand it to him, he could be an entertaining fellow."

"And then he was fired."

"Yeah. It was stupid, it didn't have to happen. The guy was producing; he made sales when nobody else could. What Howie did, he took a vacation to Mammoth to ski. When his week was up, he started calling in, saying he was sick with some bug he caught down there. This went on for weeks, and the boss got suspicious, so he checked out Howie's apartment. The manager said he hadn't been back since he drove off with his ski gear the month before. So a few days after that, when Howie strolled in here all innocent and business-as-usual, the boss had no choice but to can him."

"What happened to him? Do you know where he's working now?"

Swenson stared thoughtfully at me. "You know, I meant it when I said I liked the guy."

"I don't mean him any harm, Mr. Swenson."

"No?" He waited.

Quickly I considered several stories, rejected all of them, and told Swenson the truth. He reacted with glee, laughing loudly and slapping his hand on his desk. "Good for Howie! At least he got a few weeks of the good life before everything went down the sewer."

"So will you tell me where I can find him?"

"I still don't know why you want him."

I hesitated, unsure myself as to why I did. No one was looking for Howard John anymore, and the organization that had assigned me to locate him had ceased to exist. Finally I said, "When you have a sale pending that you think is a sure thing and then it falls through, does it nag at you afterwards?"

"Sure, for years, sometimes. I wonder what I did wrong, why it didn't fly."

"I'm the same way about my cases. This is my last open file from the law firm where I used to work. Closing it will tie off the loose ends."

"Well . . ." Swenson considered some more. "Okay. I don't know if Howie's still there, but I saw him working another lot about three months ago—Roy's Motors, up in Concord."

Concord was a city to the north. I thanked Swenson and hurried out to the van.

Concord, like Walnut Creek, had developed into a metropolis since I once worked a case at its performing arts pavilion, but the windswept frontage road where Roy's Motors was located was a throwback to the early sixties. An aging shopping center with a geodesic dome-type cinema and dozens of mostly dead stores adjoined the used-car lot; both were almost devoid of customers. Faded plastic flags fluttered limply above Roy's stock, which consisted mainly of vehicles that looked as though they'd welcome a trip to the auto dismantler's; a sign proclaiming it Home of the Best Deals in Town creaked disconsolately. I could make out the figure of a man sitting inside the small sales shack, but his features were obscured by the dirty window glass.

A young couple were wandering through the lot, stopping here and there to examine pickup trucks. After a few minutes they displayed more than passing interest in a canary-yellow Ford, and the man got up and came out of the shack. He was on the short side and running to paunch, with thinning dark hair, a brushy moustache, and a face that once had been handsome. Howard John?

As he approached the couple, the salesman held himself more erect and sucked in his stomach; his step took on a jaunty rhythm and a charismatic smile lit up his face. He shook hands with the couple, began expounding on the truck. He laughed; they laughed. He helped the woman into the cab, urged the man in on the driver's side. The chemistry was working, the magic flowing. This, I was sure, was the man who years before had scammed the greedy merchants of San Francisco.

A few short weeks of living like the high rollers, I thought, then dismissal from a good job and a series of steps down to this. How did he go on, with the memory of those weeks ever in the back of his mind? How did he come to this windswept lot every day and put himself through the paces?

Well, maybe his dreams—improbable as they might seem—had survived intact. He'd done it once, his reasoning might go, and he could do it again. Maybe Howard John still believed that he was only occupying a way station on the road to the top. But what about Marnie Morrison?

I found Howard John's residence by a method whose simplicity and effectiveness have never ceased to amaze me: a look-see into the phone book. The listing was in two names, and the wife's was Marnie.

The shabby residential street was not far from the used-car lot: a two-block row of identical shoebox-style tract homes of the same vintage as the shopping center. The pavement was potholed and the houses on the west side backed up on a concrete viaduct, but big poplars arched over the street and, in spite of the hum of nearby freeway traffic, it had an aura of tranquility. The house I was looking for was painted mint green and surrounded by a low chain-link fence. A sign on its gate said Sunnyside Daycare Cen-

ter, and in the yard beyond it sat an assortment of brightly colored playground equipment.

It was close to five o'clock; for the next hour I watched a steady
stream of parents arrive and depart with their offspring. Ten
minutes after the last had left, a woman came out of the house
and began collecting the playthings strewn in the yard. I peered
through my shade-dappled windshield and recognized an older
heavier version of Marnie Morrison. Clad in an oversize sweat-
shirt and leggings that strained over her ample thighs, she moved
slowly, stopping now and then to wipe sweat from her brow.
When she finished she trudged inside.

So this was what Marnie had become since I'd last seen her:
the overworked, prematurely aged wife of an unsuccessful used-
car salesman, who operated a daycare center to make ends meet.
And one of those ends was her periodic hundred-dollar atone-
ment for the credit-card binge that had bought her a few weeks
of high living and dreams.

Unsure as to why I was doing it, I continued to watch the mint-
green house. I'd found Marnie. Why didn't I give up and go back
to the city? There were things I should be doing at the new offices,
things I should be doing at home.

But I wanted an end to the story, so I stayed where I was.

Half an hour later a Ford Bronco passed me and pulled into
the Johns' driveway. Howard got out carrying a bouquet of pink
carnations. He let himself into the yard, stopping to pick up a
stuffed bear that Marnie had missed. He held the bear at arm's
length, gave it a jaunty grin, and tucked it under his arm. His
step was light as he moved toward the door. Before he got it open
his wife appeared, now dressed in a gauzy caftan, and enveloped
him in a welcoming embrace.

I'd reached the end of the tale. Leaving Marnie and Howard
to their surviving dreams and illusions, I drove back to All Souls
for the last time.

The big Victorian was mostly dark and totally silent. Only the
porch light and another far back in the kitchen shone. It was after
eight o'clock; none of the remaining partners lived in the building,

and they rarely spent more time there than was necessary. The new corporation they'd formed had the property up for sale and would move downtown as soon as a buyer was found.

Moving on, all of us.

I was about to haul the cartons I'd left in the foyer down to the van when I heard a sound in the kitchen—the familiar creak of the refrigerator door. Curiosity aroused, I went back there, walking softly. The room was dim, the light coming from a single bulb in the sconce over the sink. A figure turned from the fridge, glass of wine in hand. Hank.

He started, nearly dropping the glass. "Jesus, Shar!"

"Sorry. I'm not up to talking to any of the new guard tonight, so I tiptoed. Why aren't you down at the pier helping everybody shove the new furniture around?"

"I was, but nobody could make up their mind where it should go, and I foresaw a long and unpleasant relationship with a chiropractor in my future."

"So you came *here?*"

He shrugged. "Why not? You want some wine?"

"Sure. For old times' sake."

Hank went to the fridge and poured the last of the so-so jug variety that had been an All Souls staple. He handed it to me and motioned for me to sit at the round table by the window. As we took our places I realized that they were identical to those we'd occupied the first afternoon I'd come here.

I said, "You still haven't told me why you're here."

"You haven't told me why *you're* here."

"I meant to be gone hours ago, but wait till you hear my news!"

I explained about closing the Morrison file.

He shook his head. "You *do* believe in tying up loose ends. So what about those two—do you think they're happy?"

I hesitated. "What's happy? It's all relative. The guy still brings her flowers. She still dresses up for him. Maybe that's enough."

"But after the scams they pulled, the style they lived in?"

"It only lasted a few weeks. Maybe that was enough, too."

"Maybe." He took a long pull at his wine, took a longer look around the kitchen. His expression grew melancholy. This room and this table had been at the core of Hank's life since leaving law school.

"Don't," I said, "or you'll get me going."

His eyes moved to the window, scanning the lights of downtown. After a moment they rested and his lips curved into a smile. I knew he was looking at the section of the waterfront where the law firm of Altman & Zahn had recently rented offices next to McCone Investigations on a renovated pier.

"File closed," he said.

We finished our wine in silence. Around us the big house creaked and groaned, as it did every evening when the day's warmth faded. I felt my eyes sting, blinked hard. Only an incurable romantic would find significance in tonight's particular creaks and groans. And I, of course, had not a romantic bone in my body.

So why had that last creak sounded like "goodbye"?

Hank drained his glass and stood. Carried both to the sink, where he rinsed them carefully and set them on the drainboard. "In answer to your earlier question," he said, "I'm here because I forgot something."

"Oh? What?"

He came over and rapped his knuckles on the table where we'd eaten and drunk, played games and talked, celebrated and commiserated, fought and made up, and—now—let go. "This table and chairs're mine. Marin County Flea Market, the week after we founded All Souls. They're going along."

"To our joint conference room?"

"Mind reader. Is that okay with you?"

I nodded.

"Then give me a hand with them, will you?"

I stood, grinning. "Sure, but only if . . ."

"If what?" It was a stupid, sentimental decision—and one I was sure to regret.

"Only if you'll give me a hand with that ratty armchair in my former office. I can't imagine why Rae forgot it."

CARIBBEAN CLUES

by Patricia McGerr

Selena was at her desk paying bills when Hugh came in and dropped an illustrated folder on top of her checkbook.

"Look that over," he said. "It's time we had a vacation."

"Vacation?"

She glanced at the red-letter headline—*Six Sun-Filled Fun-Filled Days in the Caribbean*—then raised her eyes to regard her husband with skepticism. "While I bask in the sun, what will you be doing for Section Q?"

"Nothing consequential. A little courier duty."

"Really? I know budgets are being cut all over Washington, but I didn't think it had reached the point where agency heads have to run their own errands."

"What's the good of being chief," he countered, "if I can't give myself a plum assignment? Read the brochure. Look at the pictures. It's a great trip. A quarter hour for business and the rest of the week to enjoy ourselves. Aren't you tempted?"

"I might be." The cover picture was of scantily clad couples holding tall glasses and reclining in deck chairs around a sun-drenched pool. It was in sharp contrast to the snow and ice and blistering winds outside their door. "But only if you tell me the real reason for the trip."

"I have a piece of paper to deliver, that's all."

"That's not all." She swiveled her chair to look at him directly. "This is a secret operation and it's important enough, or risky enough, for you to go yourself. If I'm to be involved, even if only

25

as part of your cover as a cruising couple, I've a right to know what I'm walking—or sailing—into."

"In intelligence work," he reminded her, "nobody has rights. Information is given on a need-to-know basis and for this trip you only need to know what to pack."

"I can refuse to go."

"And send me off alone?" He grinned at her. "They say these cruise ships are filled with seductive females lying in wait for unattached men."

"In that case you might like to withdraw your invitation."

"What do you say we compromise?" Hugh said. "I'll give you a rough outline of the mission and you do without names or specific details."

"Very well," she agreed. "Just tell me what's on the paper and to whom you're going to deliver it."

"O.K., here's the plan." He sat down, pulling the chair closer to her desk. "Next Friday we'll fly to Miami and sail from there. The ship stops in four ports. During the second stop, a leader of the resistance forces of one of the Latin American countries will come aboard. There's a heavy price on his head, so his movements must be kept top secret. Going myself keeps the people who know about the meeting to a minimum."

"And when you meet, what then?"

"I have a list of names to give him and a map. People who are sympathetic to the cause, and dates and places where they will make contact. Once delivery is made, he'll get off the ship and my job is ended. You see, it's a very simple operation."

"You make it sound that way," she conceded, then let enthusiasm override her misgivings. "All right, Hugh, I'd love to cruise the Caribbean with you."

The first two days lived up to the brochure's promise. It was an unaccustomed luxury to wake in the morning with no plans, no appointments, no deadlines. They were free to concentrate on such important decisions as whether to take a brisk walk around the deck, play shuffleboard, or lie immobile and watch the smooth sea blend with an almost cloudless sky. In the evening they danced to the accompaniment of a five-piece band whose repertory bridged the generations from the waltz through ragtime to the latest hard rock. It was an idyllic time, the first extended period since their marriage that they could count on uninterrupted time together, their tranquility unbroken by newspapers or telephones. The single distraction was the list that Hugh was carrying with him. Soon, Selena told herself, he'll pass that on. Then we'll have the rest of the cruise to rest, relax, and enjoy each other.

Early in the morning of the third day the ship sailed into its first port. Many of the passengers boarded buses for a guided tour of the small island republic. Hugh and Selena chose to explore on their own, shop for souvenirs, and lunch at a restaurant recommended by friends. They were walking up the broad tree-lined avenue when a young boy, running fast, brushed Hugh's right hip and sped on to disappear up a side street.

"Your wallet!" Selena exclaimed. "Did he—"

"No, that's inside my coat. But I think—" he reached into his back pocket and pulled out a screwed-up paper"—yes, he left a message." Unfolding it, he read the words, "Call your office."

"Trouble," Selena said. "I knew things were going too well."

"Not necessarily," he returned. "It may be a minor change of plans. I've been out of touch for two days."

They reversed their steps and went to the American consulate, where Hugh's credentials procured a private room with a secure phone. Selena drank coffee with the consul's wife while he made his call. Soon he joined them, looking grim.

"Bad news?" she asked when, having declined an invitation to lunch, they were outside the consulate.

"The worst." He said no more until they were seated on a bench in the center of a small park where they could talk without fear of eavesdroppers.

"Raul," he told her then, "has been taken."

"Raul? Is that the man you're supposed to meet?"

"Yes. Word reached headquarters yesterday that he was caught in an ambush and delivered to the security police."

"Then your meeting is canceled."

"Not exactly. According to our source—an informer with links to the security forces—his capture has been kept secret. He was compelled, probably under torture, to give them full details of tomorrow's rendezvous. They're sending one of their own people in his place."

"Then you can at least be thankful that you found out in time. I gather it would be unfortunate if the data you're carrying went to the other side."

"A disaster," he confirmed. "In the wrong hands, my list would endanger some very good men."

"Will you meet the impostor or just let him dangle?"

"Oh, I'll keep the appointment. But I'll draw up a new list of names. Men who are solidly behind the government, some with important jobs. If we can start them distrusting each other, that will salvage something from Raul's loss. Come on." He rose from the bench, cheered by the thought of counterattack. "We'll have to have a quick lunch or we'll miss the sailing."

After returning to the ship, Hugh went at once to their stateroom to prepare a counterfeit message for the counterfeit Raul. Selena stayed on deck to watch the liner maneuver through the harbor's narrow passage while young islanders dove for coins tossed by the passengers.

Hugh had finished his work by the time she went down to dress for dinner, but with habitual caution they did not speak of it while in their cabin or later in the dining salon.

They were finishing dinner when the room's lights dimmed and the pastry chef emerged from the galley bearing aloft a cake lighted by candles.

"Somebody's birthday," Selena guessed as, with everyone's eyes upon him, he carried his sparkling burden toward the corner where they sat. A waiter followed with a bottle of champagne and, from the opposite direction, one of the ship's musicians, guitar in hand, came to meet them. Stopping at Selena and Hugh's table, the chef, with a flourish, placed the cake before them, the waiter uncorked the champagne, and the guitarist began to play and sing the "Anniversary Waltz." Other voices, scattered around the room, joined him.

Our anniversary was last month, Selena thought. They've come to the wrong table. I hope they can correct the mistake without too much embarrassment. She looked at Hugh, expecting him to protest, but he responded with an almost imperceptible shake of his head, reminding her of an agency rule. When the inexplicable occurs, do nothing and wait for an explanation.

As the song ended, the cruise director stepped forward to hand Hugh a white envelope.

"Happy anniversary, Mr. and Mrs. Pierce," she said. "This message came through shortly before dinner and the radio operator tipped us off. I hope you don't mind our holding it back in order to arrange the surprise."

"It was indeed a surprise." Hugh's glance circled the foursome—chef, waiter, guitarist, and cruise director. "My wife and I are very grateful. Will you blow out the candles, darling?"

"It was most kind of you." Selena smiled at them, took a deep breath, and bent toward the cake. The candles flickered and went out and the other diners applauded. The waiter poured the champagne, Selena cut the cake, and the staff members, satisfied with the celebration's success, left them alone.

Hugh tore open the envelope and, with unchanging expression, read the message silently and passed it to Selena. It was brief. "Happy Anniversary. Love from Sophie, Craig, and Doris." The greeting, she assumed, was camouflage. The coded message was in the signatures.

"Sophie, Craig, and Doris," she repeated.

"Yes, aren't they the thoughtful ones." Leaning close, his mouth at her ear, Hugh translated. "Source credibility doubtful."

"Oh." For the benefit of anyone still watching, she smiled demurely and lowered her eyes.

While they ate the cake and sipped the wine, she thought about the message. The source referred to must be the informer who had reported Raul's capture and replacement. That he should be of dubious credibility was not surprising. Informers are often turned into double agents. If they discovered he was sending reports to Section Q, they might well use him to feed us misinformation. But what would be the point of saying Raul was in custody if it wasn't true?

"Congratulations, you two." Passing their table with his wife in tow, a fellow passenger interrupted her thoughts. "How long since you tied the knot?"

"Fifteen years," Hugh answered.

"Let's hope you have fifteen more," he said heartily and moved on.

He was the first of a stream of well-wishers who followed them from the dining room, eager to help them celebrate the fictitious anniversary. They bought them drinks, offered toasts, shook Hugh's hand, kissed Selena.

"Next time," she suggested when they had a moment's privacy, "tell your colleagues to send condolences."

"I think," he returned, "it's time for the happy couple to take a walk in the moonlight."

They escaped from the lounge, climbed to the next deck, and walked back to the dark deserted swimming pool. There Selena was at last able to ask her question.

"If they somehow found out about Raul's mission," he explained, "but weren't able to stop him, they could plant the impostor story to block his getting the information we have for him."

"And if you give the real Raul the wrong list of names and the resistance goes to them expecting to find friends—"

"Exactly." He finished her sentence. "That would turn into a trap for him and his fellow freedom fighters."

"Then it's lucky you learned about the trick before your meeting."

"If it is a trick," he said somberly. "The message doesn't say that our source has been proved a liar, only that his credibility is doubtful. The conclusion is that the information he sent us may or may not be accurate."

"So the man coming tomorrow may or may not be Raul. Then the only safe course is to give him nothing."

"That's how it appears." He frowned, shook his head. "But if it *is* Raul, he will have taken great risks to come here. If I send him away empty-handed, all his efforts, the dangers he's faced, will be for nothing."

"There must be some way to check his identity. Aren't there pictures of him?"

"Yes, I've seen his picture. I've also seen Diego, the man they say is coming in his place. They're cousins and they look very much alike. That's one of the tragedies of civil war. It splits families. And that lets them send in a ringer who can easily pass for the man we're expecting. You can be sure he'll have all the right IDs and be fully briefed on what to say and do."

"You say you've seen pictures of both of them?"

"Pictures of Raul," he corrected. "Diego I've seen in person. So have you."

"I've seen Diego? When? Where?"

"About three years ago. Remember we went a few times to a nightclub on M Street near Wisconsin?"

"Jazz-o-mania?"

"That's the one," he said. "It's out of business now. You know how those spots come and go. But the music was good. Diego was on the drums."

"So he's lived in Washington."

"Not for long. After the club failed, he had a couple of other jobs but finally gave up and went home. They tell me he has his own band now and plays for all the official functions."

"But he's not part of the government?"

"No, his interest is music not politics. The only reason for using him as messenger is the family resemblance."

"And they'd have the same reason for giving his name as substitute if the report is a hoax. There must be some way to distinguish between them."

"I'm sure there is," Hugh agreed. "Given enough time, we could uncover the differences. But H-hour is noon tomorrow. By then I have to decide whether to give him the right list, the wrong list, or no list at all."

The ship docked at its second port at ten o'clock the next morning. Since most of the passengers would spend the day ashore, the company had sold vouchers to island residents and tourists that entitled them to a tour of the ship and buffet lunch. The arrangement supplied protective cover for the Section Q-arranged rendezvous. The scenario called for Raul to come aboard with the touring party and, shortly before noon, to go to the Carib Bar and order a drink. To assure recognition, he was to wear a bright orange shirt decorated with brown ponies. Hugh would take the stool next to his and identify himself by ordering a quinine and gin. While sipping their drinks, they would exchange comments on the weather or other small talk appropriate to strangers at a bar. And Hugh would inconspicuously pass on the list of names.

"That means I'll have approximately ten minutes to judge whether I'm talking to Raul or Diego," Hugh told Selena as they stood at the rail on the top deck watching the visitors come aboard. He shook his head.

"There ought to be something you could ask him," Selena said. "A question to which only Raul would know the answer."

"Too bad it's not the other way around," he returned. "If Raul were trying to pass as Diego, I might stump him with a musical question. But as things stand, there's no way—"

"Maybe there is," she interrupted. "There just may be."

"You've an idea?"

"I'm not sure but—yes, it might work. Anyway, it's worth a try." She turned from the rail and started away.

"Where are you going? What's your plan?"

"There's no time to explain. But I'll see you in a few minutes. Outside the Carib Bar."

Her first stop was the purser's office to ask where to find the guitarist.

"He may have gone ashore," he told her, "But I doubt it. He's probably resting in his cabin. Number 721 on B deck. Or there may be a card game going in the crew lounge."

She hurried to the cabin, knocked, and waited tensely until the shirt-sleeved young man opened the door.

"Mrs. Pierce." His tone showed surprise.

"I *don't* believe I thanked you properly for serenading us last night."

"Your husband did. He was very generous."

"I'm glad to hear it. Because I've come to ask another favor." She improvised quickly. "Actually, the celebration was a day early. This is our real anniversary. And there's a tune that has special meaning for us. *Rhapsody in Blue*. Can you play it?"

"Yes, of course."

"Then can you come right away to the Carib Bar? My husband's on his way there and I—oh, I know I must sound terribly sentimental—"

"Not at all. I'm happy to be involved in a romantic plot. Just let me get my jacket."

"I'll go on ahead," she said, "and meet you there."

She took the elevator to the Promenade Deck and looked in the small bar. There were two customers, seated at opposite ends of the counter. One was an elderly passenger, the other a dark man in an orange shirt speckled with small brown horses. She waited in the doorway for the guitarist.

"Will you sit in that alcove, please?" She indicated a spot on the other side of the room. Crossing with him, she spoke again as they passed behind the orange shirt. "I'd love to hear you play Gershwin's *Rhapsody in Blue*."

"*Rhapsody in Blue*," he repeated. "You've got it."

He sat down, strummed a few introductory notes, then began the familiar melody. Selena glanced at her watch. Two minutes to twelve.

She slipped out the other door to meet Hugh on deck.

"You have the lists?"

"Both of them. The right one here." He patted his shirt pocket. "And the other here." He touched his belt.

"I'll stand where you can see my signal. Ask him to name that tune."

"You think he'll give himself away? He's not that stupid. I don't—"

"Trust me."

"It appears," he said, "I have no choice."

She waited on deck until Hugh was seated on the bar stool, then followed him inside. Passing the guitar player, she gave him an encouraging smile, then stationed herself close enough to the bar to hear the conversation. She was behind the orange-shirted man, out of his sight, but in Hugh's line of vision.

"This is the best drink in hot weather," Hugh opened the conversation when the barman put down his quinine and gin.

"I prefer rum," the other returned, "in any weather."

"That's good, too," Hugh agreed. He picked up his glass, took a long sip, and seemed for the first time to become aware of the music. "I've heard that tune before, but I can't put a name to it. Do you recognize it?"

"Sorry. I don't know anything about American music."

Hugh glanced toward Selena. She put out her hand, thumb turned downward. He frowned, looking dubious. She repeated the gesture and he shrugged, accepting her judgment. He picked up a cocktail napkin and pressed it to his belt as if wiping off dripped liquid, then returned the crumpled napkin to the bar, near his companion's glass. A few seconds later the other man picked up both glass and napkin. He drained the glass and wiped his lips with the napkin while palming the paper Hugh had placed inside it.

"I hope you enjoy the rest of your cruise," he said politely as he got off the stool.

"Thanks," Hugh said. "Nice talking to you."

Selena watched him leave the bar, then took his place beside Hugh.

"I hope you understand what just happened," he told her. "Because I don't."

"That was Diego," she answered positively, "and you gave him the false list."

"I grant you that Diego would be suspicious of a musical clue and try to protect himself by pretending ignorance. But Raul would be genuinely ignorant. So how did that tell us which one it was?"

"Because I made sure he heard the title before our friend began to play. He knew it was *Rhapsody in Blue* and Raul would have told you so. Only Diego, needing to hide his identity, would deny his knowledge. And now your work is done, so let's thank the musician for playing our song."

JUSTINA

by Dorothy Salisbury Davis

Mary Ryan was certainly not homeless. She had lived in the Willoughby for forty-three years. Once it had been a residential hotel occupied mainly by show folk, people who worked in or about the theater at subsistence or slightly higher level. Recently it had been renovated into a stylish cooperative, but with a few small inside pockets, you might say, of people like Mrs. Ryan, who were allowed to remain on as renters by the grace of a qualified managerial charity: after all, what can you put in an inside pocket? Besides tax rebate.

The neighborhood—the West forties of Manhattan—had gone, in Mrs. Ryan's time, from respectable working class to shabby and drug-pocked misery and back again to a confusing mix of respectability, affluence, and decay. But through all the changes, the area had remained a neighborhood, with people who had lived there all their lives loyal to one another, to the shops who served them, to church and school, and who were, by and large, tolerant of the unfortunates and the degraded who came and went among them with the inevitability of time and tide.

As Mrs. Ryan got out of the elevator that January morning, she saw the nun backing off from the doorman. Louis seemed to be trying to persuade her to go out of the building by demonstrating how it could be done. He would prance three or four feet ahead of her toward the door and beckon her to follow him. The nun would take a step away from him deeper into the lobby.

Mrs. Ryan had seen the nun in the building before, and she

35

had seen her on the street, always hurrying, always laden with nondescript bundles and shopping bags. She was tall and lean and wore a habit such as most orders had stepped out of years before. Nor could Mrs. Ryan associate her garb with that of any order in her long religious acquaintanceship. "Is there any way I can help you, Sister?" she asked when she came abreast of the nun and the doorman.

"Better you can help me," Louis said, pleading with empty hands. "The super says she's not to come in, but she is in."

"You ought to show respect, Louis. A Sister is a Sister. You don't speak of her as *she*."

The nun gazed at Mrs. Ryan with large china-blue eyes that were full of pleading. "Can he put me out if I'm waiting for a friend?"

"Certainly not," Mrs. Ryan said.

Louis started to walk away in disgust and then turned back. "Miss Brennan left the building an hour ago in her nurse's uniform. Wouldn't you say it would be a long wait till she comes back, Mrs. Ryan?"

"Sheila Brennan is a friend of mine," Mrs. Ryan said. "If she said she'll be back, she'll be back. Would you like to come up to my place for a cup of tea, Sister? We can phone down to Louis and see if she comes in."

"How very kind of you, Mrs. Ryan. I would love a cup of tea." Moving with more grace than would be thought possible in the heavy, square-toed shoes, the nun collected two shopping bags from among the poinsettias. Mrs. Ryan hadn't noticed them. Whether Louis had, she couldn't know. He was standing, his back to them, looking out onto the street and springing up and down on his toes.

In the elevator, Mrs. Ryan surveyed her guest surreptitiously. She wore a full black skirt all the way to her shoe-tops and a jacket that seemed more Chinese than Christian. It buttoned clear up under her chin. The crucifix she wore was an ivory figure on what looked to be a gold or bronze cross. It put Mrs. Ryan in mind of one she had once noticed on a black man who, according to her friend Julie Hayes, was a pimp. For just that instant she

wondered if she had done the right thing in inviting the nun upstairs. What reassured her was an association from her youth in
Ireland: there was a smell to the nun only faintly unpleasant, as
of earth or the cellar, but remembered all Mrs. Ryan's life from
the Sisters to whom she had gone in infant school. Alas, it was
the smell of poverty.

Over her head of shaggy brown hair, the nun wore a thin veil
that came down to her breast. It was not much of a veil, but there
was not much breast to her, either. She said her name was Sister
Justina and her order was the Sisters of Our Lady of Hope, of
whom there were so few left each was allowed to choose her own
ministry: most, Sister Justina said, worked among the poor and
the illiterate, and often lived with them, as she herself did.

What Mrs. Ryan called her apartment was a single room into
which she had crammed a life, and which she had for many years
shared with a dachshund recently gone to where the good dogs
go. A life-size picture of Fritzie hung on the wall among a gallery
of actors and directors and theater entrepreneurs. "There's not a
face up there you'd recognize today, but I knew them all," she
said, coming out of the bathroom where she'd put the kettle on
to boil on the electric plate.

The nun was gazing raptly at the faded photographs. "Were
you an actor?"

"I was an usher," Mrs. Ryan said proudly.

"Theater people are the most generous I've ever begged from.
I am a beggar, you know," Justina said with a simplicity that
touched Mrs. Ryan to the core. There was something luminous
about her. She spoke softly, her voice throaty and low, but an
educated voice.

"The Franciscans—I always give to the Franciscans," Mrs.
Ryan said. It was the only begging order she knew.

"I feel closer to St. Francis myself than to any other saint,"
Sister Justina said. "Sometimes I pray for a mission among birds
and animals, and then I'm reminded that pigeons are birds, and
that rats and mice must have come off the ark as well as the
loftier creatures. But I think I do my best work among the poor
who ought never to have come to the city at all. They are the

really lost ones." She was sitting at the foot of the daybed, rubbing her hands together. The color had risen to her cheeks.

Mrs. Ryan thought of tuberculosis. "Don't you have a shawl, Sister?"

"I'm warm enough inside, thank you. I have so many calls to make, would you think it ungrateful of me to run off without waiting for tea?"

Or Sheila Brennan, Mrs. Ryan thought. But she had grown accustomed to visitors finding her apartment both claustrophobic and too warm. "The electric plate is terrible slow," she said, making an excuse for her guest's departure.

"You're very kind," the nun said. Her eyes welled up. "God bless!" She gathered a shopping bag in each hand and went flapping down the hall like a bird that couldn't get off the ground.

A few minutes later Mrs. Ryan was downstairs again, about to resume her trip to the Sentinal Thrift Shop. She lingered near the elevators until Louis went outdoors to look for a cab for one of the tenants with liquid assets, as Sheila Brennan liked to say of the co-op owners. She was not in the mood for a lecture from Louis, who couldn't stand street people, even if they belonged to a religious order. She was almost to the corner of Ninth Avenue when a gust of wind came up, whirling the dust before it. She turned her back, and so it was that she saw Sister Justina emerge from the service or basement entrance of the Willoughby. She clutched her veil against the wind and hurried toward Eighth Avenue, the opposite direction from Mrs. Ryan. And without her shopping bags.

Julie had the feeling that Mrs. Ryan had been waiting for her—not exactly lying in wait, but keeping an eye out for her to appear, either coming to or going from her ground-floor apartment on Forty-fourth Street. Theirs was a friendship of several years, recently broken and more recently mended. Julie still kept the tin box of dog biscuits in case the old lady appeared one day with another Fritzie in tow.

Mrs. Ryan came halloing across the street ahead of a rush of traffic. "Do you have a few minutes, Julie? There's something I need your advice on."

Julie had a few minutes. She was of the conviction that a gossip columnist hustled best who hustled least. Her visit to the rehearsal of *Uptown Downtown* could wait. She unlocked the door and led the way back into her apartment-office.

"Do you remember the day we put down the deposit here, Julie?"

Julie remembered, but it seemed a long time ago, her brief sortie into reading and advising. Sheer mischief, she'd say of it now. Now "the shop," as she'd always called it, was comfortable to live in and equipped as well with the electronics of her trade. She had learned to use the computer and rarely went near the *New York Daily* office at all.

"Friend Julie," Mrs. Ryan said, her voice lush with reminiscence. Then: "You have such good instincts about people. I want to tell you about a nun I met this morning, a beautiful person, the most spiritual eyes you ever saw." Mrs. Ryan didn't exactly proselyte, but she did propagate the faith.

"I'm not great on nuns," Julie said, and the phrase "a nun and a neck" popped into her mind. Where it had come from she had no idea.

"They're not much different from you and me," Mrs. Ryan said.

Julie raised her eyebrows.

"Her name is Sister Justina," Mrs. Ryan said, and told the story of their encounter.

"Are you sure she's a nun?" was Julie's first question.

"I'd swear to it."

"What does Miss Brennan say about her?"

"Sheila's on the day shift this week—I wouldn't go to the hospital looking for her about this. It's the shopping bags that bother me. What did she do with them?"

"And what was in them? You've got to think about drugs, Mrs. Ryan."

"It crossed my mind, may the Lord forgive me, and I suppose, to be honest, I'd have to say that's why I've come to you."

"It would seem she wanted most to get into the Willoughby," Julie reconstructed. "She tried to make it on Miss Brennan's name and then you came along. It looks as though her purpose was to deliver the shopping bags, but without the doorman or you knowing who she was delivering them to."

Mrs. Ryan agreed reluctantly.

"How did she get past the doorman in the first place?"

"She must have slipped in the way I slipped out—when he was handing someone into a cab."

"Were the bags heavy or light?"

"They flopped along, not heavy, not light."

"And why go out the basement door? Why not sail past the doorman with her head in the air?"

"Ah, she wasn't the type. She told me right out that she was a beggar—but in the way St. Francis was a beggar."

"Funny about that cross," Julie said. "I saw Goldie the other day. 'Miz Julie, I'm straight as a flagpole,' " she mimicked. "He even gave me his business card."

"Was he wearing the crucifix?" Mrs. Ryan asked disapprovingly.

Julie grinned. "I doubt it. He was wearing Brooks Brothers." She took a mug of tea from the micro-oven and set it before the older woman.

"Fancy," Mrs. Ryan said, "and me still using an electric plate." The tea was "instant" and she hated it.

Julie wondered how many like Mrs. Ryan and Sheila Brennan were still living in the Willoughby. "What was the name of your actor friend? Remember he took us down to the basement that time to look up his old notices in the trunk room?"

"Jack Carroll. He's gone now, God rest him. He was a lovely man but a terrible bore." Mrs. Ryan drank the tea down, trying not to taste it.

"That was one spooky place," Julie said. "Cobwebs and leaky pipes, and the smell of mold and old clothes when he opened the trunk."

"It's all changed down there now with the renovation. The old part's been sealed off. There's brand-new washers and dryers in the new section and it's as bright as daylight."

"She wouldn't be stealing from the dryers, would she? To give to the poor, of course."

"She would not," Mrs. Ryan said indignantly. Then, having to account to herself for the shopping bags, she added, "Besides, she'd be taking a terrible chance of being caught."

"But wouldn't that account for her going out without the bags—the fear that someone had seen her?"

"Oh, dear, I hope she doesn't come looking for me now to let her back in," Mrs. Ryan said. "I could be out in the cold myself. I'm on severance with the management. They pretend not to know I cook in my room."

"Mrs. Ryan," Julie said, "why don't you forget I said that? It's wild. I have a wicked imagination. And I'd stop worrying about the nun if I were you. She got into the building before you came along—she's not your responsibility."

Mrs. Ryan looked at her reproachfully. Then her face lit up. "Julie, I'd love you to meet her. I'll bring her around someday if I can get her to come and let you judge for yourself."

Sheila Brennan stuck her stockinged feet out for Mrs. Ryan to see. "Will you look at my ankles? You'd think it was the height of summer." The ankles were indeed swollen.

"It's being on them all day," Mrs. Ryan said. "Put them up on the couch while I pour the tea."

Sheila was younger than Mrs. Ryan, a plain, solid woman who dreaded the day of her retirement from St. Jude's Hospital. "The first I saw of Sister Justina was when she visited someone brought into the hospital with frostbite during that bad spell in December. You know the woman who tries to sell yesterday's newspapers on the corner of Fifty-first Street? The police brought her in half frozen. I told the nun that if she'd come to the Willoughby when I got off duty, and if she could promise me the woman would wear it, I'd give her a fisherman's shirt my brother brought me from Donegal. It was foolish of me to put a condition to it and what she said made me ashamed of myself. 'If she doesn't wear it, I will,' she said. I've been asking around of this one and that one to give her their castoffs ever since."

"So she's on the up and up," Mrs. Ryan said and put the teacup and saucer in her friend's hand. "But what was she doing in the Willoughby basement?"

"God knows, Mary. She may just have pushed the wrong elevator button and wound up there."

Julie and her imagination, Mrs. Ryan thought.

Sheila Brennan's explanation satisfied Mrs. Ryan because she wanted to be satisfied with it. And she did believe the nun to be a true sister to the poor. She saw her again later that week. Mrs. Ryan was herself in the habit now of taking her principal meal at the Seniors Center in St. Malachy's basement, where she got wholesome food in a cheerful environment at a price she could afford. Afterward, that afternoon, she went upstairs to the Actors Chapel and there she encountered Sister Justina kneeling in a back pew, her shopping bags at her sides.

"Sister—" Mrs. Ryan whispered hoarsely.

The nun jumped as though startled out of deep meditation and upset one of the shopping bags. Out tumbled a variety of empty plastic cups.

Mrs. Ryan went into the pew and helped her collect them, saying how sorry she was to have startled her. The containers, she noted, were reasonably clean, but certainly not new. "All I wanted to say," she explained, "is that I have a friend who would like to meet you. Her name is Julie Hayes. She's a newspaper columnist. She writes about all kinds of people, and she's very good to the needy."

"I've heard of her," the nun said without enthusiasm.

Mrs. Ryan realized she had taken the wrong tack. "Do you mind coming out to the vestibule for a minute? I can't get used to talking in church."

In the vestibule, she modified her description of Julie. "It's true that she helps people. She's even helped the police now and then. I know of at least two murders she's helped them solve. It would take me all day to tell you about her. But, Sister, she's as needy in her way as you are in yours. You both have a great deal to give, but what would you do if you didn't have takers?"

The nun laughed and then clutched at her throat to stop the cough the laugh had started. "Someday," she said when she could get her breath.

"Someday soon," Mrs. Ryan said. "She lives a few doors from the Actors Forum. You know where that is. I helped her find the place. In those days she called herself Friend Julie."

"Friend Julie," the nun repeated with a kind of recognition. Then: "I must hurry, Mrs. Ryan. They throw out the food if I don't get there in time." She ran down the steps with her bags of containers to collect the leftovers from the Seniors' midday meal.

"Nowadays it's just plain Julie Hayes," Mrs. Ryan called after her.

Julie never doubted that Mrs. Ryan would arrive one day with the nun by the hand, but what she hadn't expected was the nun's arrival alone. She didn't like unannounced visitors, but the ring of the doorbell was urgent and came with a clatter she presently attributed to the nun's use of the cross as a knocker. In fact, it was by the cross—an ivory figure on gold—that she recognized her as Mrs. Ryan's friend. She took off the safety latch and opened the door.

"Friend Julie, I need your help."

"Has something happened to Mrs. Ryan?"

"No," the nun said. "Please?"

Julie relocked the door after the nun and led the way through the apartment. She was trying to remember the nun's name.

"Mrs. Ryan has nothing to do with this, I give my word," the nun said. "She said you wanted to meet me, but that's not why I'm here. I'm Sister Justina."

Julie motioned her into a chair and seated herself across the coffee table from her. She didn't say anything. She just waited for the pitch. It was those big blue eyes, she thought, that had got to Mrs. Ryan.

"All I need to tell you about my mission, I think, is that I try

to find temporary shelter for street people who are afraid of in-
stitutional places. It's a small person-to-person endeavor, but I've
had very good luck until now. I've been keeping two people hidden away at night and in bad weather in an abandoned section
of the Willoughby basement."

"You're kidding," Julie said.

"I wish I were." The nun thrust her clasped hands between her
knees. "I went to leave them a meal this afternoon." She took a
deep breath. "One man was gone and the other one was dead.
His skull was smashed in!" Her amazing eyes were filling.

"You're lucky it wasn't you, Sister."

"I don't consider myself lucky."

"Have you gone to the police?"

Justina shook her head. "That's why I came to you. Mrs. Ryan
said you've helped the police—"

"Let's forget what Mrs. Ryan says. *You* have to go to the police. You can't just close up that part of the basement again on
a dead man as though it was a tomb."

"I don't want to do that. I only wish I could have got poor
Tim out of the city in time. He wanted to go, but he was afraid."
She looked at Julie pleadingly. "I want to do what I have to do,
but I can't."

"I'll go with you if that will help," Julie offered.

"Would you go *for* me?"

"No. If you don't show up and take the responsibility for tres-
passing or whatever it was, Mrs. Ryan and Miss Brennan could
be evicted, and where would they find a place to live?"

Justina shook her head. "Nothing like this has ever happened
to me."

"I'll say it again, then: you're lucky."

"Yes, I suppose I am," the nun said with what sounded like
heavy irony. "The habit I wear has been my salvation, my
hope in life." She drew a long shuddering breath. "Julie, I'm a
man."

For a while Julie said nothing. She was remembering where the
phrase "a nun and a neck" had come from—the poet Rilke com-

menting on one of Picasso's acrobats: "The son of a nun and a neck."

"You can use the phone there on my desk if you want to, Sister," she said.

"Thank you," Justina said. She got up. "Who do I call?"

"Try nine-one-one," Julie said.

The nun identified herself to the police dispatcher as Sister Justina, told of a body in the basement of the Willoughby Apartments, and promised to wait herself at the service entrance to the building. She gave them the address.

When Mrs. Ryan dropped in at Billy McGowan's pub for her afternoon glass of lager, Detective Dom Russo was telling of the down-and-outer his detail had taken into custody that afternoon for trying to pass a kinky hundred-dollar bill. Nobody had seen its like since before World War Two. Billy had the first dollar he made in America framed and hung above the bar. He pointed it out to the customers.

"They don't make 'em like that any more," the detective said, wanting to get on with his story. "This gingo claimed first off that he found it, just picked it up off the street. We turned him loose and put a tail on him. You know where the old railroad tracks used to run under Forty-fourth Street? He made a beeline for a hole in the fence, slid down the embankment, and led us straight to where he'd hidden three plastic containers in an old burnt-out stove. I don't need to tell you—the containers were stuffed with all this old-fashioned money."

Someone down the bar wisecracked that that was the best kind. But at the mention of plastic containers, Mrs. Ryan could not swallow her beer.

"We took him in again. This time around, he said he found the money right there in the oven of this old stove. He intended to turn it over to the police, of course," Russo repeated sarcastically, "only first he wanted to look more respectable and went to a thrift shop with one of the C-notes—a silver certificate, they used to call them."

"He should have gone right to the bank," someone else down the bar said. "They'd trade it in—dollar for dollar."

"No questions asked?" someone wanted to know.

"He should have gone to a collector and made himself some real money," Billy said.

"Look," Russo told them, "you're acting like this guy was kosher. Maybe the *money's* kosher, but he's not. I don't believe for a minute he lucked into all that old cash. Anyway, we'll hold him till we hear from the Feds."

"A developing story, as they say." McGowan moved down the bar to Mrs. Ryan. "Drink up, Mary, and I'll put a head on it for you."

"I'll take a rain check, Billy," she told him. "I've got terrible heartburn." She eased herself off the stool, and by ancient habit looked under it, half expecting Fritzie to be curled up there. Out on the street, she drew several deep breaths of the wintry air. Plastic cups, she told herself, weren't such a rare commodity.

It was almost dark and there were misty halos around the streetlights—and when she turned the corner she could see rainbows of revolving color: police activity outside the Willoughby. She approached near enough to see that the action was concentrated around the basement entrance, whereupon she reversed herself and headed for Julie's as fast as her legs would carry her.

Julie was short on patience at the arrival of Mrs. Ryan. For one thing, she was uneasy about not having followed up on the nun's story. After all, she was in the newspaper business. She ought at least to have called the city desk on a breaking story. Or covered it herself. But she had wanted to give Justina a chance to confront the police on her own. She certainly didn't want to be the person to blow her cover.

When Mrs. Ryan finished giving out her jigsaw of a tale, Julie asked her if she'd seen Sister Justina after they'd met at St. Malachy's.

"I haven't."

"Well, she's been here this afternoon, Mrs. Ryan. The police are at the Willoughby to investigate a murder that took place there in the basement. It's highly possible they'll connect it with your man with the money in the plastic cups."

"Holy Mother of God," Mrs. Ryan said.

"And they'll be looking for witnesses, for accessories."

"Sister Justina?"

"And *her* accessories," Julie said. "Your doorman isn't about to take credit for letting her into the building, is he?"

Mrs. Ryan sat a long while in silence. "Would you mind walking me home, dear? My legs are so weak I'm not sure they'll carry me."

Julie pulled on her coat, put the phone on "Service," and fastened her press card onto the inside flap of her shoulderbag.

Mrs. Ryan got weaker and weaker on the way. She suggested they stop for a brief rest at McGowan's, but Julie put a firm hand beneath the older woman's elbow and propelled her homeward.

By then word of police activity at the Willoughby had reached McGowan's and most of the patrons were there to see what was going on. Julie spotted Detective Russo as he came out of the building on the run. She planted Mrs. Ryan among her McGowan's cronies at the barricade and caught up with him as he was climbing into the back of a squad car.

"Okay if I come along?" she asked, halfway into the car behind him. They were on pretty good terms, considering that they weren't always on the same side.

"Why not?" he said ironically.

By the time they reached the precinct house, she knew how the victim and his assailant had got into that part of the Willoughby. The Environmental Protection Department had ordered a removal of old sewage pipes and part of the wall had been removed, a temporary partition put up in its place. "Like everything else in this town," Russo said, "they get the job half done and move on to the next one."

No mention of the nun. "How did they get into the building in the first place, Dom?" Julie asked.

"How the hell do I know? Somebody must've left the door open. And no wonder. It stinks to high heaven down back where they were. They buried their own shit like animals. That's how they found the body—and the tin box with the money in it."

"The money in the plastic cups you found earlier this afternoon. Do you think there's a connection?"

"You better believe it," Russo said. "The victim had one clutched in his hand when he was clobbered with the tin box."

"How did you know to go to the Willoughby in the first place?"

"We had a phone call," Russo said. "But the complainant didn't show. We'd begun to think it was a hoax—but the smell led us to him. A whole section of the wall—we just leaned on it and Jericho!"

"Jericho," Julie said. "That's nice."

So Justina had vanished. No problem: just get out of the habit and grow a beard. Until now she had carried Justina's confession of identity as a confidence, as though it had been told under a seal. It hadn't, of course, but since Detective Russo and company had the suspect in custody and enough evidence to detain him for a while, she decided to keep the matter on hold.

Mrs. Ryan and Sheila Brennan were waiting for Julie when she arrived at Mrs. Ryan's apartment. They seemed less chastened than she thought they ought to be, but there hadn't yet been time for the police to get to them.

"We're expecting them any minute," Mrs. Ryan said. "And we've decided to tell them the truth about Sister."

"And that is?"

"How she got into the building in the first place. How she used us."

Julie felt she was being used herself—that this was dress rehearsal. "Okay."

"But she would have used anybody to help those she thought

needed help." Mrs. Ryan drew a deep breath. "Julie, who would you say all that money belongs to?"

"I wouldn't say." But she was beginning to see a light.

Sheila and I have a story to tell you. Remember you mentioned Jack Carroll the other day, and his trunk in the basement? Jack lived here for years before Sheila and I ever heard of the Willoughby and he loved to tell stories of the old days—the circus people, the vaudevillians, and the chorus girls. One of his best stories, and God knows he practiced to make it perfect, was about Big Frankie Malloy. When Frankie moved in, the management renovated a whole suite for him. He had tons of money. He had his own barber sent in every day to shave him, he had his meals catered, he was always sending out for this or that, he was a lavish tipper. And the girls, there were plenty of them. But there was something wrong about big Frankie. After he moved in, he never went outdoors again—except once.

"Madge Delaney was his favorite of the girls, and she got booked into the Blue Diamond nightclub just down the street. Frankie went out the night she opened. It was said afterward that the only reason she got the booking was to lure him out. He was shot dead before he ever got to the Blue Diamond."

"Wow," Julie said.

"Don't you think it could be his money that's been hidden away all these years?"

"It's a real possibility," Julie agreed.

"You see why I asked you who it belongs to now."

"I do see," Julie assured her.

Julie's story made page 3 of the bulldog edition of the *New York Daily* and the police, discovering there was no such religious order as the Sisters of Our Lady of Hope, put out an alert for Sister Justina. The Willoughby claimed all of that very old money. It also threatened to sue the contractor whose procrastination made that part of the basement available to Sister Justina and her friends.

Mrs. Ryan's faith in the nun remained steadfast: she might herself have got the name of the order wrong. Julie thought about looking up Goldie, the reformed pimp, to ask him what became of the gold-and-ivory cross he used to wear. But she decided not to. It was one more thing she didn't have to know.

THE BOTTLE DUNGEON

by Antonia Fraser

"Quite rare nowadays, I believe," said Joss Benmuir, looking down beyond his feet at the black hole.

"It may be quite rare but it's absolutely horrible! Really, Joss, I fail to see how you can—" Lady Martin paused, then went on with fervor "—*tolerate* something so totally *foul*."

"It's not a human rights issue, Aunt May, at least not now." The intention of Robbie Benmuir was evidently to tease. May Martin was an extremely wealthy widow: since her husband's death she had occupied herself as an indefatigable campaigner for every conceivable liberal issue. Her figure was a familiar one, holding up a sandwich board of protest, spread across some newspaper.

Jemima Shore shivered as she too looked down. The Bottle Dungeon was carved—literally—out of rock. It consisted of a long narrow "neck" which bellied out into a circular "bottle," the shape of which could not be discerned from above until Joss Benmuir swung his flashlight into its depths. There were no steps cut in the "neck." The only method of getting down (or up) consisted of using a thick rope, currently coiled beside them, and fastened to an enormous iron ring in the stone.

Privately Jemima agreed with Lady Martin there was something foul about the gaping hole. She also fancied that there was a fetid smell. No light, not much air, and absolutely no sanitation beyond a tiny aperture in the rock at the bottom of the bottle which dropped to the sea—no wonder there was something dank

51

and rotten in the atmosphere of the stone cell which contained the entrance to the dungeon. But since Jemima was an outsider at this house party, she decided to stay silent. She had been working with May Martin in recent months on a project for a television series tentatively titled *A Woman's Right to Say Anything: The Female Political Voice in Various Totalitarian Countries*. She had become fond of the old lady, faintly ridiculous in her untidy appearance, certainly often ridiculed in the press for her views, yet ever gallant in her defense of those unable to speak for themselves. When her own New Year plans fell through, she had accepted Lady Martin's invitation to be her companion on the Scottish trip.

"Not really a party," Lady Martin had pronounced. "In spite of its being Hogmanay. There aren't any neighbors for miles. Plenty of time to work together." She hesitated. "Thank heaven you're not married; you'll take Joss's mind off that dreadful Clio Brown; then of course there's Robbie."

A slightly uncomfortable silence followed Robbie Benmuir's little sally about human rights. To May Martin at least such things were not a laughing matter. It was broken by Joss, who continued to gaze down into the dungeon as he spoke. "It's a tourist attraction, Aunt May. That's what it is. And a very fine one too. After all, who else would come to this desolate spot otherwise? So many finer castles, aren't there? And you know how I need the money." His tone was perfectly equable; nevertheless, the words only increased the general embarrassment. Joss was being deliberately provocative, as Jemima Shore already knew enough about the Benmuir family set-up to appreciate.

May Martin was probably rich enough to restore the crumbling castle (what remained of it) single-handed but preferred to spend her money on good causes—which did not include Castle Crask. And there was nothing to stop her doing so. Although Joss and Robbie, the children of her late brother, were her only blood relations, May Martin's money came entirely from the man she had married comparatively late in her life and very late in his, Sir Ludwig Martin, founder of LudMart. She had confided to Jemima on the way up: "Joss wants me to 'invest' in Crask—his phrase.

He should know by now that I only make strictly philanthropic investments, which does not include ancient masonry even if it is owned by my family."

As if there weren't enough tensions within the party already, thought Jemima, what with Clio Brown being once upon a time a girlfriend of Robbie. Clio Brown and her overweight and over-anxious husband, Gerald (Why on earth had she married him? The answer was, presumably, money), and now apparently—all too apparently this afternoon—Clio Brown and Joss. Jemima Shore had taken a strong dislike to Clio Brown. She hoped it was not jealousy on her part. Clio, with her cat's face and fashionably cropped dark hair, so tall, so slim, and at the same time so curved, was certainly amazingly good-looking. But there was something intensely disagreeable about her. Gerald bore the brunt of her bad moods: the sight of his red, perspiring face—even in the un-centrally heated castle he seemed perpetually hot—would remind Clio that she needed a handkerchief fetching from her bedroom. She seemed to take a malevolent pleasure in watching Gerald trying to fit his bulk up a curved stone staircase.

Joss Benmuir was right: Crask was indeed a desolate spot situated on a headland which ran out into the North Sea where even the harsh cries of the sea birds seemed to have something lonely and despairing about them. It had not always been so. Crask's moat was now dry, but its depth indicated that the castle had once acted as an important fortress, ready to repel foreign raiders and hand-off domestic assailants with equal ferocity. Its strategic position meant that some kind of defensive structure must always have existed on the site—there were even traces of a prehistoric *dun*—but the present castle had been predominantly built in the fourteenth century. It had, however, been badly battered during the Cromwellian invasion of Scotland and suffered again in the period of the Jacobite risings.

As Colonel Benmuir, father of Joss and Robbie, had been wont to lament: "It's centuries since we Benmuirs managed to find ourselves on the winning side." He sometimes added: "Perhaps that's where poor May gets her taste for losers from—the spirit of her ancestors."

Two substantial towers did, however, remain of the fourteenth century castle: but they were no longer joined by a great hall or other buildings. The space in between was occupied by grass and stones, some of which were big enough to cause unwary guests to stumble as they moved between the two separate structures which together made up the living quarters of the modern Benmuir family. There was no protection on the headland—mountains existed only in the distance—and the gusts of wind carried the sea spray inland and had been known to whirl umbrellas away. That had happened to Jemima Shore on the previous evening, so that her beautiful crushed velvet skirt had become sodden. Now, as they stood outside, a girl called Ellie Mac-Something—attached to Robbie it seemed—who had suffered similarly with her tartan wool skirt, was bold enough to ask Joss why there was no covered way.

"It would blow away like your umbrella," Joss remarked blandly. "Wouldn't it, Robbie? At least you didn't stumble over a sheep: my father used to keep sheep here to deal with the grass. I got rid of them. Besides, we chaps like leading our own lives. Robbie has always got a home here. Until I marry, that is."

"And will you and your wife have separate towers when you marry?" There was something provocative about the way Ellie MacSomething was pursuing the matter, and it occurred to Jemima that she might be thinking of transferring her affections from Robbie to his elder brother. Joss, with his pale face, the black hair falling romantically over the eyes with their heavy lids, had more the air of a Spanish grandee—an El Greco—than a Scot. Robbie, on the other hand, with his rosy, almost ruddy cheeks, his freckles, his brownish curly hair already slipping back on his forehead, and stocky figure was the same physical type as his Aunt May. Although Jemima had the impression of intelligence beneath Robbie's jokey manner, there was no doubt which brother was the better-looking and Joss was after all the owner of Crask (whatever that might mean).

"Separate towers for married couples! What a good idea!" said Clio Brown suddenly. "Gerald, I think we should get on much better like that. Towers with thick walls. Too thick for even your snores to penetrate." She smiled in her peculiar catlike manner, the corners of her small, perfectly bowed mouth turning up as though she were contemplating a small mouse before her. The mouse, however, was her large husband. One could not say that Gerald Brown flushed, since his face was red enough already, nevertheless it was clear that the remark had wounded him—but then that was presumably the intention.

By unspoken agreement, the other guests turned back to their contemplation of the Bottle Dungeon. They had all been taken on a visit to Crask's famous attraction—if a dungeon could really be so described—as a post-lunch treat by their host. The light faded early on a midwinter Scottish afternoon and as Joss Benmuir jocularly observed: "We don't want to lose one of you down the neck, not on the eve of Hogmanay anyway, it might ruin our modest celebrations."

He touched the aperture with his toe. "There's one at St. Andrew's Castle but ours is a whole foot deeper. Twenty-six foot deep." Jemima shivered again. She still could not easily bear to contemplate the idea of a prisoner lowered into the depths and left—left without light, heat, food beyond what the captors condescended to lower, left in the filth, the prey to rats . . . for there were apparently rats there in the past, probably introduced down the neck by the jailers, since the drainage hole at the bottom was minute, too small for a mouse let alone a rat to enter . . .

In desperation Jemima found herself asking, "Did anyone ever escape?" It was the best she could do to strike a more cheerful note. Before Joss could answer, May Martin said, very fiercely indeed: "The terrible thing is that people *lived*, not that they died. Death was *merciful* compared to what people endured down there. Sometimes for years. An amazing aspect of the human spirit: some people are survivors. Joss, I really think you should seal it off, not exhibit it, show some respect for the sufferings of human beings . . ." Fortunately for Joss, he was able to ignore his aunt in favor of answering Jemima. "No one escaped." He pointed to some lettering cut in the side of the stone cell. "*Initus non abeat.* Medieval Latin. It means: Once in, you can't get out. Carved shortly after the castle was built, they think." Joss paused.

"No one escaped without help, that is. Some prisoner, put down there for supporting John Knox, at the time of the Reformation, that sort of thing, did get out. But it turned out that the jailer's daughter had helped him out with a rope. Otherwise: *Initus non abeat*. That's a bottle dungeon for you."

"Just like marriage," said Clio Brown suddenly. "Once in, there's no way out. Unless you get help." At first the company assumed that this was merely one of Clio's unpleasant interjections intended primarily to bait her husband. But it turned out that she had more to say. "I want to go down, Joss. I want to see what it's like. It could be quite an experience. I want to spend the night down there. It should be—" she lifted her lips in her little cat's smile again "—gloriously private. Look how narrow that neck is. Gerald, I don't believe you could fit down there, even if the rope would hold you."

There was polite laughter from those like Ellie and Jemima who decided to pretend that Clio was joking. Gerald merely spluttered: but this time there was no doubt at all in Jemima's mind that he was seriously angry, and Clio might find she had gone for once a little too far. She did not however, act as if she was aware of her husband's rage. On the contrary, she persisted in talking about her descent, cajoled Joss into revealing that there was a rope ladder for emergencies, narrow but serviceable, in a locked cupboard in the corner of the cell, and finally provoked Gerald into shouting at her:

"If that's how you want to see the New Year in, goddamnit, don't count on finding me in a very good mood tomorrow morning."

"I don't count on finding you at all tomorrow morning, Gerald, if you go on shouting like this," replied Clio smoothly. "You're straining yourself dreadfully with all that shouting, and you know what the doctor said. Rage is not healthful." Clio sounded so primly reproachful that you might almost have thought that the previous scene in which she deliberately provoked her husband's anger had not taken place.

"And wouldn't you be pleased?" snarled Gerald. "A rich widow. Well, don't count on that either." The embarrassment continued.

Afterwards it became important as to who had first suggested the bet. Was it Joss, his eyes black as he challenged Clio in a way that seemed positively sexual even at the comparatively asexual hour of three o'clock in the afternoon? Or perhaps frivolous, giggly Ellie, seeking to stir up further trouble? Or the much calmer and more self-possessed Robbie, with exactly the opposite aim of defusing the situation? Jemima had certainly not done so—she continued to regard the Bottle Dungeon with revulsion—while Lady Martin made her indignation quite obvious.

"Sensation-monger!" she said to Jemima in an aside which was clearly intended to be heard. "The sort of person who collects Nazi mementos for kicks."

Gerald had been the first one actually to use the word "bet."

"I bet you won't stay down there for one hour, Clio, let alone for one night." Then he stumped away from the party, with the words: "Do what you damn well please! You always do." But it was after that the real bet somehow evolved: the bet that Clio would be lowered down by the little ladder, as warmly clad as possible, with sleeping bag and flashlight, and a pocket heater, generally used out shooting, to warm her hands. This lowering would take place at eleven o'clock that night. She would be formally let out—let up—one hour later, with the New Year.

"And what does she get if she wins the bet?" asked Ellie, who had gone back to twining herself round Robbie again.

"I get to choose how I spend the rest of the night." Jemima swore that Clio actually licked her lips when she said that; certainly there was a flicker of her little red tongue as she smiled. "Which means," she went on, looking at each of the three men in turn, ending with her husband, now some distance away, "I get to spend it alone."

It was not until dinnertime, when all had changed, including Clio, who wore a black lycra cat suit, that Robbie made the obvious point.

"I've just realised she's bound to win the bet, isn't she? Unless she dies of fright or something awful like that. You see, if Clio does want to come up—come up early and lose the bet—she has no way of letting us know, has she? She just has to sit it out down there—yuk—until we come and get her. Next year."

So it was agreed that Clio should be installed with a large noisy bell, which Robbie found, once used to summon laborers for lunch. If the bell was heard to ring, it would be regarded as a sign that Clio needed help and the bet was off.

"Send not to know for whom the bell tolls"—Robbie being jokey again—"because it will definitely be Clio. After all, once in you can't get out. Without help. Good family motto that, Joss, we should use it. After all, we Benmuirs are always getting into things we can't get out of, aren't we—relationships, debt, that sort of thing." Lady Martin and Joss both frowned.

The presence of the bell meant that the door to the stone cell had to be left open: Robbie was not sure the clang from the depths would otherwise be heard. But no one felt that to be a problem. The door was clearly visible across the rough grass from the Big Tower where the party was congregated in the big sitting room on the first floor, also used as a dining room on festive occasions, with its high windows and seats in the embrasures. Nobody could rescue Clio early—supposing anyone was minded to do so—without being observed.

"Not even to drop down the teeniest reviving malt whiskey"— Robbie, determinedly lighthearted again. But none of the badinage was really very lighthearted. Something—what exactly and when?—had gone too far. A troublemaking young woman, a stupid bet, what a recipe for New Year's Eve! (Jemima Shore wished she were at home, celebrating with her cat, appropriately named Midnight.) About ten-thirty both Gerald Brown and Lady Martin decided to opt out of proceedings—including the seeing-in of the New Year—and went to their respective beds. The Browns were sleeping in the Little Tower, or Robbie's Tower, together with Ellie and Robbie himself; Lady Martin and Jemima were housed still higher up in the Big Tower. Joss, as host, now politely insisted on escorting Lady Martin upstairs, despite her protests about knowing the way perfectly well.

"But Joss, I grew up here!" she exclaimed. Perhaps he intended to make his touch at this point, thought Jemima, although it was scarcely a tactful moment with her disapproval so manifest. Gerald's bulky figure could be seen crossing the grass, bending slightly as he fronted the wind. The moon, almost full, had now risen, and with its eerie glow on the stones, did something to supplement the inadequate lighting of the passage between the two towers. After a short while Clio said crossly:

"I hope he hasn't gone to sleep already. I've got to put a great many things over this." She stretched out in her skin tight black suit: she really did have the most beautiful lissome figure, small high breasts clearly visible under the lycra, and the narrow thighs and long, long legs of a model; she actually could wear her cat suit and get away with it. "I'll be back," said Clio. "May he not be *snoring*, that's all I ask."

A few moments later they watched Clio in her turn cross the grass, a cumbersome parka over her cat suit, as the winds tossed her short hair. Whatever passed between the Browns on the first floor of the Little Tower must, however, have been vaguely conciliatory because they saw Gerald at the window, raising his hand and waving. His mood must have improved since he left. Clio reappeared shortly afterward.

"Of course he's in a better temper!" she exclaimed. "He just thinks I'll lose, that's why. He's really a cunning old sod, that one. Convinced I'll panic and ring the bell. Such a downer. I really can't think why I married him." Jemima, looking at her, now more of a Michelin woman in her jerseys, thought: Why did he marry you? Do some men just like to be humiliated? Answer, I suppose: yes.

In the event, the actual descent of Clio on the rope ladder was a slight anti-climax. Her sleek head had disappeared from view into the Bottle Dungeon without anything more dramatic happening than her own voice echoing upwards: "It's great down here, the new holiday spot, can't think why those prisoners complained."

"Any rats?" called Robbie.

"They're all upstairs," Clio shouted back. "Or asleep." She was in her usual form. The flashlight was seen to cast its sepulchral glow upwards, the bell was tested (it sounded very loud), and then there was nothing to do but brave the wind and go back to the Big Tower again and wait.

There nobody could quite think how to fill in the time. The general clear view of the open door of the cell meant that it was impossible to forget Clio. Joss, their host, had fallen moodily silent, his thoughts no doubt with her. The hour looked like passing slowly until Robbie decided to organize them.

"Here we are, four people in search of an occupation. Is it to be a foursome reel or bridge?"

Although Ellie clapped her hands and voted for a reel, Jemima hastily pointed out she did not know how to dance a reel. So they all four settled for bridge. After that the time did pass a little quicker, although the fact that the bridge table was placed in the embrasure containing the big window meant that the Bottle Dungeon—and Clio—remained somewhere in Jemima's thoughts at least. Nor did the bridge prove quite the engrossing occupation for herself and Ellie they might have anticipated. The Benmuir brothers, Joss playing with Jemima, and Robbie with Ellie, played virtually every hand themselves, bidding, it seemed, with the aim of so doing. The one hand Jemima did play, Joss peered over her shoulder silently, but somehow, she felt, critically. Ellie never got to play a single hand.

It was actually Robbie who was busy making six spades—his luck was in—when they heard the bell ring. It rang loudly, the sound melted away into the wind, then it rang again. Instinctively Jemima looked at her watch: it was ten minutes to twelve. The others simply jumped up; then all of them started to run down the twisting stair, Joss pushing open the door, and out across the moonlit grass. Ellie stumbled twice but Robbie did not stop to help her. The brothers reached the cell together, leading Jemima herself by at least fifteen yards. By the time she arrived, the rope ladder was already being lowered and Joss was speaking soothing words to Clio—soothing and openly tender. But then Gerald was not present.

"Now then, darling, it's going to be all right. Trust Joss. Easy goes. Come on, my beautiful darling."

And after a few moments, Clio's head emerged once again: but it was a very different Clio, tear-stained, dirty—filthy dirty—and more or less incoherent. Jemima felt no particular pleasure at the sight; as a matter of fact, she found she preferred the confident if disagreeable Clio to this pathetic victim. Finally, how little Clio had known herself! She had been so sure of her own nerves, and so absolutely wrong when it came to the crunch. "The shadows, the ghosts of the prisoners trying to kill me" were some of the things Clio babbled about. At least Lady Martin might have been pleased at this last-minute sensitivity to the sufferings of people in the past. Still hysterical, Clio was led away in the direction of the Little Tower; it was now Robbie, not Joss, who took her arm, as though in tacit agreement that the Little Tower was "Robbie's." Joss, Ellie, and Jemima trailed after them.

"Nobody ever asked what would happen if she lost the bet!" cried Ellie suddenly: Jemima guessed she was annoyed at Robbie's attention to Clio.

"She gets to spend the night with Gerald," snapped Joss, evidently made equally tense by the sight of Robbie's arm round Clio. Ellie continued to gaze after them.

"My room is on the ground floor, overlooking the sea," she said. "I suppose I'd better go to it. It must be midnight by now. Happy New Year." Ellie did not even try to sound sincere. The door above their heads opened and shut; immediately Robbie came clattering back down the stairs; Clio had been tactfully left to face Gerald—if awake—by herself. Ellie was therefore looking slightly happier when Clio started to scream for the second time that night. This time there were no sobs, just sheer horror. What Clio was screaming over and over again, as she half ran, half fell down the stairway till she reached Robbie (and Joss), was this:

"He's dead, he's dead." Then: "Gerald, Gerald." Then more screams. It was Robbie who slapped Clio's face but it was Joss who shouted at her—almost as loudly as her own screams: "What do you mean, girl? How can he be dead?"

"He's dead," wailed Clio in a quieter tone. "I got into the bed, I touched something. It was a scarf. A long woollen scarf! A horrible thing. Red and purple squares." She gulped. "I pulled it. It didn't move. I put on the light. It was round his neck. He's dead. Gerald's dead."

"My scarf!" screamed Ellie in her turn. "That's my scarf!"

What followed was one of the most dreadful New Year's Days that Jemima had ever spent. The Crask headland and its castle was like something under an evil spell. Dawn came late and brought with it lurid red streaks over the North Sea: diabolic colors, thought Jemima.

The police in the person of one solitary officer took a long time to reach them: the nearest police station was after all over twenty-five miles away, and the force in general was occupied by drivers in distress, drunken drivers, and drunks pure and simple. The police doctor, summoned by him, took even longer to arrive; arrangements to take away the corpse—yes, Gerald had been strangled and with Ellie's woollen scarf—would take a while to make. In the meantime the corpse was locked inside the Browns' room, while Robbie, Ellie, and of course Clio took refuge in the Big Tower.

No one could leave the castle; statements would have to be made, evidence taken. The remaining occupants of Crask sat around in the big sitting room, as though in a daze.

At one point Ellie, who seemed personally angry with a situation so clearly devoid of any element of enjoyment, burst out: "It must have been some tramp. He could have got in by the back door, through that kitchenette. Some maniac. He could still be lurking. And he took my scarf!" Nobody answered her. After a while Robbie patted her hand. But nobody for the time being chose to go and sleep. When Lady Martin was wakened—by Joss—and told of the tragedy, she, too, joined them: with her curly grey hair, in her tartan dressing gown, she had the air of some cozy family nanny.

What Lady Martin said to Jemima later that morning was however, the reverse of cozy. Joss was talking to the police; Clio was lying down in his room (which he had made over to her); Robbie and Ellie were in the kitchen trying to organize some kind of meal in the absence of any local help at Hogmanay.

"She did it! Of course that wicked Clio Brown did it." Lady Martin's voice shook slightly in the passion of her conviction; she might have been lobbying a recalcitrant politician for the rights of the forgotten. "I recognize evil when I see it. People think I'm blind to the bad side of life—but what do they know about me? On the contrary, I've seen so much of it that I recognize it instantly. Clio Brown has no moral sense. She never had when she flirted with Robbie in the first place, then abandoned him for Gerald, all for the sake of the Brown money. Then she wasn't even grateful to Gerald for that—"

Jemima realized that May Martin, another woman who had married a rich man, was subconsciously contrasting Clio's behavior with her own: she gathered May had been extremely attentive to Sir Ludwig during their brief and harmonious marriage.

"Now she's done away with him in order to marry Joss and queen it here at Benmuir." Lady Martin paused in her harangue. "Yes, Jemima, I'm afraid my nephew Joss is not exactly a moral person either. Clio and Joss: they're alike in that way. Oh, ye gods! Money, and what people will do for it." An unbidden thought came to Jemima that Lady Martin could perhaps have prevented all this, whatever it was that had happened, by helping her nephew with Benmuir. She dismissed the thought. Who was she, Jemima, to say that family feeling should be put before human rights? She herself had no family.

"Listen, my friend," said Jemima in her most soothing interviewer's manner, patting the tartan-clad knee. "It's out of the question. Clio couldn't have done it. Gerald was alive when she went into the Bottle Dungeon, we know he was, and dead when she came out of it. So she couldn't have done it. No one gets out of the Bottle Dungeon without help. That motto carved in the stone—how does it go?"

All the time, however, Jemima was thinking fiercely beneath her tranquil front: I'm right, aren't I? She couldn't have done it, could she? She went over to the Little Tower, we saw her go. Gerald waved her goodbye, we saw him. A few minutes later she was back with us. Then she went down into the dungeon, we watched her, the ladder was pulled up and put aside, we could all see the stone cell from the Big Tower window. She couldn't have got out without being seen. The boys, above all *Joss*: no, he was here, we were all here. Even when Joss was dummy, he kept looking over my shoulder. Robbie never left the bridge table. If anyone went to the loo—maybe Ellie did when she was dummy— she would simply have gone to that little turret cloakroom on the same floor, one instant away; you'd have noticed a longer absence.

Jemima pursued her thoughts. And yet Gerald was dead when Clio was released. He must have been. Robbie took her up to her bedroom door and came straight down, we heard him. Besides, Gerald's body was beginning to grow cold. Jemima shuddered as she thought: I touched him.

To distract herself, she repeated. "How does the motto go?"

"Like this. *Initus*—once you're in—*non abeat*—you can't get out. The only Latin I know." Lady Martin sounded weary. "Girls in our family weren't taught Latin. Not that it would have been much use to me, as things turned out. I did learn first aid and nursing, much more useful, handling people the right way." Her voice trailed away.

Afterwards Jemima would look back on this conversation as crucial, and Lady Martin as the person who in all fairness was really responsible for solving the case. At the time she merely felt some stirring of comprehension, as though recent events, if looked at from the opposite angle, might be understood altogether differently—and correctly.

Jemima jumped up. "Will you be all right, May? I need—fresh air." On her way out of the Big Tower, Jemima stopped by the open door to the sitting room. Joss was standing there, looking out of the window. When she reached the ground floor, she could hear Robbie and Ellie in the kitchen. Jemima caught the words: "My scarf." Ellie was still complaining. She grabbed her own coat from the pile in the hall and passed rapidly out of doors. She walked across the grass, toward the stone cell, bending slightly in the wind. Jemima was conscious that Joss must be watching her from the window, as they had watched first Gerald, then Clio, the evening before. The door of the cell was still open; no one had thought to close it.

Jemima entered. The fetid reek from the open mouth of the Bottle Dungeon seemed to her stronger than ever: a reek of death. After all, if some prisoners had lived, in torment, others had died here. She remembered Clio's provocative comparison of the dungeon to marriage, a state from which she could not emerge without help. Gerald, of course, like some of the past prisoners, had emerged from it through death. The stone words were just visible above her head in the dim light. She traced them with her finger.

Initus . . . Suddenly she understood.

At that moment there was a noise behind her. Jemima turned cautiously round; she did not want to lose her footing. "Joss! You gave me a fright. I might have hurtled down into the depths."

"I wouldn't have let that happen. No more tragedies." Joss was blocking the light so that Jemima could not see his expression.

"How's Clio?"

"As well as can be expected." It was impossible to tell whether the cliché was intended sarcastically without seeing Joss's face. The effect was to make Jemima eager to get out of the cell, away from the pervasive stink which came from the dungeon, into the sea wind. She moved toward the door but Joss continued to block it.

"Any theories?" he asked. "Any theories, Jemima Shore Investigator?" He used the title of her television series by which the public generally identified her, but he made the words seem threatening. "Do you buy Ellie's tramp or Ellie's maniac?"

"*Are* there tramps in this remote spot? You tell me. But as for maniacs, I suppose you find them anywhere."

"Like criminals."

"Exactly." Jemima knew her voice was beginning to sound stifled. "The air, Joss," she began, "the air in here—" Then she realized what she must say. "One thing I do know: nobody in the party could have done it." May God forgive her for the lie: but like any prisoner she needed to get out.

"Is that so?"

"How could they? We were all together all the time, weren't we? Except for Clio, that is."

"And she was—here." Joss stepped forward as though to peer into the hole.

"Quite rare and absolutely horrible." Jemima was pleased to find her voice was under control. "No wonder Clio panicked and sounded the bell."

Joss moved aside. Jemima stepped out. She was now in the full view of the first floor of the Big Tower, where she could make out Robbie and Ellie standing together. They must be able to see her. She was safe. Nevertheless, Jemima chose to walk a number of yards away from the stone cell in the direction of the Big Tower. Then she saw Clio coming out of the great door. Her short black hair became rapidly windblown; she was wearing a parka over the black suit she had worn the night before. Clio came and leaned against Joss. He gave the impression of being quite indifferent to what anyone might think of this. Jemima had a fierce impulse to disturb that feline composure. She took a deep breath.

"Yes, you are alike," she said sharply to Joss. "Your aunt was right. Not only in your natures but physically alike. Both of you tall with short black hair. How could we tell the difference from the Big Tower? A parka over black trousers. We thought it was Clio. It was you, Joss. After you took May to her room. You killed him, didn't you?" Jemima still addressed Joss. "You took Ellie's scarf from her room to kill him. Then you made him wave out of the window, took up his arm and manipulated him, handled him. So that we were certain he was alive. Minutes later Clio came back into the sitting room, as if she'd just crossed the grass in the dark. But she'd been downstairs all along. And together you set up the bet. Another piece of handling."

"What's she saying, darling? Why is she saying these horrible things?" Clio sounded merely plaintive; she still looked perfectly, composedly beautiful.

Joss said nothing. He continued to gaze impassively at Jemima. She was glad to be under the protective gaze of Robbie and Ellie.

"*Initus non abeat.* Once in, you can't get out. The motto," cried Jemima. "But Clio wasn't actually *in* the dungeon when Gerald died. That was all a plot, a distraction to get our attention. She was lurking downstairs among all the coats, finding jerseys there, letting *you* do it, Joss. Afterward, Clio's panic in the dungeon may well have been genuine, ringing that bell that Robbie found. She was alone, she had connived at the murder of her husband: and of course the bell made for another distraction."

"Prove it," said Joss coldly to Jemima. To Clio he said: "Pay no attention, she's mad. Media people! We should never have let Aunt May bring her. Unhinged!"

"I can't prove it. That's for the police." As though on cue, Jemima was aware of the distinctive Scottish police car driving toward the gates of the castle to her right. "All I know is: you were in it together. And you're still in it together: this is one Bottle Dungeon with two prisoners inside it. A desperate kind of marriage: your word, Clio. Until one of you turns on the other, that is."

As the police car drove nearer, Jemima saw Clio's slanting cat's eyes slide away from Joss. Clio was in deep, as deep as she had been down in those fetid depths. But Clio was going to try to get out. She'll betray him, thought Jemima, and after all he did the killing. What was it May Martin said that afternoon by the dungeon? Some people are survivors.

DEATH IN SMALL DOSES

by B. K. Stevens

"You may say what you will for chemistry and sociology," Neville Carter said, his mouth puckering with mild delight as he waited for his own punchline. He was tall and mostly gray, round at the middle and soft everywhere else. His eyes couldn't quite work up a glisten, but they did sputter a bit. "You may say what you will," he continued, "for history and biology. You may praise the virtues of philosophy and sing the praises of music. I, however, shall always maintain the supremacy of English. Why, without English we couldn't even talk to each other."

People actually laughed. Not me, of course, and not Miss Woodhouse or her mother or the stern, compact woman sitting at the far end of the table. But everyone else erupted with determined glee.

"Good one, Nev!" called out a middle-aged woman. " 'Couldn't even talk to each other'! That's telling them!"

" 'Sing the praises of music,' " echoed an equally middle-aged man. "That's—well, clever. It's very—well. And so on."

"And 'the virtues of philosophy,' " a young but faded woman put in anxiously. "That was clever, too."

"Very bold," a young man said, prolonging a chuckle. "Insightful, articulate, and very bold."

It was like a scene from a nightmare. Thunder crashing outside, a gloomy dining hall lined with disapproving portraits, six English teachers, and me. I cast a resentful glance at Miss Woodhouse, who sat across the table from me, her face rigid and

68

unreadable. Why was I here? Yes, I knew this was her old prep school, I knew the woman becoming the new chairperson of the English department tonight was both Miss Woodhouse's former teacher and her mother's longtime friend, I knew Matilda Arnold had badgered both Woodhouses until they'd felt obliged to come. But I had no connection to either the school or Dr. Arnold, and Miss Woodhouse knows I hate speeches and feel insecure about my grammar. Just once, couldn't she drag someone else along to be the buffer between her and her mother?

Neville Carter emerged from his self-satisfied giggles and got ready to speak again. Didn't the man have any decency? He'd dozed comfortably through the first four after-dinner speeches, blinking himself into vaguely smiling consciousness only when the tributes his colleagues were giving him moved them to applause. Now *I* needed sleep, and I couldn't get it until he shut up.

He glanced at his notes. "These have been good years," he said. "While it has been my honor to serve as your chair, the department had prospered. We have protected the curriculum against the envy of other departments, actually increasing the number of required English courses. We have labored to ensure we are not unjustly slighted when budgets are set, leaves granted, salaries determined. So I hope you will not accuse me of arrogance if I say I look back at these years with 'modest pride.' Like Milton's Eve, you know—'modest pride.' "

The four teachers sitting nearest him hummed and nodded, impressed. Professor Woodhouse nudged me in the ribs. "Milton," she whispered, "was talking about sex. A ghastly, inappropriate allusion, little Harriet."

"And now," Neville Carter went on, "I look forward to my retirement. I hope you agree I've earned the rest—"

"Hear, hear!" the middle-aged woman cried, unable to contain herself. "Well-earned! Well-earned!"

Neville Carter flushed with pleasure. "I shall miss you all. But it's good to know I leave you in capable hands." He lifted his eyes from his notes, looking down the table at the so-far-silent woman who stared back expressionlessly. "Matilda, you have been absent from our midst too long. I remember when you first joined the English department, many years ago. I remember how sorry we were to lose you when the headmaster asked you to become dean. And although you've had your little disagreements with us over the years, I speak for everyone when I say how happy we are to have you back. I know you will be a fine leader, a firm, loyal advocate for the department and its interests. I know your tenure as chair will be accomplished and harmonious. I trust it will be as deeply satisfying as my own. Welcome, Dr. Matilda Arnold. Welcome back to our department."

There was applause, of course—I applauded wildly, too, so relieved and happy he'd sat down at last. Two white-suited waiters began setting small glasses by each place. Miss Woodhouse had told me about this part of the tradition. Drinking isn't usually allowed at faculty functions at Newton Academy, but when a department changes hands, the incoming chair is allowed to propose one toast in honor of the retiring chair. And so now one waiter circulated with a cut-glass decanter, pouring careful inches of sherry. The other waiter took a second decanter and filled Dr. Arnold's glass. That's right, I remembered. Miss Woodhouse had told me she had a heart condition and couldn't drink at all—that must be juice. Poor woman. Sitting through all those speeches and not getting even one decent belt as a reward.

Dr. Matilda Arnold stood up. She looked about sixty and was thin and short, but there was nothing frail about her. She was sturdy and energetic and intensely intelligent—you could see all that at a glance. And she was mad. You could see that, too.

"Thank you for that speech of welcome, Neville," she said, each word slow and distinct. "I doubt, however, that everyone in this department shares your professed enthusiasm about my return. One of you is trying to kill me."

Finally, action. I sat up straighter, looking to Miss Woodhouse for confirmation. But she saw me looking and shook her head. The announcement had taken her by surprise, too.

It had certainly surprised everyone else. There was a moment of absolute quiet, then a nervous giggle from the young woman. Neville Carter frowned. "You're joking, of course."

"I am not joking," Matilda Arnold said sternly, then shrugged.

"I may be exaggerating. The attempts on my life have been so clumsy and stupid it's hard to believe they were sincere. Of course, since a member of this department was behind them—well. They *may* have been sincere. At any rate, someone's trying to scare me away. In the month since the headmaster announced I'd be the new chair, I've received two anonymous threats through campus mail, each followed by an attack. The second threat arrived yesterday morning, and late last night someone got into my house and extinguished the pilot light in my oven. My cat woke me before there was any danger—indeed, it would take the house so long to fill with fumes that I probably would have arisen in time even had Boots not been so vigilant—but the attempt *was* made. And today I received another threat."

She took a sheet of paper from her purse and handed it to Miss Woodhouse. "Here, Iphigenia. Now you know why I insisted you come tonight. I've followed your career with interest. I know about your accomplishments as a police officer and a private detective. Accordingly, this morning I mailed you the other two threats and some additional documents. With luck, you'll receive them tomorrow and can begin your investigation immediately."

Miss Woodhouse shook her head. "I appreciate your confidence, but if you're right, you'll need bodyguards around the clock. We can't really—"

"I have also," Matilda Arnold cut in, "given a check to the Friends of the Seagull Society—a strange little charity, of no interest to me, but a favorite, I know, of your mother's. The check has been cashed. You are thus, I think, honor bound to consider your retainer already paid, yourself already hired."

Miss Woodhouse looked ready to protest, but her mother silenced her with a snarl. "Raise no objections, you nasty girl. Matilda needs your help, and you quite frankly need the business. Must you fuss *every* time someone hires you?"

That settled it. "I'm sorry, Mother," Miss Woodhouse said meekly. "Dr. Arnold, I'll be happy to take your case, but this isn't the time to discuss it. Perhaps tomorrow—"

"Oh, what nonsense," Neville Carter cut in. "Matilda, we cannot have private detectives meddling in our affairs and creating scandal. If someone *has* been playing pranks on you, it's undoubtedly a student, and the Dean of Students will handle it. I cannot *believe* you'd even suggest that a member of this department could wish to harm or threaten you."

"The threats are all on department stationery," Matilda Arnold countered, "and I'm sure Iphigenia will find they were typed on the department's computer, to which you all have access. Further, the threats are literary, and I hardly think students would express their hostility with line references to Shakespeare or Tennyson. And despite your saccharine speech, I know none of you wanted me as chair. You, Neville, haunted the headmaster's office for three solid weeks after he announced his decision, whining and protesting and threatening lawsuits."

Neville Carter bristled. "I made no explicit references to lawsuits. I merely pointed out that, while I bear you no animosity, departments usually select their own chairs. It is unusual and somewhat insulting for the headmaster to ignore their vote and insist on his own choice."

"It is *very* insulting," Matilda Arnold agreed, "but the headmaster hardly ignored your vote. He saw the name of the person you elected and became physically ill." She looked up at the middle-aged man. "Jeffrey Littel—Neville Carter's listless clone. The predictable successor to your legacy, Neville, the first person you hired when you seized control of the department twenty years ago and set about filling it with weaklings you could control, with people so relentlessly mediocre they would make even you look good by comparison."

Jeffrey Littel flushed. "I—well. I resent that."

She raised an eyebrow. "You recognized it as an insult, then? Good. A flicker of intelligence. Cultivate that spark, Jeffrey, if you hope to teach anything but ninth-grade grammar for the rest of your life. I probably can't get you dismissed, but tenure won't protect you from dreary teaching assignments. I know how lazy and incompetent you are, how you recycle lectures for decades and won't allow students to ask questions because you haven't a clue about how to answer them."

"That's his teaching style," the middle-aged woman said angrily. "You have no right to criticize it."

"Ah, yes," Matilda Arnold said, smiling. "Valerie Littel, devoted sister of Jeffrey—not quite as stupid and inert as he, but twice as scheming, twice as vicious. You used your brother to wheedle your way into a position for which you are not even remotely qualified, and ever since, you've neglected your students and concentrated all your efforts on school politics, made so frantic by your guilty knowledge of your incompetence that you couldn't rest secure even after you bullied the school into granting you tenure. You thought you'd be the power behind the throne, didn't you, when Jeffrey was named chair? Think again, Valerie. As of now, you've lost your influence. For one thing, I'll have the final say on hiring. No longer will you be allowed to fill the department with creatures like Adam Pulen."

The young man at the table shook his head sadly. "You're just revealing your own bitterness, Matilda."

"Yes, I'm bitter," Matilda Arnold said. "Bitter at seeing a man like you teaching at this fine old academy, at seeing your corruption tolerated and allowed to spread. You are even more worthless than the other untenured person in the department, than Carla Perry, who caters to every student whim, who shows movies in class three times a week so she needn't bother to prepare and her students needn't bother to open a book—"

"But my students don't *like* books," Carla Perry said peevishly. "They'd *rather* watch movies. And I'm so busy with student committees and organizations, with Delta Phi Phi and the Student Affairs Committee, and the Sunshine Squad—"

"That's right," Matilda Arnold said, nodding. "Use that as your excuse—and be sure to mention all the memorable projects you've sponsored, such as last year's Self-Esteem Carnival. You can list them on your *vita* when you apply for your next job. By the way, Iphigenia, I've sent you the *curriculum vitae* of all the members of the department. Study them closely, to familiarize yourself with the backgrounds of these mediocrities. We'll meet soon. And now," she said, lifting her glass, "the traditional toast.

Neville, you drove me from teaching two decades ago, by making this department so abominable I could no longer stand to be part of it. Now I return, and as you and all your cronies know, I do so with the single intention of purging the department before I too retire. The person behind these ridiculous threats shall be the first to go, but none of you will be allowed to neglect your duties any longer, to nap through your classes and devote all your time to scheming for selfish, petty advantages. And so, beloved colleagues, I drink to you."

She drained her glass, frowned, and set it down. "Shockingly bitter apple juice," she observed and clutched her throat, and gasped, and crashed forward over the table, dead.

At nine the next morning, I sat in the spacious, sunny parlor that serves as the office for Woodhouse Investigations, typing the final report for an insurance case. Miss Woodhouse walked in briskly—six feet tall, broad-shouldered, lean, her black-gray frizz of hair pulled back tightly and fastened with a thick blue rubber band. She cast a deferential glance at her mother, who sat in a rocking chair framed by the big bay window. Today, the professor was whittling potatoes into the profiles of presidents, completing a model of Mount Rushmore.

"Harriet," Miss Woodhouse said, "I'll be busy in the kitchen for the next two hours. I have, of course, informed the police about the materials Dr. Arnold sent me. An officer will come by for them at eleven."

I frowned at her. "But the mail always arrives by ten."

She frowned back. "I know that. I told the police that. And Lieutenant Glass—and the police said someone would come by at eleven. When the mail arrives, you must open it as usual, and make copies of anything important. You must not by mistake open the envelope from Dr. Arnold—it is, after all, evidence in a possible homicide—and you must not copy anything to which only the police should have access at this point."

God, I hate it when she pulls these stunts. I knew what was going on. Lieutenant Glass had been her fiancé fourteen years ago, before the professor had had her breakdown, before Miss

Woodhouse had felt obliged to break off her engagement, resign from the police force, and start a private detective agency so she could devote more time to her mother. And I knew that Lieutenant Glass was still in love with Miss Woodhouse, and that she was too proud to accept the help he was frantic to give her, and that they had come up with all sorts of dodges to disguise the fact they were cooperating. And always, when they staged one of their charades, I was cast as the stooge.

I sighed. "All right, Miss Woodhouse. When the mail comes, I'll be careful not to open the envelope from Dr. Arnold. And I won't make copies of any documents we shouldn't have."

The professor sniffed loudly. "Clumsy," she said, defining Teddy Roosevelt's mustache with short, sure swipes of her knife. The charade was partly for her sake—she knew that—and if she wanted it to continue, she'd have to play almost as dumb as me. "I am morally certain, Iphigenia, that Matilda did not die of natural causes. She was poisoned. You must prove that."

"I'll try, Mother," she said, and hid in the kitchen.

The mail came promptly at ten. I whistled obliviously, keeping my face stupidly limp as I opened each envelope and made copies of everything—the electric bill, a subscription offer from *National Geographic*, everything Matilda Arnold had sent us. Promptly at eleven a uniformed policeman arrived, and Miss Woodhouse emerged from the kitchen, smelling of ammonia.

"Here you are, officer," she said. "The envelope from Dr. Matilda Arnold, containing—good God, Harriet! You didn't accidentally open it, did you?"

I shrugged. "I guess," I said. "Silly me."

The policeman blushed. He was very young, very embarrassed. "Lieutenant Glass asked me to give you this," he said. "It's a letter, I think, thanking you for your cooperation."

She slit open the envelope. One sheet of stiff police stationery and a few typed lines—and stuck to the back of it, with maple syrup, a sheet from a yellow scratch pad. "What's this?" she said, feigning surprise. "Let's see—'Death from massive overdose of digitalis. Victim's digitalis prescription refilled one week ago, five pills unaccountably missing from bottle in her medicine cabinet.

Possibly stolen during burglary at her house, night before her murder. Find the burglar, find the murderer.' Goodness, officer. I don't think I was supposed to see this. You'd better return it to Lieutenant Glass."

The officer took the yellow sheet from her awkwardly. "The lieutenant also said to ask if you'd like a key to Dr. Arnold's house, since your mother's an old friend of hers and since Dr. Arnold has a cat—he thought you might want to feed the cat. And he asked me to say he looked the house over this morning but didn't touch anything, won't take anything away until tomorrow. So he said maybe you'd like to feed the cat tonight."

Somberly, Miss Woodhouse took the key from him. "I shall," she said, "feed Dr. Arnold's cat tonight. Thank you."

He left, looking glad to escape. "I hope, Harriet," Miss Woodhouse said severely, "you were not so very careless as to accidentally copy the contents of Dr. Arnold's envelope."

I tried to look confused. "Gosh. Maybe. At least, I *think* these are copies of the things she sent you. What do *you* think?"

I handed her the copies, and she took them to her desk. "Well, these *could* be copies of the threats she received—they're similar to the ones she gave me last night, which I of course turned over to the police. What do you think, Mother? 'T. Wolfe 1940'— does that sound like a threat?"

The professor didn't look up. "A reference to a Thomas Wolfe novel, *You Can't Go Home Again*. Yes, in the context of Matilda's return to her department, that might be a threat."

"And this note was attached to it," I said, handing Miss Woodhouse the copy. " 'Received Monday morning, April 19. That evening, as I worked in library, bust of Sir Isaac Newton toppled from its stand in upper balcony, crashing inches from my feet. Library nearly deserted—no culprit in sight.' "

"Interesting," Miss Woodhouse said. "And here's the next one. '*Richard II*, III, ii, 103'—should I look it up?"

The professor glared at her. "Do you doubt me, Iphigenia? Let's see—ah, yes. Most likely, 'The worst is death, and death will have his day.' A more specific, more serious threat."

"Yes, they do seem to be escalating," Miss Woodhouse agreed. "What does Dr. Arnold say about that one, Harriet?"

I read from the photocopy. " 'Received second threat May 10. That night, sat up until one, making notes for talk with I. W. At four, Boots woke me. Pilot light out, gas fumes. No break-in, but faculty secretary keeps key in her desk, for feeding Boots when I'm out of town. Easy for any faculty member to take.' "

"Just as it would have been easy for any faculty member to slip into the dining hall last night while we were having punch in the lobby," Miss Woodhouse said, "and poison the decanter of apple juice—from which, of course, only Dr. Arnold would be drinking. I'm sure her heart condition was common knowledge. And then there's the final threat, the one Dr. Arnold showed me last night. I've looked it up already—it refers to Tennyson's 'Charge of the Light Brigade,' the lines about riding 'Into the jaws of death/Into the mouth of hell.' Any thoughts, Mother?"

"Just that this person shows a slight preference for British authors—but that, of course, could have been done intentionally, to mislead us. What else did Matilda send, Harriet?"

I looked through the copies. "A brief cover letter, saying she hopes to talk to Miss Woodhouse soon. Aside from that just the resumes of the English teachers, with some penciled notes on them. I'm surprised she didn't send more—aren't you?"

"Oh, Matilda would be discreet about what she'd commit to writing," the professor said. "She wouldn't send an outsider, even a detective, written records of confidential information she'd learned in her capacity as dean. The *vitae*, however—and they *are* called *vitae*, dear Harriet, not resumes—are essentially public documents. There's no impropriety in showing them to us—and little chance they'll reveal much. People seldom put damaging information about themselves on their *vitae*. To uncover *that*, we must persuade the department members to inform on each other."

"They won't," I said, shaking my head. "They're so close, so fond of each other—they couldn't say enough good things about each other last night. I bet they'll all refuse to talk to us, put up a really solid front."

The professor smiled. "Don't be too sure, little Harriet. Judging from my years in academia, I'd venture—"

The doorbell rang. Neville Carter was standing on the front porch, wearing a black suit, looking somber.

"I've been to the funeral home," he said when I let him into the office, "to check on the arrangements. Poor Matilda has no family, you know. She devoted her entire life to the Academy."

"It's very sad," Miss Woodhouse agreed, and waited.

"Indeed." Neville Carter took the chair near her desk. "And I thought I should stop by here. I spoke to the police last night, but it *does* seem a private detective—well, we must guard the Academy's reputation, and since you're a loyal alumna, I'm sure you'll be more discreet. Can I help you in any way?"

"I hope so," Miss Woodhouse said, and shot a knowing glance at her mother. The professor, grinning, had gone back to her potato-sculpting, straightening the lines in Lincoln's beard. "Now, Mr. Carter, do you know anything about the attempts on Dr. Arnold's life? No? Then do you know if anyone in the department had a special grudge against her, a special reason to fear her?"

He seemed to think it over. "Not really. Certainly *I* had no reason to fear her—I'm retiring, you know, and so would be quite beyond her reach. Jeffrey and Valerie Littel are tenured, so they're safe, too. And they're such fine people, such dear old friends— it's absurd to imagine either would harm her. As for Carla Perry, her tenure decision *is* coming up next year, but she's done so well here that I'm sure it's just a formality. No, none of us had any reason to fear Matilda."

"You haven't," Miss Woodhouse said, "mentioned Adam Pulen."

He fidgeted with his tie. "Didn't I? Well, he's a true scholar, completing his dissertation at a first-rate university. True, he *did*—but I'm sure he wouldn't *murder* anyone."

Miss Woodhouse picked up Adam Pulen's *vita*. "I notice he graduated from college in 1984 and began graduate school in 1989. That leaves several years unaccounted for. See? Dr. Arnold circled those dates, and wrote 'gap' in the margin."

"So she did," he said, peering. "Well. This is awkward. I *do* know what he was doing during those years—but I didn't, you understand, when we hired him. I found out just this fall, when a woman wrote to Matilda, trying to track him down. Some tale of a broken engagement and an illegitimate child. The young woman's name was Rebecca Carswell. You may have heard of her father, the Reverend Edward Carswell?"

"The one who ran that television ministry?" Miss Woodhouse asked. "The one who's now serving twenty years for fraud?"

He nodded. "Yes. Adam worked for the Reverend Carswell for several years, and was named in the indictment after the *60 Minutes* piece and all the disclosures. But Adam was never convicted, you understand—never convicted. He wanted to start over, and that, apparently, entailed breaking his engagement to Miss Carswell, who claimed Adam had fathered her child. But the tests were inconclusive—you see—inconclusive. When we learned all this, we were naturally dismayed. Still, he was so young when it happened—early twenties—and we all make errors in judgment, so who are we to condemn others? The department voted to keep Adam on. But Matilda wanted him dismissed. She was quite frustrated when the headmaster sided with us."

"And I see from these notes," Miss Woodhouse said, "that Dr. Arnold also had doubts about his teaching, and his critical approach. Do you share those reservations?"

Neville Carter shrugged. "Oh, well. His approach—I couldn't say what it is, really. I haven't much interest in such matters, or much time to supervise teaching. Other duties keep me too busy—I have to protect the department's interests, you know. I'm sure his teaching and approach are fine."

"But Dr. Arnold *did* care deeply about such matters," Miss Woodhouse said. "If she'd become the new chair, she would presumably have again tried to get rid of Mr. Pulen."

"Perhaps." He shifted in his chair. "Although I wouldn't conclude he'd therefore—no. I won't point an accusing finger at anyone. Still, if one *did* feel compelled to search for someone with a motive, and if one *did* feel his youthful indiscretions indicate a lack of character—but I'm sure not."

"Thank you for your candor, Mr. Carter," Miss Woodhouse said solemnly, standing up. "I know this was painful for you."

As soon as he was gone, I threw my hands in the air. "His own colleague! And Carter served him up to us on a platter."

"Well, he was almost bound to serve *someone* up to us," Miss Woodhouse said. "I'm sure he wants this case concluded quickly, before police and detectives poke around in his department too much and uncover any little secrets *he's* hiding. And Adam Pulen was the natural choice as sacrificial victim. He's been in the department only two years—his arrest would be embarrassing, but not as bad as the arrest of one of Carter's longtime cronies. And Carter—Harriet, will you see who's at the door?"

This time it was Carla Perry. She was barely thirty but already looked about half used up, her movements small and nervous, her face drawn into a permanently resentful expression. She looked me over and sniffed, unimpressed.

"I want to talk to someone important," she said.

She didn't much like having Professor Woodhouse in the office, too, but the professor didn't budge. The professor never budges. Anyone who wants to talk to Miss Woodhouse had better get used to that. Carla Perry fussed briefly and gave up.

"I wanted to see if I could help," she said. "With your investigation, I mean. If you need information or anything."

"We do," Miss Woodhouse said. "For example, is there anyone with a special reason to resent Dr. Arnold?"

Carla Perry laughed harshly. "You mean *besides* Jeffrey?"

Even Miss Woodhouse seemed surprised the accusation had come so quickly. "I assume you mean Jeffrey Littel?"

"Well, I don't know of any *other* Jeffrey I could mean, do you?" The sarcasm seemed automatic and unconscious. "Yes, I mean Jeffrey Littel. I'm not saying he killed her, but obviously he had the most reason to resent her. He was sure he'd be the new chair, and then the headmaster names Dr. Arnold. It was a real slap in the face. Jeffrey was livid that day, and he said some things—but I wouldn't want to repeat them."

"Then you shouldn't have alluded to them, little girl," the professor commented, rocking steadily in her corner. "Now, I suppose, you want us to tease you out of your feigned reluctance. Let us deny her the pleasure, Iphigenia. Let us ask instead about the tenure decision facing her next year."

Carla Perry flushed. "That's no big deal. I mean, it's all sewn up. I mean, I've got a Ph.D., which is more than *some* people in the department can say, and I've done lots of extra stuff with the student clubs and committees and things."

"Dr. Arnold didn't seem impressed with your efforts," Miss Woodhouse said, looking over Carla Perry's *vita*. "She's bracketed your list of the projects you sponsored and written 'excessive, detrimental' in the margin."

"Well, she didn't care for Assertiveness Awareness Week," Carla Perry admitted, "and she had reservations when we put the Inter-Active Video Arcade in the library. But students love things like that, and students come first, right? It's just that Dr. Arnold was old-fashioned and put all this emphasis on teaching, like we can expect students to *study* all day. So we disagreed, but we never, like, argued. She respected my philosophy."

"Which you describe so eloquently," the professor observed. "We shall give all your comments due weight." As soon as Carla Perry was gone, the professor shuddered. "And some university awarded a Ph.D. to *that*. I tremble for the academy, Iphigenia."

"As do we all," Miss Woodhouse agreed. "And yet Carla Perry's natural stupidity is probably no greater than Neville Carter's. It's just that she went through the schools thirty years later, and thus received no education. Well, I suppose that visit was predictable. Perry's an obvious suspect, since she's coming up for tenure and Dr. Arnold couldn't stand her—naturally, she'd want to point us toward someone else."

"Do you think she picked Jeffrey Littel at random?" I asked.

"Possibly. Or perhaps she honestly *does* suspect him, or perhaps she hopes to get him out of the way and become chair herself." She picked up Valerie Littel's *vita*. "His sister's the only other possible candidate, and all she's got is a B.A.—Perry's degree makes her a likelier choice."

"I guess," I said, "but even so—"

The phone rang. It was Valerie Littel, whispering, asking if I could slip away for lunch. I repeated the question, looking at Miss Woodhouse for a decision. She nodded, and I accepted.

I went to Chic and Ruth's, a justly popular deli in Annapolis's historic district, and spotted Valerie Littel in a corner booth. Or rather, I sniffed her out—even the rich fragrance of pastrami couldn't keep me from zeroing in on her perfume. I'm not a squeamish person. Secondhand smoke doesn't faze me, I visited L.A. for a week and never noticed the smog, I drive by chemical factories and fields of grazing cows without rolling up my window. But last night, sitting next to Valerie Littel at dinner, I'd nearly passed out from the perfume.

Today she was wearing sunglasses, and a scarf covered her too-curled, too-teased, implausibly black hair. "I'm glad you came," she whispered. "I feel awful about this—I don't know if I should come forward or not. I want you to advise me."

"I'll try," I said, "but if you have some information, why don't you tell Miss Woodhouse and—"

"No, no. I'm not ready to take that step." She bit her lip. "He was my teacher, after all, and my friend."

God. What next? "You mean Neville Carter?"

"Yes," she said miserably, and took a thick bite of her egg salad sandwich. "He *did* hire me, after all—even though he's held me back all these years, and not given me the teaching schedules and committee assignments I deserve—so I suppose I owe him something. But murder! That's very serious, isn't it?"

I solemnly agreed that murder was very serious. "You think Mr. Carter murdered Dr. Arnold?"

She nodded, still munching. "Neville hated Matilda, and he hated having a woman take over the chair—that's why he backed Jeffrey and not me, even though I've done a *lot* more for the department. Well that's how men are. The headmaster's sexist, too. He didn't want me as chair, either."

"He picked Dr. Arnold," I pointed out. "She's a woman."

"A woman he could control. I liked Matilda very much, but

she was a traditionalist. The headmaster wouldn't want to stir things up by giving a woman like *me* any power."

This was awkward. "Or maybe he picked Dr. Arnold because she had a Ph.D. I saw your *vita*, and—"

Her head jerked up, and I felt the anger burning through the sunglasses. "It wasn't about degrees. It was about power. The headmaster wanted to rule through Matilda, and Neville wanted to rule through Jeffrey. It'd kill Neville to give up control, even after he retires. He shaped the department in his own image and ran it for decades. If Matilda had taken over, all that would have changed. That's why he had to kill her."

At least she was blunter than the others had been. "Do you know of any proof?" I asked.

She hesitated. "Not exactly. But before dinner, when we were all having punch in the lobby, I went to the ladies' room to freshen my perfume, and I saw a man sneak into the dining room. I didn't see him clearly—I was at the far end of the hall, I never went *near* the room myself—but I *think* it was Neville."

All through the rest of her egg salad sandwich and my turkey club, I tried to get her to say something more definite. No luck. She told many tales of Neville Carter's tyranny and mental instability but wouldn't get more specific about the person she'd seen last night. Well, I thought as I walked back to the office, possibly she hadn't seen anybody. Possibly, she was just afraid someone had seen *her* leave the lobby, and wanted to get her own accusation on record before someone hurled one at her.

When I got back to the office, Adam Pulen was already seated in the chintz armchair near Miss Woodhouse's desk. He was by far the most stylish-looking member of the department—blond hair slicked straight back like a male model, three-piece gray suit with a vaguely continental look, designer tie with Windsor knot. I wouldn't have called him handsome, though. There was an evasiveness about his features that had made me rule him out immediately the night before, even without making my usual wedding ring check.

"I'm glad you're back, Ms. Russo," he said, standing up as I entered. Well, he got points for remembering my name. "I was just telling Ms. Woodhouse and her mother about the rumors flying around campus today. They can't be true, can they?"

"I'm afraid so," Miss Woodhouse said. "Dr. Arnold died of a massive digitalis overdose. She was murdered."

He frowned slightly, as if reluctant to contradict her. "Well, that's one way to read it, I suppose. But it could just as easily have been an accident—or suicide."

"Certainly not!" the professor cried indignantly. "I have known Matilda Arnold for decades, young man, and she was not such a fool as to accidentally drop five digitalis pills into her apple juice. And she would never take her life intentionally."

He shrugged. "Intentionally, unintentionally—it's impossible to know, isn't it? Look at it this way. She'd committed herself to being the chair, and I'm sure she wanted to shake things up, but at her age she must have dreaded the thought of a daily struggle with colleagues who didn't want her back. So she sends herself threatening letters, fakes murder attempts—there were no witnesses, were there?—and poisons her juice. She gives a grand speech, telling us all off, and dies. Now she's a martyr, and everyone in the department is a murder suspect. She's succeeded in shaking things up, but spared herself the slow drudgery of reform. Who's to say that's not the way to read it?"

The professor glared. "*I* say it. I knew my friend, and what you suggest is impossible. You seem eager to spread this theory of yours, young man. You couldn't be trying to create a distraction, could you, to divert attention from incriminating evidence about yourself—some youthful indiscretion, perhaps?"

He nodded in gracious knowledgment. "So you already know about that. But that's the point—everybody already knows. I have nothing left to hide, and I had nothing to fear from Matilda Arnold. She'd have no reason to drag out old secrets and risk creating a scandal for the Academy, when everybody knows I'll be leaving Newton after one more year anyway."

"You will?" Miss Woodhouse said. "Why?"

"Because my dissertation is nearly complete. Once I have my Ph.D., I'll move to university teaching. I have no desire to stay at

Newton forever, teaching nothing but literature and writing. My real interest is critical theory. Check with my graduate professors—they'll tell you I'm doing very well on my dissertation and have excellent prospects for finding a position. While you're at it, check Matilda's appointment calendar. You'll find I went to see her after she was named chair, to make sure we agreed about letting sleeping dogs lie. She assured me that she had no interest in the past, that she was far more concerned about certain things going on at Newton right now."

"Certain things?" the professor echoed. "Clarify, please."

He went through the same little fake-hesitation act the others had performed. "Well, I'm not accusing anyone of murder, but Matilda *did* mention Carla Perry—Carla's—well, to be frank, she's been sleeping with students. She loves all those little committee projects of hers, and I guess that's one way of getting students to cooperate. And Matilda *did* say she planned to bring all this up at Carla's tenure hearing, and she'd already warned Carla about it. Of course, even if that might *look* like a motive, I'm not saying Carla's the one."

"Of course you're not," Miss Woodhouse said, nodding. "I understand perfectly. And I—Harriet, would you get the door?"

Naturally, I had to get the door again. There was still one loyal member of the English department left, and he had to spread his bit of dirt, too. It was awkward, though—ushering Jeffrey Littel into the office even before Adam Pulen left.

Adam Pulen sprang to his feet. "Jeffrey! What a surprise!"

Jeffrey Littel frowned. "Yes. Well. I was just coming to tell the Woodhouses about visiting hours at the funeral home."

"And I was just leaving," Adam Pulen said, and fled.

"Please, sit down, Dr. Littel," Miss Woodhouse said. "You wanted to tell us about visiting hours?"

"Well, yes—that is, yes." Jeffrey Littel lowered himself into the armchair. He was absolutely the dullest human being I had ever met. His face was pushed-in and pasty, his hair was scant and limp, his voice never aspired to anything beyond a drone. "That is—well. Visiting hours are from four to six tomorrow, and we're all going around five, then going to my house—mine and Valerie's—for sherry, and cheese, and—well, and so on. And—well, since your mother was a friend of Matilda's, and—well. Perhaps you'd like to come. And so on."

The speech took five minutes. My eyelids were already drooping. "Thank you," Miss Woodhouse said. "We'll come."

"Good. That's very—well, good." He paused for a solid two minutes, and I nearly dozed off. "And I—well, I hate to say this, but—well, duty, and such, and the law, and—well. And so on. So I thought I should come forward."

Even Miss Woodhouse was yawning. "About what, Dr. Littel?"

"Well, about—well, about Valerie, you know. My sister? Well. I love her, of course, but I—well. I thought you should know. She and Matilda—well. Valerie always wanted to be chair herself, but without a suitable degree—well. The headmaster would never—well. And to see another woman, one she despised—well. And so on. Not that I'd want to—of course not. But she's been staying out late for no reason, and being secretive, and—well. I thought you should know. And so on."

Professor Woodhouse let out a loud hiss, and her daughter snapped into awareness. "Yes. Thank you. And we'll be at visiting hours tomorrow. Harriet, please see Dr. Littel out."

I stumbled across the office and nudged him through the door. I was rubbing my eyes as I went back to join the Woodhouses. "His own sister!" I said. "I don't believe it."

"Believe it," Miss Woodhouse said grimly. "I'd guess she's been bullying him all his life, and he's sick of it and wants his freedom—even weaklings *do* want freedom, you know, even if they wouldn't know what to do with it. Well, we now have some leads. Our next step is to feed Dr. Arnold's cat. But since Barry—since Lieutenant Glass said to feed it tonight, I'll wait until after dark. It could be the police would find it awkward if we showed up while it's still light. So I'll—"

"You will not go to Matilda's house at all," the professor said severely. "You know how frightfully allergic to cats you are, Iphigenia, and I am *not* about to nurse you through another attack. We will send little Harriet."

Miss Woodhouse balked. "But she's a secretary. I'm sorry, Harriet—you know I have great respect for you, but you're not trained as a detective. You won't know what to notice."

"Then she must notice everything," the professor said firmly. "You shall not go to that house, Iphigenia. Give dear Harriet what instructions you will, but you shall not go."

And that's why, at ten that night, I drove to Dr. Matilda Arnold's house alone, armed with a Polaroid camera, a legal pad, detailed instructions, and a sack of Meow Mix. I was determined to notice everything.

Boots was curled up just inside the front door. I scratched him behind the ears and reveled in his purr. "Oh, you're a fat, fine cat," I said, "and I'd love to take you home, but I can't have a pet in my apartment. Don't worry, though. We'll find *just* the right home for you. I hope you like Meow Mix."

I filled his bowl and changed his water, then got to work. Dr. Arnold's desk first—the professor had warned me it'd be messy, and she hadn't exaggerated. Apparently, Dr. Arnold never cleared off her desk, just let things accumulate in layers. The top layer featured an open copy of *The Sorrows of Young Werther* and a yellow pad with the heading "Notes for Meeting with I. W." I copied down the block-letter jottings on each page—notations about Neville Carter's flagrant incompetence and indifference to teaching, Jeffrey Littel's numbing laziness, Valerie Littel's viciousness and politicking, Carla Perry's committee projects, Adam Pulen's unsound theories and spotted past. I took a picture of the desk, then moved to the dining room and took a picture of the stereo topped by an album cover for a recording of *Tosca*.

And then there was a noise upstairs. My hands tensed so sharply that I snapped another picture without meaning to. It's the killer, I thought. The killer came back here for some reason, and heard my car pull into the driveway, and didn't have time to get out of the house, and ran upstairs to hide. And now the killer's waiting for the right moment to sneak up on me with a gun, or a knife, or a syringe of digitalis, or something.

Oh, nonsense. Don't be a fool, Harriet, I told myself sternly. It's just the cat. And I am *not* going to act like the thriller heroine who slowly inches her way up the staircase, only to scream stupidly when the harmless cat leaps at her.

All the same, I had to see what that noise was. Slowly, I inched my way up the staircase. The noise had come from the left, I thought, so I turned that way and stepped cautiously into the first room I came to. I switched on the light, the harmless cat leapt at me, and I screamed stupidly.

"Oh, you silly Boots," I said, and took a moment to glance around the room. This must have been Dr. Arnold's bedroom, I thought, noting the narrow bed with its Spartan white spread, the well-stocked bookshelves, the clutter-free bureau, the fiercely polished hardwood floor and old-fashioned braided throw rugs. Just the sort of bedroom you'd expect her to have.

I reached for Boots, but he slipped away, heading purposefully for a closed door in the room and rubbing his back against it, purring reproachfully. "Is that her closet?" I asked, smiling. "Is that where she keeps your catnip? Your toys? Is that the problem? Well, we can take care of that."

I walked over to the closet, pausing before the heavy oak door to bend over and scoop Boots up. I heard a click and looked up—just in time to be hit full in the face by the door as it was shoved open suddenly. I don't really remember falling backwards, but I do remember hitting my head on that gleaming floor—I don't think I'll ever forget that—and then I must have blacked out for a few seconds. I woke up to darkness, to Boots licking my face and meowing in disapproval, and to the sound of footsteps pounding down the stairs.

"Rats!" I cried, and got to my feet. Desperately, I stumbled through the darkness, slipping on a braided throw rug, colliding with the bookcase, finally tripping over Boots and falling against the wall and finding my hand on the light switch. I turned it on, the room sprang into view again, I flung open the door and ran down the stairs. But the intruder was gone.

"Oh, rats again!" I cried, then apologized to Boots, who seemed offended by that particular curse. Mumbling an assortment of other curses, I spent the next hour moving from room to room, taking pictures and filling my pad with notes.

It was midnight when I got to Woodhouse Investigations. Miss Woodhouse was waiting in the kitchen, smoking Marlboros and drinking Diet Coke—two vices she can indulge in only when her mother isn't around. She listened silently to my description of what had happened as she leafed through the Polaroids.

"Any sign of a break-in?" she asked, fingering the picture of the stereo.

"Not that I could see. And the doors were locked."

"Then we have to wonder how the intruder got in. It wasn't the key in the faculty secretary's desk this time—I'm sure the police took that." She paused to gaze at the notes about Dr. Arnold's desk. "Well, if it's the same person who got in the other night and blew out the pilot light, he or she may have had a copy made—an incautious, arrogant thing to do. We also have to wonder *why* this person risked going to the house again."

"To remove incriminating evidence?" I suggested.

She nodded, barely listening. "Possibly. Not necessarily. Harriet, you've had a long day and done well. Get some rest."

As I left, she was reaching for the telephone. I know who she's calling, I thought. Well, he'll be glad to hear from her, even at this hour. And she must have noticed something really important in those notes and pictures, if she's willing to put aside her pride and ask him for help directly.

When I returned in the morning, she was in a fine mood.

"It's a beautiful day, Harriet," she observed. "And that's a beautiful dress you're wearing. But you'll have to change it later—it's not dreary enough for a funeral home."

Oh, good. I'd been hoping she'd ask me along for that. "Do we keep working on the Arnold case today?" I asked.

"Oh, no need," she said cheerily, flipping through her address book. "We can concentrate on locating a suitable home for Boots. By the way, Mother, I know you'd like to come to the visiting hours, but perhaps it would be safer for you to stay home. Things may reach something of a climax at that point."

The professor looked up from the pâpier-maché duck she was making and scowled. "I shall certainly honor my old friend by attending the visiting hours. And your professed concern for my safety doesn't deceive me you nasty girl. You've engineered something, haven't you? Will That Man be there?"

Miss Woodhouse looked abashed. "Not if you object, Mother."

"I most definitely object." She slapped a bill on the duck, so hard she nearly crushed its face. "If you are too inept and lazy to handle the situation on your own, have someone else sent. The city *does* employ more than one police officer, does it not?"

That put a damper on the morning, but a reasonable level of harmony had resurfaced by the time we set out for the funeral home. Miss Woodhouse looked crisply mournful in a tailored black suit, my navy-blue dress was undisgraceful, and the professor was magnificent—a long black silk dress, high-buttoned black shoes, black lace gloves, black shawl, black hat with face-covering black veil. No doubt about where she was headed.

The members of the English department stood in a knot in the reception room, competing to produce the loudest sigh and the longest face. Neville Carter pointed sadly toward a side room.

"Poor Matilda's in there," he said.

The three of us walked in slowly, the professor in the middle as we stood by Matilda Arnold's casket.

"Dear Matilda," the professor sighed. "Not the very nicest person, true—a hasty temper, an inclination to vindictiveness—but a woman of integrity, and a fine teacher. I am glad you had the opportunity to be her student, Iphigenia. Since taking her classes, you have not, I believe, ever once dangled a modifier."

"I don't believe I have, Mother," Miss Woodhouse agreed. "She was fierce about modifiers—no student dared dangle one in her presence. I feared her then, but thank her now."

The professor sobbed softly—the first time I ever heard such a sound come from her. There was an impatient cough behind us, and I turned around to see Carla Perry standing in the doorway, her arms folded across her chest, her face sullen.

"We're leaving for the Littels' house," she said. "Neville told me I should tell you. If you're going to come, come now."

"In a moment," Miss Woodhouse said, not turning around,

and we lingered by the casket. Don't worry about Boots, Dr. Arnold, I thought, looking down at her. We found him a good home.

As we drove to the Littels' house, Miss Woodhouse explained her plan, giving us careful instructions. By the time we arrived, all the members of the English department were gathered in the tiny living room. Neville Carter aimed himself straight at Miss Woodhouse and hung on her arm, trailing after her whenever she tried to turn away, droning on sonorously and endlessly about his grief, his respect for Dr. Arnold, his eagerness to help bring her killer to justice. Carla Perry sat hunched in a corner of the sofa, taking resentful sips of her sherry and looking like she wished it was something stronger. Professor Woodhouse sat down next to her, undeterred by her scowls, and eventually succeeded in drawing her into a grumpy, halting conversation. I spotted Adam Pulen standing off by himself and walked over to join him. Since I was still teary after seeing Dr. Arnold, he offered me a tissue, patted my shoulder, and made sympathetic mumbles. Time to be nice, I decided, and asked him a random question about his dissertation. That set him off. He talked nonstop, gesturing eagerly, his face glowing with animation. I nodded in vigorous agreement with everything he said, letting my eyes grow wide with admiration, pretending I understood.

As for our hosts, Jeffrey Littel was in fine spirits. His usually ashen complexion had brightened so much that you could almost call it beige, and his walk—well, I won't go so far as to say there was a bounce to it, but his feet scarcely dragged at all. Quite a contrast to the way he had looked just yesterday. He passed from guest to guest with a decanter, urging everyone to have more sherry, trying to make lively small talk and sometimes averaging as many as three syllables a minute. His sister, however, didn't really seem to be in the mood for entertaining. Valerie Littel's face grew grimmer by the second as she circulated among her guests, shoving cheese trays at us, yanking empty glasses from our hands, barking at her brother to be quicker with the refills. Once, I caught her glaring at me. I shot her my brightest smile and was rewarded with a snarl.

Finally, Neville Carter released Miss Woodhouse's arm, picked up his glass, and cleared his throat.

"We meet," he said, "on a sad occasion. Let me propose a toast to the memory of our revered colleague, Matilda Arnold."

We all took mournful sips. "And now," Neville Carter said, "we must look to the future. As you know, Jeffrey, spoke to the headmaster, and he agreed to appoint you department chair. Even in these regrettable circumstances, we congratulate you."

So that's why Jeffrey Littel was looking so happy today. He blinked and smiled, smiled and blinked, bobbing his head jerkily to signify his readiness for leadership.

Carla Perry, by contrast, looked ready to implode with envy. "But what about the murder?" she demanded. "We can't move on till that's settled. Have the police discovered anything?" She turned to Miss Woodhouse. "Have *you*?"

"Oh, I don't—well," Jeffrey Littel cut in, turning pale. "What I mean to say is—well. Not the time or place, and so on. The funeral home, and poor Matilda, and—well. And so on."

Valerie Littel drained her glass. "*I* say we get things out in the open. Everybody seems to think one of us killed Matilda. If that's true, I don't see how we can talk about the future. If there's a villain in our midst, I want to know about it."

Adam Pulen shook his head regretfully. "Can we ever *really* know, Valerie? Can we ever be sure it was murder at all, and not suicide or an accident? And even if it *was* murder, who's to say who the villain is, who the victim is? If Matilda drove someone to murder, doesn't she share the responsibility for—"

"Quiet, silly man," the professor cut in angrily. "This is not some text for you to deconstruct; this is a real woman, whose life was taken from her. Matilda was murdered—*she* is the victim. Someone murdered her—*that* person is the villain. Have I made those points sufficiently clear?"

Adam Pulen shrugged, and half smiled, and looked away. Miss Woodhouse took over. "In fact," she said, "both the police and I *have* made some discoveries. And although in some ways this *is* an inappropriate time to discuss such matters, a police sergeant will arrive here soon, and perhaps I should prepare you."

"A police—here?" Jeffrey Littel said numbly. "But I don't—well, that is—I don't—"

"Stop sputtering, Jeffrey," Valerie Littel said, and turned to Miss Woodhouse. "Is he coming to make an arrest?"

Miss Woodhouse raised a noncommittal eyebrow. "Perhaps. She—it *is* she, by the way—will try to locate one final piece of evidence, and an arrest may follow. Both the police and I believe the person who entered Dr. Arnold's house the night before she died is the murderer. We have made a tentative identification of that person, and may soon confirm it."

"But who *is* it?" Carla Perry demanded impatiently.

"Not until the police arrive," Miss Woodhouse said, and made them wait. Ten minutes later, the police car pulled up. Miss Woodhouse greeted Sergeant Judith Hoffer and her partner, conferred with them for several minutes, then introduced them.

"Sergeant Hoffer has brought with her several photographs of Dr. Arnold's house," she said. "Some Ms. Russo took last night, and some the police took yesterday morning. Although Dr. Arnold's house was not the scene of the murder, it *was* the scene of an alleged burglary, and Lieutenant Glass—and the officer in charge took full precautions. It's fortunate he did." She spread four pictures on a coffee table. "Here are two shots of Dr. Arnold's desk and two of her stereo. You'll see they're almost identical, with two differences—in the pictures taken last night, an open copy of *The Sorrows of Young Werther* appears on the desk, and an album cover for the opera *Tosca* appears on the stereo. Neither appears in the pictures taken yesterday morning. Ms. Russo did not place those items on the desk and the stereo, and neither did the police. We must assume they were placed there by the intruder who was in the house last night, who knocked Ms. Russo out with a closet door and then escaped. Now, what do *The Sorrows* of *Young Werther* and *Tosca* have in common?"

Professor Woodhouse sniffed disdainfully. "Sentimentality," she said. "Mediocrity."

Miss Woodhouse smiled. "Perhaps. But aside from that, in both works the protagonists end their troubles by committing suicide. It seems to me our intruder put those items on display to suggest that Dr. Arnold was thinking of ending her troubles in the same way."

Adam Pulen could recognize a direct attack. "That's ridiculous," he said. "Would I have talked about suicide openly if I intended to plant false evidence suggesting the same thing? That wouldn't be very subtle, would it?"

Miss Woodhouse shrugged. "I don't accuse you of subtlety, Mr. Pulen—only of murder, and of arrogance. I don't think there's any limit to your arrogance. Everything about this case points clearly to murder, but you reentered the house to force conflicting evidence into the scene to confuse us, to make us think suicide might be a possibility, too."

"It *is* a possibility," he insisted. "Everything's a possibility. At any rate, *I* had no motive to murder her. She couldn't have hurt me. I'm leaving Newton next year anyway."

"Yes," she agreed, "to seek a university position. And to secure such a position, you'll need a recommendation from the chair of Newton's English department. With Dr. Arnold out of the way, the chair was bound to be Jeffrey Littel—and I think you had good reason to believe you'd get a stellar recommendation from him. If Dr. Arnold were chair, you'd get no recommendation. She'd have gone out of her way to call any university to which you applied with details about your past, and to kill any chances of a position—an intolerable prospect for an ambitious young person. I think *that's* what she said when you had your appointment with her. I don't think she said one word about Dr. Perry's alleged sexual misconduct with students."

"What!" Carla Perry cried, stricken.

Adam Pulen turned to her, still not blushing. "I'm sorry, Carla. It looked like a motive, so I felt obliged to inform Miss Woodhouse. Matilda told me about your affairs with students, and she said she'd bring them up at your tenure review."

"Impossible," Professor Woodhouse said firmly. "Matilda would never share confidential information with a junior member of the faculty—it would violate all her standards of propriety. And if she suspected Dr. Perry of sleeping with students, she would not wait until her tenure review. She would insist on immediate dismissal. Academies such as Newton cannot tolerate such misconduct for a minute, let alone a full year."

"But it isn't true!" Carla Perry wailed. "I haven't slept with any students. I would never—"

Miss Woodhouse held up a hand. "I believe you, Dr. Perry. I'm sure your sexual conduct is completely beyond reproach. We must wonder, then, how Mr. Pulen got the idea that you'd been having affairs with the students, that this was a weapon he could use to deflect suspicion from himself. There is, of course, his own record of abusing sexual relationships for his own advantage— the deserted daughter of the Reverend Carswell comes to mind, and there's at least one other woman he may have used to advance his career. He may have naturally assumed you, too, were unscrupulous about your relationships. But there is something more." She held up a sheet of paper. "This is a copy of a page from a pad on Dr. Arnold's desk, a page a curious intruder might have read when he entered her house to blow out her pilot light. It says, 'CARLA PERRY—STUDENT AFFAIRS. EXCESSIVE, DETRIMENTAL.' "

"But that didn't mean I was having affairs with students," Carla Perry protested. "I'm sure she just meant she didn't like my work on the Student Affairs Committee, and—oh." She looked with wonder at Adam Pulen, suddenly understanding.

"That's right," Miss Woodhouse said. "You misread what Dr. Arnold had written, Mr. Pulen. You were in her house the night before she was murdered, you saw her notes, and you misread them. Her remarks at the dinner, along with her penciled comments on Dr. Perry's *vita*, reveal her true intentions. You misinterpreted them, and that led you to falsely accuse Dr. Perry."

"To accuse—well!" Jeffrey Littel cried. "I mean to say—that is, a colleague, a member of this—well! Bad form, Adam! I mean to say, loyalty, and decency, and—well! And so on!"

"Very articulate, as always," Professor Woodhouse observed. "But in this one respect, Mr. Pulen is not unique. Each of you came to us yesterday with damaging information about a colleague. Each of you took turns as both accuser and accused. Think of *that* at your next department tea."

"True enough, Mother," Miss Woodhouse agreed. "In other respects, however, Mr. Pulen *is* uniquely despicable. He saw a chance to benefit by murdering another human being, and there was nothing to hold him back—no moral standards, no belief that moral standards of any sort are desirable or real. He tormented Matilda Arnold for a month, and then he killed her."

Adam Pulen looked at her coolly. "Prove it," he said.

"All right." Miss Woodhouse looked to Sergeant Hoffer.

Sergeant Hoffer stepped forward. "I'd like to see your key ring, please, Mr. Pulen."

He hesitated, shrugged, and handed it over. "This doesn't prove anything," he said.

She looked through the keys, found an especially shiny one, and compared it to a key from her pocket. "Identical," she announced. "Mr. Pulen, I'm reading you your rights."

"Bastard!" Valerie Littel cried out suddenly. "Murderer! I loved you, you said you loved me, and I lied for you. I saw you sneaking out of the dining room that night, and I lied to protect you and said it was Neville. And the next thing I know, you're flirting with some stupid little secretary!"

"You said it was *me*?" Neville Carter cried.

Miss Woodhouse nodded, satisfied. "A final confirmation—I wasn't positive, but I was hoping. Thank you for that deft little job of seduction, Harriet. I know it was distasteful to you, but you prompted Ms. Littel to respond in exactly the way I thought she would. Mr. Pulen, you're finished."

He looked back at her. Even the handcuffs didn't seem to frighten him or shame him. "Don't be sure of that. And don't you act so self-righteous. You want to destroy me, don't you? What you're doing is essentially the same as what you say I did."

Miss Woodhouse smiled grimly. "No, Mr. Pulen," she said. "There is a difference. There is most definitely a difference."

That wasn't quite the end of the story. Adam Pulen pled not guilty, of course, concocting a story about why Dr. Arnold gave him a key to her house, why she'd confided only in him about Carla Perry's student affairs. He reconciled with his deserted fiancée, Rebecca Carswell, and she and Valerie Littel took out loans to pay his bail. Then he disappeared, leaving both women dazed and in debt. Months later, California police picked him up in the coffee house of a university where he'd been using a false name, playing up to graduate professors, regaling them with stories about how the records of his degrees at a European university had been destroyed in a fire. He's been brought back to Annapolis for trial. This time, there will be no bail.

On the evening of his capture, the Woodhouses and I celebrated with a bottle of champagne and a chicken stuffed with olives and onions. "He *could* still get out of it," I said, pulling off a drumstick. "He *could* fool a jury. He's so good at twisting things around. He comes up with these stories and you know they're outrageous, but it's impossible to prove it."

"It is quite possible to prove, little Harriet," Professor Woodhouse said serenely. "Not easy, but possible. Cling to common sense, and never fear to call absurdity and evil by their true names, no matter how cleverly and confidently they may present themselves. That is, I feel sure, what the members of the jury will do. They are bound to be less sophisticated than the English faculty at Newton, and therefore less likely to tolerate nonsense. They will see through Mr. Pulen and his stories. Have no fear, little Harriet. They will convict him."

Miss Woodhouse smiled slightly. "And so Adam Pulen will at last become," she said, "a man of conviction."

For some reason, that struck me as terribly funny, and I started to laugh; but the professor frowned. "Do not feed her delusions, little Harriet. Iphigenia has no sense of humor. She has never once in her life made a tolerable pun."

"It wasn't *that* bad, Mother," Miss Woodhouse protested. "I've heard worse."

The professor shrugged, unconvinced, and Miss Woodhouse chuckled. We toasted Matilda Arnold's memory, and finished the chicken.

SKIN DEEP

by Sara Paretsky

I

The warning bell clangs angrily and the submarine dives sharply. Everyone to battle stations. The Nazis pursuing closely, the bell keeps up its insistent clamor, loud, urgent, filling my head. My hands are wet: I can't remember what my job is in this cramped, tiny boat. If only someone would turn off the alarm bell. I fumble with some switches, pick up an intercom. The noise mercifully stops.

"Vic! Vic, is that you?"

"What?"

"I know it's late. I'm sorry to call so late, but I just got home from work. It's Sal, Sal Barthele."

"Oh, Sal. Sure." I looked at the orange clock readout. It was four-thirty. Sal owns the Golden Glow, a bar in the south Loop I patronize.

"It's my sister, Vic. They've arrested her. She didn't do it. I know she didn't do it."

"Of course not, Sal—Didn't do what?"

"They're trying to frame her. Maybe the manager . . . I don't know."

I swung my legs over the side of the bed. "Where are you?"

She was at her mother's house, 95th and Vincennes. Her sister had been arrested three hours earlier. They needed a lawyer, a good lawyer. And they needed a detective, a good detective.

Whatever my fee was, she wanted me to know they could pay my fee.

"I'm sure you can pay the fee, but I don't know what you want me to do," I said as patiently as I could.

"She—they think she murdered that man. She didn't even know him. She was just giving him a facial. And he dies on her."

"Sal, give me your mother's address. I'll be there in forty minutes."

The little house on Vincennes was filled with neighbors and relatives murmuring encouragement to Mrs. Barthele. Sal is very black, and statuesque. Close to six feet tall, with a majestic carriage, she can break up a crowd in her bar with a look and a gesture. Mrs. Barthele was slight, frail, and light-skinned. It was hard to picture her as Sal's mother.

Sal dispersed the gathering with characteristic firmness, telling the group that I was here to save Evangeline and that I needed to see her mother alone.

Mrs. Barthele sniffed over every sentence. "Why did they do that to my baby?" she demanded of me. "You know the police, you know their ways. Why did they come and take my baby, who never did a wrong thing in her life?"

As a white woman, I could be expected to understand the machinations of the white man's law. And to share responsibility for it. After more of this meandering, Sal took the narrative firmly in hand.

Evangeline worked at La Cygnette, a high-prestige beauty salon on North Michigan. In addition to providing facials and their own brand-name cosmetics at an exorbitant cost, they massaged the bodies and feet of their wealthy clients, stuffed them into steam cabinets, ran them through a Bataan-inspired exercise routine, and fed them herbal teas. Signor Giuseppe would style their hair for an additional charge.

Evangeline gave facials. The previous day she had one client booked after lunch, a Mr. Darnell.

"Men go there a lot?" I interrupted.

Sal made a face. "That's what I asked Evangeline. I guess it's part of being a yuppie—go spend a lot of money getting cream rubbed into your face."

Anyway, Darnell was to have had his hair styled before his facial, but the hairdresser fell behind schedule and asked Evangeline to do the guy's face first.

Sal struggled to describe how a La Cygnette facial worked—neither of us had ever checked out her sister's job. You sit in something like a dentist's chair, lean back, relax—you're naked from the waist up, lying under a big down comforter. The facial expert—cosmetician was Evangeline's official title—puts cream on your hands and sticks them into little electrically heated mitts, so your hands are out of commission if you need to protect yourself. Then she puts stuff on your face, covers your eyes with heavy pads, and goes away for twenty minutes while the face goo sinks into your hidden pores.

Apparently while this Darnell lay back deeply relaxed, someone had rubbed some kind of poison into his skin. "When Evangeline came back in to clean his face, he was sick—heaving, throwing up, it was awful. She screamed for help and started trying to clean his face—it was terrible, he kept vomiting on her. They took him to the hospital, but he died around ten tonight.

"They came to get Baby at midnight—you've got to help her, V. I.—even if the guy tried something on her, she never did a thing like that—she'd haul off and slug him, maybe, but rubbing poison into his face? You go help her."

II

Evangeline Barthele was a younger, darker edition of her mother. At most times, she probably had Sal's energy—sparks of it flared now and then during our talk—but a night in the holding cells had worn her down.

I brought a clean suit and makeup for her: justice may be blind but her administrators aren't. We talked while she changed.

"This Darnell—you sure of the name?—had he ever been to the salon before?"

She shook her head. "I never saw him. And I don't think the other girls knew him, either. You know, if a client's a good tipper or a bad one they'll comment on it, be glad or whatever that he's come in. Nobody said anything about this man."

"Where did he live?"

She shook her head. "I never talked to the guy, V. I."

"What about the PestFree?" I'd read the arrest report and talked briefly to an old friend in the M.E.'s office. To keep roaches and other vermin out of their posh Michigan Avenue offices, La Cygnette used a potent product containing a wonder chemical called chorpyrifos. My informant had been awestruck— "Only an operation that didn't know shit about chemicals would leave chorpyrifos lying around. It's got a toxicity rating of five—it gets you through the skin—you only need a couple of tablespoons to kill a big man if you know where to put it."

Whoever killed Darnell had either known a lot of chemistry or been lucky—into his nostrils and mouth, with some rubbed into the face for good measure, the pesticide had made him convulsive so quickly that even if he knew who killed him he'd have been unable to talk, or even reason.

Evangeline said she knew where the poison was kept—everyone who worked there knew, knew it was lethal and not to touch it, but it was easy to get at. Just in a little supply room that wasn't kept locked.

"So why you? They have to have more of a reason than just that you were there."

She shrugged bitterly. "I'm the only black professional at La Cygnette—the other blacks working there sweep rooms and haul trash. I'm trying hard not to be paranoid, but I gotta wonder."

She insisted Darnell hadn't made a pass at her, or done anything to provoke an attack—she hadn't hurt the guy. As for anyone else who might have had opportunity, salon employees were always passing through the halls, going in and out of the little cubicles where they treated clients—she'd seen any number of people, all with legitimate business in the halls, but she hadn't seen anyone emerging from the room where Darnell was sitting.

When we finally got to bond court later that morning, I tried to argue circumstantial evidence—any of La Cygnette's fifty or so employees could have committed the crime, since all had access and no one had motive. The prosecutor hit me with a very unpleasant surprise: the police had uncovered evidence linking my client to the dead man. He was a furniture buyer from Kansas City who came to Chicago six times a year, and the doorman and the maids at his hotel had identified Evangeline without any trouble as the woman who accompanied him on his visits.

Bail was denied. I had a furious talk with Evangeline in one of the interrogation rooms before she went back to the holding cells.

"Why the hell didn't you tell me? I walked into the courtroom and got blindsided."

"They're lying," she insisted.

"Three people identified you. If you don't start with the truth right now, you're going to have to find a new lawyer and a new detective. Your mother may not understand, but for sure Sal will."

"You can't tell my mother. You can't tell Sal!"

"I'm going to have to give them some reason for dropping your case, and knowing Sal it's going to have to be the truth."

For the first time she looked really upset. "You're my lawyer. You should believe my story before you believe a bunch of strangers you never saw before."

"I'm telling you, Evangeline, I'm going to drop your case. I can't represent you when I know you're lying. If you killed Darnell we can work out a defense. Or if you didn't kill him and knew him we can work something out, and I can try to find the real killer. But when I know you've been seen with the guy any number of times, I can't go into court telling people you never met him before."

Tears appeared on the ends of her lashes. "The whole reason I didn't say anything was so Mama wouldn't know. If I tell you the truth, you've got to promise me you aren't running back to Vincennes Avenue talking to her."

I agreed. Whatever the story was, I couldn't believe Mrs. Barthele hadn't heard hundreds like it before. But we each make our own separate peace with our mothers.

Evangeline met Darnell at a party two years earlier. She liked him, he liked her—not the romance of the century, but they enjoyed spending time together. She'd gone on a two-week trip to Europe with him last year, telling her mother she was going with a girlfriend.

"First of all, she has very strict morals. No sex outside marriage. I'm thirty, mind you, but that doesn't count with her. Second, he's white, and she'd murder me. She really would. I think that's why I never fell in love with him—if we wanted to get married I'd never be able to explain it to Mama."

This latest trip to Chicago, Darnell thought it would be fun to see what Evangeline did for a living, so he booked an appointment at La Cygnette. She hadn't told anyone there she knew him. And when she found him sick and dying she'd panicked and lied.

"And if you tell my mother of this, V. I.—I'll put a curse on you. My father was from Haiti and he knew a lot of good ones."

"I won't tell your mother. But unless they nuked Lebanon this morning or murdered the mayor, you're going to get a lot of lines in the paper. It's bound to be in print."

She wept at that, wringing her hands. So after watching her go off with the sheriff's deputies, I called Murray Ryerson at the *Herald-Star* to plead with him not to put Evangeline's liaison in the paper. "If you do she'll wither your testicles. Honest."

"I don't know, Vic. You know the *Sun-Times* is bound to have some kind of screamer headline like DEAD MAN FOUND IN FACE-LICKING SEX ORGY. I can't sit on a story like this when all the other papers are running it."

I knew he was right, so I didn't push my case very hard.

He surprised me by saying, "Tell you what: you find the real killer before my deadline for tomorrow's morning edition and I'll keep your client's personal life out of it. The sex scoop came in too late for today's paper. The *Trib* prints on our schedule and they don't have it, and the *Sun-Times* runs older, slower presses, so they have to print earlier."

I reckoned I had about eighteen hours. Sherlock Holmes had solved tougher problems in less time.

III

Roland Darnell had been the chief buyer of living-room furnishings for Alexander Dumas, a high-class Kansas City department store. He used to own his own furniture store in the nearby town of Lawrence, but lost both it and his wife when he was arrested for drug smuggling ten years earlier. Because of some confusion about his guilt—he claimed his partner, who disappeared the night he was arrested, was really responsible—he'd only served two years. When he got out, he moved to Kansas City to start a new life.

I learned this much from my friends at the Chicago police. At least, my acquaintances. I wondered how much of the story Evangeline had known. Or her mother. If her mother didn't want her child having a white lover, how about a white ex-con, ex-(presumably) drug-smuggling lover?

I sat biting my knuckles for a minute. It was eleven now. Say they started printing the morning edition at two the next morning, I'd have to have my story by one at the latest. I could follow one line, and one line only—I couldn't afford to speculate about Mrs. Barthele—and anyway, doing so would only get me killed. By Sal. So I looked up the area code for Lawrence, Kansas, and found their daily newspaper.

The *Lawrence Daily Journal-World* had set up a special number for handling press inquiries. A friendly woman with a strong drawl told me Darnell's age (forty-four); place of birth (Eudora, Kansas); ex-wife's name (Ronna Perkins); and ex-partner's name (John Crenshaw); Ronna Perkins was living elsewhere in the country and the *Journal-World* was protecting her privacy. John Crenshaw had disappeared when the police arrested Darnell.

Crenshaw had done an army stint in Southeast Asia in the late sixties. Since much of the bamboo furniture the store specialized in came from the Far East, some people speculated that Crenshaw had set up the smuggling route when he was out there in the service. Especially since Kansas City immigration officials discovered heroin in the hollow tubes making up chair backs. If

Darnell knew anything about the smuggling, he had never revealed it.

"That's all we know here, honey. Of course, you could come on down and try to talk to some people. And we can wire you photos if you want."

I thanked her politely—my paper didn't run too many photographs. Or even have wire equipment to accept them. A pity—I could have used a look at Crenshaw and Ronna Perkins.

La Cygnette was on an upper floor of one of the new marble skyscrapers at the top end of the Magnificent Mile. Tall, white doors opened onto a hushed waiting room reminiscent of a high-class funeral parlor. The undertaker, a middle-aged highly made-up woman seated at a table that was supposed to be French provincial, smiled at me condescendingly.

"What can we do for you?"

"I'd like to see Angela Carlson. I'm a detective."

She looked nervously at two clients seated in a far corner. I lowered my voice. "I've come about the murder."

"But—but they made an arrest."

I smiled enigmatically. At least I hoped it looked enigmatic. "The police never close the door on all options until after the trial." If she knew anything about the police she'd know that was a lie—once they've made an arrest you have to get a presidential order to get them to look at new evidence.

The undertaker nodded nervously and called Angela Carlson in a whisper on the house phone. Evangeline had given me the names of the key players at La Cygnette; Carlson was the manager.

She met me in the doorway leading from the reception area into the main body of the salon. We walked on thick, silver pile through a white maze with little doors opening onto it. Every now and then we'd pass a white-coated attendant who gave the manager a subdued hello. When we went by a door with a police order slapped to it, Carlson winced nervously.

"When can we take that off? Everybody's on edge and that sealed door doesn't help. Our bookings are down as it is."

"I'm not on the evidence team, Ms. Carlson. You'll have

to ask the lieutenant in charge when they've got what they need."

I poked into a neighboring cubicle. It contained a large white dentist's chair and a tray covered with crimson pots and bottles, all with the cutaway swans which were the salon's trademark. While the manager fidgeted angrily I looked into a tiny closet where clients changed—it held a tiny sink and a few coat hangers.

Finally she burst out, "Didn't your people get enough of this yesterday? Don't you read your own reports?"

"I like to form my own impressions, Ms. Carlson. Sorry to have to take your time, but the sooner we get everything cleared up, the faster your customers will forget this ugly episode."

She sighed audibly and led me on angry heels to her office, although the thick carpeting took the intended ferocity out of her stride. The office was another of the small treatment rooms with a desk and a menacing phone console. Photographs of a youthful Mme. de Leon, founder of La Cygnette, covered the walls.

Ms. Carlson looked through a stack of pink phone messages. "I have an incredibly busy schedule, Officer. So if you could get to the point . . ."

"I want to talk to everyone with whom Darnell had an appointment yesterday. Also the receptionist on duty. And before I do that I want to see their personnel files."

"Really! All these people were interviewed yesterday." Her eyes narrowed suddenly. "Are you really with the police? You're not, are you? You're a reporter. I want you out of here now. Or I'll call the real police."

I took my license photostat from my wallet. "I'm a detective. That's what I told your receptionist. I've been retained by the Barthele family. Ms. Barthele is not the murderer and I want to find out who the real culprit is as fast as possible."

She didn't bother to look at the license. "I can barely tolerate answering police questions. I'm certainly not letting some snoop for hire take up my time. The police have made an arrest on extremely good evidence. I suppose you think you can drum up a fee by getting Evangeline's family excited about her innocence, but you'll have to look elsewhere for your money."

I tried an appeal to her compassionate side, using half-forgotten arguments from my court appearances as a public defender. Outstanding employee, widowed mother, sole support, intense family pride, no prior arrests, no motive. No sale.

"Ms. Carlson, you the owner or the manager here?"

"Why do you want to know?"

"Just curious about your stake in the success of the place and your responsibility for decisions. It's like this: you've got a lot of foreigners working here. The immigration people will want to come by and check out their papers.

"You've got lots and lots of tiny little rooms. Are they sprinklered? Do you have emergency exits? The fire department can make a decision on that.

"And how come your only black professional employee was just arrested and you're not moving an inch to help her out? There are lots of lawyers around who'd be glad to look at a discrimination suit against La Cygnette.

"Now if we could clear up Evangeline's involvement fast, we could avoid having all these regulatory people trampling around upsetting your staff and your customers. How about it?"

She sat in indecisive rage for several minutes: how much authority did I have, really? Could I offset the munificent fees the salon and the building owners paid to various public officials just to avoid such investigations? Should she call headquarters for instruction? Or her lawyer? She finally decided that even if I didn't have a lot of power I could be enough of a nuisance to affect business. Her expression compounded of rage and defeat, she gave me the files I wanted.

Darnell had been scheduled with a masseuse, the hair expert Signor Giuseppe, and with Evangeline. I read their personnel files, along with that of the receptionist who had welcomed him to La Cygnette, to see if any of them might have hailed from Kansas City or had any unusual traits, such as an arrest record for heroin smuggling. The files were very sparse. Signor Giuseppe Fruttero hailed from Milan. He had no next-of-kin to be notified in the event of an accident. Not even a good friend. Bruna, the masseuse, was Lithuanian, unmarried, living with her mother. Other than the fact that the receptionist had been born as Jean Evans in Hammond but referred to herself as Monique from New Orleans, I saw no evidence of any kind of cover-up.

Angela Carlson denied knowing either Ronna Perkins or John Crenshaw or having any employees by either of those names. She had never been near Lawrence herself. She grew up in Evansville, Indiana, came to Chicago to be a model in 1978, couldn't cut it, and got into the beauty business. Angrily she gave me the names of her parents in Evansville and summoned the receptionist.

Monique was clearly close to sixty, much too old to be Roland Darnell's ex-wife. Nor had she heard of Ronna or Crenshaw.

"How many people knew that Darnell was going to be in the salon yesterday?"

"Nobody knew." She laughed nervously. "I mean, of course *I* knew—I made the appointment with him. And Signor Giuseppe knew when I gave him his schedule yesterday. And Bruna, the masseuse, of course, and Evangeline."

"Well, who else could have seen their schedules?"

She thought frantically, her heavily mascaraed eyes rolling in agitation. With another nervous giggle she finally said, "I suppose anyone could have known. I mean, the other cosmeticians and the makeup artists all come out for their appointments at the same time. I mean, if anyone was curious they could have looked at the other people's lists."

Carlson was frowning. So was I. "I'm trying to find a woman who'd be forty now, who doesn't talk much about her past. She's been divorced and she won't have been in the business long. Any candidates?"

Carlson did another mental search, then went to the file cabinets. Her mood was shifting from anger to curiosity and she flipped through the files quickly, pulling five in the end.

"How long has Signor Giuseppe been here?"

"When we opened our Chicago branch in 1980 he came to us from Miranda's—I guess he'd been there for two years. He says he came to the States from Milan in 1970."

"He a citizen? Has he got a green card?"

"Oh, yes. His papers are in good shape. We are very careful

about that at La Cygnette." My earlier remark about the immigration department had clearly stung. "And now I really need to
get back to my own business. You can look at those files in one
of the consulting rooms—Monique, find one that won't be used
today."

It didn't take me long to scan the five files, all uninformative.
Before returning them to Monique I wandered on through the
back of the salon. In the rear a small staircase led to an upper
story. At the top was another narrow hall lined with small offices
and storerooms. A large mirrored room at the back filled with
hanging plants and bright lights housed Signor Giuseppe. A dark-
haired man with a pointed beard and a bright smile, he was min-
istering gaily to a thin, middle-aged woman, talking and laughing
while he deftly teased her hair into loose curls.

He looked at me in the mirror when I entered. "You are here
for the hair, signora? You have the appointment?"

"No, Signor Giuseppe. Sono qui perchè la sua fama se è sparsa
di fronte a lei. Milano è una bella città, non è vero?"

He stopped his work for a moment and held up a deprecating
hand. "Signora, it is my policy to speak only English in my
adopted country."

"Una vera stupida e ignorante usanza io direi." I beamed sym-
pathetically and sat down on a high stool next to an empty customer chair. There were seats for two clients. Since Signor
Giuseppe reigned alone, I pictured him spinning at high speed
between customers, snipping here, pinning there.

"Signora, if you do not have the appointment, will you please
leave? Signora Dotson here, she does not prefer the audience."

"Sorry, Mrs. Dotson," I said to the lady's chin. "I'm a detective. I need to talk to Signor Giuseppe, but I'll wait."

I strolled back down the hall and entertained myself by going
into one of the storerooms and opening little pots of La Cygnette
creams and rubbing them into my skin. I looked in a mirror and
could already see an improvement. If I got Evangeline sprung
maybe she'd treat me to a facial.

Signor Giuseppe appeared with a plastically groomed Mrs.
Dotson. He had shed his barber's costume and was dressed for

the street. I followed them down the stairs. When we got to the bottom I said, "In case you're thinking of going back to Milan— or even to Kansas—I have a few questions."

Mrs. Dotson clung to the hairdresser, ready to protect him.

"I need to speak to him alone, Mrs. Dotson. I have to talk to him about bamboo."

"I'll get Miss Carlson, Signor Giuseppe," his guardian offered.

"No, no, signora. I will deal with this crazed woman myself. A million thanks. *Grazie, grazie.*"

"Remember, no Italian in your adopted America," I reminded him nastily.

Mrs. Dotson looked at us uncertainly.

"I think you should get Ms. Carlson," I said. "Also a police escort. Fast."

She made up her mind to do something, whether to get help or flee I wasn't sure, but she scurried down the corridor. As soon as she had disappeared, he took me by the arm and led me into one of the consulting rooms.

"Now, who are you and what is this?" His accent had improved substantially.

"I'm V. I. Warshawski. Roland Darnell told me you were quite an expert on fitting drugs into bamboo furniture."

I wasn't quite prepared for the speed of his attack. His hands were around my throat. He was squeezing and spots began dancing in front of me. I didn't try to fight his arms, just kicked sharply at his shin, following with my knee to his stomach. The pressure at my neck eased. I turned in a half circle and jammed my left elbow into his rib cage. He let go.

I backed to the door, keeping my arms up in front of my face and backed into Angela Carlson.

"What on earth are you doing with Signor Giuseppe?" she asked.

"Talking to him about furniture." I was out of breath. "Get the police and don't let him leave the salon."

A small crowd of white-coated cosmeticians had come to the door of the tiny treatment room. I said to them, "This isn't Giuseppe Fruttero. It's John Crenshaw. If you don't believe me, try speaking Italian to him—he doesn't understand it. He's probably never been to Milan. But he's certainly been to Thailand, and he knows an awful lot about heroin."

IV

Sal handed me the bottle of Black Label. "It's yours, Vic. Kill it tonight or save it for some other time. How did you know he was Roland Darnell's ex-partner?"

"I didn't. At least not when I went to La Cygnette. I just knew it had to be someone in the salon who killed him, and it was most likely someone who knew him in Kansas. And that meant either Darnell's ex-wife or his partner. And Giuseppe was the only man on the professional staff. And then I saw he didn't know Italian— after praising Milan and telling him he was stupid in the same tone of voice and getting no response it made me wonder."

"We owe you a lot, Vic. The police would never have dug down to find that. You gotta thank the lady, Mama."

Mrs. Barthele grudgingly gave me her thin hand. "But how come those police said Evangeline knew that Darnell man? My baby wouldn't know some convict, some drug smuggler."

"He wasn't a drug smuggler, Mama. It was his partner. The police have proved all that now. Roland Darnell never did anything wrong." Evangeline, chic in red with long earrings that bounced as she spoke, made the point hotly.

Sal gave her sister a measuring look. "All I can say, Evangeline, is it's a good thing you never had to put your hand on a Bible in court about Mr. Darnell."

I hastily poured a drink and changed the subject.

SOLITARY JOURNEY

by Shizuko Natsuki

"Miss Kayama, Miss Kayama!"

I was just leaving the entrance to the inn when I realized someone was calling me. I turned to find the landlady kneeling on the raised section of the entrance hall with a young girl of about twelve or thirteen standing behind her. It was easy to see that they were mother and daughter, as they shared the same delicate, refined features. It was the mother who had called me.

"You've forgotten something; this is yours, isn't it?" she said, taking a small wine-red handbag from her daughter and showing it to me.

I gave a weak smile and nodded.

"You left it over there," the young girl said and pointed to the rear of the lobby which was built out over the river. They had both seen me carrying the bag several times and as the only other guests were an elderly couple, it was obvious who it belonged to.

Looking at the young girl, my smile became much brighter, as I have a soft spot for children.

"You are right, I must have left it when I was reading the newspaper. Thank you," I said, taking it from her. My smile grew even broader. "What year are you in at school?"

"The sixth grade."

"So you will be going to high school soon; is it far to school?"

"No, I just take the bus to Shuzenji."

"I see." Today was Sunday, which must be why she was at home. I put the small handbag into my case and looked out

113

through the glass doors. A tree-lined drive wound its way up the steep hill toward the bus stop and sun shone brightly on the buds of the cherry trees. It was still only the beginning of March, but already the wind that blew over the River Kano held the promise of spring.

"It must look really beautiful when the cherry trees are in full bloom."

"Yes, there are some more trees a little farther down the Shimo Road, too, and when they all bloom at the end of March or the beginning of April, it is really superb. It's difficult to say just when they will bloom, though," the landlady said.

"I see, I'd appreciate it then if you could send me a postcard when they are about seventy percent in bloom," I said, repeating my request of the previous night. "Then I can take some time off work and come and see them. There is nothing I like better than the signora of cherry blossoms," I said brightly. The landlady answered me with a slight bow.

"Well, I'll see you again in the spring then."

I waved goodbye to the little girl and turned toward the road.

"Thank you very much," they called out to me, and I could tell from their tone that I had made a good impression on them. I walked slowly up the hill, feeling very pleased with myself.

Weekend trips from Tokyo like this are one of my favorite pasttimes. I work in a high-class boutique in the city center and live alone in an uptown apartment. My father is a doctor in a village in Gunma prefecture and recently my brother joined him in the practice, but I have not been to see them for two years now. Although I like children as a rule, I cannot seem to get on with those that are related to me, and I find my brother's children very noisy. Although I never go home these days, I often make short trips out from town. The boutique where I work is in an office building which is closed on Sundays and the other two salesgirls and I take it in turns to have the Saturday off.

I don't like hotels or inns that cater for group holidays but rather small, exclusive places where the owners only have two or three staff and can offer their customers personal treatment. These places are often very expensive but are frequented by executives and famous people, so they seem to have no shortage of guests. A friend of mine from university worked for a travel agency and she kept finding new places near Tokyo for me to try.

When I arrived at an inn, I generally made friends with the owner's wife or one of the older maids, so when I asked them to write and let me know when the cherry trees would be in bloom or the maple leaves would turn red, they usually agreed, and I felt sure that a letter would arrive for Reiko Kayama at the beginning of April to tell her about the cherry blossoms.

I had not done so well with the handbag, though. I changed my Boston bag to the other hand and gave a bitter smile. It would seem that things that are forgotten on purpose have a way of finding their way back to their owners.

It was just after the New Year's holiday when I had left a yellow pen case in the bathroom of the inn I was staying in at Kyoto. It had contained a Swiss army knife and a rather expensive ballpoint pen, and although I rather grudged leaving them there, I could easily buy new ones when I got back to Tokyo. I had written my name inside, so I knew that as soon as the staff at the inn found it they would send it to the address I had written in the register.

However, I had only got as far as the Togetsu Bridge when a small boy of about nine called out to me. It was a boy I had played with at the inn the night before. He was very well behaved and I got the impression that he had been brought up in a good household.

"Are you leaving now?" he asked.

"Yes, and you?"

"No, we will be staying a little longer, but I was bored so I came along here to play."

He looked up at me and fidgeted for a few minutes before producing the yellow pen case from the pocket of his blazer.

"Isn't this yours?"

I gave a weak smile and opened it to check the contents. As I did so, I felt his eyes lock onto the red army knife. It was the kind with scissors, a tin opener, and countless other blades folded into the handle. I gave him the knife and then left him with a wave. I would probably have given the girl in the inn my handbag, too, if her mother had not been there. It always makes me feel good when I give a present to a child like that.

However, thanks to her finding it, it would not be sent on to Reiko Kayama as I had planned. Still, it had given me the chance to remind them to let me know when the cherry trees came into blossom, so it wasn't a complete waste of time.

At this point, I think I should mention that I do not know anyone named Reiko Kayama, which is why I failed to answer the landlady straightaway when she called me. I do know a Reiko Kagawa, however: she is twenty-four and works in the same boutique as me. Although she is five years younger than me and joined the show much, much later, she wasted no time in picking up one of the men who worked in another company situated in the same building, and at the end of last year they announced their engagement. They plan to hold the wedding in September, but at the moment her fiancé is abroad on a business trip and as a result I get shown postcards of Paris or London every day.

When I filled in the register at the inn, not only did I use a name similar to hers, I also used her fiancé's address, so at the end of March or the beginning of April he will receive a card from the landlady telling him that the cherry trees are almost in full bloom. He will probably guess that Reiko made a trip while he was away and not only used a false name, but his address as well. He'll conclude she would only have done this because she had another love and even if he doesn't reach that conclusion straightaway, I will have managed to sow the first seeds of doubt between them. That was the secret pleasure I enjoyed on my trips away from town.

It was about ten days after I got back from Izu, a Thursday in the middle of March at a little before seven o'clock, when the boutique was due to close, that the manager looked at the calendar in the back of the shop.

"Mrs. Sugimori has been off for three days now," he said half to himself.

Kozue Sugimori was the third assistant in the boutique. She had telephoned on Tuesday morning to say that she had a cold, but we had not heard anything since then. Mr. Ohki, the manager, had taken the call.

"She sounded very hoarse and said that she had a temperature so I suppose she might still be in bed."

"Yes," I added, "they say that there is a very bad strain of Hong Kong flu around at the moment."

I don't know if Reiko was even listening. She was rearranging some scarves in a showcase, and by the blank look on her face seemed that she was already on a date with her fiancé, in spirit if not body.

"If she is very bad, maybe I should go and see her." Mr. Ohki was in his forties and beginning to bald. He looked over at me for my opinion.

"Isn't her husband at home?"

"No, he has gone to Southeast Asia on business and won't be back until the fifteenth."

"She is on her own then."

Kozue was the only one of us who was married. She was younger than me, only twenty-seven, and she and her husband lived together in an apartment in the trendy part of town. He was a merchandiser or something for a clothing company and often had to travel both domestically and internationally, and as a result Kozue was left on her own a lot.

"If you have time, you couldn't pop in on her on your way home, could you? It is on your way . . ."

I could tell from the sly look on his face that he knew that I was single and would not have a date for the night and so had all the time in the world.

"Has she got a sore throat?"

"Yes, she was very hoarse; it sounded painful for her to speak."

That would probably mean that she was not faking. Her husband being away from home a lot, she had taken a clothes designer as a lover and often hinted about him to me.

"That is probably why she hasn't phoned," I said casually. "Okay, I'll stop by on my way home then."

"I'd be very grateful. It's a bit tricky for me to go, being a man and all. . . . you can leave early if you like."

"I'll do that then. I'm beginning to get a bit worried myself," I said, frowning with apparent concern as I made my way into the back room to get ready.

I looked in the mirror and had to admit that the face I saw there was beautiful. I am a well-built person and my face is also large and well defined, making me easily the best-looking person in the shop. The only problem was that my large well-shaped eyes slanted upward slightly and my well-shaped mouth also turned up in the corners, giving me a slightly satanic look. When I go on my weekend trips, one of the things I enjoy is to talk to people and see their image of me change as they find out what a nice person I really am.

I took the subway to Aoyama, and by the time I arrived at the four-story building where Kozue lived it was about ten past seven. The building was surrounded by a wrought-iron fence and border, by a small lawn, making it look very exotic. Kozue had once mentioned to me that most of the occupants of the building were both hostesses or rich men's mistresses, and it would appear that it was still a bit early in the day for them to be up and about as the bright lit entrance hall was quite deserted.

I went up to the elevators and was just about to press the call button when one of them started to descend. I waited for it to arrive.

As soon as the door started to open a woman rushed out, almost bumping into me. She looked up at me for an instant, then turned away and hurried across the hall. She had a very nice russet-brown coat slipped over her shoulders and I got the impression that she probably worked in a bar or something.

I stepped into the empty elevator and pressed the button for the fourth floor.

The fourth floor was deserted but I had been to visit Kozue two or three times before and found her apartment without any difficulty.

I rang the bell but there was no answer. I knocked, but still the apartment was silent.

So, Kozue had gone off with her lover for a few days after all—or then again, she might be so ill that she could not come to the door. Maybe she had caught pneumonia and was unable to call for help. . . . I panicked and tried the door, and to my surprise it opened. The lights were on in the apartment.

"Kozue . . . how are you feeling?" I called out as I entered the apartment. I walked into the living room and there she was.

She was lying facedown on the floor next to the table, looking as if she had fallen out of her chair. There was blood pouring out of neck of the grey turtleneck sweater she was wearing and it ran down her head and formed a large pool on the carpet below.

I called an ambulance, but the hospital telephoned to say that she died before she arrived there. By this time the flying squad and local police had arrived and were making door-to-door inquiries.

I was questioned for some time by an assistant inspector from the local station called Takahama.

"So you say that she had caught a cold and had not been to work?" he asked. He was a good-looking, well-built sportsman-type of about thirty-five or thirty-six.

"Yes, but it looks as if she felt well enough to get up, although judging by the turtleneck pullover her throat must still have been painful."

Seeing that I was comparatively calm, he said, "She was stabbed with a sharp knife just above the neck of the pullover. The carotid artery was cut, and that is what led to her death, although she was stabbed in three other places around the head and face. It was a very vicious crime," he explained. "Since the room has not been disturbed at all, we are inclined to think that the crime was committed by an acquaintance with a grudge against the victim. Have you any idea who might have wanted to harm her?"

"No, not at all, she was liked by everyone she met."

"And you have not heard any rumors about anyone wanting to get even with her husband?" When I said I hadn't, he asked me where her husband worked, and after I told him, he had one of his men get in touch with the company.

After thinking about it for a while, I told him that I believed Kozue had a lover who was a clothes designer called Sugimoto or something. I told them everything I knew or suspected, although this was only to help their investigations, and I made them promise to keep it all confidential unless her lover had actually been responsible. After all, I did not want to ruin Kozue's reputation now that she was dead.

Assistant Inspector Takahama seemed very interested in all I had to say and told me what he thought had happened.

"I think the victim showed the murderer into the living room and was attacked while they talked—which means that she knew her assailant. Not only that, but considering that she was still alive, even though she had been wounded so seriously, I think you must have arrived on the scene almost immediately."

The fact that the blood had not completely soaked into the carpet was also proof of this.

"Are you sure that you did not hear or see anything suspicious when you arrived?"

I suddenly realized with a jolt something I should have thought of earlier.

"Now you come to mention it, I did see something, in fact, I almost got knocked over. . . ." I went on to tell him about my encounter at the elevator and he leaned forward eagerly.

"You are sure the elevator came from the fourth floor?"

"Yes, without a doubt. I was just about to press the call button when I saw the light for the fourth floor go out and it did not stop anywhere else."

"And you say that she looked as if she worked in a bar or something?"

"Yes, that is the impression I got. Not many people wear their hair up these days, and as we passed I noticed the smell of perfume."

"How old was she?"

"I think she must have been over forty; she had very beautiful eyes but there were small wrinkles around them."

"Had you ever seen this woman before?"

"No, never."

"Would you know her if you met her again?"

"Yes, I might."

Assistant Inspector Takahama snapped his fingers and nodded.

"This is a very difficult case. We haven't got any evidence; even the murder weapon is missing, and you are our only witness at the moment—we might ask for your assistance again in the future."

He said it in a very offhand manner, but after that I was called down to the local police station regularly, and while I was there other detectives came to the boutique and interviewed the manager and Reiko Kagawa. Not only was I their most important witness, but as the person who first discovered the crime, I was also their main suspect. However, no matter how they searched, they could find no motive for me to kill Kozue, or anyone else for that matter, and if I was innocent, it meant that my evidence became all the more important.

The police finally decided that the woman I had bumped into outside the elevator was the murderer, and they repeatedly asked me to come to the police station to see if I could identify any of the women they were investigating.

I would arrive at the station and a detective would show me to a small dark room with curtains across one wall. The detective would draw the curtain and I would see the next room through a sheet of glass, where another detective would be interrogating a woman who sat facing me.

"They can't see you from in there. To them, this window looks like a mirror, so take your time and study them to see if any of them are the woman you saw in the lobby."

I was not told why these particular women had been chosen as suspects, but I felt sure that Kozue's lover's wife or her husband's lover must have been amongst them. However, although I tried to match their features to those of the woman I saw, it was impossible.

One day, about ten days after the murder, I was called down to the station for the seventh time. Assistant Inspector Takahama showed me through to the little room and drew the curtain. I took one glance at the woman in the next room and gave a gasp, then started to feel a little faint. She wore her hair up over a narrow forehead and finely penciled eyebrows. Today she was wearing an imported blouse like the ones I sell in the boutique and a suede vest, but there was no mistaking her.

"Have you seen her before?" Takahama asked, watching my face closely.

"Yes, that's her. That is the woman who almost bumped into me when the elevator doors opened."

"Are you quite sure?"

"Yes, absolutely, she is just as I remember her, in her forties, sophisticated, and she looks as if she works in a bar."

"It is true that she works in a bar in Ginza. . . ." Takahama seemed to find it hard to believe that this was the murderer, and judging from her relaxed manner and the way she smiled every now and again, she did not seem to be undergoing a very severe interrogation.

"Have you ever heard the surname Fukao?" Takahama asked.

"No."

"Kozue Sugimori didn't mention her at all?"

"Not as far as I can remember." I did remember, however, that he had asked me the same question on another occasion. "Does that name hold some special significance?"

"Well actually, the victim had scribbled the name down on a pad next to the phone. It seems likely that someone called Fukao telephoned her and she jotted the name down, but neither her husband nor anyone else has been able to tell us who it may be."

"I see."

"Anyway, Fukao sounds like a surname, and put together with your statement about a woman in her forties who looked as if she worked in a bar, we decided to check all the bars in Tokyo for people who matched that description and were called Fukao. It was a big job, but luckily it is quite an unusual name and to date we have only come across three people who fit the description and we are presently making secret inquiries about them."

"Does that mean that this woman is called Fukao, too?"

"Yes, but as far as we have been able to ascertain, Kozue's husband has never been to her bar and she denies any knowledge of him. She lives in an apartment in Uguisudani with a young son and although she does not have any regular male friends at the moment, I find it hard to believe that she has any relationship with the victim's husband. All the same, you are quite sure that this is the woman you saw in the lobby of the victim's building?"

"Yes," I said forcefully. The more I looked at her, the surer became that this was the woman I had seen.

The woman lit a cigarette, and as she blew out a stream of smoke she stared me right in the eye. Even though she could not possibly see me, I felt a cold hatred in her look that seemed to be aimed directly at me.

Next day, I read in the evening newspaper that Terumi Fukao had been arrested, and next to the report was a photo of the woman I had seen the day before through the two-way mirror. It said that she had admitted to killing Kozue, but there were several points that were not clear and these were being investigated by the police.

The following day Assistant Inspector Takahama came to the boutique to see me, and I could tell from his relaxed attitude that the case had been cleared up.

"It is entirely thanks to your cooperation that we were able to catch the culprit, so I thought the least I could do would be to come and thank you," he said in a free and easy way.

"So that woman was the murderer then."

"Yes, when we started interrogating her she denied all knowledge of the affair, but when we told her that we had a witness who had seen her in the lobby of the victim's building and pressed her for an explanation, she became very agitated and finally admitted everything."

"So she was having an affair with Kozue's husband or something . . . ?"

"No, she was not lying when she said that she did not know either of the Sugimoris. That day was the first time she had ever met Kozue. She had telephoned before she visited, and that was when Kozue had jotted down the name, just as we guessed. However, when they were talking she lost her temper and stabbed Kozue with the Swiss army knife she had with her."

"Army knife?"

"Yes, she took us to her apartment where she had hidden it in the back of a drawer. It was one of those fat ones with scissors, nail clippers, and all kinds of blades that fold into the handle. There was also some dried blood on one of the blades and that matched the blood type of the victim."

"But didn't you say she had a young son? What is he going to do now that she has been arrested?"

Takahama gave me a funny look and I realized it must have sounded a rather strange thing to say, but I was only trying to change the subject to something I could cope with. Also, for some reason, the boy's fate seemed important to me.

"Actually he is in hospital at the moment. I suppose it is a good thing in a way, as it means he was not there to see us take his mother away in handcuffs."

"In hospital?"

"Yes, in fact it is very easy to sympathize with Fukao. Since she separated from her husband, she has devoted herself to raising her son, Akio, and in order that he would not miss his father, she lavished all her love on him. He is ten years old and he attends an exclusive private school. Although his mother has to leave him alone a lot while she is at work, her greatest pleasure is to close the bar and take him somewhere on a trip during the school holidays.

"However, she came back to her apartment one night in the beginning of February to find Akio, who should have been in bed, lying in the hall, his face covered with blood. She rang for an ambulance and got him to a hospital where he was treated. When he recovered consciousness he told her that he had tried to open a parcel that had been delivered with his knife, but he slipped and it went into his left eye. Luckily, he was not in a critical state, but there was a chance that he might lose his left eye."

"Oh, no . . ."

"Terumi went home where she found the knife lying on the floor of the hall and had another shock. She had never given her son a knife—you often read about children with overprotective parents who have never held a knife and can't even sharpen a pencil without an electric sharpener—well, Akio was one of these."

"I see . . ."

"She asked him where he had got it, and he said that he was given it. During the New Year's holidays, she had taken him for a trip to Kyoto and a young woman who was staying in the same inn had left a pen case in the toilet. Akio found it, and when he gave it back to her she gave him the knife as a reward. He knew that his mother would take it away from him if she saw it, so he kept it hidden and played with it while she was out. That night he had tried to use it to open a parcel when he slipped and stabbed himself."

"I see . . ." I answered automatically.

"Anyway, after about a month of treatment, Akio lost the use of his left eye. His mother told herself that she should be glad that at least he still had his right eye, when the child started to complain that that had become blurred, too. The doctor told her that it was only an inflammation and would soon heal, but she took it very hard.

"She found herself hating this stranger who would casually give a dangerous weapon to her precious son. She went down to the inn in Kyoto, and after explaining the circumstances got them to show her the guest book. The only person who fit the dates was a woman called Kozue Sugimoto, but the address belonged to a Kozue Sugimori. She guessed that this person had probably gone to Kyoto with her lover and changed her name slightly so her husband would not find out, but she was convinced that Kozue Sugimori was the person responsible for her son's injuries. She looked up her telephone number and after phoning, she went to visit her."

"But I suppose Kozue denied it."

"Exactly. Fukao had not meant to get revenge on her when she first went. If she had, she would hardly have used her real name on the phone. She just wanted Kozue to know what she and her son had been through and make her apologize. However, even when she was presented with the knife, Kozue denied all knowledge of it and denied even having been to Kyoto at the New Year. Finally she accused Terumi of trying to blackmail her, and that was when Terumi lost control of herself and struck out blindly with the knife she was holding in her hand."

I heard a kind of explosion in my head and all the color seemed to fade away. I knew then that I would be locked in this gray loveless world until the day I died. Needless to say, the person who had been to Kyoto and signed the guest book with Kozue's name in the hope that Kozue's husband would hear about it was none other than myself . . .

—translated by Gavin Frew

UNACCEPTABLE LEVELS

by Ruth Rendell

"You shouldn't scratch it. You've made it bleed."

"It itches. It's giving me hell. You don't react to mosquito bites the way I do."

"It's just where the belt on your jeans rubs. I think I'd better put a plaster on it."

"They're in the bathroom cabinet," he said.

"I know where they are."

She removed the plaster from its plastic packaging and applied it to the small of his back. He reached for his cigarettes, put one in his mouth, and lit it.

"I wonder if you're allergic to mosquito bites," she said. "I mean, I wonder if you should be taking antihistamine when you get bitten. You know, you should try one of those sprays that ease the itching."

"They don't do any good."

"How do you know if you don't try? I don't suppose smoking helps. Oh, yes, I know that sounds ridiculous to you, but smoking does affect your general health. I bet you didn't tell the doctor you had all these allergies when you were examined for that life insurance you took out."

"What do you mean, 'all these allergies'? I don't have allergies. I have rather a strong reaction to mosquito bites."

"I bet you didn't tell them you smoked," she said.

"Of course I told them. You don't mess about when you're taking out a hundred thousand pounds' worth of insurance on

127

your life." He lit a cigarette from the stub of the last one. "Why d'you think I pay such high premiums?"

"I bet you didn't tell them you smoke forty a day."

"I said I was afraid I was a heavy smoker."

"You ought to give it up," she said. "Mind you, I'd like a thousand pounds for every time I've said that. I'd like a *pound*. You smokers don't know what it's like living with it. You don't know how you smell, your clothes, your hands, the lot. It gets in the curtains. You may laugh, but it's no joke."

"I'm going to bed," he said.

In the morning she had a shower. She made a cup of tea and brought it up to him. He stayed in bed smoking while he drank his tea. Then he had a shower.

"And wash your hair," she said. "It stinks of smoke."

He came back into the bedroom with a towel round him. "The plaster came off."

"I expect it did. I'll put another one on."

She took another plaster out of its pack.

"Did I make it bleed?"

"Of course you make it bleed when you scratch it. Here, keep still."

"You'd think it would stop itching after a couple of days, wouldn't you?"

"I told you, you should have used an antiallergenic spray. You should have taken an antihistamine. You've got a nasty sore place there and you're going to have to keep it covered for at least another forty-eight hours."

"Anything you say."

He lit a cigarette.

In the evening they ate their meal outdoors. It was very warm. He smoked to keep the mosquitoes away.

"Any excuse," she said.

"One of those little buggers has just bitten me in the armpit."

"Oh, for God's sake. Just don't scratch this one."

"Do you really think I should have told the insurance people I'm allergic to mosquito bites?"

"I don't suppose it matters," she said. "I mean, how could anyone tell after you were dead?"

"Thanks very much," he said.

"Oh, don't be silly. You're much more likely to die of smoking than of a mosquito bite."

Before they went to bed she renewed the plaster on his back and, because he had scratched the new one, gave him another. He could put that one on himself.

He had to get up in the night, the bites drove him mad and he couldn't just lie there. He walked about the house, smoking. In the morning he told her he didn't feel well.

"I don't suppose you do if you didn't get any sleep."

"I found a packet of nicotine patches in the kitchen," he said. "Nicotend or something. I suppose that's your latest ploy to stop me smoking."

She said nothing for a moment. Then, "Are you going to give it a go then?"

"No, thanks very much. You've wasted your money. D'you know what it says in the instructions? 'While using the patches it is highly dangerous to smoke.' How about that?"

"Well, of course it is."

"Why is it?"

"You could have a heart attack. It would put unacceptable levels of nicotine into your blood."

"Unacceptable levels—you sound like a health minister on telly."

"The idea," she said, "is to stop smoking while using the patch. That's the point. The patch gives you enough nicotine to satisfy the craving *without* smoking."

"It wouldn't give me enough."

"No, I bet it wouldn't," she said, and she smiled.

He lit a cigarette. "I'm going to have my shower and then perhaps you'll redo those plasters for me."

"Of course I will," she said.

A FINE SET OF TEETH

by Jan Burke

I saw Frank drop two cotton balls into the front pocket of his denim jacket, and I made a face. "Those won't help, you know."

He smiled and said, "Better than nothing."

"Cotton is not effective ear protection."

He picked up his keys by way of ignoring me and said, "Are you ready?"

"You don't have to go with me," I offered again.

"I'm not letting my wife sit alone in a sleazy bar. No more arguments, all right?"

"If I were on a story—"

"You aren't. Let's go."

"Thanks for being such a good sport about it," I said, which made him laugh.

"Which apartment number?" Frank asked as we pulled up to the curb in front of Buzz Sullivan's apartment building. The building was about four stories high, probably built in the 1930s. I don't think it had felt a paintbrush along its walls within the last decade.

"Buzz didn't tell me," I answered. "He just said he lived on the fourth floor."

Frank sighed with long suffering, but I can ignore someone as easily as he can and got out of the car.

As we made our way to the old stucco building's entry, we

dodged half a dozen kids who were playing around with a worn soccer ball on the brown crabgrass lawn. The children were laughing and calling to one another in Spanish. A dried sparrow of a woman watched them from the front steps. She seemed wearier than Atlas.

For the first of the three flights of stairs Frank muttered at my back about checking mailboxes but soon followed in silence. Although Buzz had moved several times since I had last been to one of his apartments, I knew there would be no difficulty in locating the one that was his. We reached the fourth floor and Frank started to grouse, but soon the sound I'd been waiting for came to my ears. Not just my ears: I heard the sound under my fingernails, beneath my toes, and in places my mother asked me never to mention in mixed company. Three screeching notes strangled from the high end of the long neck of a Fender Stratocaster, a sound not unlike those a pig might make—if it were having its teeth pulled with a pair of pliers.

I turned to look at Frank Harriman and saw something I rarely see on his face: fear. Raw fear.

I smiled. I would've said something comforting, but he wouldn't have heard me over the next few whammified notes whining from Buzz's guitar. A deaf man could have told you they were coming from apartment 4E. I waited until the sound subsided, asked, "Should we drop you off back at the house?," and watched my husband stalk over to the door of number 4E and rap on it with the kind of ferocious intensity one usually saves for rousing the occupants of burning buildings.

Q: What's the difference between a dead trombone player and a dead snake in the middle of a road?
A: The snake was on his way to a gig.

The door opened, and a thin young man with a hairdo apparently inspired in color and shape by a sea urchin stood looking at Frank in open puzzlement. He swatted a few purple spikes away from his big blue eyes and finally saw me standing nearby. His face broke into an easy, charming smile.

"Irene!" He looked back at Frank. "Is this your cop?"

"No, Buzz," I said, "that's my husband."

Buzz looked sheepish. "Oh, sorry. I've told Irene I'm not like that, and here I am, acting just exactly like that."

"Like what?" Frank asked.

"I don't mind that you're a cop," Buzz said proudly.

"That's big of you," Frank said. "I was worried you wouldn't accept our help."

Buzz, who is missing a sarcasm detection gene, just grinned and held out a hand. "Not at all, man, not at all. It's really good of you to offer to take me to the gig. Guess Irene told you my car broke down. Come on in."

Buzz's purple hair was one of two splashes of color in his ensemble; his boots, pants, and shirt were black, but a lime-green guitar—still attached by a long cable to an amp—and matching strap stood out against this dark backdrop.

There was no question of finding a seat while we waited for Buzz to unhook his guitar and put it in a hard-shell case. The tiny apartment was nearly devoid of furniture. Two plastic milk crates and a couple of boards served as a long, low coffee table of sorts. Cluttered with several abandoned coffee mugs and an empty bowl with a bent spoon in it, the table stood next to a small mattress heaped with twisted sheets and laundry. The mattress apparently served as both bed and couch.

There were two very elegant objects in the room, however—a pair of Irish harps. The sun was setting in the windows behind them and in the last light of day they stood with stately grace, their fine wooden scrollwork lovingly polished to a high sheen.

"You play these?" Frank said in astonishment.

Without looking up from the guitar, which he was carefully wiping down with a cloth, Buzz said, "Didn't you tell him, Irene?"

"I first met Buzz at an Irish music festival," I said. "He doesn't just play the harp."

"Other instruments, too?" Frank asked.

"Sure," Buzz said, looking back at us now. "I grew up in a musical family."

"That isn't what I meant," I said. "He doesn't just play it. He coaxes it to sing."

"Sure and you've an Irish silver tongue now, haven't ye, me beauty?" Buzz said with an exaggerated brogue.

"Prove my point, Buzz. Play something for us."

He shook his head. "Haven't touched them in months except to keep the dust off them," he said. "That's the past." He patted the guitar case. "This is the future." He laughed when he saw my look of disappointment. "My father feels the same way—but promise you won't stop speaking to me like he has."

"No. What you play is your choice."

"Glad to know at least one person thinks so. Shall we go?"

"Need help carrying your equipment?" Frank offered. I was relieved to see him warming up a little.

"Oh no, I'm just taking my ax, man."

"Your ax?"

"My guitar. I never leave it at the club. My synthesizer, another amp, and a bunch of other stuff are already at the club—I leave those there. But not my Strat."

Q: How do you get a guitar player to turn down?
A: Put sheet music in front of him.

On the way to Club 99, Buzz talked to Frank about his early years of performing with the Sullivan family band, recalling the friendship his father shared with my late mentor, O'Connor.

"O'Connor told me to go to this music festival," I said. "There was a fifteen-year-old lad who could play the Irish harp better than anyone he'd ever met, and when he got to heaven, he expected no angel to play more sweetly."

"Oh, I did all right," Buzz said shyly. "But my training wasn't formal. She tell you that she helped me get into school, Frank?"

"No—"

"It was your own hard work that got you into that program," I said.

"Naw, I couldn't have done it without you. You talked that friend into teaching me how to sight-read." He turned to Frank.

"Then she practically arm-wrestled one of the profs into giving me an audition."

Frank smiled. "She hasn't changed much."

"Sorry, Buzz," I said. "I thought it was what you wanted."

"It was!" Buzz protested. "And I never could have gone to college without your help."

"Nonsense. You got the grades on your own, and all the talent and practice time for the music was your own. But when your dad told me you dropped out at the beginning of this past semester, I just figured—"

"I loved school. I only left because I had this opportunity."

"What opportunity?" Frank asked.

"The band you're going to hear tonight," he said proudly.

I was puzzled. "It's still avant-garde?"

"Yes."

"Hmm. I guess I never thought there was much money in a avant-garde."

"Not here in the U.S. Locally, Club 99 is about the only place we can play regularly, and they don't pay squat there. Our band is too outside for a lot of people."

"Outside?" I asked.

"Yeah, it means—different. In a good way. You know, we push the envelope. Our music's very original, but for people who want the Top Forty, we're a tough listen. That's the trouble with the music scene here in the States. But Mack—our bass player—came up with this great plan to get us heard over in Europe. We made a CD a few months ago, and it's had a lot of air play there. We just signed on for a big tour, and when it's over, we've got a steady gig set up in a club in Amsterdam."

"I had no idea all this was happening for you, Buzz. Congrats."

"Thanks. I'm so glad you're finally going to get to hear us play—three weeks from now we'll be in Paris. Who knows when you'll get a chance to hear us after that. Frank, it's been awhile since Irene heard me play and—oh!" He pointed to the right. "Here's the club. Park here at the curb. There's not really any room in back."

He had pointed out a small brown building that looked no

different from any other neighborhood bar on the verge of ruin. A small marquee read: LIVE MUSIC. WAST LAND. NO COVER CHARGE BEFORE 7 P.M.

"Wast Land?" Frank asked. "Is that your band?"

"The Wasteland. The 'e' is missing. And the word 'The.' "

"You named the band after Eliot's poem?"

"You've read T. S. Eliot's poetry?" Buzz asked in unfeigned disbelief.

"Yeah. I think it made me a more dangerous man."

I rolled my eyes.

Buzz sat back against the seat and grinned.

"Cool!"

Q: What band name on a marquee will always guarantee a crowd?

A: Free Beer.

As we pushed open the padded vinyl door of Club 99, our nostrils were assailed by that special blended fragrance—a combination of stale cigarette smoke, old sweat, splitbeer, and unmopped men's room that is the mark of the true dive. I was thinking of borrowing Frank's cotton and sticking it in my nose.

Behind the bar a thin old man with tattoo-covered arms and a cigarette dangling from his mouth was stocking the beer cooler, squinting as the cigarette's smoke rose into his face. He nodded at Buzz, stared a moment at Frank, then went back to his work. We were ignored completely by the only other occupant, a red-faced man in a business suit who was gazing into a whisky glass.

"I thought you said the band was meeting here at seven," I said as we walked along the sticky floor toward the stage.

I glanced at my watch. Seven on the dot.

"The others are always late," Buzz said. He set up his guitar, then invited us into a small backstage room that was a little less smelly than the rest of the bar. It housed a dilapidated couch and a piano that bore the scars of drink rings and cigarette burns. The walls of the room were covered with a colorful mixture of graffiti, band publicity photos, and handbills.

"Is there a photo of your band up here?" Frank asked.

"Naw. Most of those are pretty old. But I can show you photos of the other members of the band. Here's Mack and Joleen, when they were in Maggot." He pointed to two people in a photo of a quartet. Everyone wore the pouting rebel expression that has become a standard in band photos. The man Buzz pointed out was a bass player about Buzz's age with long, thick, black hair. The woman, boyishly thin, also had long, thick, black hair.

"That photo's about ten years old. Mack and Joleen were together then."

"Together?"

"Yeah. You know, lovers."

"They aren't now?"

"No, haven't been for years. But they get along fine."

Q: What's the difference between a drummer and a drum machine?

A: With a drum machine you only have to punch in the information once.

"Over here's a photo of Gordon. He's a great drummer," Buzz said. "He hates this photo. He said the band stank. Its name sure did." He pointed to a photo of a band called Unsanitary Conditions.

Buzz was right—I didn't think too many club owners would be ready to put that on their marquees.

The drummer, a lean but muscular man, wasn't wearing a shirt over his nearly hairless chest. He had also shaved all the hair from his head. He held his drumsticks tucked in crossed arms. He was frowning. It didn't look like a fake frown.

Live, updated versions of two of the band members arrived a few minutes later. Gordon looked pretty much the same as he did in the Unsanitary Conditions photo. He was wearing a shirt and he had short orange hair on his head, but the frown gave him away.

"Her Royal Highness is late again, I see," he seethed, adding a couple of colorful phrases before he realized that Buzz wasn't alone. He then smiled and said politely, "Hi, I'm Gordon. Are you Buzz's folks?"

Frank snorted with laughter behind me.

"Oh, man!" Buzz said in embarrassment. "These are my friends. They aren't *that* old!"

"Sorry," Gordon said. "Buzz, did you listen to that tape I gave you?" He broke off as the door opened again.

Preempting a repeat of Gordon's mistake, Buzz quickly said, "Mack, these are my *friends*. Frank and Irene, this is Mack."

It was a good thing Buzz introduced us. Mack was now balding, and his remaining hair was very short, including his neatly trimmed beard. I judged him to be in his midthirties, closer to our age than Buzz's, with Gordon somewhere in between the two.

"Hi, nice to meet you," he said, but seemed distracted as he looked around the small room.

"No," Gordon said, "Joleen isn't here yet." He shook his head. "Can you imagine what touring with her will be like?"

"Don't worry about it," Mack said placatingly. "She'll be very professional."

Gordon didn't look convinced.

"Uh, Buzz," Mack said, "the house is getting full. Maybe you should find some seats for your friends."

I thought Mack was just trying to make the band's infighting more private, but when Buzz led us back into the club, a transformation had taken place. Taped music was playing over the speakers, a recording of frenzied sax riffs that could barely be heard above people talking and laughing and drinking.

There was an audience now. The man in the business suit had left the bar, and the place was starting to fill up with a crowd that seemed mainly to be made up of young . . . as I sought a word for the beret-clad, goatee-wearing men and their miniskirted female companions, Frank whispered, "Beatniks! And to think I gave away my bongo drums."

"Poetry and bongo drums?" I whispered back. "Did Kerouac make you want to run away from home?"

"As Buzz said, I'm not *that* old."

Buzz wanted us to sit near the stage, but I knew better. I muttered something about acoustics, and we found a table along the back wall next to the sound man. Buzz sat with us for a few minutes, and I was pleased to see that Frank was starting genuinely to like him.

Buzz might not be sarcastic but he is Irish, and he was spinning a tale about learning to play the uilleann pipes that had us weeping with laughter. Just then a woman walked onstage, shielded her eyes from the lights, and said over one of the microphones, "Buzz! Get your behind up here—now!"

Q: *What's the difference between a singer and a terrorist?*
A: *You can negotiate with a terrorist.*

The club fell silent, and there was a small ripple of nervous laughter before conversation started up again. The sound man belatedly leaned over and turned off her mike. He shook his head, murmured, "*Maybe* I'll remember to turn that on again, bitch," and upped the volume on the house speakers. I could hear the saxophone recording more clearly now, but I was distracted by my anger toward the woman.

She was thin and dressed in a black outfit that was smaller than some of my socks. Her hair was short and spiky; I couldn't see her eyes, but her mouth was hard, her lips drawn tight in a painted ruby slash across her pale face.

"Joleen," Buzz said as if the name explained everything. He quickly excused himself and hurried up to the stage as Joleen stepped back out of the lights. The other members of the band soon joined them onstage. If Buzz had been bothered by her tone, he didn't show it.

The group did a sound check, only briefly delayed while Joleen cussed out the sound man and proved she might not need a mike. The members of the band then left the stage with an argument in progress. Although I couldn't make out what they were saying, Gordon and Joleen were snapping at one another, the drummer looking ready to raise a couple of knots on her head. Mack was making "keep it quiet" motions with his hands, while Buzz seemed to be lost in his own thoughts, ignoring all of them.

"I think I'm going to need a drink," Frank said. "You want one?"

"Tell you what—I'll drive home. Have at it."

Frank spent some time talking to the bartender, then came back with a couple of scotches. He downed the first one fairly quickly and was taking his time with the second when the band came back onstage.

Q: How can you tell if a stage is level?
A: The bass player is drooling out of both sides of his mouth.

The sound man turned on his own mike and said, "Club 99 is pleased to welcome The Wasteland." There was a round of enthusiastic applause.

Joleen held the mike up to her lips and said softly, "We're going to start off with a little something called 'Ankle Bone.'" Amid hoots and whistles of approval the band began to play.

The music was rapid-fire and intricate and quite obviously required great technical skill. Joleen's voice hit notes on an incredible range. There were no lyrics (unless they were in some language spoken off-planet), but her wild mix of syllables and sounds was clearly not sloppy or accidental.

The rest of the band equaled her intensity. As Mack and Buzz played, their fingers flew along the frets; Gordon drummed to complex and changing time signatures. But at the end of the first song and Frank's second scotch, he leaned over and whispered, "Five bucks if you can hum any of that back to me."

He was right, of course, but out of loyalty to Buzz I said, "They just aren't confined by the need to be melodic."

Frank gave an emperor's-new-clothes sort of snort and stood up. "I'm going to get another drink. I'll pay cab fare for all three of us if you want to join me."

Figuring it would hurt Buzz's feelings if we were both drunk by the end of his gig, I said, "No, thanks."

Q: What do you call someone who hangs out with musicians?
A: A guitar player.

By the end of the set I was seriously considering hurting Buzz's feelings. "Get outside!" one member of the audience yelled in encouragement to the band, and when the sound man muttered, "And stay there," I found myself in agreement. The crowd applauded wildly after every piece (I could no longer think of them as songs, nor remember which one was "Jar of Jam" and which was "Hangman's Slip Knot"), but long before the set ended I had a headache that could drive nails.

Buzz grabbed a bottle of beer at the bar and came back to our table, smiling. Frank surprised me by offering the first compliment.

"You're one hell of a player, Buzz."

"Thanks, man."

They proceeded to go through an elaborate handshaking ritual that left me staring at my husband in wonder. I was spared any comment on music or male ceremonial greetings when Gordon grabbed the seat next to Buzz.

"Excuse us," Gordon said, turning his shoulders away from us and toward Buzz. "You never told me—did you listen to that tape?"

"Keep your voice down," Buzz said, glancing toward the stage, where Joleen was apparently complaining about something to Mack. He turned back to Gordon. "Yeah, I listened. Your friend's got great keyboard chops."

"Yeah, and you have to admit Susan's also got a better voice than Joleen's. Great bod, too."

Buzz glanced at the stage. "Joleen's bod isn't so bad."

"No, just her attitude. Think of how much better off our band would be with Susan."

"But Joleen started this band—"

"And she's about to finish it, man. She rags on all of us all the time. I'm getting tired of it. This band would be better off without her."

"But they're her songs."

"Hers and Mack's. He has as much right to them as she does."

Buzz frowned, toyed with his beer. "What does Mack say?"

Gordon shrugged. "I'm working on him. I know he was knocked out by Susan's tape. If you say you're up for making the change, I know he will be, too."

"I don't know . . ."

"Look, Buzz, I really love playing with you. Same with Mack. But I can't take much more of Joleen."

"But Europe . . ."

"Exactly. Think of spending ten weeks traveling with that bitch. You want to be in a car with her for more than ten minutes?"

I looked up and saw Joleen walking toward us with purpose in every angry stride. "Uh, Buzz—" I tried to warn, but she was already shouting toward our table.

"I know exactly what you're up to, you jerk!"

Gordon and Buzz looked up guiltily, but in the next moment it became clear that she was talking to the sound man. He didn't seem impressed by her fury.

"You're messing around with the monitors, aren't you?"

The sound man just laughed.

Joleen stood between Frank and me and pointed at the sound man. "You won't be laughing long, you—"

"Joleen," Buzz said, trying to intercede.

"Shut up, you little twerp! You don't know the first thing about music. If you did, you'd understand what this jerk is doing. You try singing while some clown is fooling around with your monitor, making it play back a half-step off."

The effect the sound man had created must have been maddening; the notes she heard back through the speaker at her feet on stage would be just slightly off of the notes she sang into the mike. Still, I couldn't help but bristle at her comments to Buzz.

Instead of being angry with her, though, Buzz turned to the sound man. "Dude, that's a pretty awful thing to do to her. She's singing some really elaborate stuff, music that takes all kinds of concentration, and you're messing with her head."

The sound man broke eye contact with him, shrugged one shoulder.

"See?" Buzz said to Joleen. "He's sorry. I'm sure it won't happen next set." Before Joleen could protest, Buzz turned to us. "How's it sounding out here?"

Picking up my cue, I said, "Wonderful. He's doing a great job for you guys."

"And what the hell would you know about it?" she said.

"Joleen," Buzz said, "this is my friend from the paper."

She stopped in midtant and looked at me with new interest. "A reviewer?"

"No," I admitted.

"Well, I was right, then. You don't know what you're talking about." She eyed Frank and said, "You or this cop."

"How did you know he's a cop?" Buzz asked, but before she could answer, Frank took hold of her wrist and turned it out so the inside of her arm was facing Buzz.

"Oh," he said, "junkies just seem to have a sixth sense about these things."

She pulled her arm away. "They're old tracks, and you know it. I haven't used in years."

Frank shrugged. "If you say so. I really don't want to check out the places I'd have to look if I wanted to be sure."

She narrowed her eyes at him but stomped away without another word. "Hell," Gordon said. "You need anything else to convince you, Buzz?"

"She brought me into the band, man. It just doesn't seem right."

"If another guitar player came along, she'd do this to you in a minute," Gordon said. "You know she would."

Buzz sighed. "We've got three more nights here. Let's at least wait until we finish out this gig to make a decision."

Gordon seemed ready to say more but then excused himself and walked backstage. The minute he was out of earshot, Buzz turned to Frank. "Were they old tracks?"

"Yes."

"I feel stupid not noticing. Not that it matters. If they're old, I mean." His face turned red. "What I mean is, she can really sing."

I watched him for a moment, then said, "You like her."

"Yeah." Buzz forced a laugh. "It's obviously not mutual." He looked toward the stage, then rubbed his hand over his chest as if easing an ache. "Well, I better get ready for the next set."

Frank watched him walk off, then looked over at me. He pushed his drink aside, moved his chair closer to mine.

Q: What do you call a guitarist without a girlfriend?
A: Homeless.

Buzz seemed to recover his good humor by the time he was onstage. There was an air of anticipation in the audience now. It seemed that most of them had heard the band before and were eagerly awaiting the beginning of this set.

As the band members took their places, I sat wondering what Buzz saw in Joleen. My question was soon answered, though not in words.

Buzz and Joleen stood at opposite ends of the stage facing straight ahead, not so much as glancing at one another. She sang three notes, clear and sweet, and then Buzz began to sing with her, his voice blending perfectly with hers. It was a slow, melodic passage, sung a cappella. The audience was absolutely silent— even Frank sat forward and listened closely.

They sang with their eyes closed as if they would brook no interference from other senses. But they were meeting, somewhere out in the smoky haze above the room, above us all, touching one another with nothing more than sound.

The song's pace began to quicken and quicken, the voices dividing and yet echoing one another again and again until at last their voices came together, holding one note, letting it ring out over us, ending only as the instruments joined in.

The crowd cheered, but the musicians were in a world of their own. Buzz turned to Gordon and Mack, all three of them smiling as they played increasingly difficult variations on a theme. I watched Joleen; she was standing back now, letting the instrumentalists take center stage, her eyes still closed. But as Buzz took a solo, I saw her smile to herself. It was the only time she smiled all evening.

The song ended, and the crowd came to its feet, shouting in acclaim.

Q: Did you hear about the time the bass player locked his keys in the car?
A: It took two hours to get the drummer out.

Mack joined us during the second break between sets. With Buzz's encouragement he told us about the years he'd studied at Berkeley, where he met Joleen, and about some of the odd day jobs and strange gigs he had taken while trying to make headway with his music career—including once being hired by a Washington socialite to play piano for her dog's birthday party.

We spent more time talking to Mack than to Buzz, whose attentions were taken by another guitar player, a young man who had stopped by to hear the band and now had questions about Buzz's "rig."

"That means his equipment, right?" I asked.

"Not just the equipment," Mack explained. "I play my bass with a really straight-ahead setup; just my bass and my amp." He pointed out his large Peavey amplifier, about four feet tall. "But Buzz's rig is much more complicated," he said. He went on to tell us that a rig-referred not just to the equipment—the guitar, an amp, a set of speakers, a synthesizer, rack effects, and an array of foot pedals—but also to the ways in which the guitar had been modified, the setup for the synthesizer, and all the other mechanical and electronic aspects of Buzz's playing.

"None of which will ever help that poor guy play like Buzz does," he said. "Buzz has the gift."

"He feels lucky to be in this band," I said. "He has great respect for the other players."

Mack smiled. "He's a generous guy." As Joleen walked over to Buzz and handed him a beer, Mack added softly, "He's a little young yet, and I worry that maybe he has a few hard lessons to learn. Hope it won't discourage him."

"How do you two manage to work together?" I asked.

He didn't mistake my meaning. "You mean because of Joleen's temper? Or because we used to be together?"

"Both."

"As far as the temper goes, I'm used to her. Over the years we've played with a lot of different people; I've outlasted a lot of guys who just couldn't take her attitude. Great thing about Buzz is that he's not just talented, he's easy to get along with. He's able to just let her tantrums and insults roll off him."

"And Gordon?" Frank asked.

"Oh, I don't think Gordon is going to put up with it much longer. The musician's lot in life, I guess. Bands are hard to hold together. Talk to anybody who's played in them for more than a couple of years, he'll have more than a few stories about band fights and breakups."

"But from what Buzz tells us, you've worked hard to reach this point—the CD, the tour, the gig in the Netherlands—"

"Yeah. I'm hoping Joleen and Gordon will come to their senses and see that we can't let petty differences blow this chance. I think they will." He paused, took a sip of beer. "You were also asking about how Joleen and I manage to work together after being in a relationship, right?"

I nodded.

"Well, she and I have always had something special. We write songs together. Musically, we're a good fit. When we were younger, when we first discovered that we could compose together, there was a sort of passion in the experience, and we just assumed that meant we'd be a good fit in every other way. But we weren't."

"Still," I said, "I'd think it would be painful to have to work with someone after a breakup."

He smiled. "I won't lie. At first it was horrible. But what was happening musically was just too good to give up. The hurt was forgotten. Over the years we each found other people to be with. And like I said, we have something special of our own, and we'll always have that."

He glanced at his watch. "Better get ready for the last set. You two want to come out to dinner with us afterward?"

"Thanks for the invitation," Frank said, "but I'm wearing down. Irene, if you want to stay—"

I shook my head. "Thanks, but I'll have to take a rain check, too."

"Another time, then. I forget that other people aren't as wired after a gig as the band is. I'll check with Buzz—I can give him a lift home if he wants to join us."

I toyed with the idea of heading home early if Buzz should

decide to go out to dinner with the band. But my mental rehearsal of the excuses I'd make on my way out the door was cut short when Buzz stopped by the table and said, "They asked me if I wanted to go to dinner with them but they're just going to argue, so I'd rather go home after this last set. Is that okay?"

"Of course," I said, hoping my smile didn't look as phony as it felt.

We went backstage after the last set, but it was clear the band was not going to linger. Joleen and Gordon were already on their way out the door, saying they'd see Mack at a nearby all-night coffeeshop. Buzz and Mack stood near one another, guitar cases in hand. Mack asked us to excuse them for a moment and started to take Buzz aside.

"That's okay," I said. "We'll wait for Buzz at the car—nice meeting you, Mack."

When he caught up with us, Buzz was smiling. "Mack fronted me some of what we're owed by the club—knew I was running a little short because of the car." He sighed in relief, then frowned. "Hope he checked it out with Joleen first. They're supposed to decide things together."

"I don't think she'd mind," I said. "Sounds as if it's a personal loan from him, not the band."

Q: Why did God give drummers ten percent more brains than horses?

A: So no one would have to clean up after them during the parade.

"What was the name of the first song in the second set?" Frank asked Buzz as we drove him home. Buzz was being uncharacteristically quiet, staring out the car window. But at the question he smiled.

"It's called 'Draid Bhreá Fiacla.' That's Irish for 'a fine set of teeth.' "

"How romantic," I said.

"It is, really. Joleen rarely smiles, but once I said something that made her laugh and she had this beautiful grin on her face after. When I saw it, I said, 'Well, look there! You've a fine set of teeth. I wonder why you hide them.'"

"Did she have an answer?"

He laughed. "In a way. She bit me. Not hard, just a playful little bite. So the next time I saw her, I gave her the song and told her its name and got to see the smile again."

"You wrote that song?" Frank asked.

"She worked on it some after I gave it to her, made it better. It belongs to both of us now, I suppose."

"Of all the ones we heard tonight, that one's easily my favorite," I said.

"Mine, too," Frank said.

"Joleen says it's too melodic," he said. "But I don't think she means it. She just doesn't want me to think too highly of myself."

Q: What's the difference between a viola and an onion?
A: Nobody cries when you chop up a viola.

"Thanks again for the ride," he said when we pulled up in front of his apartment.

"You have a way to the club tomorrow night?" Frank asked. "I could give you a ride if you need one."

"The Chevette is supposed to be ready by late afternoon. I'm kind of glad it broke down. It was great to meet you, man."

"You too. Stay in touch."

"I will. You take care, too, Irene."

After Buzz closed the car door, Frank said, "Let's wait until he's inside the building."

Having noticed the three young toughs standing not far down the sidewalk, I had already planned to wait. But Buzz waved to them, they waved back, and he made his way to the door without harm.

It was about three in the morning when we got to bed. When Buzz called at ten o'clock, we figured we had managed to have almost a full night's sleep. Still, at first I was too drowsy to figure out what he was saying. Then again, fully awake I might not have understood the words that came between hard sobs. There were only a few of them.

"She's dead, Irene. My God, she's dead."

"Buzz? Who's dead?" I asked. Frank sat up in bed.

"Joleen."

"Joleen? Oh, Buzz . . ."

"She . . . she killed herself. Can you come over here? You and Frank?"

"Sure," I said. "We'll be right over."

By the time we got there, he was a little calmer. Not much, but enough to be able to tell us that Gordon had found her that morning, that she had hanged herself.

"It's his fault, the bastard!" He drew a hiccuping breath. "Last night, when they went out to dinner, he told Joleen he was quitting the band. Mack tried to talk him out of it, but I guess Gordon wouldn't give in."

"Gordon called you?"

"No, Mack. He told me she made some angry remark, said we'd just find a new drummer. Mack was upset and said he didn't want to try to break in a new drummer in three weeks' time, that he was going to cancel the tour. He told her he was tired of her tantrums, tired of working for months with people only to have her run them off. It must have just crushed her—she worked so hard—"

I held him, let him cry, as Frank went into the kitchen. I could hear him opening cupboards. Finally he asked, "Any coffee, Buzz?"

Buzz straightened. "Just tea, sorry. I'll make it."

He regained some of his composure as he went through the ritual of making tea. As the water heated, he turned to Frank. "The police will be there, won't they?"

"Yes. It's not my case, but I'll find out what I can for you. The detectives will want to talk to you—"

"To me? Why?"

"Standard procedure. They'll talk to the people closest to her, try to get a picture of what was going on in her life."

"Do you think she—I mean, hanging, is it quick?"

"Yes, it's quick," Frank said firmly. I admired the authority in it, knowing that he was probably lying. Suicide by hanging is seldom an efficient matter—most victims slowly suffocate. But if Joleen's suffering hadn't been over quickly, at least some small part of Buzz's was.

"Thanks," Buzz said. "I thought you would know." He sighed and went back to working at making tea. I straightened the small living room, made it a little more tidy before Buzz brought the tea in and set it on the coffee table.

We sat on the floor although Buzz offered us the mattress-couch. He took two or three sips from the cup, set it down, then went to stand by the window. The phone rang, but he didn't answer it. "Let the machine get it," he said in a strained voice. "I can't talk to anybody else right now."

The answering machine picked up on the fourth ring. We heard Buzz's happy-go-lucky outgoing message, then the beep, then, "This is Parker's Garage. The part we were waiting for didn't come in, so the Chevette won't be ready today. Sorry about that."

"Aw, Christ, it only needed that!"

"Look, Buzz," I said, "if you need a ride anywhere, we'll take you."

"I've imposed on you enough. And after the last twenty-four hours, Frank has undoubtedly had his fill of Buzz Sullivan."

"No. Not at all," Frank said.

The phone rang again. This time he answered it. "Hi, Mack." He swallowed hard. "Not too good. You?" After a moment he said, "Already? . . . Yeah, all right."

He hung up and shook his head. "The club wants us to have our stuff out of there before tonight. They've already asked another band to play. Guess it's the guys who were going to start there when we went to Europe."

"You need a ride?" Frank asked.

"Yeah. I hate to ruin your weekend—"

"We're with a friend," I said. "It isn't ruined. What time do you need to be there?"

"Soon as possible. He said the detectives want to talk to us there. Club owner, too—he told Mack, 'I'm not too happy about any of this!'—like anybody is!"

Q: *What's the difference between a bull and an orchestra?*
A: *An orchestra has the horns in the back and the ass in front.*

We arrived before the others and found the door locked. We walked around to the narrow alley, reaching the back door just as the owner pulled up—the bartender from the night before. He looked like he wanted to give Buzz a piece of his mind but thought better of it when he took a look at Frank. Frank is six four, but I don't think it's just his height that causes this kind of reaction among certain two-legged weasels. (I asked him about it once, and he told me he got straight A's in intimidation at the police academy; I stopped trying to get a straight answer out of him after that.)

The owner grumbled under his breath as he unlocked the door and punched in the alarm code, then turned on the lights. I walked in behind him. I had only taken a couple of steps when I realized that Buzz was still outside; without being able to see him, I could hear him sobbing again. Frank stepped into the doorway, motioned me to go on in. I heard him talking in low, consoling tones to Buzz, heard Buzz talking to him.

I squelched an unattractive little flareup of jealousy I felt then; a moment's dismay that someone who had known Buzz for only a few hours was comforting him when I had been his friend for several years. How stupid to insist that the provision of solace be on the basis of seniority.

My anger at myself must have shown on my face in some fierce expression because the owner said, "Look, I'm sorry. I just didn't get much sleep. This place don't close itself, and now at eleven o'clock I've already had a busy morning. But I really am sorry about that kid out there. He's the nicest one of the bunch. And I think he had eyes for the little spitfire." He shook his head. "I never would have figured her for the type to off herself, you know?"

"I didn't really know her," I said. "I just met her last night."

"She had troubles," he said. "But she was always the type to get more mad than sad." He shrugged "I don't know. She was complicated—like that music she sang."

He started moving around the club, taking chairs off tabletops. I helped him, unable to stand around while he worked. In full light the club seemed even smaller and shabbier than it had in the dark.

Soon Buzz and Frank came in. Frank started helping Buzz pack away his equipment. Within a few moments other people arrived: the detectives, then Mack and Gordon.

None of the band members seemed in great shape. The detectives recognized Frank and pulled him aside, then asked the owner if they could borrow his office.

They asked to talk to Mack first. He went with them. Gordon climbed the stage steps and began to put away his cymbals.

Frank surreptitiously positioned himself between Buzz and Gordon. They worked quietly for a while, then Gordon said, "I'm sorry, Buzz. I—I never would have said anything to her if I'd thought . . ."

"It's not your fault," Buzz said wearily, contradicting his earlier outburst. He finished closing the last of his cases and began helping Gordon.

Mack came out and told the bar owner that the detectives wanted to talk to him next. By then most of the equipment had been carried into the backstage room. All that was left was a single mike stand—Joleen's.

I walked onto the stage and stood where she had stood during "A Fine Set of Teeth." I thought of her voice, clear and sweet on those first notes, her smile as she listened to Buzz's solo. I looked out and wondered how she saw that small sea of adoring faces that must have been looking back at her; wondered if she had known of Buzz's loyalty to her; remembered the bite and figured she had. I thought of her giving the sound man hell; she had both bark and bite.

I saw Mack, standing at the bar, at about the same moment he saw me. He stared at me, making me wonder if I was causing him to see ghosts.

Feeling like an interloper, I stepped away from the empty mike stand, then paused. I had the nagging feeling that something about the stage wasn't right. Something was missing. Of course, most of the equipment had been packed up already—it was that thought which made me realize what was bothering me. I glanced back at Mack, then called my husband over.

"Tell your friends not to let Mack leave," I whispered. "There's something he needs to explain."

"Are you going to tell me about it, or has being on this stage gone to your head?"

"Both. Where is Mack's big Peavey amp?" I asked. "Or Joleen's mike and monitor?"

Frank looked around, then smiled. "I'll be right back. And maybe you should try to stand close to Buzz. This will be hard on him." He took a step away, then turned back. "How did you know it was murder?" he whispered.

"I didn't. Not until just now. Ligature marks?"

He nodded.

I walked into the backstage room. Gordon sat on the couch. Buzz was sitting on the piano bench. I sat down next to Buzz and lifted the keyboard cover. "You play?" he asked.

"Sure." I tapped out the melody line of "Heart and Soul." "It's one of two pieces I can play," I said.

A corner of his mouth quirked up. "The other being 'Chopsticks'?"

"How did you know?"

"People just seem to know those two," he said, reminding me about the missing sarcasm gene.

"Come on," I said. "Play the other half."

"Half?" he said, filling in the chords.

"Okay, three-quarters."

Gordon laughed.

"Come on," Buzz said, "there's room for you, too."

"I'll pass," he said, "I don't even know 'Chopsticks.' "

We stopped when we heard Gordon shout, "What are you doing to Mack?" We turned to see Mack being led out in handcuffs.

"They're arresting him," Frank said as they left. "For Joleen's murder."

"So tell me again how you figured this out," Buzz asked later when we were back at his apartment. We were sitting on the floor around the coffee table.

"Okay," I said. "We were the first ones at the club this morning, right?"

He nodded.

"You and Gordon both had equipment to pack up. Your equipment was still on the stage because when you left Club 99 last night, you had every intention of coming back tonight. But one band member knew he wouldn't be back. Mack was the last band member to leave the club. He packed up his amplifier and took it home."

"You figured that out just standing there?"

"I was thinking about that dirty trick the sound man pulled on her—making her hear her own voice a half-step off through the monitor. But the mike and monitor were gone, and so was Mack's amp. I knew you didn't pack them up, neither did Gordon. You had only worked on your part of the stage, or to help Gordon. So Mack must have taken his equipment and Joleen's from the stage. But then I realized that he hadn't been on the stage this morning—he was questioned by the police as soon as he got there. I didn't notice what was missing at first—his equipment isn't as elaborate as your rig, or Gordon's kit. Neither was Joleen's."

"And the marks you were talking about?" he asked Frank.

"You're sure you want to hear about this?"

"Yeah."

"There were two sets of marks on her neck—the type of mark known as ligature marks. One set was horizontal, across her neck—the other was V-shaped, from her chin to behind her ear. The second set of marks would be typical of a suicide by hanging, but they were postmortem—they were made by the rope some-

time after she was dead. The first marks—the horizontal ones—
were the ones that were made by the pull, of the rope when she
was alive—made when someone stood behind her and strangled
her."

Buzz was silent for a long time, then asked, "Why?"

"Mack probably told her the truth at the restaurant," Frank
said. "He had lost a lot of good players because of her attitude.
Just as it looks as if things have stabilized and The Wasteland's
big break is coming along, she starts making trouble with
Gordon."

"But she was the heart of the group! Her voice."

"Gordon was going to offer him a new singer," Frank reminded him.

"Susan?"

"I suppose he would have worked with Susan on the songs he
had already written with Joleen, then taken Susan with the band
to Europe."

Buzz frowned. "You're right. He had already given her a couple of them to learn. Susan sang them on the tape Gordon
brought last night."

"Mack wanted to make sure he had sole rights to the songs."

"Oh, and then what?" Buzz asked angrily. "What did he think
would happen down the road? Have you ever heard one of
Mack's songs? Dull stuff. Technically passable, but nothing more.
He just provided the wood. She set it on fire. With her dead, who
would have provided that fire?"

"Now," I said, "I think you're getting closer."

They both stared at me.

"Buzz," I asked, "until you wrote 'A Fine Set of Teeth—' "

"You mean 'Draid Bhreá Fiacla'?"

"Yes. Until then had anyone other than Mack written a song
with her?"

"No, but he didn't understand that either, did he?" he said,
and looked away. "No, he couldn't."

I didn't contradict him, but I wondered if he was right. Perhaps
Mack understood exactly what it meant, and perhaps Joleen, who
had known Mack better than the others, also believed that the

safest course was to hide any affection she felt for Buzz. I kept these thoughts to myself; bad enough to second-guess the dead, worse if the theory might bring further pain to the living.

When we were fairly sure he'd be all right, and had obtained promises from him that he'd call us whenever he needed us, we left Buzz's apartment.

We were in the stairwell of the old building when we heard it— the first few notes of 'Draid Bhreá Fiacla,' the notes a woman with a fine set of teeth used to sing with eyes closed.

The notes were being played on an Irish harp, and a young man's voice answered them.

THE ROOTS OF DEATH

by Margaret Maron

I was dawdling over a second cup of coffee, rereading Marcie's letter and despairing anew at today's mobility, which can put the width of a whole continent between a woman and her first grandchildren, when I noticed activity at the old Brockman house next door. I put down the letter.

The mock orange hedge that separates our two yards was too high for me to see the ground floor, but the shutters on a second-floor window suddenly flew back, framing a young, very pretty girl with uptilted chin and sleek dark hair. Resting firm, capable hands on the windowsill to smile at someone below, she seemed so utterly, blissfully happy that I, too smiled involuntarily. She saw me sitting in our sunny breakfast nook and threw a friendly disarming smile in my direction. I liked her at once.

People in the Brockman house again, and young people at that! I could hardly wait for Frank to come home that night to tell him the good news.

It had been a long, lonesome winter for me, with Marcie and her husband transferred to a branch office in Oregon and Frank, Jr., away at college. Brampton is a small Southern town in the outermost suburbs of Washington, D.C., and doesn't offer too many diversions. Besides, I never was much for ladies' clubs, for listening to a flock of elderly hens cackle about their grandchildren or preen themselves on growing old gracefully.

"We should have had a dozen children," Frank often said that winter. "A natural-born mother like you misses having someone to cluck over."

Well, I *do* like young folks, and the next morning I made up a fresh batch of oatmeal cookies and stepped through a gap in the mock orange to ring their back bell.

Anne Jordan opened the door instantly. "I was just going to come borrow a cup of something and invite you over," she smiled, wiping dusty fingers on the seat of her blue stretch pants before taking the cookies. "Come on in and have some coffee."

I saw that my first impression across the widths of our yards had been deceiving. Her slender figure, good bones, and open smile had given an appearance of extreme youth, but up close, tiny lines around her wide gray eyes revealed that she was past thirty.

"I'm thirty-two," she told me that day, "and I feel like a nineteen-year-old bride. After twelve years of marriage, we finally have our first real home."

"Her husband was in the army," I told Frank at dinner, "and you know what that means: military housing, packing up and moving every time you've just got used to a place."

My younger brother Don, who teaches botany at the college here and lives in a neat bachelor apartment on campus, was over for dinner that night, and he grinned at my enthusiasm. "Sounds as if you've adopted her."

"Oh, you know Alicia," Frank teased. "All strays and orphans."

Although Anne *was* orphaned at an early age and shunted from one indifferent relative to another while growing up, she was by no means a stray. Her marriage to John Jordan was a rock upon which to anchor, and now that he had finally fulfilled the promise he'd made when they were first married—the promise of permanency, a proper home, civilian life—she had fallen in love with him all over again.

"He never minded army life, but I hated it," Anne confided. "Most people got two-or three-year assignments to one spot, but our limit always seemed to be eighteen months. Once, in Germany, I planted rose-bushes. I thought that even if I only saw them bloom one spring, it would be worth it. New orders came six months later for Japan. After that I just stuck to zinnias and petunias."

Standing at her kitchen window that first day in early spring, she gestured happily to the deep back yard and its long-neglected garden where a few scattered crocuses poked up through the dead grass. "I noticed a little nursery on the edge of town the other day. Do you suppose I could find a Dorothy Perkins rosebush there? It's an old-fashioned rambler. My grandmother had one."

All my frustrated maternalism went out to her, and after that I was over almost every day, lending a hand with painting cabinets, washing crystal from Germany, polishing brass trays from India, and helping Anne decide where all the accumulation of twelve years of travel could be positioned to best advantage through the Victorian-size Brockman house.

I remember her satisfaction as she stood a massive pair of heavy iron candlesticks on either side of the wide center staircase in the entrance hall.

"I bought them in Spain," she said. "I knew how perfect they would look someday in this exact position," and they were the right touch: thickly twining tendrils and grape leaves of black iron formed a stubby five-inch diameter and stretched up nearly four feet from a heavy block base, enhancing the formal red and black wallpaper of the entrance hall. Her decorative sense was superb, and the Brockman place bloomed and took on new beauty under her sure touch.

"Don't forget I've had years to plan it," she said once, and showed me a thick looseleaf notebook bulging with ideas and pictures he'd clipped from a long line of homemaking magazines. "It's just as well John didn't resign his commission any sooner. Look how my taste ran in those early days. Ultra-super-modern. Ugh!"

I had a sudden heart-wrenching picture of a trickling stream of bright women's magazines following her around the world; of the days spent dreaming over, choosing and rejecting from, their shiny pages. It was as if she had held her life suspended, refusing to become attached to any place or unmovable thing or person until now, when she could let herself begin to live.

Throughout the long slow spring, I showed her the town, introduced her to Mr. Higgins at the greenhouse, and rummaged with her in the secondhand shops where we found several lovely chests to refinish. It was like having Marcie back, furnishing her first home, all over again.

We saw little of John at first. He was a stocky, capable man, not quite six feet tall, with an aura of restless energy. He helped move the heavier furniture, then absented himself, relieved to escape the endless discussions of the best color for the den, of whether the dining room should be papered or the badly scratched paneling replaced.

He told Anne cheerfully, "Two things: stay inside our budget and no pink ruffles in the den."

As he left for Washington one day, he said to me, "It's wonderful of you to take her under your wing. She's needed a friend for a long time, and I'm afraid I just can't work up much interest in interior decorating." He smiled at Anne, happily engrossed with fabric swatches. "I haven't seen her so excited since we were married."

"Darling," Anne said, holding out two pieces of fabric, "do you think the federalist blue or—"

"Ask Alicia," he protested and blew her a kiss. "I'm off to my office. I didn't know civilians worked so hard!"

John had found an excellent job in Washington as personnel manager of a small but growing paper products firm. It had recently merged with a larger business, and John had been brought in as a neutral outsider to smooth over the merger and effect a friction-free working relationship between the two groups of employees. So far, he had managed to preserve his neutrality, but he was constantly being faced with complaints as old precedents and outmoded traditions were changed for progress' sake.

"I only hope it continues to be hectic for a good long time," Anne said. "At least until John gets used to the placidity of civilian life. He's always enjoyed settling flaps. That's why he made such a good administrator in the army." For a moment there was a shadow of apprehension in her voice. "I just hope he doesn't start missing it when the office settles down."

During April and May, John's office continued to demand long hours, and Anne began to join us for bridge on Friday nights when Don was over for dinner, a regular habit with him. Yet it was understood that even if she held seven no-trump, doubled, redoubled and vulnerable, the moment John's car could be heard in the drive she would leave us, running across our backyard, cutting through the hedge to greet him.

Looking at the handful of face cards she had flung down one night, Don said wistfully, "It must be nice to have a wife who would leave a hand like that to welcome you home."

Frank and I looked at him in surprise. It was the first time we had ever heard him regret his choice of bachelorhood, and Frank chuckled, "Better take warning, Don. Another remark like that and Alicia'll have you marching down the aisle. Like tomorrow, possibly."

Frank was so close to the truth that I could feel myself blushing as I pushed down the mental list of eligible females that I'd been checking off. "It's no disgrace to want my brother happily married," I argued. "He's forty now. How's he going to feel at fifty, with no family to cherish and to be cherished by?"

"Lucky!" Don answered. "Admit it, my dear. How many women do you know like Anne who are content to center their lives around making a home for their husbands?" And he cut the deck for three-handed rummy.

By June, the main improvements to the house were complete. There remained only the small additions and deletions of decor that would allow a dedicated homemaker a lifetime of happy puttering.

The yards and flower gardens were to have been John's project, but as, the office yet demanded long hours, Anne tackled it under Don's supervision. Despite his lack of a garden of his own, Don has a bright green thumb and keeps our garden in a constant state of upheaval, shifting bulb beds and shrubs like a housewife rearranging furniture.

He often dropped in to help Anne repot the begonias into hanging baskets for the patio or to prune back an overgrown lilac, and he even found the exact rambling rosebush Anne had longed for. The exuberant hug she gave him in enthusiastic gratitude sent him stumbling through a border of sweet williams.

He and John devoted several Sundays to digging up young dogwood sprigs in the surrounding woods to transplant along their back fence. Anne had volunteered to help but was instantly voted down by everyone, for by this time, her condition was decreed too delicate to allow unwarranted strain.

All of us were delighted at the prospect of a baby. Frank and I had hardly got used to the idea of grandchildren before Marcie and her family had moved so far away, and Don had already decided that he would plant a Japanese walnut in the back corner that fall. "It should be just right for easy climbing in five or six years," he declared.

John was happiest of all. He had wanted a child for years, but Anne had held back.

"How heavenly it sounds to say so confidently, 'In five or six years our child will be climbing a tree planted this fall,' " she glowed. "To know that he isn't going to be dragged all over the world, transferred from one school to another."

"For heaven's sake, Anne!" John exploded in exasperation. "You always make military life sound like existence in a concentration camp. What's so terrible about raising a child in the service? Think how much more sophisticated all the kids were that we knew, how quickly they learned a bit of foreign languages."

"A bit is right," Anne said hotly. "Kitchen vocabularies learned from the maids they were constantly left with. No chance to form ties or build a feeling of belonging."

"But they learned to belong anywhere, honey. And most of them were as well adjusted as any kids in Brampton."

"And what of the ones who weren't, John? You can't have forgotten little Kevin Lentz, whose bedroom was over ours in Japan. The way he cried for hours every night."

"He was an emotionally disturbed child, and you can't know he wouldn't have been the same if his father had been an accountant in Brampton. Besides, it was his first move and he was just upset at leaving his dog behind. He's probably learned to adjust by now, just as our child—"

He laughed abruptly. "Look at us! Our first fight since we came to Brampton, and it has to be in front of Alicia and Frank." The talk moved lightly on to other subjects, and I was the only one who even noticed what John had almost said, though Anne's large gray eyes had been momentarily puzzled.

From that moment on, I began to distrust John vaguely, and once started, many small incidents seemed to take on uneasy significance. I noticed a restlessness about him, his lack of real interest in the house, and one day in July, I heard him remark that with all the improvements they'd made, the house had easily doubled in value.

By late fall, the office merger had settled down into a smooth routine, and as John became a normal nine-to-fiver, a bored impatience seemed to grow in him.

Anne put it down to the adjustment to civilian life and prospective fatherhood, but I was not so sure, and early one November day when he came over to return a pair of pliers, my concern for Anne's happiness lost its discretion.

"John," I said hesitantly, "I know it's none of my business, but are you happy here in Brampton?"

He shrugged. "Oh, I suppose I'm as content here as I would be in any one place."

"But you don't like being in just one place forever?"

He sighed. "I wish Anne could see me as clearly as you do. She's so intoxicated with this house, this town, with you. Oh yes, most definitely with you," he repeated irritably, noting my look of surprise. "You're the closest thing to a mother she's ever known. She'll miss you the most."

"*Miss* me!" I exclaimed, aghast.

"Look, Alicia, I know I must seem like a heel, but I've tried to live like Anne wants and I just can't. I said I would try civilian life and I have. That was our deal. But I see it just isn't my bag."

"But it's only been a few months," I protested.

"Months of knowing that I'll be doing the same thing for the rest of my life, the same job, the same place, the same people. No offense to you or even to this town, but in the service you have the adventure of never knowing where your next assignment is going to be. How much excitement do you think I can get out of watching leaves fall off the same tree year after year after year?"

"But Anne—"

"I know, but she's a good sport, and frankly I don't think she actually hated the army as much as she says now. I never heard her do much complaining before."

"Because she loved you," I pleaded; "because she knew you'd keep your promise and give her a home."

"But I have and I will. We can keep the house, rent it out during our overseas tours. We're bound to be stationed in Washington once in a while if I request it. And even if we don't she'll get over it."

"The way that child Kevin got over the loss of his dog?" I asked him caustically.

"Now, Alicia," he said, grinning boyishly at me, but I was not about to be gotten around so easily.

"I think it was nasty of you to wait until she was pregnant at last."

"I didn't plan that, honest. But I won't pretend I'm sorry. I've wanted a son for years, but Anne would never agree to it before."

"When will you be leaving?" I asked bleakly, suddenly feeling older than my fifty-two years entitled me to feel.

"It's too soon to say. I've started the paperwork, but I don't know if they'll let me reenter at my former rank. That's why I haven't told Anne yet."

"You needn't worry about *my* telling her," I assured him. "I couldn't bear it."

Anne's love and trust in John were painful to remember. In such a short time she had become a dearly-loved daughter to me and I cried as I thought of the baby I might never see, who would be born in some goodness-knows-where base hospital.

"It isn't fair," I raged that night to Frank as we lay in the darkness of our bedroom. "He talks of Anne's not understanding him and thinks that because he wants a thing, she will come to want it, too. And he's wrong-wrong-*wrong!*"

Frank put a comforting arm around me. "You're getting too worked up, honey. You forget that she's his wife and not your daughter. Why, you didn't get this upset when Marcie moved to Oregon."

"Marcie was different. She was excited about going. Anne won't be."

"Maybe when the baby is born—"

"It will be worse. Oh, Frank," I sobbed, "I was so looking forward to that baby."

In the next few days, I found many reasons to be out of the house. I didn't want to see Anne's face, so full of luminous content, knowing what I did, but as I was leaving one morning, Anne intercepted me. With a child's anxious directness, she asked, "Have I done something, Alicia? You act as if you're avoiding me."

"Of course not, dear. I've been catching up on a lot of shopping. Thanksgiving sales, you know." But I had missed our long talks, and when she wistfully invited me to come in for coffee, I couldn't resist.

As we were entering the house, I saw Mr. McKeon, our mailman, trudging up my front walk. "You go ahead and pour," I called to Anne. "I want to see if there's a letter from Frank, Jr., or Marcie."

"Just a postcard from Frank, Jr.," Mr. McKeon greeted me. "He needs more money. Say, he sure does go through a lot."

I agreed that he did indeed. We're all so used to Mr. McKeon's reading any unsealed mail that no one bothers to get angry about it any more.

"If you're going back to Mrs. Jordan's, you can take her these and save me a few steps. Just bills and circulars and a letter from the army marked 'Official Business.' "

"They never stop." Anne smiled as she left the mail on a small hall table for John. "You wouldn't believe how endlessly the army tries to keep you involved. This one probably says, 'Are you sure you don't want to stay active by joining the reserve?' "

Yet the envelope filled me with apprehension. Its bulk was greater than that of a normal form letter, and I couldn't help wondering if this might be the last time I would see Anne so serenely happy.

As I drew the living room drapes that evening, I saw John drive in. He gave me a cheery wave, but I stared back coldly. That he could be so callous! Moving jerkily around our kitchen, slamming silverware on the table, pounding the veal as I would have enjoyed pounding John, I could imagine Anne going through similar movements next door, graceful despite the eight-months' burden she carried within her. I could almost see her dashing upstairs for a quick dab of lipstick as she heard John's car, making herself pretty for an adored husband who was about to smash her ordered dreams.

Then Frank came home and I forced myself to push down the hatred I felt for John and the compassion for Anne, to make light conversation over our meal. Frank was fond of Anne, but old-fashioned enough to hold that a wife's place was by her husband wherever he wanted to go, and that, after all, it was really none of my business. I was too depressed to court a lecture from him.

We were just beginning our dessert when I heard running footsteps across our backyard and Anne burst into the kitchen without knocking. Her voice was ragged and she gasped from the exertion.

"Alicia—Frank—you've got to help me. It's John. He—he slipped—he fell—on the stairs. I think he's dead."

She stumbled to a chair, crying wildly, as Frank sprang up and rushed out the door. Her gray eyes almost black, she clutched at my hand sobbing, "Please—*please* help me!"

Instantly my mind shot back twenty years to the day a crash from the den brought me on the run to find Frank's most cherished possession—his great-grandfather's gold watch, which hung inside a bell-shaped glass—lying smashed on the hearth and a shaken six-year-old Marcie terrified by the enormity of her guilt.

She had looked at me with the same expression as was now in Anne's eyes and whispered, "What will Daddy say? Mommy, please help me."

I hugged Anne briefly, fiercely. "Go lie down on the couch," I ordered. "You must think of the baby. I'll take care of everything," and I ran to follow Frank across the yard.

We found John at the foot of the wide staircase, his body twisted at a grotesque angle. His head lay against the foot of one of the heavy iron candle-sticks and a small pool of blood had oozed out from the wound where he had struck.

Frank knelt briefly, listening for a pulse beat.

"Is he alive?" I whispered.

"Can't tell," he grunted, rising heavily. "If he is, it's just barely. Where's the phone? I'll call a doctor."

"In the den," I gestured. As Frank moved past me, I went nearer to look down at John lying there so quietly, and hated him even more than before. If dead, I thought, especially if dead by Anne's push, he would be an even more destructive force in her life than alive.

Then I saw the crumpled letter in his hand, half under his body. Frank's voice called from the den, "The doctor says I'd better call Chief Norton, under the circumstances, but Doc's on his way."

The sound of the dial clicking out the numbers of our local police station spurred me into what had to be done to protect Anne.

By the time Frank returned, I had finished and the official army letter, now smooth and flat, lay casually among the other opened bills and circulars on the hall table.

"I'll stay here," Frank said. "You'd better go to Anne. Poor kid! Damn shame this had to happen now."

Anne sat in the same chair as I had left her, her eyes still dark with horror. "He's dead, isn't he?" she asked numbly. "He was coming up the stairs behind me. He couldn't understand why I was so furious. I didn't know I could feel that much anger. That letter! The army—and he expected me to be pleased because it was Germany again. *Germany!* But I didn't mean to—I didn't want—"

"Hush!" I said sharply. "Shut up and think about the baby for a minute."

Her voice cracked with tension. "You think I *haven't* been thinking of my child while you were over there?" She was on the ragged edge of hysteria.

"He slipped," I said deliberately. "He slipped and fell and struck his head on the candlestick. It was an accident. Do you understand, Anne? It was only an accident."

I couldn't be sure that she heard me. She had the withdrawn look of one listening for a faint, faraway sound. Suddenly, she clutched her abdomen and slumped across the table in pain.

I sat there beside her, stroking her hair and repeating slowly over and over, as to a retarded child, "It was an accident. He slipped and fell. You loved him. You were happy together. It was an accident." At last I saw the lights of a car swing in next door, and I ran across to bring back the doctor.

He ordered an ambulance immediately, and little Todd was born that night. It was a near thing for Anne and him, and hours passed before we were sure both would live.

By the time Chief Norton could question her about that night, it was just a brief formality, and John's death was put down as a regrettable accident. I think even Anne eventually convinced herself that John had fallen unaided.

When she was home, at last, with her young son, I asked, "You *will* stay on here, won't you, Anne?"

Her clear gray eyes widened in surprise. "Why, of course. This was our first real home, our only home." She blinked away the tears before they had a chance to form.

So Anne has stayed in Brampton and become a very dear part of our lives. Little Todd is beginning to talk now, and it's adorable to hear him try to say Alicia; it comes out "Weesha." He's almost as precious to me as Marcie's children, whom I see so seldom.

And Don! He spoils Todd dreadfully, always bringing him toys and sweets. He's planning to adopt Todd when he and Anne are married next spring. It will be a fine marriage; they have so many common interests, not least of which is Don's love of Brampton and complete lack of wanderlust.

Why, if I'd had any doubt but that their happiness would be the final outcome, I'd never have given the iron candlestick a low swinging putt into John's head when he moaned lightly, lying at the foot of the staircase, while Frank phoned the police.

THE MAGGODY FILES:
SPICED RHUBARB

by Joan Hess

"I haven't seen Lucinda Skaggs since a week ago Tuesday," Lottie Estes mentioned to a friend in the teachers' lounge. The fourth period bell precluded further analysis. Although it was of no botanical significance, the next morning it was discussed at the garden club meeting. It took several hours to reach the Emporium Hardware Store, but then the pace picked up and by midafternoon it was one of the topics at Suds of Fun Launderette next to the supermarket, in the supermarket proper, and even at the Dairee Dee-Lishus (although the teenagers moved on to more intriguing topics, such as blankets alongside Boone Creek and which minors had been caught in possession of what illegal substances).

Thus the tidbit—not a rumor, mind you—crept up the road, moving as slowly and clumsily as a three-legged dog on a frozen pond, until it reached Ruby Bee's Bar & Grill. This is hardly worthy of mention (nor was the fact that Lottie had not seen Lucinda Skaggs since a week ago Tuesday, but for some reason it was being mentioned a lot), since Ruby Bee's Bar & Grill was the ultimate depository of all gossip, trivial or boggling or outright scandalous, within the city limits of Maggody, Arkansas (pop. 755). Despite occasional attempted coups, it was acknowledged by almost everybody that the proprietress, Ruby Bee Hanks, was the guardian of the grapevine.

"So?" Estelle Oppers responded when she was presented with the tidbit. She took a pretzel from the basket on the bar, studied it for excessive salt, and popped it into her mouth.

"So I don't know," said Ruby Bee. "I was just repeating it, for pity's sake."

"Has Lucinda Skaggs disappeared, or has Lottie lost her bifocals?"

"All I know is that Lucinda hasn't been seen in nearly two weeks now." In retaliation for the skeptical reception, Ruby Bee pretended to polish the metal napkin holder while surreptitiously inching the pretzels out of Estelle's reach. "Lottie said you can set your watch by Lucinda's comings and goings. She's real big on 'early to bed, early to rise,' and Lottie says not one morning goes by that Lucinda doesn't snap on the kitchen light at six sharp, put out the garbage at six-fifteen, and—"

Estelle recaptured the pretzels. "I'm not interested in Lucinda Skaggs's schedule, and I'm a mite surprised Lottie and certain other people, present company included, find it so fascinating. If you're so dadburned worried about Lucinda—and I don't know why you should be, what with her being so holier-than-thou and more than willing to cast the first stone—why don't you call her and ask her if she's had a touch of the stomach flu?"

"I might just do that," Ruby Bee muttered, wishing she'd thought of it herself but not about to admit it. "When I get around to it, anyway."

She went into the kitchen and stayed there for a good five minutes, rattling pots and pans and banging cabinet doors so Estelle would know she was way too busy to fool with calling folks on the telephone to inquire about their health. When she returned, the stool at the end of the bar was unoccupied, which was what she'd been hoping for, so she hunted up the telephone number and dialed it.

"Buster," she began real nicely, "this is Ruby Bee Hanks over at the bar and grill. I was wondering if I might speak to Lucinda about a recipe?"

Estelle pranced out of the ladies' room and slid onto the barstool. She waited with a smirky look on her face until Ruby Bee hung up the receiver. "Glad you found time in your busy schedule to call over at the Skaggses' house. What'd she say?"

"I didn't talk to her. Buster says she's gone to visit her sister up in Hiana." She hesitated, frowning. "I seem to recollect Lucinda telling me that her sister was doing so poorly they had no choice but to put her in a nursing home in Springfield."

"Maybe she's back home now."

Ruby Bee tapped her temple with her forefinger. "It was a case of her being able to hide her own Easter eggs, if you know what I mean. Lucinda was real upset about it, but there wasn't any way her sister could take care of herself. 'God helps those who help themselves,' Lucinda said to me awhile back at the supermarket, over in the produce section, 'but all my sister's helping herself to is costume jewelry at the five and dime when she thinks nobody's watching.' Why would Buster lie about it?"

"He's most likely confused," Estelle said, yawning so hard her beehive hairdo almost wobbled, but not quite. "She could have gone to visit her sister in the nursing home, or she had to see to some family business in Hiana, or—"

"I don't think so," said Ruby Bee. She picked up the damp dishrag and began to wipe the counter, drawing glittery swaths that caught the pastel light from the neon signs on the wall behind her.

I stared at my mother, who, among other things, is the infamous Ruby Bee. The other things include being a dedicated and undeniably adept meddler, an incurable gossip, and a critic of my hair, my clothes, my face, and my life in general. I'll admit my hair was in a no-nonsense bun, my pants were baggy, my use of makeup was minimal, and my life was as exciting as molded gelatin salad, but I didn't need to hear about it on a daily basis.

I took a gulp of iced tea and said, "You want me to arrest Buster Skaggs because you couldn't get Lucinda's recipe for spiced rhubarb conserve? Doesn't that seem a little extreme—even to you?"

"I didn't say to arrest him," Ruby Bee said. "I said to question him, that's all."

"He probably doesn't know her recipe. Why don't you wheedle it out of the chef herself?"

Ruby Bee sniffed as if I were a stalk of ragweed polluting the barroom. "I would, Miss Smart Mouth, but no one's laid eyes on Lucinda for a good two weeks, and when I called and asked to speak to her, Buster had the audacity to say she was visiting her sister in Hiana."

"Oh," I said wisely. "How about a grilled cheese sandwich and a refill on the tea?"

"I wish you'd stop worrying about your stomach and listen to me," Ruby Bee said in her unfriendliest voice. "You are the chief of police, aren't you? It seems to me you'd be a little bit worried when someone ups and disappears like this, but all you care about is feeding your face and hiding out in that filthy little apartment of yours. That is no kind of life for a passably attractive girl who could, if she'd make the slightest effort, find herself a nice man and settle down like all her high school friends have. Did I tell you that Joyce is expecting in October, by the way?"

I was torn between stomping out in a snit and staying there to feed my face, about which I cared very dearly. For the record, my apartment was dingy but not filthy, and I may have been reading a lot lately, but I was in no way hiding out. Hiding out would imply someone was looking for me, and as far as I could tell no one was.

"Okay," I said, "you win. I'll put a real live bullet in my gun and march over to the Skaggses' house. If Buster refuses to divulge the recipe for rhubarb conserve, I'll blow his head off right there on the spot. About that sandwich . . ."

"I just told you Buster said Lucinda was visiting her sister in Hiana. I happen to know Lucinda's sister is in a nursing home in Springfield."

The conversation careened for a while, with me being called various names and being accused several times of failing to behave in a seemly fashion (a.k.a. one resulting in wedding vows and procreation). I participated only to needle her, and when the dust settled back on the barroom floor, I was standing on Lucinda Skaggs's front porch. The paint was bubbling off the trim like crocodile skin and the screen was rusted, but behind me the grass was trimmed, the flower beds were bright with annuals, and the vegetable garden in the side yard was weedless and neatly mulched.

"Hey, Arly," Buster said as he opened the door. "What can I do for you?" He was a small but muscular man with short gray hair and a face that sagged whenever his smile slipped. He was regarding me curiously, but without hostility.

I could have saved time by asking him if he'd murdered his wife, but it seemed less than neighborly. "Do you mind if I visit for a minute?"

"Sure, come on in." He pulled the door back and gestured at me. "You'll have to forgive the mess. Lucinda's been gone a couple of weeks, and I'm not much of a housekeeper."

With the exception of a newspaper and a beer can on the floor, the living room was immaculate. The throw pillows on the sofa were as smooth and plump as marshmallows, the arrangement of wildflowers was centered on the coffee table, the carpet still rippled from the vacuum cleaner. No magazines or books were in view, and unlike most living rooms in Maggody, no television set dominated the decor. On one wall an embroidered sampler declared that this was home, sweet home. Another hypothesized that a bird in the hand was worth two in the bush, and a third, ringed with coy pink storks, proclaimed that Shelley Belinda Skaggs had weighed seven pounds two ounces on November third, 1975.

"Lucinda's hobby," Buster said as I leaned forward to feign admiration for the tiny stitches. "She says that it relaxes her, and that the devil finds work for idle hands."

"They're very nice," I murmured. I sat down on the sofa and declined iced tea, coffee, and a beer. "I understand Lucinda's visiting her sister."

He gave me a wary look, but I chalked it up to the inanity of my remark. "Yeah, she's strong on family ties. There's a sampler in the kitchen that says, 'The family that prays together stays together.' I guess she and her sister have been on their knees going on two weeks now."

"I don't think I've seen Shelley around town in a while. Did she go with her mother?"

"Not hardly," he said with a brittle laugh. "Shelley took off a couple of weeks ago. I keep thinking we'll get a call from her, but we haven't had so much as a postcard."

"Took off?"

He shrugged, but he didn't sound at all casual as he said, "Ran away is more like it, I suppose. She and Lucinda had an argument, and the next morning there was a note on the kitchen table. According to Lucinda, the acorn can't stray far from the oak, but she may be wrong this time."

I glanced at the sampler behind me and did a bit of calculation. "Shelley's a minor. Have you notified the police in the nearby towns and the state police?"

"I wanted to, but Lucinda kept saying good riddance to bad rubbish. She was real upset with Shelley for coming home late one night and called her a slut and a lot of other nasty names. She's always been real stern with Shelley, even when she was nothing but a little girl in pigtails. When Lucinda wasn't whipping her, she was making her sit in a corner in her room and embroider quotations from the Bible. I can't tell you how many times I've heard Lucinda say—" He broke off and covered his face with his hands.

It was not a challenge to complete his sentence: Spare the rod and spoil the child. I barely knew Lucinda Skaggs, but I was increasingly aware of how much I disliked her. She seemed to live from cliché to cliché, and I suspected she would have some piercing ones for yours truly.

I waited until Buster wiped his eyes and attempted to smile. "I'll call the state police and alert them about Shelley. While you make a list of the names and addresses of your family and friends, I need to look through her things to see if I can find any leads. Also, we'll need a recent photograph."

Buster nodded and took me to Shelley's bedroom. It was as stark as the living room, with dreary beige walls, a matching bedspread, a bare lightbulb in the middle of the ceiling, and only the basic pieces of furniture. A brush and comb were aligned on the dresser. The drawers contained a meager amount of folded underthings, sweaters, and T-shirts. In the closet, skirts and blouses were separated and hung neatly; had it been plausible, I was sure they would have been alphabetized. There were no boxes on the the shelf, no notebooks or diaries in the drawers, no letters hidden under the mattress. The only splash of color came from a braided rug on the hardwood floor. The room, I concluded, could have passed inspection in a convent. Handily.

I paused to see which pithy statements Lucinda had chosen for her daughter's walls. "Pride goeth before a fall." "Honor they father and thy mother." "For dust thou art, and unto dust shalt thou return." Not quite as lighthearted as posters and pinups of movie stars, I thought as I returned to the living room.

Buster gave me a photograph of a teenaged girl, her smile as starched as her white blouse. Her hair was pulled back so tightly that there were faint creases at the corners of her eyes, which regarded the camera with contemptuous appraisal. I was not surprised that she wore no makeup or jewelry.

I put the photograph in my shirt pocket. "I'll return this to you as soon as possible."

"Here are a few addresses of relatives," he said as he handed me a piece of paper, "but I've already spoken to them and they promised to let me know if Shelley shows up."

I skimmed the list. "What about Shelley's aunt in Hiana?"

"She wouldn't set foot in that place, not with her mother being there." He looked down for a moment. "The telephone was disconnected, but I'll run up there this evening and fetch Lucinda. It's getting too quiet around here with both of them gone."

I promised to let him know what the police had to say, although I doubted it would amount to much. As I drove away, it occurred to me I'd exchanged a pseudo-missing person for a real one. The reverse would have been more palatable. And Ruby Bee's scalloped potatoes would have been more palatable than the can of soup I planned to have for dinner, but I wasn't quite prepared to deal with the thumbscrews served alongside them.

*   *   *

"Guess we got all excited over nothing," Ruby Bee said with a sigh. "Lucinda came home last night, and sent Buster by first thing this morning with the recipe." She squinted at the index card. "This won Lucinda a blue ribbon at the county fair last fall. As soon as I get a chance, I'm going to try it."

Estelle pensively chewed a pretzel. "What did Arly have to say about her little visit yesterday?"

"I haven't laid eyes on her," Ruby Bee admitted, wondering if she could get decent rhubarb at the supermarket across the road. "But now that Lucinda's back, I guess it was nothing but a wild-goose chase. Of course, we only have Buster's word that she really is back."

"Lottie said she caught a glimpse of her at six-fifteen, putting out the garbage by the back door like she always does. She thought Lucinda looked thin, but I suppose all that bother with her sister must be worrisome."

Ruby Bee put down the recipe, propped her elbows on the bar, and tugged on her chin. "I still don't know why Buster lied about that. It doesn't make a whisker of sense, him saying Lucinda was in Hiana with her sister."

"He was addled," Estelle said firmly.

This time Ruby Bee did not resort to wiping the counter. Instead, she picked up the card, studied it with a deepening frown, and then, in a peculiar voice, said, "I don't know, Estelle. I just don't know."

I figured I had two options. I could park up by the skeletal remains of Purtle's Esso Station and nab speeders, or I could sit in the PD and swat flies. Both required physical exertion, and I was taking a nap when Ruby Bee and Estelle stormed through the door.

Ruby Bee banged down a small bowl on my desk. "I told you so."

In that she told me some fool thing every hour, I wasn't sure how to field this one. "Told me what?" I finally said.

"I told you that Lucinda Skaggs didn't visit her sister in Hiana. Just taste this."

"And don't be all day about it," Estelle added. "This is an emergency."

I leaned forward and studied the goopy red contents of the bowl, then shook my head. "Sorry, ladies, I never taste anything that could be a living organism. A primeval one, to be sure, but perhaps in the midst of some sort of evolutionary breakthrough."

Ruby Bee put her hands on her hips. "Taste it."

"Oh, all right, but it better be good." Trying not to wince, I put my fingers in the goop, plucked out a bite-size lump, and conveyed it to my mouth without dribbling on my shirt. I regretted it immediately. My lips were sucked into my mouth, and the interior of my cheeks converged on my retreating tongue. Only decorum prevented me from spitting it out. "Yuck! This is awful!"

"No, it's not," Ruby Bee said, "or it's not supposed to be, anyway. It's Lucinda Skaggs's spiced rhubarb conserve, and it won a blue ribbon at the county fair last year."

I washed out my mouth with lukewarm coffee. "If it did, there was a good deal of bribery. This is absolutely awful. Maybe you didn't follow the recipe correctly, because this nasty stuff could turn someone's face inside out."

Estelle flapped an index card at me. "Are you saying Ruby Bee doesn't know how to follow a recipe, Miss Cordon Blue? There's not much to it—you slice your orange and your lemon, add your water, your vinegar, and your rhubarb, put in a little bag with gingerroot, cinnamon candies, mace, and cloves, and simmer until it gets nice and thick." She paused so dramatically that I realized I was holding my breath. "Your raisins are optional."

"And I followed the recipe right down to the cup of raisins," Ruby Bee snapped. "Now what do you aim to do about Lucinda Skaggs?"

I was still sipping coffee to get rid of the painfully tart taste in my mouth. "Decapitation? Force feeding?"

"She never came home," Estelle said, enunciating slowly so that the less perceptive of us in the PD could follow along. "This spiced rhubarb conserve proves it."

"Wait a minute," I said. "She came home yesterday evening. Buster told me he was driving to Hiana to fetch her, and she did give you the recipe for this vile concoction, didn't she?"

Ruby Bee glowered at the offending goop, and then at the offending chief of police. "Buster said she copied it down for me, but she didn't. She may not be the most charitable woman in town, but she did win a blue ribbon and there's no way on God's green earth that she sent this recipe to me."

"Why not?" I asked meekly.

Estelle stuck the card under my nose. "Just take a look for yourself, missy. Where's the sugar?"

"That's right," Ruby Bee said, looming over me like a maternal monolith. "Where's the sugar?"

This time I was standing on Lottie Estes's front porch, knocking on her door. A curtain twitched; and shortly thereafter, Lottie opened the door, gave me a crisp smile, and said, "Afternoon, Arly."

"I wanted to ask you a few questions about your neighbors," I began. Before I could continue, I was pulled inside, placed on the sofa, and cautioned to stay quiet until the shades were lowered and the curtains were drawn.

"We can't be too careful," Lottie whispered as she sat down beside me and patted my knee. "Now, what would you like to know?"

"Is Lucinda Skaggs home?" I asked.

"Why, I believe she is. This morning when I happened to be in my guest bedroom hunting for a pattern, I noticed that the light went on at six and she put out the garbage at exactly six-fifteen. At seven-thirty, Buster came out and got in his truck, then stopped and went back to the door. Lucinda handed him a card, and he returned to the truck and left, giving me a little wave as he drove by."

"And you saw her?"

Lottie's wrinkled cheeks reddened as she took off her bifocals and cleaned them with a tissue that appeared almost magically from her cuff. "I didn't want them to think I was spying on them, so I did stay behind the sheers. But, yes, I saw Lucinda for a second when she put out the garbage, and I heard her speak quite sternly to her husband when she gave him the card. She said something along the lines of 'a friend in need is a friend indeed.' I couldn't hear Buster's response, even though I had opened the window just a bit to enjoy the morning breeze."

I was amazed that she hadn't used binoculars and a wiretap. I thanked her for her information, but as I started for the door, an unpleasant thought occurred to me. "Two weeks ago," I said, "did you happen to be hunting for a pattern in the guest bedroom and see Buster carrying a duffel bag or a rolled carpet to his truck?"

"Oh, heavens no," she said with a nervous laugh. "However, I was doing a bit of dusting one morning when I saw him carry a braided rug *into* the house."

I could feel bifocaled eyes on my back as I walked across the yard to the Skaggses' house. I knocked on the door, then turned around to gaze at the garden. The bushy bean and pea plants were already thick, and the zucchini leaves were broad green fans. The tomato plants, although not yet a foot high, were encased with cylindrical wire cages.

The door opened behind me. Without turning back, I said, "Your garden's coming along nicely. I suppose Lucinda does a lot of canning in the fall."

"Tomatoes, beans, beets, turnips, greens, all that," Buster murmured. "A penny saved, you know . . ."

"Is a penny earned," I said, now looking at him. "I thought of another one while I was walking over here. Like to hear it?" He nodded unenthusiastically. "Little strokes fell great oaks."

"Is there something you wanted, Arly?"

"I'd like to speak to Lucinda about her recipe for spiced rhubarb conserve. Ruby Bee made a batch of it this afternoon, and it was inedible."

"I can't imagine that. It won a blue ribbon at the fair."

I opened the screen door, but he remained in the doorway, his arms folded. "I brought it with me so Lucinda could check it," I said, showing him the card.

"She's asleep. She's real fond of the one about the early bird catching the worm. I'd rather have ham and eggs myself." He reached out to take the card, but I lowered my hand. "I'll have her take a look at it in the morning. If there's something wrong, she can fix it up and I'll get it back to Ruby Bee."

"I had a call from the state police," I said, ignoring his vague attempt to reach the recipe card. "You'll be delighted to know they've located Shelley at a shelter in Farberville."

"They have?" he said uncertainly. He swallowed several times and licked his lips until they glistened like the surface of the rhubarb goop. "That's great, Arly. I was really worried about her. So was Lucinda, although she won't admit it. That was the reason she left the next day to visit her sister in Hiana. I'll tell her first thing in the morning."

"You said something interesting when we were discussing where Shelley might have gone," I continued. "You said Shelley wouldn't go to Hiana because her mother was there. How would Shelley have known her mother was there?"

He shook his head and gave me a bewildered look, but I wasn't in the mood to play Lieutenant Columbo and drag the ordeal out until the last commercial.

I held up the card once more and said, "The handwriting matches the list you wrote for me yesterday. You copied the recipe, but omitted the sugar. Lucinda wouldn't have, since she's made it often and is a meticulous person. Let's return to Mr. Franklin's 'Little strokes fell great oaks.' Lucinda might not have cared to be characterized as a tree, but I doubt it took little strokes to fell her. What did it take?"

His face and everything else about him sagged. "She was screaming at Shelley, spitting on her and slapping her. I couldn't stand it any more. I told her to shut up. She started screaming at me, and I pushed her away from me. She fell, hit her head on the edge of the kitchen table."

"I don't think so. When we do an investigation, we'll determine the details, but it didn't happen in the kitchen. It happened in

Shelley's room, which is why you took Shelley to Hiana and brought back a braided rug to cover the bloodstains."

"It was an accident," a defiant voice said. Shelley joined her father in the doorway, dressed in a dowdy robe. Her head was covered with hair rollers and a scarf; no doubt Lottie was convinced she'd spotted Lucinda for a second at the back door. "I was the one who pushed her, but I didn't mean for her to hit her head. Or maybe way in the back of my mind, I wanted it to happen." Although her expression did not change, her eyes filled with tears that began to slink down her cheeks.

Buster put his arm around his daughter. "I pushed her. God knows she's had it coming for twenty years."

Shelley looked up at him. " 'The heart of the fool is in his mouth.' "

" 'But the mouth of the wise man is in his heart,' " he countered sadly.

"We'll sort those out later," I said before we got lost between quotation marks. "Where's the body?"

Neither answered, but both of them glanced furtively over my shoulder. I studied the neat rows of tomato plants, each ringed with mulch and exuding the promise of a rich red crop later in the summer. I cast around in my mind for a suitable quote, and although my biblical training was sparse, I found one. " 'They that sow in tears shall reap in joy.' "

Buster managed a wry smile. "Lucinda would have appreciated it. As she was so fond of saying, 'Waste not, want not.' "

THE LAST, BEST CHANCE

by Suzanne Jones

He hadn't looked like the last, best chance to Duffy in the beginning. When he knocked her out of the path of the on-coming car, he had seemed less heroic than interfering. She might have saved herself, and with less damage. She found herself bruised against the opposite curb, her knee scraped and bleeding. Her lips felt numb. Her whole body felt numb.

"That guy never even stopped! It's like he tried to run her down!" An indignant voice. Then other disembodied, indignant voices. Concerned voices. Hands pulling her to a sitting position, then upright. Where she swayed, looking down stupidly at her torn stockings and bloody knee.

"Is she all right? Does she need a doctor?"

"No, she's just drunk." Another voice. *His* voice, flat and un-emotional. Harsh. She twisted her head around to look at him and found that she had torn the earring from her ear and was bleeding from there as well.

"I'll see that she gets home," he said.

She could not now remember if he had said anything else to her then. He had half-dragged, half-supported her when she stumbled the remaining distance to the parking lot at Alfalfa's. When they reached her car, he opened her purse and extracted her keys and wallet—she supposed to find out where she lived. Duffy hadn't much noticed or cared what he did. She supposed this not-caring was part of the incremental progress of the pilgrim on the road to not-being—which she knew was an achievable goal. God knows, if Jeff could attain it, in time anyone could.

The man drove her home in the "previously owned" BMW Gregory had bought her last year. She tried to concentrate on the myriad of lights on the dash, but the tears kept rolling down her cheeks. The ergometric arrangement of the dash had particularly impressed Gregory's son: Jeffrey in the cold, cold ground.

Poor Jeff. Gregory's son never had been much good at anything, yet he had managed his end with an efficiency she would not have expected. It made her think that it must have been an accident. They say most suicides are. And Jeff was said to have had an astonished look on his swollen face, as if his success had taken him by surprise, as though the consequence of stepping off a chair with his neck in a noose should have surprised anyone.

It was now the week before Labor Day, and in a few weeks the aspen would begin to turn gold in the high country, and the grass would stiffen and brown on Jeff's grave. The funeral hadn't beer that long ago. A month? Two months? The only thing she could remember from it was Jeff's friend Matthew coming up to her at the grave site and pushing his owlish face into hers and telling her that he wished her as dead as Jeff.

Which was unfair of him. He hadn't known the half of it. Besides, she had tried to find a little sorrow within herself for Jeff, but by the time he had dangled and danced in the air of the attic of her sister's large old house on Mapleton, there wasn't any. All gone. No sorrow or affection tucked away in any corner of her soul. Perhaps Matthew was right, and her indifference was what had led him up to the attic, but she doubted it. Jeff had better reasons than Duffy to do himself in.

Though she might have been a contributing factor. But then, wasn't everything? Carcinogens. The rape of the environment. Cruelty to animals. Haiti, or the little war of the month.

She felt little guilt concerning Jeff's end in the attic. He had effectively removed himself from the people she cared about on that twisting road down the Big Thompson Canyon. She felt a surge of anger at the memory, which she supposed should remind

her that she was not as far along as she might be on the true path
to not-caring, pilgrim that she was, if she could still feel that much
anger.

She wondered if it had been Matthew who had been behind
the wheel of the car which had almost run her down. Or another one of Jeff's friends. She had seen only a blurred shape
bearing down on her, but then her eyes had been full of angry
tears. No one had gotten the license number of the car. But she
doubted it was Matthew. It was probably just someone who
hadn't seen her crossing blindly in the middle of the block until
too late, someone who had made a mistake and didn't want to
stop to live with the consequences. Duffy could sympathize with
that position.

Her rescuer came into the elevator with her and up to the
apartment Gregory had leased for her near Boulder's mall. He
unlocked the door, pushed her into the bathroom, into the shower
still fully clothed, turned on the water, and left her there.

The drug-and alcohol-induced ennui dissipated in the shock of
the cold water, leaving her exhausted, and her body sore and stiff.
She shed her sodden clothes and dabbed some antiseptic on her
knee and ear. She wrapped a towel about her wet blond hair and
put on a robe. When she came into the living room, she had
almost forgotten about him. She hadn't expected to find him still
there.

He was a tall, lean man with broad shoulders and angry eyes.
He was looking closely at the wall of photographs: Duffy in a
sailplane. Duffy in a kayak. On the tennis court. On Hallet's third
buttress. On Shasta on crampons. And et cetera. Fragments of
her life. Most of the high points.

"Almost getting run over—almost getting yourself killed
wouldn't rattle you much, would it?" He waved a hand at the
photographs. "It's what you do for fun."

"That's right," she said. "I'm just plucky as anything."

He took hold of her robe at the throat and pushed her against
the wall of photographs. The frames dug painfully into her back.

"If you're not afraid to die, then what *are* you afraid of?"

His face was very close to hers. The irises of his eyes were caramel colored with red flecks in them. His grip on her was painfully tight. She had to force herself not to look away.

"Are you afraid of mutilation?" He moved his hand to her face. "You're a good-looking girl. Afraid of being slashed?" He drew a finger lightly across her cheek. "Of being blinded?" He tapped the corner of her eye. She made herself gaze steadily at him.

A weirdo. A freak. The world was full of them. Rescued by a pervert. Just her luck.

"No," he said, releasing her abruptly and turning away. "It's not so much that you're *not* afraid of death, is it? It's more that life doesn't matter that much to you. So you could always find another car to step in front of. Mutilation would just be a painful stop on the way to oblivion."

"I'd just as soon avoid it, thanks."

She relaxed a little. He was talking too much to be a real threat. They say real threats don't talk—they just do.

She rubbed her throat and pulled the robe closer about her. Her head ached. Too much wine, too many pills. She wanted to tell him to go, but was cautious. The violence in him seemed very close to the surface.

"Who pays for this place?" he asked. "And all of those?" He indicated the pile of credit cards he had emptied from her wallet onto the neat and orderly surface of her desk.

He looked at her, but she said nothing.

"You're a student at the university, and these digs are too pricey for a student. Besides, you're kind of old for a student, aren't you? Pushing thirty," he said, picking up her student ID.

"Slow learner," she said then, cautiously. There was something about him that was disturbing, dangerous. On the edge. Maybe she was wrong. Maybe he was a doer. "So you should let me get back to my books. I've got three cantos of the *Faerie Queene* that I should be galloping through as we speak. Anyway, you've done your good deed for the week. You can go about your business full of self-congratulations."

She opened the door for him.

He didn't move. "What if no one is there to push you out of danger the next time you cross a street?"

She fingered her torn ear. "I'll have to fall back on using the crosswalk and going with the light. Not to worry. I'll get by."

"The Chinese say that if you save a life, you become responsible for it."

She wondered whether anyone would come if she screamed into the hall. Probably not. The inhabitants of the building carefully kept themselves remote from one another. A respect for privacy was as much a requirement for living at that fashionable address as the hefty deposit.

"I'm not Chinese, and neither are you," she said evenly. "Consider yourself absolved of any responsibility. Thanks for everything."

He nodded. "And have a nice day." He tossed her keys on the desk, took one last look about the room, and left.

She put the chain on the door and clicked the deadbolt into place. Rescuer or no, she knew he had wanted to see if he could frighten her. Consider it done.

He hadn't looked like the last, best chance then.

Duffy had gone through the next few days of classes numbly. Despite the ugliness of the quarrel with Gregory which had propelled her in front of that car, she expected to hear from him. As usual. She had wanted the telephone to ring. Not wanted it to ring. Wanted it to ring. For almost a week.

Then when it did ring, the man's voice wasn't Gregory's.

"This is Richard Anderson." There was a pause while she tried to place the voice. It sounded familiar.

"I'm the guy who isn't Chinese. The one who kept you from becoming roadkill. Remember me?"

Remember those angry eyes inches from her own, wanting—no, demanding—to know what she was afraid of?

"Yes, I remember you."

"Dodged any speeding cars lately?"

"Lately I haven't had to."

"I noticed from one of the hero shots on your wall that you're a tennis player, and I've got tickets to the Volvo tournament. They're playing the first few rounds at the Event Center this weekend. Do you want to go?"

Was it the challenge in his voice that made her accept? Or that Gregory hadn't called? She didn't know. Though she was a little afraid of Richard Anderson, at that particular moment he hadn't seemed nearly as dangerous to her as Gregory. And she had wanted to see the tennis.

"No good deed should go unpunished," she told him. Of course she would go.

Out of deference to Gregory (who by the weekend had brought her flowers and stayed over), but mostly because she had little interest in Richard Anderson, she didn't dress with any particular care and wore no makeup and her heavy glasses instead of contacts. She supposed she looked like the English graduate student that she was. Richard Anderson didn't comment on her appearance.

He was knowledgeable about tennis, and she enjoyed the event more than she would have had she stayed home and watched it on television. Which was the reason she agreed to see him again. He had tickets to one of the Artist Series concerts at Macky, the auditorium on campus. Some Japanese violinist. Who was marvelous. This time Duffy dressed for the occasion.

They went for coffee afterwards, went for lunch the next day. He asked many questions of her, but she learned little about him. He had been a software designer but was on some sort of disability leave from his company for a bad back. He had been married once but was not married once but was not married now. He seemed to have plenty of time, money, and no particular girlfriend.

The persistency with which he pursued certain subjects irritated her. He seemed fascinated by her need to put herself at risk. And he kept asking her—in different ways—who the man was in her life. A girl like her always had someone.

Though she was candid with him in most things (she used candor as a measure of her indifference), she refused to answer those questions. Besides, the reason she put herself at risk was so personal and so mundane it embarrassed her: She was afraid to be afraid. The only thing worse than fear was giving in to it. And she refused to tell him about Gregory. Gregory was nobody's business but her own.

Sometimes she found Richard staring at her in a way which made her uneasy. She had expected him to make some sort of pass at her on any one of the times she had gone out with him, and she had been prepared for that, but he had not. That puzzled her a little more each time she saw him, and finally offended her vanity.

After a discussion they had on Renaissance architecture and Northern Italy, he asked her to his apartment to partake of something he called his "ancestral spaghetti," which he alleged was a familial recipe from Italy, but from an area so far north it was almost Swiss.

His apartment was comfortably and expensively furnished, but modern and not particularly Italian or anything else. The furnishings were obviously rented. There was so little in it that was personal, the place had a temporary feel.

The spaghetti sauce, he assured her, was ninety-percent bacon fat and butter, and not for anyone who had a concern for health or long life. Its excellence was reserved only for those fearless enough (or stupid enough) to consume that much fat at one sitting.

They drank white wine during the preparation—he chopped the bacon and onion and green peppers and mushrooms while she sat on a stool in the kitchen and watched. She accused him of the Tom Sawyer ploy: He was trying to make the activity of chopping all those vegetables look fascinating enough to emulate. But he could not tempt her. Chopping was cooking, and Duffy didn't cook.

With only one person doing the chopping—and many vegetables to be chopped—there was time for a considerable amount of white wine to be consumed before they sat down to eat. He opened a good bottle of Chianti Classico for the meal itself, and by the time they got to the after-dinner brandy, they were both a little drunk. Which may explain what happened next.

She heard him mutter that he should never have gone near her, should never have touched her. He hadn't intended this. And afterwards he looked so sad, she almost believed him.

He said, "I'm sorry. I haven't been with a woman for some time."

"I have to go," she said, gathering up her clothes.

"Not yet," he said. This time his hands were not rough.

It was late by the time she got back to her apartment. There was a message from Gregory on her answering machine. He had wanted to meet her for a drink after work. Wherever she was, he hoped she was safe and warm and thinking of him. She erased the message and stood for a time in the dark, not thinking of anything at all.

The next day she went to class and the library. She had a paper for her Spenser seminar due the first week in October. When she came back to the apartment, she thought she would hear from Richard. She didn't.

Gregory had left her a message, affectionate and concerned, but Richard hadn't called. A week passed without her hearing from him. And then two.

His not calling her put her a little off balance. It was not what she expected. She tried to call him, and found that he had no answering machine. She was more puzzled than hurt and then annoyed with herself that she felt anything at all.

But it had shaken her confidence and left her uneasy. The world wasn't working quite the way it should.

She put it down to her state of mind when she thought that someone might be following her. She'd glimpse movement out of the corner of her eye, but would turn to find no familiar face among the students hurrying to their classes. Still, her life seemed to move as smoothly along its customary way as it ever had. She went to class. She saw Gregory when he was free. Had her wine when she was alone. Nothing had changed, apart from this uneasiness.

Her sister Mary called, wanting to know who she was bringing with her the next weekend to Grand Lake. Closing the summer house was a ritual in which Duffy had participated almost every

year since their father died. Two weeks after Labor Day, when
the aspen were brilliant against the dark green forests of pine and
fir and spruce on the side of the mountain, the family—Mary and
Gregory, their three daughters, and Gregory's mother—went to
Grand Lake to close the house for the summer. This would be
their first year without Jeff, Mary had said sadly. She had been
fond of Gregory's son by his first marriage, that is, as fond as
Mary was of anyone. It was something which Duffy had admired
for years. Mary's reserve, her incredible poise, the way she glided
through her life, kind, unruffled, and serene, leaving the worries
of the world to work themselves out as best they might.

The past couple of years Duffy had taken one of Jeff's friends
with her to the lake. They were pleasant, clean-cut, well-behaved
boys who had little interest in her. Mary expected Duffy to take
someone, so she might as well take one of Jeff's friends. It was
someone to sail and fish with and someone to help them pull the
boats out of the water and help make the house ready for winter.

Now she knew she should call someone to go to the lake with
her, but not one of Jeff's friends. She seemed to have become the
center of their anger at his loss. Like Matthew. Their resentment
made her impatient. But she should take someone.

The day after Mary's call was a raw, windy day, a day which
was more typical of November than the last of September. Duffy
had been on her way to the library on campus amid swirls of
leaves when someone caught her arm. As she tried to pull away,
he forced her to look at him.

"Remember me?" he asked.

"Let's see now. I'm older, and my recall isn't what it once was.
'Richard,' isn't it?" She freed her arm. "Long time no see, Richard. Whatever have you been doing with yourself? You look awful."

He did look awful. His eyes were bloodshot, he needed a shave.

"I've been out of town," he said.

" 'Out of town,' he said, as if it excused anything, as if it were
a reason in and of itself," she said. "It's bad manners, Richard,
after plying a girl with Chianti and cholesterol and boffing her

brains out, not even to call to see if she got home. It's ungentlemanly. Worse, it's bad luck."

"Let's get some coffee," he said.

She hadn't intended to go with him, but the intensity of her feeling had surprised her. She had wanted to cause him pain. And she wasn't through wanting to.

But by the time they had found a table in the crowded student union, and he had gone to get their coffee, her anger had dissipated. She only felt a little tired and wondered what she was doing there when she ought to be studying. Worse, by the time he had made his way back to the table, she had begun to feel sorrier for him than for herself. It was hardly his fault he wasn't Gregory. Or that she had chosen to romanticize an evening of frenzied, drunken couplings, and he had not. Now he seemed to be a scapegoat to which she had been trying to tie her several sins. Nice try at being seduced and abandoned, Duffy. Quit looking for men on white horses to take you away from all this. If you don't like your life, get yourself out.

"I was afraid you might not still be here," he said, as he set the mug in front of her.

She hadn't said anything, but found she wasn't expecting him to say anything, either. And he hadn't. He hadn't explained or apologized. He didn't elaborate on the "trip out of town." He seemed as remote as any stranger. Which, she reminded herself, he pretty much was.

He asked her about her classes, her instructors. Later she wouldn't be able to recall much of the conversation.

As they parted, she said carelessly, "Call me." But realized as she hurried in the direction of the library, that she had no real expectation that he would do so. Nor did she care.

But he did call her, and she asked him to go with her to Grand Lake for the weekend—to help close the summer house. After she hung up, she felt she had done a most unwise thing and was uneasier than ever.

The drive over did little to relieve that feeling, though the scenery through Estes Park and over Trail Ridge was as spectacular as ever and usually had a calming effect on her. The mountains didn't care, they just were. Always the same and ever different.

The aspen had been showy that fall, but wind had created patches of gray, leafless trees which lay against the dark green of the mountains like clouds of smoke.

He had said little on the way up Trail Ridge, that high road which would shortly close for the year with the first major snow. They were on the way down the other side toward Grand Lake when he said, "What do you dream of when you dream?"

The intimacy of the question disconcerted her. Their conversation had been carefully impersonal since he had stopped her on campus.

"You mean as in 'perchance to' or as in 'aspiration'?"

"Either. Both."

She shrugged. "Of being free, I guess. Isn't that what everyone dreams of?"

"Aren't you free now?"

"Almost no one is. Everyone has obligations, if only to himself. Oneself," she corrected herself irritably.

He nodded.

"What do *you* dream of?" she asked.

"I don't dream."

"Everyone dreams. At least when they sleep. You just don't remember—" She glanced sideways at him, but his face was smooth and as untroubled as she had ever seen it as he stared at the high valley before them.

"Duffy, thank God you've come. Ruth and I are boring the hell out of each other. We're on our billionth game of gin."

"Speak for yourself, Mary. Work does not bore me. And winning this much money at these stakes is work. But what's an old woman to do for a little pin money?"

"So how much are you up now," Duffy said as she embraced her sister and the old woman who was dark, like a gypsy.

"One hundred twenty-three thousand and some change," Ruth said, consulting a scorepad.

Mary rolled her eyes. She was a beautiful woman, blond and tall and as thin as if she hadn't had three children.

"Richard, this is my sister Mary and her mother-in-law, Ruth Bellflower. Richard Anderson. Don't believe what either one of them says about the other."

Her duty done, Duffy went to find some wine as her sister helped Richard take their things upstairs.

"She cheats," Mary confided to Richard as they mounted the stairs.

Ruth craned her neck to follow their progress.

"Nice-looking boy," Ruth said as Duffy came back to her. "Better than those noodles you been bringing up here. When you gonna marry? You girls, you let your best chances pass you by. It's not healthy for a woman to live alone. I should know."

"Don't overdo it, Ruth. Want to scare him off? Anyway, you should be ashamed of yourself. Mary is a lousy card player. You shouldn't have to cheat to beat her."

"You shouldn't believe everything you hear. Anyway, I only cheat to add a little interest. We spend so much time with each other, it makes us tired. My son is always dragging off my little ones to be on the lake with him. They could be a comfort to their grandmother—"

"—if only they'd stay home and learn to tat."

"What's wrong with learning a few skills? The problem with you girls is you got too much learning. Thinking too much will make anyone choleric."

"Choleric? God, Ruth. I'm going down to the boathouse."

Gregory was bringing the old inboard alongside the dock as Duffy reached it. The girls, ages four, seven, and eight, and blond as their mother, were as happy to see her as ever, scrambling out of the boat and banging into each other to hug her as she held her wine up out of harm's way. They wanted to know all about the man Duffy had brought with her. When she told them Richard had saved her from being flattened by a car, they tore away to the house to see a real live hero.

Gregory watched them scurrying up the hill.

"I thought you said you could have saved yourself."

"Having a hero makes for a better story."

"He's not one of Jeff's friends?"

"No. I'm not very popular with Jeff's friends at the moment. They've nominated me for prime mover in Jeff's trip to the attic."

She watched his face darken.

"None of the boys has said anything to me," he said. "Why should they think you had anything to do with Jeff's death?"

Duffy hesitated, looking at the wine in her hand. It was the color of blood. She had not betrayed Jeff before his death, and Gregory had seemed in too much pain at the funeral to add more. She wondered why she was ready to tell him now. Maybe because she was tired of Jeff and his friends and their ignorance.

She drew him into the shade of the boathouse and out of view of the house above.

"Jeff and I were in an accident in July."

He looked at her questioningly.

"Do you remember the day I gave Jeff a ride back to Boulder? I had come up during the week for one of the kids' birthdays—Marianne's."

He leaned close to her and brushed her hair back from her face. "It was the last time Jeff was at the lake," he said. "This accident, it happened on your way back to Boulder?"

She nodded. "I let Jeff drive the BMW. He took the wrong road out of Estes, the road along the Big Thompson instead of back through Lyons. But it was such a lovely day, we didn't mind and didn't turn around. It's not that much farther. We were driving fast on a good road on a sunny day, and there was almost no traffic."

She offered him some wine, but he shook his head.

"Jeff passed a car and pulled in too closely. Cut the guy off and pissed him off, I guess. I wasn't paying a whole lot of attention. Before I knew anything was wrong, the guy had pulled alongside and then swerved in front of us. Stupid play. Jeff didn't brake in time to avoid hitting the rear fender, and their car spun over the bank and into the river."

Gregory frowned. "He should have told me."

"He was afraid to. Jeff stopped on the shoulder—the BMW didn't have a scratch on it—and I ran back to where they had gone over. We could hear them yelling for help. Then he dragged me back to the car and took off. I finally got him calmed down enough to let me call the highway patrol from a gas station—"

"What was so wrong in that? What else could you have done?"

"Oh, Gregory, we left the scene, and they were pinned in the car and were drowning! There wasn't time to call anyone. We should have stayed and at least tried to help. The woman died. I read about it in the paper. They were tourists from Illinois."

He didn't say anything for a long moment.

"What does this have to do with the way Jeff's friends are treating you? Why should they blame you for his death?"

"Because I couldn't bear to be around Jeff afterward. They knew that Jeff had been like a brother to me, that we were close, and then I wouldn't see him. I wouldn't return his calls."

"Why didn't you tell me there was trouble between you and Jeff?"

She looked away from him across the lake. "Because I'd have had to tell you about the accident, and I was ashamed. Leaving those people was such a weak thing for us to have done."

"*Us?* 'A weak thing for us to have done'? And what did you do that *you* regret? You said you weren't driving. You didn't run anyone off the road. You didn't panic. What has our brave Duffy to reproach herself for?"

She wanted to say, "I let him make me a coward," but Gregory's tone made her cautious. "I didn't have to get back into the car, but I did."

"Ah," he nodded. "Instead of plunging into the water, and effecting a single-handed rescue, you mean."

Duffy was very still.

He paced to the dock and came back to her. "You didn't tell me about this before Jeff's death, when I might have helped him, nor afterwards, when we all needed to know a reason—some reason—why he might have taken his own life. Instead of imagining all sorts of things. So why tell me now?"

And why had she? Because she was tired of Jeff's friends trying to make her feel guilty? They weren't her friends, and she didn't feel guilty. Or because she couldn't bear the sight of Gregory just now, happy with his children. Content with his life.

"I don't know."

He slapped her. She hadn't seen it coming and was stunned.

"You think about it," he said, "and let me know."

He turned on his heel and went up the slope to the house.

She tried to catch her breath.

"Lovers' quarrel?"

She hadn't heard him come along the dock. He peered at her through thick glasses.

"Matthew, what are you doing here?"

"Jeff found out you were sleeping with his daddy, didn't he? Isn't that what broke his heart?"

"Get out of here, you little creep," she said fiercely. "Stop spying on me."

He blinked at her. "You can't possibly know how much I want you dead. It's my dearest wish."

"Put it with a tooth under your pillow," she said and brushed past him. She didn't look back until she got to the steps of the porch. By then he had disappeared.

The girls had taken Richard for a walk, and Mary and Ruth had started supper. Gregory was alone on the porch, but she walked past him without looking in his direction. She poured herself another glass of wine. Through the glass between the living room and the porch she saw Gregory get up and go back down the slope to the boathouse.

She looked at him dispassionately, the dark curly hair, the broad shoulders and heavy neck, the waist that was already beginning to thicken. He was almost fifteen years older than she was, but none of that mattered. She knew he had only to look over his shoulder at her for her to follow. There didn't seem to be much she could do about that. But he didn't look back, and she sat on the porch, drinking her wine until she heard the racket the girls made coming into the house.

Dinner was as subdued an affair as eating with three lively

young girls could make it. Duffy had yet to attain that wine as-
sisted moment when nothing mattered and was very aware of
Richard's silence as the girls prattled on about the walk they had
taken with him. Gregory did not look at her.

Duffy helped the girls clear the table and stayed in the kitchen
mostly to supervise, while the adults took their coffee on the
porch. When the kitchen was about as clean as it was going to
get, she started the girls on Monopoly and took her wine onto
the patio nearest the road. She thought it prudent to stay out of
Gregory's way for a while.

"He's the one, isn't he?" Richard had come up silently behind
her.

"I don't know what you're talking about."

"The man in your life. Him. Gregory."

"I wish you'd let that alone. And let me alone."

"I couldn't be sure until I saw you together. There's a lot of
heat between you, even though he seems pretty out of sorts at
the moment. Did bringing me here upset him?"

"You don't know what you're talking about."

"The old woman knows, even if she doesn't say. The wife
chooses not to notice."

"And the kids? Have you decided whether they know or not,
or do you plan to interrogate them on the subject?"

"You're with him a lot, aren't you? You travel with him. He's
the one who pays for your apartment."

"Shut up. It's none of your business."

*Shut up before one of the girls comes onto the patio, looking
for us. Or before Gregory wonders where we are.*

"I had to be sure. I had seen him going into your building. I
thought he was the one."

Then she was aware she was alone. She sat for a while, finishing her wine. Then she went into the kitchen for another glass
and heard Mary taking the children upstairs for their baths. Only
Ruth sat alone on the porch, looking over the lake in the dimming
light.

"There you are. Your young man asked my Gregory to show

him the boats. He said he likes to sail. Used to sail on Lake Michigan, he said. He's a strange one, isn't he? Such a quiet boy. Broody. Choleric. He probably thinks too much."

Lake Michigan. Duffy had gone to Chicago to meet Gregory on one of his business trips in June, before the accident, and they had a room overlooking the lake. There had been sailboats on it, and it looked like a vast, gray, inland sea.

It might have been possible, Duffy thought, if one had a vision of a gray BMW with Boulder County plates seared into the brain—even if one couldn't remember all the numbers—to go to the license bureau in Boulder and look through all those BMW registrations. There couldn't be that many gray BMW's in Boulder County. A hundred? Two hundred? Then check out each owner until he found a blonde who looked like the woman in the canyon. If one were very patient and very dedicated. But how to find the man?

She had drunk too much wine to think clearly. She tried to remember Richard's helping her to her car after he had knocked her against the curb. She was fairly certain that he hadn't opened her purse until then. How had he known which car was hers? Had he been following her, waiting for her to lead him to the man? What had he just said to her? "I saw him going into your building."

"Where you going? You're gonna kill yourself running around like that in the dark!"

The dark wasn't the danger. She wasn't afraid of the dark. She hurled herself down that familiar path to find what she was afraid of, to break herself against it, if she had to. She didn't think she could make him believe her, but she could stop him. She had to stop him.

He met her at the door of the boathouse, and she knew she was too late. His face was pale. He was sweating and breathing hard.

"He wasn't the one," she panted, seizing his shoulders. "It was Jeff." She shook him. "It was his son who was driving."

"You'd have said anything to save him, wouldn't you? Anything."

He put his hands about her throat. In the dying light, his eyes looked as black as obsidian. Her mind was detached. So this was what death looked like. But her body had not lost its will to live. She tore frantically at his wrists.

"But he's dead, as dead as she is."

She hammered at his face as she lost consciousness, black streaked with red and a roaring in her ears. Then she was aware of her cheek hard against the rough planking of the dock.

She got to her knees, gasping, trying to pull the air into her burning lungs.

"I thought I wanted you dead, but I couldn't let him kill you, and he wouldn't let go." It was Matthew. "I had to keep hitting him. Weird. Is he dead? Did I kill him?"

He stood above Richard's body, the bloody oar still in his hands.

"I don't know," she said. "I don't think so."

She got to her feet and stumbled against the boathouse, groping inside the door for a light. Gregory was floating facedown in one of the slips, rocking gently deeper and deeper into the water.

"Oh, God," Matthew said. "I'll get someone. I'll get the police."

He ran up the slope to the house and disappeared in the dark.

Duffy sat on the dock beside Richard and waited. Her throat ached and she couldn't swallow. She closed her eyes. She heard the familiar sounds of the lake: the slap of the waves and the creak of the dock. An owl. The sounds she had heard when she was a child, when all she had to do was come in before dark. When she was free.

After a time, she put out a hand to his battered head and stroked his hair. Tenderly. Like a lover.

ACCOMMODATION VACANT

by Celia Fremlin

"I'm sorry . . ." The woman's eyes slithered expertly down Linda's loose, figure-concealing coat, and her voice hardened. "No, I'm sorry, the room's been taken . . . No, I've nothing left at all, I'm afraid. . . . Good afternoon. . . ."

Familiar enough words, by now. Goodness knows we ought to be used to it, thought Linda bitterly, as she and David trailed together down the grimy steps. She dared not even look up at him for comfort, lest he should see the tears stinging and glittering in her eyes.

But he had seen them anyway. His arm came round her thin shoulders, and for a moment they leaned together, speechless, in the gray, mean street, engulfed by a disappointment so intense, so totally shared, that one day, when they were old, old people, they might remember it as an extraordinary joy . . .

"Lin—Lin, darling, don't cry! It'll be all right, I swear it will be all right! I promise you it will, Lin . . . !"

The despairing note in his young voice, the pressure of his arms round her, destroyed the last remnants of Linda's self-control. Burying her face against the worn leather of his jacket, she sobbed, helplessly and hopelessly.

"It's my fault, David, it's all my fault!" she gulped, her voice muffled amid the luxuriance of his dark, shoulder-length hair. "It was my fault, it was me who talked you into it. You said all along we shouldn't start a baby yet, not until you've got a proper job. . . ."

At this, David jerked her sharply round to face him.

"Lin!" he said, "never, never say that again! I want this baby as much as you do, and if I ever said different, then forget it! He's *our* baby, yours and mine! I'm his father, and I want him! Get it? I *want* him! And I'm going to provide a home for him! A smashing home too," he proclaimed defiantly into the dingy, uncaring street. "—A home fit for my son! Fit for my wife and son . . . !" His voice trailed off as he glared through the gathering November dusk at the closed doors, the tightly curtained windows, rank on rank, as far as they could see. "My God, if I could only get a decent job!" he muttered, and grabbing Linda's hand in a harsh, almost savage grip, he hurried her away—back to the main road, back to the lighted buses, back "home."

That's what they still called it anyway, though they both knew it wasn't home anymore. How could it be, when they had to steal in through the front door like burglars, closing it in a whisper behind them, going up the creaking stairs on tiptoe in the vain hope of avoiding Mrs. Moles, the landlady, with her guarded eyes and her twice-daily inquisitions: "Found anywhere yet? Oh. Oh, I see. Yes, well, I'm sorry, but I'm afraid I can't give you any more extension. Six months you've had (to the day, actually; Linda remembered in every detail that May morning when she had come back from the doctor's bubbling over with her glorious news, spilling it out, in reckless triumph, to everyone in the house). Six months, and I could have got you out in a week if I'd been minded! A week's notice, that's all I'd have to've given, it's not like you're on a regular tenancy! Six months I've given you, it's not everyone'd be that patient, I can tell you! But I've had enough! I'm giving you till Monday, understand? Not a day longer! I need that room. . . ."

Sometimes, during these tirades, David would answer back. Standing in front of Linda on the dark stairs, protecting her with his broad shoulders and his mass of tangled, caveman hair, he would storm at Mrs. Moles face-to-face, giving as good as he got; and Linda never told him that it only made matters worse for her afterward. His male pride needed these shows of strength, she knew, especially now, when his temporary job at the Rating Office had come to an end, and the only money he could count on was from his part-time job at the cafeteria—three or four afternoons at most.

If only he had finished his course and got his engineering degree instead of dropping out half way!—Linda silenced the little stir of resentment, because what was the use? No good needling him *now* about his irresponsible past. Poor Dave, responsibility had caught up with him now, all right, and he was doing his best—his unpractised best—to shoulder it. Doing it for *her*. For her, and for the baby . . . recriminations don't help a man who is already stretched to his limit. Besides, she loved him.

Monday, though! Mrs. Moles really meant it this time! *Monday*—only four days away! That night, Linda cried herself to sleep, with David's arms around her and his voice, still shakily confident, whispering into her ear: "Don't you worry, Lin! It'll be all right. I promise you it'll be all right. . . ."

It wouldn't, though. How could it? They had been searching for months now, in all their free time and at weekends, lowering their standards week by week as the hopelessness of the search was gradually borne in on them. From a three-room flat to a two-room one . . . from one room with use of kitchen to anything, anything at all. . . . If all these weeks of unflagging effort had produced nothing, then what could possibly be hoped from four more days . . . ?

The next morning, for the first time since their search began, David set off for the estate agent's alone. After her near-sleepless night, Linda had woken feeling so sick, and looking so white and fragile, that David had insisted on her staying in bed—just as, a couple of weeks earlier, he had insisted on her giving up her job. Before he left, he brought her a cup of tea and kissed her goodbye.

"Don't worry, love, I'll come up with something *this* time, just you see!" And Linda, white and weak against the pillows, smiled and tried to look as if she didn't know that he was lying.

After he had gone, she must have dozed off, for the next thing she knew, it was past eleven o'clock, pale November sunshine was glittering on the wet windows, and the telephone down in the hall was ringing . . . ringing . . . ringing . . .

No one seemed to be answering. They must all be out. With a curious sense of foreboding (curious, because what bad news could there possibly be for a couple as near rock bottom as herself and David?), Linda scrambled into dressing gown and slippers and hurried down the three flights of stairs.

"Darling! I thought you were never coming . . ." It was Dave's voice all right, but for a moment she hadn't recognized it, so long was it since it had sounded buoyant and carefree like that—"Darling, listen! Just *listen*—you'll never believe it. . . ."

And she didn't. Not at first, anyway; it was just too fantastic; a stroke of luck beyond their wildest dreams! In those first moments, with the telephone pressed to her unbelieving ear, she couldn't seem even to take it in.

What had happened, she at last gathered, was this: David had been coming gloomily out of the estate agent's with the familiar "Nothing today, I'm afraid" still ringing in his ears, when a young man, red-haired and strikingly tall, had stepped across the pavement and accosted him.

"Looking for somewhere to live, buddy?" he'd asked; and before David had got over his surprise, the stranger was well and thoroughly launched on his amazing, incredible proposition.

A three-room flat, self-contained, with a balcony, and big windows facing south—all for five pounds a week!

"And he'd like us to move in *today!*" David gabbled joyously on. "Just think of it, Lin! *Today!* Not even one more night in that dump! No more grovelling to the old Mole! God, am I looking forward to telling her what she can do with that miserable garret—"

"But . . . but, darling . . . !" Linda could not help breaking in at this point. "Darling, it sounds fantastic, of course it does! But . . . but, Dave, are you sure it's *all right*? I mean, why should this—whoever he is—why should he be letting the flat at such a ridiculously low rent? And—"

"Just what *I* wanted to know!" David's voice came clear and exultant down the line. "But it's quite simple really—he explained everything! You see, he's just broken up with his girl, she's gone off with another man, and he just can't stand staying on in the place without her. He's not thinking about the money, he just wants OUT—and you can understand it, can't you? I mean, he was nuts about this girl, they'd been together for over a year, and he thought she was just as happy as he was. The shock was just more than he could take . . ."

"Yes . . . Yes of course . . ." Linda's excitement was laced with unease. "But—David—I still don't quite understand. Why *us*? Why isn't he putting it in the hands of the agents . . . ?"

"Darling!"—there was just the tiniest edge of impatience in David's voice now—"Darling, don't be like that! Don't spoil it all! Anyway, it's all quite understandable, really—Just think for a minute. A chap in that sort of emotional crisis—the bottom just knocked out of his life—the last thing he needs is a lot of malarky about leases and tenancy agreements and date of transfer and all the rest of it. So he decided to bypass the whole estate agent racket and simply—"

"So what was he doing, then, just outside an estate agent's?"

The words had snapped out before Linda could check them. She hated her own wariness, her inability to throw herself with total abandon into David's mood of unquestioning exultation.

But this time David seemed to enjoy her hesitation: it was as if she had played, unwittingly, the very card that enabled him to lay down his ace.

"Aha!" he said—and already she could hear the smile in his voice—the bold, cheeky, self-congratulatory smile with which he used to relate the more outrageous exploits of that bunch of tear-aways he used to go around with—"*Aha*, that was cleverness! Real cleverness. Just the sort of thing that *I* might have thought of"—how wonderful it was to hear his cocky, male arrogance coming alive again after all these months of humiliation and de-feat!—"He did just the thing that *I* always do in a tricky situa-tion—he asked himself the right questions! Like, what's the quickest way to clinch a deal—any deal? Why, find a chap who's desperate for what you've got to offer. And when the thing on offer is a roof over the head—then where do such desperate chaps come thickest on the ground? Why, outside an estate agent's, just after opening time! So that's what he did—just hung about waiting for someone to come out the door looking really sick. . . ."

It made sense. Sense of a sort, anyway. Linda felt her doubts begin to melt. Joy hovered like a bright bird, ready to swoop in.

"It—Oh, darling! It seems just too good to be true!" she cried. "Oh, Dave, I'm so happy! And this young man—once we're settled, and you've got another job, we must insist on him taking more than five pounds—we mustn't take advantage of his misery! Not when *we're* so happy . . . so lucky . . . ! Oh, but we don't even know his name . . . !"

"We do! It's Fanshawe!" David countered exultantly. "It's on the name-slip outside the door—R. Fanshawe. But I've changed it, darling, I'm right here, and I've changed it already! It says 'Graves' now! 'David and Linda Graves'! Oh, Lin, darling, how soon can you get here . . . ?"

It was bigger even than she'd imagined, and much more beautiful. It was on the fifth floor of a large modern block, and even now, in winter, the big rooms were filled with light. The sunshine hit you like a breaking wave as you walked in, and through the wide windows, far away above the roofs and spires of the city, you could see a blue line of hills.

Linda and David could hardly speak for excitement. They wandered from room to room as if in a trance, exploring, exclaiming, making rapturous little sounds that were hardly like words at all; more like the twittering of birds in springtime, the joyous nesting time.

Deep, roomy shelves. Built-in cupboards and wardrobes. Bright, modern furniture—and not too much of it; there would be plenty of room for their own few favorite pieces.

"Your desk—it can go just here, Dave, under the window. It'll get all the light!" exclaimed Linda: and, "See, Lin, this alcove— I can build his cot to exactly fit in! This will be *his* room . . . !" and so on and so on, until at last, exhausted with happiness, one of them—afterward, Linda could never remember which, and of course, at the time, it did not seem important—one of them suddenly noticed the time.

"Gosh, look, it's nearly two!" exclaimed whichever one it was; and there followed quite a little panic. For by two-thirty David was supposed to be at the cafeteria, slicing hard-boiled eggs, washing lettuces, sweeping up the mess left by the lunchtime customer. . . . It would never do for him to lose this job, too. Hand in hand they raced out of the flat . . . raced for the bus . . . and managed to reach home in time to get David out of his leather jacket and into a freshly ironed overall just in time to be not much more than ten minutes late for work. Kissing him goodbye, Linda was careful not to muss up his hastily smoothed hair—the curling, shoulder-length mane was a bone of contention at the cafeteria—as, indeed, it had been at all his other jobs—but *she* loved it.

At the door, he paused to urge her to rest while he was gone; to lie down and take things easy.

"You weren't too good this morning," he reminded her, "so whatever you do, don't start trying to do any packing—we'll do it this evening, together. Oh, darling, just imagine Mrs. M's face when she sees us bumping our suitcases down the stairs this very night! Monday, indeed! *I'll* give her Monday . . . !"

Obediently, after he'd gone, Linda pulled off her dress and shoes and climbed into bed. It was quite true, she *was* tired. For a few minutes she lay staring up at the ceiling, trying to realize that she was looking at those familiar cracks and stains for the very last time. She couldn't believe it, really; the change in their fortunes had been so swift, so dreamlike somehow, that she hadn't really taken it in.

"Rest," David had urged her, but it was impossible. Excitement was drumming in her veins; it was impossible to be still, with all this happiness surging about inside her. She must *do* something. Not the packing—she'd promised to wait for David before starting on that—but there'd be no harm in getting things sorted out a bit . . . get rid of some of the rubbish. Those torn-off pages of Accommodation to Let, for a start: they'd never need *those* again . . . !"

Clumsily—for she was nearly eight months gone now—she heaved herself off the bed, and as she did so, David's leather jacket, hastily flung aside when he'd changed for work, cascaded off the bed onto the floor, with a little tinkling, metallic scutter of sound.

The keys, of course. The keys of the new flat: and as she picked them off the floor, Linda was filled with a surge of impatience to see again her beautiful new home—"home" already, as this place had never been. She ached to look once more out of the wide, beautiful windows, to gloat over the space, the light, and the precious feeling that it was *hers!* Hers and David's, and the new baby's as well! She wanted to examine, at leisure and in detail, every drawer and cupboard; to make plans about where the polished wooden salad bowl was to go, and the Israeli dancing girl . . . and the books . . . and the records . . .

Well, and why not? The whole afternoon stretched ahead of her—David wouldn't be home till nine at the earliest. What was she waiting for?

The flat did not seem, this time, quite the palace of light and space that it had seemed that morning, but it was still very wonderful. The rooms were dimmer now, and grayer, because, naturally, the sun had moved round since this morning, and left them in shadow.

But Linda did not mind. It was still marvelous. Humming to herself softly, she wandered, lapped in happiness, from room to room, peering into cupboards, scrutinizing shelves and alcoves, planning happily where everything was to go.

What space! What lovely, lovely space! Opening yet another set of empty, inviting drawers, it occurred to Linda that, for a man with a broken heart, their predecessor had left things quite extraordinarily clean and tidy. In the turmoil of shock and grief, how on earth had he forced himself to clean up so thoroughly— even to Hoover the carpets, and dust out the empty drawers? Or maybe the defecting girlfriend had done it for him? A sort of guilt offering to assuage her conscience . . . ?

Musing thus, Linda came upon a cupboard she had not noticed before—it was half hidden by a big, well-cushioned armchair pulled in front of it. It looked as if it might be big enough to store all the things for the new baby. . . . Linda took hold of the handle and pulled—and straightaway she knew that it was locked. This, then, must be where the ultra-tidy Mr. Fanshawe had stored away his things? Spurred by curiosity, Linda tried first one and then another of the keys on the bunch David had been given—and at the third attempt, the door gave under her hand. Gave too readily, somehow. It was as if it was being pushed from inside . . . a great weight seemed to be on the move . . . and just as the fear reached her stomach, making it lurch within her, the door swung fully open, and the body of a girl slumped out onto the floor. A blonde girl; probably pretty, but there was no know- ing now, so pinched and sunken were the features; already mot- tled with death.

Linda stood absolutely still. Horror, yes. In her recollections afterwards, and in her dreams, horror was the emotion she re- membered most clearly. And what could be more natural?

But not at the time. At the time, in those very first seconds, before she had had time to think at all, it was not horror that had overwhelmed her at all, it was fury. Sickening, stupefying fury and disappointment.

"Damn you, damn you, damn you!" she sobbed, crazily, at the silent figure on the floor "I *knew* it was too good to be true! I *knew* there would be a snag . . . !" And it was the sound of her own voice, raised in such blind, self-centered misery, that brought her partially to her senses.

She must *do* something. Phone somebody. Scream "Murder!" out of the window. Get help.

Help with what? How can you help a girl who is already dead . . . ? With the strange, steely calm that comes with shock, Linda dropped to her knees and peered closely at the slumped, deathly figure. No breath stirred between the bluish lips; no pulse could be felt in the limp, icy wrist. The girl lay there lifeless as a bundle of old clothes, ruining everything.

Because, of course, the flat was lost to them now. Had, in fact, never been theirs to lose. The whole thing had been a trick, right from the beginning. What they had walked into, so foolishly and trustingly, was not a flat at all, but a dreadful crime. Presently, the police would be here, cordoning everything off, hunting down the real owner of the flat, bringing him back for questioning. They would be questioning herself and David, too. . . . That, of course, had been the whole point of the trick! Linda could see it all now. They had been lured here deliberately by the phony offer of a home, in order that they should leave their fingerprints all over the place and be found here when the police arrived. A pair of trespassers, roaming without permission or explanation around someone else's flat! Because that's how it would look: why should the police—or indeed any other sane person—believe such a cock-and-bull story as she and David would have to tell? A ridiculous, incredible tale about having been offered, by a total stranger, an attractive three-room flat in a pleasant neighbourhood for only five pounds a week. All that this Fanshawe man had to do now was to deny totally the encounter with David outside the estate agent's, and it would be his word against David's—with, to him, the overwhelming advantage that his denials would sound immeasurably more plausible than David's grotesque assertions!

Neat, really. "*Aha*, that was cleverness!" as David had so lightheartedly remarked, only a few hours ago!

At the thought of all that happiness—of David's pride, his triumph, all to be so short-lived—a cold fury of determination seized upon Linda's still-shocked brain, and she knew, suddenly, exactly what she must do.

The dead cannot suffer. They are beyond human aid, and beyond human injury, too; so it wasn't really so terrible, what she was going to do.

Cautiously, and without even any great distaste, so numbed was she with shock, Linda got hold of the limp figure by the thick polo neck of its woollen sweater and began to pull.

Luckily, at this dead hour of the afternoon, the long corridors were empty as a dream. The lift glided obediently, silently downwards with its terrible burden . . . down, down, past the entrance floor, past even the basement . . . down, down to the lowest depths of all . . . and there, in an icy, windowless cellar, stacked with old mattresses and shadowy lengths of piping, Linda left her terrible charge.

It would be found—of course it would be found—but now there would at least be a sporting chance that the clues—now so thoroughly scrambled—would no longer lead so inexorably to the fifth floor flat into which the new tenants had just moved. It would be just one more of those unsolved murders. There were dozens of them every year, weren't there?

It would be all right. It *must* be all right. It must, it must . . .

All the same, Linda couldn't get out of the beautiful flat fast enough that afternoon. While the gray November day faded— she dared not switch on any lights for fear of advertising her presence here—she pushed the big chair back in front of the cupboard again, and set the room to rights. Then, still trembling, and feeling deathly sick, she set off for home. It was only five o'clock: four whole hours in which to recover her composure before David got back from work.

And recover it she must. At any cost, David must be protected from all knowledge of this new and terrible turn of events. She recalled his triumphant happiness this morning, the resurgence of his masculine pride. . . . She pictured how he would come bounding up the stairs this evening, three at a time, carrying a bottle of wine, probably, to celebrate . . .

And celebrate they would, if it killed her! Not one word would she breathe of her fearful secret—not one flicker of anxiety would she allow to cross her face.

Celebrate! Celebrate! Candles; steak and mushrooms, even if it cost all the week's housekeeping! She would wash and set her hair, too, as soon as she got in, and change into the peacock-blue maternity smock with the Chinese-y neckline. . . . She thought of everything, hurrying home through the November dusk that evening, except the possibility that David would be in before her . . .

She stood in the doorway clutching her parcels, speechless with surprise, and staring at him.

"Where the hell have you been?"

Never had she heard his voice sound so angry. How long had he been here? Why had he come back so early . . . ?

"I said you were to *rest!*" he was shouting at her. "You promised me you'd stay here and rest! Where have you *been?* I've been out of my mind with worry! And where are the keys? The keys of the flat? They were here . . . in my pocket . . . !"

He was sorry, though, a minute later; when she'd handed over the keys, and had explained to him about her excitement, about the sudden, irresistible impulse to go and look at the beautiful new flat once more. He seemed to understand.

"I'm sorry, darling, I've been a brute!" he apologized. "But you see it was so scary, somehow, coming in and finding the place all dark and empty! I was afraid something had happened. I thought, maybe, the baby . . ."

The reconciliation was sweet: and if he questioned her a little over-minutely about her exact movements that afternoon, and exactly how she had found things in the flat—well, what could be more natural in a man thrilled to bits about his new home, into which he is going to move that very night?

And move that very night they did.

No more Mrs. Moles! No more tiptoeing guiltily up and down dark stairs! Everywhere, light and space and privacy! And on top of this, a brand-new, modern kitchen, and a little sunny room exactly right for the baby—only a month away he was, now! For a day or so, Linda had feared that the birth might be coming on prematurely; she had been having odd, occasional pains since dragging that awful weight hither and thither along cement floors, through shadowy doorways. But after a few days it all seemed to settle down again—as also, amazingly, did her mind and spirits.

At first, she had been full of guilt and dread: it was all she could do not to let David notice how she started at every footfall in the corridor . . . every soft moan from the lift doors as they closed and opened. Sometimes, too, she was aware—or imagined she was aware—of David's eyes on her, speculative, unsmiling. At such times she would hastily find occasion to laugh shrilly . . . clatter saucepans . . . talk about the baby . . . Anything.

But presently, as the days went by, and nothing happened, her nerves began to quieten. Indeed, there were times when she almost wondered whether she hadn't imagined the whole thing. Because there was nothing in the papers, nothing on the radio—though she'd listened, during those first few days, like a maniac, like a creature obsessed, switching on every hour on the hour.

Nothing. Nothing at all. Had the body, conceivably, not been found yet? Surely it was *someone's* business—caretaker, nightwatchman, or someone—to go into that cellar now and again. Or—was it possible that the murderer himself had discovered where it had been moved to—had, perhaps, even watched her moving it, from some hidden vantage point . . . ? The lift, the corridors had all *seemed* to be totally deserted, but you never knew . . .

To begin with, weighed down as she was by guilt and dread, Linda had tried as far as possible to avoid contact with the neighbors; but inevitably, as the days went by, she found herself becoming on speaking terms with first one and then another of them. The woman next door . . . the old man at the end of the corridor . . . the girl who always seemed to be watering the rubber plant on the second-floor landing. Bits of gossip came to her ears, of tenants past and present, including, of course, snippets of information about hers and David's predecessor in the flat . . . And slowly, inexorably, it was borne in on her that practically none of it fitted with David's story in the very least degree. The previous tenant had been neither red-haired nor tall—hadn't, in fact, been a man at all, but a woman. A young, blonde woman, Linda learned, who had rather kept herself to herself. . . . Oh, there's been goings-on, yes, but there, you have to live and let live, don't you? Quite a surprise, actually, when the young woman gave up the flat so suddenly, no one had heard a thing about it, but there you are, the young folk are very unpredictable these days. . . .

And it was now, for the very first time, that it dawned on Linda that she only had David's word for it that the bizarre and improbable encounter with "Mr. Fanshawe" had ever taken place at all. Or, indeed, that any "Mr. Fanshawe" had ever existed!

This terrible, traitorous thought slipped into her mind one early December evening as she sat sewing for her baby. And having slipped in, it seemed, instantly, to make itself horribly at home . . . as if, deep down in her brain, there had been a niche ready-prepared for it all along.

Because everything now slid hideously, inexorably into place: David's disproportionate anger when he found she had visited the flat by herself that first afternoon: his unexplained, mysteriously early return from work on that same occasion. Perhaps, instead of going to the cafeteria, he had slipped off that working overall the moment he was out of sight and gone rushing off to devise some means of disposing of the body: his preparations completed, he would have arrived at the flat, scared and breathless—to find that the body had already disappeared! What then? Bewildered and panic-stricken, he would have hurried home—only to find that she, Linda, had been to the flat ahead of him! Had he guessed that she must have found the body? And if so, what had he made of her silence all these days? What did he think she was thinking as she sat there, demure and smiling, evening after evening, sewing for the baby? No wonder he had been giving her dark, wary glances! What sort of a look would it be that he'd be giving her tonight, when he came in and saw the new, terrible fear in her eyes, the suspicion flickering in her face and in her voice?

Suspicion? No! No! She *didn't* suspect him—how could she? Not *David!* Not her own husband, the man she loved! How *could* she, even for an instant, have imagined that he might be capable of . . . !

Well, and what *is* a man capable of? A proud, headstrong young man who not so long ago was the daredevil leader of the most venturesome teenage gang in his neighborhood? To what sort of lengths *could* such a young man go, under the intolerable lash of humiliation? He, who had set out in proud and youthful arrogance to conquer the world, and now finds he cannot even provide any sort of home for his wife and child? Such a young man—*could* he, in such extremities of shattered pride and of self-respect destroyed—*could* he simply walk in a strange flat, murder the occupant, and coolly take possession . . . ?

And even if he couldn't—couldn't, and hadn't, and never would—what then? What about *her?* How could she, having once let the awful suspicion cross her mind, ever face him again? How was she to behave . . . look . . . when he came in from work tonight? What sort of supper should one cook for a suspected murderer . . . ?

And as she sat there, crouched in the beautiful flat, while outside the evening darkened into night, she heard the soft whine of the lift—the opening and closing of its doors.

And next—although it was only a little after five, and David shouldn't be home till nine—next there came, unmistakably, the sound of the key in the door.

Afterwards, Linda could never remember what exactly had been the sequence of her thoughts. *Why?* had been one of them, certainly—*Why* is he arriving home so early?—and then, swift upon the heels of this, had come the blind, unreasoning panic. . . . What is he *doing* out there? Why doesn't he come right in . . . shut the front door behind him? Why isn't he calling, "Lin, darling, I'm back," the way he always does? Why is he being so quiet, so furtive . . . ? Lurking out there . . . standing stock-still, to judge by the silence . . .

But after that, in Linda's jumbled memory, all was confusion. Had she recognized the blonde girl at once—so different as she now looked—or had there been several minutes of stunned incomprehension as they gaped at one another in the little hall, all at cross-purposes in their questions and ejaculations?

Because, of course, this was the rightful tenant of the flat, Rosemary Fanshawe by name; as astounded (on her return from a stay in hospital and a fortnight's convalescence) to find a strange girl in possession of her flat as Linda was at this sudden invasion by a stranger. Linda could never remember, afterward, who it was who finally made coffee for whom, or in what order each had explained herself to the other; but in the end—and certainly by the time David got back at nine o'clock—all had been made clear, and a sort of bewildered friendship was already in the making.

For this bright, well-groomed girl was indeed the same that Linda had found and taken for dead; and there had indeed been a terrible lovers' quarrel, just as the red-haired young man outside the estate agent's had affirmed. What he had told David hadn't been a lie, exactly; rather a sort of mirror image of the truth, with all the facts in reverse. Thus it had been he, not Rosemary, who had ended the relationship: it had been her heart, not his, that was broken. It was she, not he, who had declared that she couldn't bear to stay in the flat for so much as another day. Hysterically, she had flung her things into cases . . . ordered a car to take them to a friend's house . . . and then, in less than an hour, had returned, half crazy with grief and fury, to storm at him for not having tried to prevent her going. There had been a final, terrible quarrel, at the climax of which Rosemary had threatened dramatically to take a whole bottle of sleeping pills. Enraged by this bit of melodramatic blackmail (as he judged it), the red-haired boyfriend—Martin by name—had slammed out of the flat; but later, growing scared, he had crept back, and found to his horror that she really *had* taken the pills, and was lying—dead, as he thought—on the floor. (Actually, as they'd explained to Rosemary in the hospital, she'd only been in a deep coma, but a layman could not be expected to realize this, as both breath and pulse would be too faint to be discerned.) Appalled—and terrified at the thought that he might be blamed—Martin had bundled the "body" out of sight in the nearest cupboard, and set himself frantically to cleaning up the flat and removing all traces of their joint lives. All night it had taken him; and while he packed and scrubbed, his brain had been afire with desperate schemes for shuffling off the responsibility—preferably onto some anonymous outsider—while he, Martin, got clean away. By the time morning came, and his task was finished, his plans were also ready; he washed, shaved, and off he went to the estate agent . . .

And in fact, it all worked out much as he had hoped—with the fortunate addition that, as it turned out, it was probably Linda's action in dragging the "body" down to the basement that had saved Rosemary's life—the jolting, the knocking about, and the icy chill of the cellar had prevented the coma becoming so deep as to be irreversible. That same night, she had recovered consciousness sufficiently to stagger out into the deserted street and wander some way before being picked up and taken to hospital.

And David, when he came home and heard the whole story? He was unsurprised. David was no fool, and he had realized right from the start (despite his show of bravado) that there was something very phony indeed about that offer outside the estate agent's, but had decided (being the kind of young man he was) to gamble on the chance of being able to cope with the tricksters, whatever it was they were up to, when the time came. However, with his mind full of the possible hazards of the venture, he had naturally been thrown into a complete panic by the discovery that Linda had gone off alone that first afternoon into what might well prove to be a trap of some kind; and even after his immediate fears had been set at rest, he had not failed to notice, in the succeeding days, that Linda was oppressed and ill-at-ease. He knew nothing, of course, about the "body," but he could see very well that there was something . . .

Now, he shrugged. He'd gambled and lost before in his short life.

"Oh, well. It's back on the road for us, then, Linda, my pet," he said, reaching out his hand toward her . . . but at that same moment Rosemary gave a squeal as if she'd been trodden on.

"Oh, *no!* Not *yet!* Oh, *please!*" she cried. "I can't possibly stay on in the flat by myself, I *must* have someone to share, now that . . ."

Of course, it wasn't quite the same as having the place to themselves; but it was much, much better than living at Mrs. Moles's. And for Rosemary, likewise, it wasn't quite the same as having Martin there; but it was much, much better than having to pay the whole of the rent herself. She found, too, that she enjoyed the company; and when, soon after his son was born, David resumed his engineering studies and began bringing friends home from college, she found she enjoyed it even more.

"Wasn't it lucky that I took those pills just when I did?" she mused dreamily one evening, after the reluctant departure of one of the handsomer of the embryo engineers; and Linda, settling her baby back in his cot, had to agree that it was.

Indeed, when you thought of all the ways the thing *might* have ended, "lucky" seemed something of an understatement.

SIC TRANSIT GLORIA

By Barbara Paul

"*Sic transit gloria mundi*," Roberts read from the paper. "On Monday, Gloria threw up in the subway."

"Ha ha," said Gloria Sanchez, not looking up from the typewriter.

"You don't think that's funny?"

"It's Friday afternoon, Roberts. *Nothing* is funny." They'd flipped a coin to decide who'd write the report on the arson in the project houses; Gloria lost.

No one else was in the police detective unit room on the second floor of the ninth precinct stationhouse. The other detectives all managed to be out on cases as the work week drew to a close; that phone call coming in ten minutes before the shift change could wreck your weekend. But this time Gloria and her partner had misjudged; they'd wound up their investigation into the projects fires about an hour too early. The place had been an oven even after the flames were extinguished; the city's charitable impulse had not extended to air-conditioning the falling-down project houses. Roberts had been antsy to get out of that depressing place, but no more so than Gloria herself. She'd once lived there.

"DiFalco in?" she asked.

Roberts craned his neck to look through the glass partition of the captain's office. "Yep."

She'd finish the report but not turn it in until Monday. If DiFalco saw her leaving a report on the lieutenant's desk, he'd keep them there quizzing them about meaningless details until

218

well after their shift had ended; it was one of the captain's little ways of reminding them who was boss. The Great White Father needed lots of props.

The phone rang; they both groaned. "I'm typing," Gloria pointed out.

Her partner took the call. "Detective Roberts."

Gloria concentrated on finishing the report, only half listening as Roberts asked a question or two, jotting down the answers. When he'd hung up, he cleared his throat, something he did only when he was nervous. *Uh-oh.*

"They just fished a burlap bag out of the East River," he said in a tight voice. "Three kids inside. All dead."

Gloria's hand reaching for the finished report froze in midair. "Jesus Christ!" The two partners stared at each other. "Dead before they were tossed in?" *She hoped.*

"Don't know yet." He cleared his throat again. "Lieutenant's not here."

"Yeah." She rolled the report out of the typewriter and signed it hastily, dropping it off in the lieutenant's office on their way to see DiFalco.

The captain had watched their approach, sitting in one of his power poses—bent forward, weight supported by two fists pressing down on the surface of his desk. "Was that the project-fires report?" he asked. "What did you—"

"No fatalities," Gloria interrupted. "Bomb and Arson is taking it. Listen to Roberts, Captain."

"Call just came in," her partner reported. "Three dead kids were just pulled out of the river. They'd been stuffed into a burlap bag."

Gloria watched as DiFalco's expression turned to one of disgust. Not shock . . . disgust. He stood up abruptly, making the legs of the chair squeal against the floor. "Fill me in on the way." He charged past them out the door.

Gloria stopped at her desk long enough to call Gran Fran and tell her she'd be late getting home. Then she had to run to catch up with the two men.

The late-afternoon heat was oppressive to the point of making breathing difficult. "Sanchez, you drive," DiFalco instructed. "Okay, Roberts, what have they got?"

Gloria started the car and sped out of the parking lot across the street from the ninth precinct stationhouse. Anyone watching would think the two white men in the backseat had a black female chauffeur. Chauffeuse? She didn't mind driving, but damned if she'd let anyone call her a chaufferette.

Roberts was consulting his notebook. "A fry cook named Wiechowski was smoking a joint in East River Park and watching this homeless pair . . . they had some kind of hook on a pole and they were snagging things out of the river. They pulled in this big burlap bag—but after they opened it, they both took off running. Wiechowski went down to take a look. He saw the dead kids, called the cops. That's all so far."

DiFalco grunted. "Crime Scene Unit?"

"Called from the site."

Roberts read out directions to the exact location. As Gloria pulled the car onto a grassy place not meant for parking, they could see the CSU was already there. The usual crowd of onlookers was abnormally quiet. Violent death always brought the voyeurs out of the woodwork; but even they were subdued when the victims were children.

Small children, Gloria saw with a further shock. When Roberts had said kids, she'd visualized teenagers, or near-teens. But these three, two boys and a girl, were much younger than that; one of the boys looked like a preschooler. White kids. Looked well nourished. She couldn't tell much about the quality of their clothing; too much river dirt. The small bodies, bloated now, had been removed from the burlap bag and were laid out in a row.

Captain DiFalco went off to talk to the first officer on the scene while Roberts was interviewing the fry cook who'd called the police. The man kneeling by the girl's body was from the medical examiner's office, an Asian Gloria knew slightly. She hunkered down next to him. "Dr. Wu."

He glanced up. "Hello, Sanchez." He shook his head. "Isn't this about the ugliest thing you've ever seen?"

Just about. "Tell me they were dead when they went into the water."

Another headshake. "I wish I could. But there are no wounds on the bodies. A few superficial scratches they probably inflicted on each other while they were struggling to get out of the bag. The autopsy will show whether there's river water in the lungs or not—that's all we'll have to go on."

"That's enough. How long they been dead?"

"They'd been in the water long enough for the decomposition gases to make them float. But not long enough for the fingernails to loosen. Hot weather speeds everything up, so my guess is from three days to a max of three weeks. And before you ask—no, the autopsy won't pin it down any more than that."

Gloria nodded. "Call me when you've finished the autopsy?"

Dr. Wu stood up tiredly and peeled off his latex gloves. "Remind me . . . where am I?"

"Ninth precinct."

"Right. I'll call."

Gloria left to find Roberts and Captain DiFalco. Neither the first officer nor the fry cook had had anything to add; the latter had never gotten a good look at the faces of the two homeless he'd been watching. "Don't waste time looking for them," DiFalco instructed. "They don't know anything. Sanchez, you're the primary on this one. Start with Missing Persons."

"We'll need pictures," she said. "Cleaned-up ones." They couldn't go to parents of missing children and show photos of the dead kids the way they were now.

"Tell the CSU you want morgue shots. And you two can forget about your weekends—I want you on it until you catch the bastard who did this. Now, I've got to go make sure our PR flack gets his facts straight."

Like spelling your name right. Gloria told the photographer they'd need morgue shots by early tomorrow morning and trailed after DiFalco back to the car. She and Roberts would spend the evening going through Missing Persons reports, looking for possible matches.

Gloria dropped the Great White Father off at the stationhouse on East Fifth and headed the car downtown toward Police Plaza and Missing Persons.

Gran Fran was waiting up for her when she got home a little before eleven. "You work too hard, chile," the old woman said.

"Yeah, I keep telling 'em that," Gloria replied, "but they just don't listen."

"You hungry?"

"Naw, I ate. What you doing up so late?"

"I got somethin' on my mind, Gloria."

At that moment Gloria wanted a shower more than anything in the world, but she sat down to listen to what her grandmother had to say. "What's troubling you, Gran?"

The old woman leaned forward in her chair. "I don't wanna go into that home you took me to see. I go in there, I'll die. An' those people in there, they all yell at you all the time. I ain't deaf. And I ain't gonna end up just one more old black woman sittin' around waitin' to pass on. I just cain't do it, chile. Don't make me."

Gloria's heart sank. "You know you need somebody with you all the time. I worry about you here alone all day."

The old woman lifted her chin. "I ain't gonna go die just to save you the trouble of worryin'," Gran Fran snapped. "And I know I cain't take care of myself no more, you don't have to tell me that." Her tone softened. "But they's another way. I want to go back to Alabama. I want to go home."

"Alabama!"

"You remember Estelle, Sister Charlayne's chile?"

Gran Fran had a lot of relatives in the South that Gloria had never met, but Estelle had come to New York for a visit about five years ago. "Sure, I remember."

"I done called her and ast, and she say if I turn my Social Security check over to her, she'll take me in."

Gloria didn't care for the sound of that. "Why you wanna go back? You never lived in Alabama long as I know you, Gran. And you don't visit, haven't for years."

"But it's where I was born, an' thass where I wanna be when my time comes." The old woman reached out and took Gloria's hand.

"Gloria, honey, you been real good to me for a lot of years, and I loves you for it. But it's time for me to go home. Let go, chile."

Stall. "Lemme call Estelle tomorrow. Then we talk about it. Okay?"

A big smile split Gran Fran's wrinkled face. "Okay. Then we talk about it."

To change the subject, Gloria got up and turned on the television. "I got a new case today," she said. "Let's see if it made the news."

It did. Eventually Captain DiFalco's serious face filled the screen, revealing the fate of the three as yet unidentified children. He announced pompously that he promised the city of New York that whoever perpetuated such a monstrous act would be brought to justice. No mention of the name of the detective who would be leading the investigation. As usual.

"That man sho' do love hisself," Gran Fran commented. "Those poor littl'uns! Who'd do such a thing to chirrun?"

"Some sick sonuvabitch," Gloria said, wishing now she hadn't let her grandmother watch. She helped the old woman get ready for bed, making sure she took her medication; Gran Fran sometimes forgot.

After finally getting her shower, Gloria crawled into bed and tried to shut out the sound of the rock music pounding away in the apartment below. Over the sound of the music she could make out angry shouting from the outside hallway; but she'd double-checked all six locks on the steel door before she went to bed. The building was only one step up from a tenement, but it was all she could find within walking distance of the stationhouse on East Fifth. Gloria frequently used her lunch break to run home and check on the old woman. It was why she'd never asked to transfer out of the Ninth, one of the worst precincts in the city. The Ninth was an area of town where she could afford an apartment with two bedrooms.

Her grandmother had had several bad falls. She couldn't use her walker in the crowded apartment, and her cane wasn't always enough to keep her balanced and upright. She needed to make frequent trips to the bathroom, each one a hazardous journey for her, alone. And that was the old woman's life these days: making it safely to the bathroom and back again.

Gloria remembered when she was still in the police academy how Gran Fran always had friends dropping by, or she herself was off to see somebody or other. But most of those friends were dead now, or in the same condition Gran Fran was in; visiting days were over for all of them. Now her grandmother never left the apartment, sitting there alone in fear and pain all day, just waiting for Gloria to get home. That was no kind of life. Gloria had thought Gran would welcome the idea of a nursing home— someone to help her when she needed it, people to talk to again.

And Gloria could visit. But if she took her grandmother to Alabama, she might never see her again. Gran Fran didn't have much time left, and that ailing old black woman was the only person in the world Gloria could call family.

Gloria was the product of a mixed marriage. Her father was a Puerto Rican named Carlos Sanchez who'd run out on her mother when she became pregnant, so Gloria had never known him. Her black mother, LuAnn, had been sixteen years old when Gloria was born; she stuck around four more years before she, too, took off for parts unknown, leaving her young daughter with Gran Fran. The two had been on welfare and living in the project houses off and on all through Gloria's childhood; Gran did domestic work when she could get it.

Gloria's only memory of her mother was of a pretty young woman crying her heart out. Gloria had once asked Gran if LuAnn and Carlos had really been married. "LuAnn say they were" was the old woman's reply.

Gloria had soon learned that a half-black, half-Hispanic child was not welcome in either community. But she did not suffer a lonely childhood; the aggressiveness that the Lower East Side breeds into all its children let her make it clear to the other kids that they ignored Gloria Sanchez at their peril. She even bullied her way into the home of a Latina schoolmate and there, slowly and laboriously, learned to speak Spanish.

Gloria was tolerated, but she was never really accepted. Only her black grandmother had not held her mixed heritage against her; Gran Fran had even been proud of Gloria's lighter skin—an attitude that at one time had irked her granddaughter, on days she felt more black than Hispanic. But as she grew into adulthood, Gloria learned she could put on the persona of either culture with equal ease. And that was something she'd put to use many a time, ever since deciding her best chance for survival was to put on a badge and carry a gun.

She'd been black the last three days. Tomorrow, she'd be Rosie Perez.

Dr. Wu had called early. River water in the lungs; the kids had been tossed in alive. The CSU had provided them with the requested morgue shots and the added information that the three children had been wearing good-quality clothing. No welfare family getting rid of unwanted mouths to feed, then. They'd have to depend on the Missing Persons reports for their leads.

"Forty-two names," Gloria said. "I guess we'd better divide these up." They got busy calling the names on their separate lists, making sure the various parents would be at home before paying their grim visits.

It was a pain-filled morning. The families had had their anxieties aroused by the phone calls; their guilty relief that the drowned children were not theirs was heartbreaking to see. One divorced mother asked if the children had been sexually abused. Gloria told her the medical examiner had said no.

By noon, Gloria was on the Upper West Side, too far away to check on Gran Fran in person. A phone call assured her the old woman had had a good morning watching cartoons. Then Gloria spread out a pile of change, pulled out her address book, and called Gran's niece Estelle in Canoe, Alabama.

After the necessary amenities, Gloria asked if Estelle had really agreed to give Gran Fran a home.

Yes, indeed she had. "I allus like Fran," Estelle said. "My kids is gone, Gloria, moved to Mobile or N'Yawlins, most of 'em. Kids don't like being stuck in a place like Canoe no more. But it's a good slow place for old folks like your gran."

Cautiously, Gloria brought up the matter of Gran's signing her Social Security check over to Estelle. "Wouldn't it be better to charge her a flat fee for room and board?"

"Oh Law', Gloria honey, your gran never did eat much. And I got the room now that the kids is gone. No, what I'm worryin' about is all those pills old folks has to take. They costs a lot of money. And what if she needs an operation? I can give her good meals and a place to stay, but I cain't pay for no operation."

Gloria started to say she'd pay for the medical expenses, but paused; Estelle couldn't be calling her for money every time Gran needed a prescription filled. "Yeah, that makes sense," she agreed.

"I tell you what you can do," Estelle went on. "Send her a li'l spendin' money ever' month. Ever'body feel better with cash in their pocket. You bring your gran on down here. She can have the boys' room now they gone."

Estelle's "boys" were close to forty; Estelle herself must be pushing sixty. "Estelle, you understand what you're taking on? Gran Fran is feeble and has to be watched. She needs help just going to the bathroom."

A throaty laugh filled the receiver. "Tell me about it. I already got one just like that livin' here—my daddy's in the same way. Him and Fran'll be company for each other." Another laugh. "Hey, Gloria? They might fall in love and get married."

Gloria had to smile at that. She told Estelle she'd call her back in a day or two and hung up. Gran Fran was lucky. She had two places where she was welcome; she wasn't one of those debilitated old people who were just a burden no one wanted. And Estelle's place sounded right for Gran, away from the noise and dirt and constant fear the city generated. She'd have someone of her own generation to talk to, someone she already knew. Clearly, taking Gran to Alabama would be the best thing for her.

But I can't do it, Gloria thought in sudden anguish. *I just can't give up the only person in the world I have to love.*

At that moment her pager went off. When she called in, she learned that Roberts had found the parents of the two boys who'd been in the burlap bag.

"Darren and Jamie Bellamy," Roberts told her, back at the stationhouse. "Aged nine and six. Mrs. Bellamy knew the name of the girl, too . . . Kyra Waterman. She's not on my list."

Gloria quickly scanned her own list of missing children. "Not here, either." The two exchanged a puzzled glance. "Her family didn't report her missing?"

"Lemme check." Roberts phoned Missing Persons; they had no report on a Kyra Waterman.

"Fill me in," Gloria ordered.

The boys had been missing for two weeks, Roberts said. "Darren Bellamy and Kyra Waterman were buds. Jamie Bellamy was the tagalong younger brother. The last the Bellamys saw of their boys was on a Monday when Mrs. Bellamy dropped them off at the Claymore School on East Eightieth."

Gloria raised an eyebrow. "Upscale-uppity."

"Yeah, the Bellamys have money. But when the housekeeper went to pick them up in the afternoon, a school official said that the boys and Kyra had left with Kyra's mother, Mrs. Waterman."

"They call the Watermans?"

"Mrs. Waterman says she let the boys out in front of their building. Mrs. Bellamy blames Mrs. Waterman for not watching to see they got inside safely."

Gloria shook her head, making her gold loop earrings dance. "Doesn't make sense, man," she said, her soft Latin lilt making the words sound like a song. "If the two boys disappear' then, and Kyra disappear' later—how come they all end up in that same burlap bag?"

"Yeah. And why didn't the Watermans report Kyra missing?"

"Let's go ask. They both work?"

"Just him."

"We talk to the lady firs'. Where they live?"

The Watermans had a townhouse on East Eighty-fifth. The

door was answered by a uniformed Jamaican maid; Gloria flashed her detective's shield and asked in Spanish to see Mrs. Waterman.

The minute or so before the lady of the house joined them was enough to tell the two detectives the place reeked of money. They looked in as many rooms as they could in the time they had, and everything they saw looked brand new. Pricey modern furniture, original contemporary art on the walls. No antiques, no identifiable family heirlooms. The place was a showroom for success symbols.

Janine Waterman was an attractive, well-cared-for woman in her early to mid thirties who had a polished persona for dealing with strangers. "Is it my husband you want to see?" she asked. "I'm afraid he had to go into his office this afternoon."

"We'll talk to you, ma'am," Gloria said. "Does Mr. Waterman often work on Saturdays?"

"Almost never." She graciously offered them seats and then sat quietly, her head tilted to one side, waiting to hear what they had to say. Posing for them. The two detectives automatically catalogued details: five feet five inches, a hundred and twenty pounds, short black hair expensively styled, luminous hazel eyes that not only made eye contact but held it. Her at-home Saturday afternoon clothes were a stylish two-piece dress and mid heels.

Gloria looked at the woman's hands; they lay perfectly still in her lap. But Mrs. Waterman was affecting a composure that Gloria sensed was not real. Something was bothering the woman.

Gloria leaned back in a chair that would have cost her six months' rent and let Roberts explain that the two Bellamy boys had been found drowned; he made no mention of young Kyra Waterman.

Kyra's mother expressed shock, then grief, then self-recrimination. "I feel responsible," she said with a catch in her voice. "I didn't wait until they were safely inside. Oh, those poor boys! Do you have any idea who did it?"

"Not yet," said Roberts. "We just got an ID on them an hour ago."

"Those poor boys," she repeated.

"Where's Kyra?" Gloria asked abruptly.

The question didn't *quite* take Janine Waterman by surprise. "Why, she's staying with my sister for a while, in upstate New York."

Gloria pulled out her notebook. "What's your sister's phone number?" She made a point of pronouncing it *seestuh*.

The woman paled. "Really, Detective, er . . ."

"Sanchez."

"Detective Sanchez, what's this all about? Why should I give you my sister's phone number?"

"So I can check an' make sure Kyra's really there."

"Well, I just told you she was there! Really, Detective, this is too much."

Gloria leaned forward and said in a soft, accent-free voice: "We both know she's not there, Mrs. Waterman. Kyra was kidnapped, too, wasn't she?"

The other woman's eyes grew large. "Kidnapped! I don't know what you're talking about. Kyra's with my sister."

Gloria and Roberts exchanged a glance. Then, as gently as she could, Gloria told Janine Waterman that her daughter had been found dead with the Bellamy boys.

At first she was so still that Gloria was beginning to wonder if she'd understood. Then Mrs. Waterman stood up and walked stiffly out of the room.

Gloria turned to Roberts. "Did the Bellamys tell you where the husband works?"

"Yeah, he's CEO of some firm on Madison, part of a conglomerate." He pulled out his notebook and flipped a page. "Bracewell Communications."

She pointed to a phone. "Get him here."

Gloria spent the next ten minutes outside the door of the room Mrs. Waterman had retreated to, listening to the choking, whimpering sounds coming from inside. Finally the door opened and Mrs. Waterman stared at her blankly. "I tried to call Harris at his office. He wasn't there."

"My partner called him. He's on his way home." Gloria led her back to the living room, asked if she could get her anything; received a headshake in reply.

Roberts gestured Gloria out to the hallway. "I had to tell him. He wouldn't come without knowing why."

She nodded. "Prolly just as well." Department policy was to break the news of the death of a loved one in person whenever possible. "How long a drive from his office?"

"Another five minutes."

It was closer to ten when Harris Waterman came bursting in. He ignored the two detectives and went straight to his wife. They clung to each other silently for a moment, and then murmured a few things Gloria couldn't catch. Waterman was a handsome man, not yet forty, bulky in the chest and shoulders. Brown hair and eyes, gold wire glasses, enormous hands. He was as expensively garbed as his wife.

Finally Waterman acknowledged their presence. "You're sure it's Kyra?"

Silently Roberts took out the morgue shot of the girl and said, "Brace yourselves," before handing it to the Watermans.

Mrs. Waterman dropped her face into her hands and began to cry. Clenching his jaw, Mr. Waterman thrust the photo back at Roberts. "Yes," he said. "That's Kyra."

"I know you want us out of here," Gloria said to them, "an' I don' blame you. But if we're gonna catch this guy, we gotta have some answers. Okay?"

The couple looked repelled, but both nodded agreement.

"Awright . . . first, did you get a ransom call?"

They did, Harris Waterman said. The kidnapper had wanted an even million. It had taken Waterman a few days to convert some stock, but he'd got the million; it filled two large suitcases. He was told to take the money to an abandoned gas station on Staten Island; the kidnapper said the public phone there still worked. Waterman was to wait by the phone for further instructions.

"I waited two hours," the man said. "Nothing. I tried the phone and got a dial tone, so it wasn't that. I finally gave up and came home." They'd had no further word from the kidnapper.

"Why didn't you call the police?"

"Because he said he'd cut Kyra's throat if we did!" Mrs. Waterman answered faintly.

"We couldn't take the chance," Waterman added. "The police would be in on it, the FBI would be in on it . . . We didn't want to scare him into doing something rash."

"The Bellamys called the police."

Mrs. Waterman put a hand to her forehead. "Oh, that was just a . . . a fluke. The Bellamys learned the boys were missing right away, when their housekeeper got back from the school. Before we knew Kyra was gone. The Bellamys called the police before the kidnapper had a chance to call *them*. They didn't tell him they'd already reported the boys missing."

"And when did you find Kyra was missing?"

Mrs. Waterman hesitated; her husband murmured, "Tell them."

She took a deep breath. "I didn't drop off just the boys at the Bellamys' place—I left all three of them there, Kyra, too. The kids often played in one another's houses. The first hint I had that something might have happened to Kyra came when Rose Bellamy called wanting to know where her boys were. But I thought nothing of it then—I just assumed the kids had slipped out of the house without Rose's seeing them."

"So how did you find out?"

"It wasn't until the kidnapper called that we actually knew he had Kyra." She established eye contact, first with Roberts and then with Gloria. "I apologize for telling you that story about Kyra's visiting my sister. Harris and I thought Kyra would have a better chance of surviving if we just went on as if nothing had happened. But her absence had to be explained somehow."

"That's what you told the school? That she was out of town?"

She nodded. "Oh, it's my fault! I should have stayed until they were inside!" But even while blaming herself, Mrs. Waterman was looking for exoneration. "I've done it dozens of times, dropping them off like that! It's never been a problem. It was broad daylight, a good neighborhood. Nobody else was around. And I still don't see how the kidnapper could have grabbed them in so short a time . . . unless he was hiding there waiting."

"Or mebbe the kids didn't go straight into the buildin'. Coulda gone someplace in the neighborhood firs'—that's somethin' we can check. You got a recent picture of Kyra?"

Mrs. Waterman left the room and returned with a five-by-seven of a chubby little girl with a sad face. "It's not very flattering, I'm afraid. But it's the most recent we have."

When asked, the Watermans described the kidnapper's voice as harsh and low-pitched . . . almost as if he were hoarse. Neither of them recognized the voice.

The detectives told the Watermans they'd keep in touch and left.

Roberts said, "We're gonna need help on this one."

Gloria agreed. "I'll ask DiFalco for some men to canvass the neighborhood where the Bellamys live. Where *do* they live?"

Roberts pointed. "One short block down, three long blocks across. Same neighborhood."

"Let's pay 'em a visit."

On the way, Gloria said, "If you learned that some children were missing—children you'd just left your own child with— would you think 'nothing of it' at first?"

"Yeah, that's kind of odd. Maybe it just didn't sink in on her that Kyra might be in danger."

"Huh. Me, I'd be yellin' and screamin' *Where's my kid??*" Gloria said. "But then, me and Janine Waterman ain't exactly two of a kind."

"Not exactly," Roberts agreed.

Gloria shot him a look.

No one was home at the Bellamy house. Not even a maid, Jamaican or otherwise, to answer the door. "Back to the station-house?" Roberts asked. "Can we stop somewhere on the way? I didn't get any lunch."

Neither did Gloria. They stopped for greaseburgers and coffee in a cafe where Gloria tried to lighten her mood by flirting with the Puerto Rican behind the counter.

Roberts, who spoke no Spanish, said, "I hate when you talk dirty." He finished a burger and cleared his throat. "I've made up my mind. I'm gonna take the Sergeants Exam in September."

Gloria nodded slowly. "Good move, dude."

"It's the only way I'm ever gonna get out of the ninth precinct."
He cleared his throat. "Sanchez, I don't get it. You could ace that
exam, but you've never taken it. You got something against being
a sergeant? You *like* it in the Ninth?"

"I got my reasons," she replied automatically. Then it hit her:
If Gran Fran went to live with Estelle, Gloria would have no need
to stay in the ninth precinct any longer. The thought made her
dizzy . . . mostly with guilt. "You finished? Let's go."

Back at the stationhouse, they found a message from Captain
DiFalco demanding a progress report. Gloria was surprised to be
able to reach him at home; DiFalco liked to spend his weekends
playing.

When she told him they had a kidnapping-for-ransom on their
hands, he grunted. "That's what I was afraid of. Nail this one
fast, Sanchez. I don't want the FBI horning in. What do you
need?"

"Manpower. We oughta show photos of the kids 'round the
neighborhood. In case they didn't go straight into the Bellamys'
buildin'."

"That was two weeks ago. Not much chance of anybody remembering. But yeah, check it out. Who's there?"

Gloria looked around the PDU squadroom. "Faulkner, Goetz,
and Minutello."

"Put Goetz on."

She called the detective to the phone. Goetz bitched about
being pulled off his own case, but it was protest for form's
sake. He handed the phone back to Gloria and went to tell
Faulkner and Minutello they were to drop everything to do a
door-to-door.

"What's your next move?" DiFalco wanted to know.

"We haven't seen the Bellamys since we learned this was a
kidnappin'. They're next."

"Right. I'll be in later. Sanchez, you and Roberts can take time
off to sleep, but nothing else. You hear?"

"I got it, I got it."

She briefed the other three detectives and handed over the photos of the kids. Then Roberts made a phone call. The Bellamys were home.

Jack and Rose Bellamy could have passed as brother and sister. Same dark coloring, same small, wiry build, same rapid way of talking. Their home, unlike the Watermans', looked as if children had lived there; comfort was more important to the Bellamys than maintaining a showplace. Nor were they as self-consciously fashionable as the Watermans; both wore sneakers and sweats.

A picture of the two boys was prominently displayed in the living room. They'd been good-looking kids, more attractive than the rather dumpy Kyra Waterman.

Gloria and Roberts had no difficulty in getting them to talk; the Bellamys had already decided to go to the police with the whole story even before the detectives got there. They'd lived in utter panic ever since the kidnapper had called and said don't go to the police . . . after they'd already done so. But there was no longer a reason for them to keep quiet.

The Bellamys had their own import company, which they both worked at full-time. Occasionally one of them would leave early to pick Darren and Jamie up from school, but they weren't fanatic about it. The housekeeper usually went to fetch them.

"We'd like to talk to her," Gloria said.

"She's not a live-in," Rose Bellamy explained, her words coming out in a rush. "She just works weekdays. She stayed with the boys until either Jack or I got home from work." Roberts took down the housekeeper's name and address.

They'd received one phone call from the kidnapper demanding a million dollars. "We couldn't raise the entire million in the time he gave us," Jack Bellamy said, "but we did get half of it. I put a note in with the money pleading for more time to raise the rest." He'd taken the cash to an abandoned gas station on Staten Island where he'd waited for a phone call that never came. They hadn't heard from the kidnapper since.

"But why?" Mrs. Bellamy demanded, her voice strident. "Did he mean to kill them all along? Was he just playing games with us?"

"Somethin' musta gone wrong," Gloria said, "and he couldn't leave any witnesses. We prolly got more'n one kidnapper here. Did the voice on the phone sound familiar at all?"

No, Mr. Bellamy said. The voice had been growly, hoarse. "Sounded phony as hell to me."

Gloria leaned forward. "Phony? As if he was trying to disguise his voice?"

"Yeah. So?"

"So why would he disguise his voice unless he was afraid you'd recognize it?"

His mouth fell open. "It's someone we know?"

"Maybe he was just being cautious, but the chances are you do know the kidnapper."

"Oh, good God," Mrs. Bellamy said.

"All right, then. Who do you and the Watermans know in common?"

"No one!" Mrs. Bellamy exclaimed. "Our only connection with the Watermans is through the kids. Darren and Kyra were in the same fourth-grade class at Claymore . . . Jamie was a first grader. We know the Watermans through school functions, of course. And the boys sometimes went to their place to play after school, although more often Kyra came here. But outside of that, nothing."

"There's got to be some link between you," Gloria insisted. "The Watermans described the kidnapper's voice in much the same terms you did. Which suggests he knew both—" She broke off when she saw Jack Bellamy staring at her. "What?" she demanded.

"What happened to your accent?" he wanted to know.

Roberts grinned crookedly. "It comes and goes. But you never had any contact with the Watermans outside of school functions?"

It had been building up a long time: Rose Bellamy finally exploded. "That stupid, *stupid* woman! Just driving off and leaving them on the street! If Janine Waterman paid half as much attention to her child as she did to her . . . her *glamour*—none of this would have happened!"

"Wait a minute," Roberts interrupted. "Are you saying Kyra Waterman was a neglected child?"

She waved a hand at him. "No, no, nothing like that. But Janine never listened to Kyra. She never even looked at her during school functions—her eyes were always someplace else. Sometimes I thought she was ashamed of Kyra. Janine is so absorbed in herself she can't even do a simple thing like making sure children get inside safely." Her voice was bitter.

"It's a strange family," Jack Bellamy agreed. "Harris and Janine are so glitzy, and Kyra . . . wasn't. She wouldn't have spent so much time over here if she was happy at home, would she? Kyra just didn't fit the rich and glamorous image her parents projected." He shook his head. "Poor kid. I wish now I'd paid more attention to her myself."

Gloria felt a flash of respect for Jack Bellamy. Here both his sons had just been killed, but he could still spare some sympathy for a misfit little girl he hadn't even known very well. "I know how rough this has to be on you both," she said, "but if you do think of some other link between you and the Watermans, give me a call." She handed Jack Bellamy her card. "Any time of the day or night."

He took the card without looking at it. "Find him," he said in a voice that was almost a hiss. "That bastard wiped out half our family. Find him."

The two detectives muttered reassurances and left. Neither one of them said anything for a moment, and then Roberts let out a breath. "Whew. I'm drained."

"Yeah." She knew what he meant. "Look, I'll drop you off at the stationhouse. There's something I gotta take care of at home."

"DiFalco's probably there by now."

"I won't be long."

On the drive back downtown Gloria kept hearing Jack Bellamy's voice in her head: *That bastard wiped out half our family.* "We need to talk to that housekeeper. How did they make arrangements about who picked up the kids when? You got an address on her?"

"Yeah, in the Bronx. How will that help finger the guy who did the killing?"

Gloria didn't answer, thinking. "Janine and Harris Waterman had a story made up to tell us, about the girl visiting upstate."

"That was before they knew she was dead. Trying to explain her absence."

"Yeah, but if they made up one story, couldn't they make up another? The first one for us to see through, so we'd accept the second?"

"Huh? What are you getting at?"

Gloria shook her head. "I dunno. Just thinking out loud." *That bastard wiped out half our family.*

Roberts got out on East Fifth and Gloria drove on to a ribs joint. Gran Fran sometimes had trouble digesting ribs, but she did love them so. During the day she nibbled on whatever was in the fridge, when she remembered. But Gloria tried to make sure she ate every night.

The first thing Gloria did when she got home was go over and hug the other half of her family as hard as she could without hurting the old woman. Then she sprinkled Beano liberally over the ribs and made her grandmother promise not to wait up for her.

Back to the stationhouse. She was in luck; Captain DiFalco got there two minutes after she did.

"The commissioner wants to know why I haven't called in the FBI on a kidnapping case," DiFalco said. "I told him the FBI is most effective in trapping the perp at the ransom drop. But we're investigating murder now. The kidnapping part is over and done with."

"Did he buy it?" Gloria asked.

The captain grimaced. "He's given us twenty-four hours. If we don't have a suspect by this time tomorrow, the FBI takes over."

Gloria and Roberts exchanged a look. Twenty-four hours. And they didn't have a clue.

*　　*　　*

The sun was barely up, but already heat was shimmering up from the sidewalks: another scorcher. Gloria took a swallow of her coffee and wished she'd brought something cold to drink.

She was sitting in the car about four houses down from the Waterman place. Roberts had said he'd be at the stationhouse by seven; she still had plenty of time. The main problem was going to be staying awake.

Last night had been a bust. The three detectives who'd done a door-to-door in the Bellamy neighborhood had come up empty. Not many stores in the area—an art gallery, a gourmet foods shop. Most of the neighbors had no idea who the Bellamy kids were. The few that did remember seeing the boys around couldn't pinpoint the last time they'd seen them.

Gloria and Roberts had driven out to the Bronx to interview the Bellamys' housekeeper. How did the housekeeper know when someone else was picking up Darren and Jamie from school? Mr. or Mrs. Bellamy told her. Did Mrs. Waterman ever call and say she'd drive the boys home? No, Mrs. Bellamy always told her. Then she'd never spoken to Mrs. Waterman? No. Has this kind of mix-up ever occurred before? Never.

One final question: How long had she been working for the Bellamys? Nearly ten years, ever since Darren was born.

There was nothing more to be learned. Roberts grumbled all the way back to the ninth precinct about the waste of time. Next up: They'd done a search through old case records for an instance in which kidnap victims had been drowned. Nothing. At one in the morning they'd given up and gone home to grab a few hours sleep.

Gloria saw the door of the Waterman house open and was instantly out of the car. It was the Jamaican maid, on her way to early Mass. Gloria hurried to catch up with her and spoke to her in Spanish.

The first thing the maid said when she saw Gloria's detective shield was: "I have my green card!"

"Relax," Gloria told her. "I'm not from Immigration. I just want you to tell me a little about Kyra."

The maid—whose name was Veronica—didn't want to talk to her at first, but eventually Gloria persuaded her that all she was interested in was the child.

Veronica shrugged. "She was a fat little girl."

"That's it?"

"She was sullen. She looked at her feet when someone spoke to her. Not a pleasant child. And she had no sense of style at all."

"Not like her parents, huh?"

"Not like them at all. Do you know what I think? I think she was a changeling. Babies get mixed up in hospitals all the time!"

Gloria walked along with her as she talked, piecing together a picture of an unhappy child who'd failed to measure up to her parents' standards in just about every way. Not once did the maid express any sympathy for the girl's lot.

"They bought her her own Nordic Track," Veronica said. "They put it in her room so she'd see it every day and remember to exercise. Mrs. Waterman, she even framed some calorie-counter charts and hung them on the wall so Kyra would learn which foods were fattening. But did it do any good? No! How many times do I catch that girl in the kitchen stuffing food in her mouth?" She sighed in exasperation. "Why did she do that, eat all the time?"

Because she wasn't getting enough nourishment elsewhere. Gloria wondered what it would be like waking up every morning to find an exercise machine staring at you accusingly. She thanked Veronica for her help and went back to the car.

Roberts wasn't there yet when she got to the stationhouse. When he did come stumbling in, eyes still puffy with sleep and carrying a Styrofoam cup of coffee, she said, "Don't get comfortable. We're leaving."

"Where we going?"

"That school official who told the Bellamys' housekeeper that the kids had left with Mrs. Waterman—we want to talk to her. You got her name and address?"

"Yeah, but . . . why do we want to talk to her?"

"She can give us an objective picture of the kids."

"Fer gawd's sake, Sanchez, why do we keep going after the victims? That's not going to point us toward the killer."

"It might. I tell you right now, I think the Watermans' story sucks. They're holding something back."

He looked baffled. "What they told us dovetails with the Bellamys' story."

"Yeah, well, I don't have that part figured out yet. Come on, where does this woman live?"

Vice Principal Elizabeth Jasper lived in Chelsea, and she'd been asleep when the detectives rang her doorbell. "I can't offer you coffee," she said wryly, "because there's none made yet."

Gloria apologized for rousing her so early on a Sunday morning and promised not to take much of her time. "Just tell us what you can about Kyra Waterman."

"That poor child. And Darren and Jamie." Once the parents had been notified, the names of the victims had been made public. "Kyra was a problem. Oh, I don't mean she was disruptive in the classroom. But bringing her out of herself was a challenge for her teachers." She frowned. "Kyra was not a good student, and she had no social skills whatsoever. She didn't know how to interact with the other children and just stared at her feet whenever an adult said something to her. She sulked a lot, and wouldn't answer half the time she was spoken to. But she was showing improvement . . . a very slow improvement, but a steady one. She responded to praise and encouragement."

"But she made friends with Darren Bellamy," Roberts said.

Elizabeth Jasper's expression changed from a frown to a sad smile. "That was all Darren's doing. Darren was a lovely child—I think he was the *nicest* little boy I've ever known. Very considerate of others. He was the most popular boy in the class. Do you know, some of the other children used to stand by the door waiting for him to get there in the mornings?"

"Wow," said Gloria. "So what was it, opposites attract?"

"Their teacher says at first Darren probably just felt sorry for Kyra. He saw her alone and miserable, and his natural instinct was to reach out. But eventually something clicked between them and they became real friends. That's when Kyra started responding to her teachers' encouragement. Having a friend made all the difference."

"You talked to the parents about Kyra's problems?"

The Vice Principal looked uncomfortable. "The Watermans were very concerned that Kyra 'improve'—they used that word a lot. They were attentive parents, I'll give them that. They wanted her to be attractive and full of personality . . . which is not unreasonable. But they never seemed concerned with what Kyra might want."

She went on to explain that the children were not just turned loose at the end of the day; the school made sure every child had transportation or an escort. Mrs. Bellamy had called the school several months ago to say it was okay to let Darren and Jamie ride home with Mrs. Waterman and Kyra. So their door monitor had no reason to object when the boys told her they were going home with Kyra.

"Whoa," Gloria said. "Going home *with Kyra*? Mrs. Waterman dropped them all off at the Bellamys' place."

Elizabeth Jasper spread her hands and smiled. "Maybe they changed their minds."

They thanked her and apologized again for disturbing her so early. Gloria was silent as they started the drive back to the stationhouse; something Elizabeth Jasper said had hit home, the part about Kyra's parents not caring what she wanted. Was that what Gloria was doing to Gran Fran? Catering to her own wants instead of her grandmother's needs? *Why was it so hard to let go?*

Roberts broke the silence. "I had no idea Kyra was like that."

Gloria came out of her funk. "Wait till I tell you about Veronica." She repeated her conversation with the Watermans' maid.

"Sounds like a pretty grim life for the kid," Roberts commented. "How does this get us any closer to the killer?"

Gloria wasn't yet ready to articulate the horror of what was becoming increasingly obvious to her. "This next part's gonna be tough. Even though it's Sunday, we gotta get hold of people in that company where Waterman's the CEO—Bracewell Communications? Find out his status in the conglomerate that owns the company. What kind of man he is. Whether he's considered ruthless."

She watched his face as it dawned on Roberts what she was getting at. He was aghast.

It took them the rest of the morning and most of the afternoon, but Gloria and Roberts were able to track down enough of Bracewell Communications' executives to get a clearer picture of Harris Waterman. Every one of them found it most interesting that the police were asking questions about him.

They all agreed that Waterman was clever and competent, but they all found some way to hedge on their praise; it wouldn't do to make a rival look *too* good. They all lived in a post-yuppie world built on rivalry; it was survival of the fittest in a way Darwin had never envisioned. How important was a man's family in the corporate scheme of things? The family a man built around him was a good measure of the man himself, was the reply.

They all had been in each other's houses, knew what decorators they all used, what cars they drove. They belonged to the same clubs, used the same caterers, carried the same credit cards. Presenting a successful, prosperous face to the world was very much a part of Bracewell's game plan.

And Harris Waterman played the game well. The president of the parent company that owned Bracewell Communications was retiring next year, and Waterman was in the running to take over the whole shebang. And yes, he was ruthless in getting what he wanted.

Gloria and Roberts did most of their interviewing over the phone, but they paid visits to a couple of the higher-ranking executives. In both places they saw alert, outgoing, attractive children . . . who wore their designer clothes well. They were all the things that Kyra Waterman could not be.

Not all of the execs had met young Kyra; one of them expressed the opinion that the Watermans had kept her hidden away as much as possible. Those who had seen her couldn't quite keep the smirk out of their voices, even while murmuring conventional expressions of sympathy for the Waterman family. But all that was secondary; their primary concern was that what had happened to the Watermans could also happen to them. *Protect your own turf at all costs.*

Both Gloria and Roberts had ended their interviews with bad tastes in their mouths. When they called Captain DiFalco, he came in immediately.

"Let me get this straight," he said. "You're saying the Watermans killed their own daughter . . . because she was *unsatisfactory?*"

Gloria sighed. "You don't know these people, Captain. To them, appearance is everything. The whole world they live in is like that. I don't know whether they really thought Kyra was enough of a drawback to keep Harris Waterman from getting his promotion. More likely she just didn't fit into the picture of the ideal life they were building for themselves. Kyra was a . . . an inconvenience."

DiFalco rubbed his hand over his mouth. "Jesus Christ. Now I've heard everything."

"It's sick," Roberts said in the understatement of the year.

"Evidence. You've got no evidence."

"We got *pointers*," Gloria said. "The door monitor at the school said the Bellamy boys told her they were going home with Kyra. Janine Waterman said she dropped them off at their own house."

"Soft, Sanchez."

"Okay. The voice of the 'kidnapper' on the phone sounded disguised, the Bellamys said. It was Waterman who called them, pretending Darren and Jamie were being held for ransom. He was afraid Jack Bellamy would recognize his voice."

"So those boys died only because they happened to be with Kyra at the time the Watermans had planned to kill her?"

"Looks like it. The man is ruthless, Captain."

He was silent for a while. Then: "What about the wife? Is she as ruthless as the husband?"

"She's more a go-along type, I'd say. Not exactly a birdbrain, but she's none too quick. Janine would follow Harris's lead."

"Bring her in," the captain ordered. "Lean on her. I don't care how you do it, but get her to say something incriminating. I'll get someone from the D.A.'s office in here. Let's see if we have a case."

"Sick," Roberts repeated.

Janine Waterman was openly appalled by her surroundings; Gloria thought she'd probably never been in a police station in her life. And the ninth precinct stationhouse was worse than most. Their suspect stared at the one-way mirror in the wall, aware that they were being watched.

They'd brought in both the Watermans. Harris had insisted on calling their lawyer and was left to stew in a different interrogation room under guard until the attorney got there. They didn't have much time.

Gloria sat across a table from Janine Waterman, while Roberts stayed on his feet, ready to bark a question at the suspect from behind her. Gloria plunged right in: "You didn't drop the three kids off at the Bellamy place. You took them home with you."

The other woman started to protest, but Roberts snapped, "Don't interrupt!"

"We have witnesses, Mrs. Waterman. Two of them." Gloria was a good liar. "Witnesses who saw you bring the kids to your place on the Monday they supposedly disappeared. The day you and your husband killed them."

Janine Waterman's pretty face was stricken; she looked as if she couldn't believe this was happening. Finally she managed to ask, "Who?"

"Who are the witnesses? A neighbor across the street and a street cleaner."

"A what?"

"Street cleaner. One of those no-name guys who keep your street prettier than my street. And both the witnesses will testify in court that you had the two Bellamy boys with you when you brought Kyra home. You've been lying to us all along."

Mrs. Waterman didn't answer, her eyes darting around the small interrogation room, looking for escape, not knowing what to say.

"We know what you did. And we know why you did it. And in case you hadn't heard, the state of New York has brought back the death penalty."

That got to her. Her eyes focused on Gloria, trying to make sense of what was happening. "How . . . how could you know . . ." She trailed off.

When she didn't continue, Roberts said, "Best scenario, you're going to live the rest of your life in prison. Get used to the idea."

She gasped. "The rest of my life?"

"You were expecting time off for good behavior?" Gloria asked drily. "Forget it. Look around you, Mrs. Waterman. You don't like the looks of this place? This is the Taj Mahal compared to where you're going."

The woman burst into tears. When she'd regained some measure of control, she said, "You've got it wrong! We didn't kill Kyra. We *loved* Kyra!"

"No, you didn't. You were ashamed of her. She embarrassed you. And she was in the way. So you got rid of her."

She buried her face in her hands.

First Gloria and then Roberts kept pounding away at her, not about what she'd done but about what was going to happen next. They told her about her temporary stay at Rikers Island with the pushers and the whores, followed by the shame and humiliation of a public trial. They made her see how degrading and dangerous her life in prison would be. They kept at it until Gloria judged the time was right.

"You're going to prison, no question—but you don't have to be a gray-haired old lady when you come out," Gloria told her. "There's a way."

It took a moment to sink in. Janine Waterman stared at her blankly and then said, "A way?"

"A way to shorten your sentence. You'd get out while you're still young enough to build a life."

She moistened her lips. A whisper: "How?"

"Help us. Give us details, testify against Harris." Gloria switched to sympathetic mode. "We know this wasn't your idea.

You were just helping your husband, right? Maybe he even talked you into it. Why should you pay the same penalty as him?"

Roberts said, "Cooperate with us now, and you're out in a few years. Your attorney can make a deal with the D.A. It's done all the time."

A gleam of hope appeared in Janine Waterman's eyes.

Gloria saw it. "Start by telling us why the Bellamy boys were killed, too. Why not just tell them they couldn't come over that day?"

One last moment of hesitation, and then she decided. "It would look suspicious—something I'd never done before. You know. It might call attention to me. Harris said do everything the same as usual."

"Then why not postpone your plans for Kyra until the boys weren't there?"

"The alibi. Harris had an alibi established for that afternoon. It had to be then."

"Uh-huh. And what kind of alibi did he have established for you?"

Their suspect's face slowly turned appalled, then frightened, then angry.

Good God, Gloria said to herself. *She hadn't even thought of that.* Rose Bellamy was right; Janine Waterman was a stupid woman.

But it had the effect of strengthening her resolve to cooperate. Harris Waterman had flown to Boston on business that morning. He'd checked into a hotel and then flown right back under a different name. He'd made his third flight of the day, back to Boston, after the deed was done.

The children had all been alive the last time she'd seen them; the delicate, sensitive Mrs. Waterman couldn't bear to watch. Harris had told the kids he was taking them for a boat ride.

"A boat ride? Where?"

"Oh, from the boathouse, of course. The docks are enclosed, so no one could see Harris when . . . when he did it."

"*What boathouse?*"

Janine Waterman flinched. "Bracewell maintains boating facilities for its executive officers," she said, "in a little town upriver called Fremont. An hour's drive, about. But you don't—"

The door burst open and a stocky, gray-haired man erupted into the room. "Janine, don't say another word. Detectives, I need to speak to my client alone. Not here—in a room without one of those." He gestured in annoyance at the one-way mirror.

"Certainly," Gloria replied smoothly. She called in an officer to escort them to a room where they could talk—and to stand guard outside. "Mrs. Waterman," Gloria asked, "this is your husband's attorney? He's looking out for your *husband*'s best interests?"

Janine Waterman stared at the man wide-eyed.

"Don't pay any attention to them, Janine," he said. "They're playing at divide-and-conquer." The two of them left with their police escort.

Gloria and Roberts exchanged a look and both heaved a sigh of relief. They went into the observation room on the other side of the one-way mirror.

DiFalco and a woman named Perry from the D.A.'s office were still staring through the glass at the now-empty interrogation room. "Well?" DiFalco asked.

"You'll need to place him at the boathouse on the day in question," Perry said.

"We'll do it," the captain said quickly. "Now that we know where to look. We'll get you a witness."

"Get two. All right—charge them. I'll get things started at my end."

DiFalco smacked his fist against his palm. *Yes!*

"We're going for maximum sentencing on this one," Perry went on.

"For him?"

"For both of them."

DiFalco scowled. "She won't sign a statement without a deal. She—"

"I'm making no deals with a bitch who would help kill her own child. You get me those witnesses." Perry's gaze turned inward.

"Those two—they're not quite human, are they?" She pressed her lips together and made her way out of the room.

The three cops she left behind shared a moment of grim satisfaction. "That was good work, Sanchez," DiFalco said. "You, too, Roberts. *Real* good work."

Roberts mumbled something, pleased.

"Thanks, Captain," Gloria said. "I guess this is the right moment to tell you—I need some personal time. A week."

"Take it later. You've got witnesses to find."

Gloria sighed. "Captain, you send two men with Roberts and it's a one-day job. You don't need me."

"Half a day," Roberts promised.

DiFalco never gave in easily. "A week all at once? Couldn't you spread it out a little?"

Gloria shook her head. "I'm going to Alabama. I need a full week."

Roberts helped out again. "We can handle it, Captain."

"Okay, then," DiFalco agreed. "Visiting the old homestead, are you?"

Gloria had never been to Alabama in her life. "Yeah. That's right."

"Well, have a good trip."

She nodded toward his departing back. "It will be." *Now that I've finally let go.*

FAIR AND SQUARE

By Margaret Yorke

Mrs. Ford stepped aboard the *S.S. Sphinx*, treading carefully along the ridged gangplank, her stick before her. It would be unfortunate if she were to stumble and injure herself before her holiday had properly begun.

Her holiday.

Mrs. Ford had developed the custom of avoiding some bleak winter weeks by going abroad. While ostensibly seeking the sun, she sought to give her family some relief from having to be concerned for her. She tried hard not to be a burden to her middle-aged sons and daughters and their spouses.

She had been cruising before. She had also stayed in large impersonal hotels in the Algarve and Majorca, where it was possible to spend long winter weeks at low cost, enduring a sense of isolation among uncongenial fellow weather refugées. On her cruise, Mrs. Ford knew she could expect near insolence from certain stewards because she was a woman traveling alone. With luck, this would be counterbalanced by extra thoughtfulness from others because of her age.

Her cabin steward would be an important person in her life, and she had learned to tip in advance as a guarantee of service and her morning tea on time. There would be patient tolerance from couples who were her children's contemporaries; they would wait while she negotiated stairways and would help her in and out of buses on sightseeing excursions ashore. Older passengers in pairs would be too near her in age and too fragile themselves to spare her time or energy, and the wives would see her as an alarming portent of their own future.

There would be plenty of older spinster ladies in cheerful groups or intimately paired. Eleanor Ford would not want to join any such coterie.

The best times would be if the sun shone while the ship was at sea. Then, in a sheltered corner, she would read or do her tapestry while others played bridge or bingo or went to keep-fit classes. She would have her hair done once a week or so, which would help to pass the time. She hoped she had brought enough minor medications to last the voyage. The ship's shop would certainly sell travel souvenirs and duty-free scents and watches but might be short on tissues, indigestion remedies, and such.

Each night Mrs. Ford would wash her underthings and stockings and hang them near the air-conditioning to dry by morning. For bigger garments she would be obliged to use the laundry service. She would go on most of the shore excursions, though they tired her and she had been to all the ports before, because to stay on board would be to mean she had abandoned all initiative. She would send postcards to her smaller grandchildren and write letters to her sons and daughters.

She would long for home and her warm flat with all her possessions round her and her dull routine—yet this morning she had been pleased, leaving it in driving sleet, at the prospect of escaping to the sun. Most people would envy her, she told herself, wondering which of her fellow-passengers, who had looked so drab waiting at the airport, would, by the whim of the head steward, be her table companions throughout the cruise. She had requested the second sitting and been assured by the shipping office that this wish would be granted—otherwise what did you do in the evening after an early meal? As it was, Mrs. Ford would be able to go to bed almost at once when dinner was over with a book from the ship's library, which was likely to be one of the best features of the vessel.

Her cabin was amidships, the steadiest place in bad weather, and not below the dance floor, where she might hear the band, nor the swimming pool, where the water might splosh to and fro noisily if the ship rolled. She had been able to control these points when booking. What she could do nothing about was her neighbors. They might be rowdy, reeling in at all hours from the discotheque, or waking early and chattering audibly about their operations or their love lives—Mrs. Ford had overheard some amazing stories on other voyages.

As she unpacked, she thought briefly about Roger, her husband, who had died six years ago. He had been gentle and kind, and she had been lucky in her long life with him. He had left her well provided for, so that even now, with inflation what it was, she could live in modest comfort and put aside enough funds for such an annual trip. She had so nearly not married Roger, for it was Michael whom she had really loved, so long ago. Setting Roger's photograph on her dressing table, she tried to picture Michael, but it was difficult. She seldom thought of him after all this time.

That night climbing into her high narrow bunk, she had a little weep. It was like the first night away at school, she thought, when you didn't yet know the other pupils or your way around. It would all be better in a day or two.

In the morning she had breakfast in her cabin. The ship had sailed at midnight, and beyond the window the sun shone on a gently rolling sea. Mrs. Ford had taken a sleeping pill the night before, and so she felt rather heavy-headed, but her spirits lifted. She would find a place on deck in the sun.

On the way, she stopped at the library and selected several thrillers and a life of Lord Wavell, which should be interesting. She found a vacant chair on a wide part of the promenade deck and settled down, wrapped in her warm coat. After a while, in the sunlight, she slept.

The voice woke her.

"You're not playing properly," it charged. "Those aren't the right rules."

Mrs. Ford's heart thumped and she sat upright in her chair, carried back by the sound to when she was twelve years old. She was playing hopscotch with Mary Hopkins, and Phyllis Burton had come to loom over them threateningly—large, confident, and two years older, disturbing their game.

"This is how *we* play" came the present-day response, in a male voice, from the deck quoit player now being challenged on the wide deck near Mrs. Ford's chair.

"They're not the right rules," the voice that was so like Phyllis's insisted. "Look, this is how you should throw."

Long years ago Mrs. Ford's tennis racket had been seized from her grasp and a scorching service delivered by Phyllis Burton. "You played a footfault," she had accused—and later, umpiring a junior match, she had given several footfaults against Eleanor Luton, as Mrs. Ford was then, in a manner that seemed unjust at the time and did so still. All through Mrs. Ford's schooldays, Phyllis Burton's large presence had loomed and intervened, interfered and patronized, mocked and derided.

She was good at everything, but though she was older she was in the same form as Mrs. Ford. She wasn't a dunce, however—it was Eleanor who was a swot, younger than everyone else in her form. In the library she was unmolested; her head in a book, she could escape the pressures of community life she found hard to endure. Eleanor was no joiner, and neither was she a leader—it was Phyllis who became, in time, head girl.

There came the sound of a quoit, thudding.

Mrs. Ford opened her eyes and saw large buttocks before her, shrouded in navy linen, as their owner stooped to throw.

"We enjoy how we play," said a female voice, but uncertainly.

"Things should always be done the right way," said the owner of the navy-blue buttocks, straightening up.

In memory, young Eleanor in her new VAD uniform stooped over a hospital bed to pull at a wrinkled sheet and make her patient feel easier. Phyllis, with two years' experience, told her to strip the bed and make it up over again, although this meant moving the wounded man and causing him pain.

"But the patient—"

"He'll be much more comfortable in the end, it's for his own good," Phyllis had said. And stood there while it was done, not helping, although two could make a bed much more easily than one.

Phyllis had contrived that Eleanor was kept busy with bedpans and scrubbing floors after that, until more junior nurses arrived and she had to be permitted to undertake other tasks.

Michael had been a patient in the hospital. He'd had a flesh wound in the thigh and was young and shocked by what he had seen and suffered in the trenches. He and Eleanor had gone for walks together as he grew stronger. When he cast away his crutches, he took her arm for support—and still held it when he could walk alone. They strolled in the nearby woods, and had tea in the local town. Phyllis saw them once and told Eleanor so, and soon after that Eleanor was switched to night duty so that she scarcely saw Michael again before he went back to the front. She didn't receive a single letter from him, and after months of waiting, although she never saw his name on the casualty lists, she decided he had been killed.

Later she met Roger, who was large and kind and protected her from the harshest aspects of life for so many years, leaving her all the more ill prepared to battle alone, as now she must.

"Games are no fun unless you play fair and square," said the sturdy woman with Phyllis's voice.

Mrs. Ford looked away from her and saw a thin girl in white pants and a red sweater and a young man in an arran pullover and clean new jeans—the deck quoit players. The older woman was leaving, walking away, but the damage was done.

"Come on, Iris, your turn," said the man.

"No, I don't want to play any more," the girl said.

That had happened long ago, too. Eleanor had not wanted to play games after Phyllis Burton's derisive interventions.

There was some murmuring between the two. The man put his arm round Iris's shoulders but she flung it off and, head down, mooched off along the deck, disappearing eventually round the corner. The man watched her go, then moved to the rail and leaned over it, gazing at the water.

Mrs. Ford was trembling. The woman was so like Phyllis,

whom she hadn't heard of since "their" war, so long ago. Strange that someone else should waken her memory. Phyllis, if she were still alive, must be well over eighty now—eighty-four, in fact—and this woman was what? Getting on for sixty? It was hard to tell these days.

Mrs. Ford found it difficult to settle back down after that, and spent a restless day.

Proper table allocations, not prepared the night before when seating had been informal as passengers arrived, had now been made, and Mrs. Ford was pleasantly surprised to find that she was at the doctor's table, with two couples past retirement age and a younger pair. The doctor was also young, reminding Mrs. Ford of her eldest grandson, who was thirty-five. She didn't know that her elder son, that grandson's father, now chairman of a group of companies, had personally visited the shipping office to request special attention for his mother, particularly a congenial place for meals. He and his wife had been on a cruise the year before—their first—and had seen for themselves what Mrs. Ford's fate could be. Her children all loved their timid mother and respected her desire to maintain her independence—and, far from relaxing about her when she went away, they worried. On a ship, however, there was constant attention at hand, a doctor immediately available, and swift communication in an emergency.

Mrs. Ford felt happy sitting next to the doctor, waiting for her soup. She would eat three courses merely, waiting while others ate their way through the menu like schoolboys on a binge. The doctor told her he was having a year at sea before moving, in a few months' time, into general practice. It was a chance to see the world, he said.

He was a tall blond young man with an easy manner and he liked old ladies, who were often valiant, building walls of reserve around themselves as a defense against pity. Mrs. Ford, he saw, was one like that. There were others who thought great age allowed them license to be rude, and took it, and the doctor liked them, too, for he admired their spirit. He ordered wine for the whole table and Mrs. Ford saw the other three men nod in agreement; they would all take their turn to buy it and so must she. This had happened to her before and it was always difficult to insist, as she must if she intended to accept their hospitality. She liked a glass of wine.

Phyllis Burton, if she were a widow, would have no difficulty in dealing with such a problem. She would, early on, establish ascendancy over the whole table.

After all these years, here was Phyllis Burton in her mind, and just because of the dogmatic woman on the deck this morning.

Conversation flowed. The doctor asked about Mrs. Ford's family and listened with apparent interest to her account of her grandchildren's prowess in various activities. It was acceptable to brag of their accomplishments, but not of one's children's successes, Mrs. Ford had learned. Everyone disclosed where they lived and if they had cruised before—or, failing that, what other countries they had visited. Both retired couples had been to the Far East, the younger pair to Florida. The doctor revealed that he was unmarried, but his face briefly clouded—then he went on to describe the ship making black smoke off Mykonos (such a white island!) due to some engine maintenance requirement. He laughed. It had looked bad from the boats taking the passengers ashore.

Mrs. Ford had enjoyed her meal. The passenger list was in her cabin when she returned after dinner but she didn't look at it. She read about Lord Wavell, falling asleep over him and waking later with her spectacles still on. Then, with the light out and herself neatly tucked under the bedclothes, she dreamed about Michael. They were walking in the woods near the hospital, holding hands, and he kissed her sweetly, as he had so long ago, her first kiss from an adult male, right-seeming, making it easy when afterwards Roger came along.

She woke in the morning a little disturbed by the dream, but rested.

The next night the captain held his welcoming party, and at it

Mrs. Ford, hovering on the animated fringe of guests, saw the doctor talking to a pretty girl in a flame-colored dress. She saw them together again in Athens, setting off to climb the Acropolis.

Mrs. Ford decided not to attempt the ascent—she had been up there with Roger on a night of the full moon and preferred to hold that memory rather than one of a heated scramble that would exhaust her. She waited in a tourist pavilion by the bus park, drinking coffee, till the groups from the ship returned. This time the doctor was alone. With her far-sighted eyes, Mrs. Ford peered about for the girl but did not see her.

Then she heard the voice again.

"What a clumsy girl you are. I don't know why you can't look where you're going," it said, in Phyllis's tones. "Look at your trousers—they're ruined. Scrambling about like a child up there!"

"I'm sorry, Mummy." Mrs. Ford heard the tight high-pitched reply of someone in a state of tension. "I slipped. It will wash out."

Mrs. Ford, on her way to coach number four, glanced round. The tourists wouldn't pause for coffee—meals were paid for on the tour and they were returning to the ship for lunch before taking other excursions before the *Sphinx* sailed that night. Behind her she saw a tall, well built woman with carefully coiffed iron-grey hair in a tweed skirt, sensible shoes, and an expensive pigskin jacket. Beside her was the girl Mrs. Ford had witnessed talking to the doctor, her blonde hair caught back in a slide at the nape of her neck. On her pale trousers there was a long, dirty smear.

It was to the mother, however, that Mrs. Ford's eyes were drawn. Just so might Phyllis Burton have looked in middle age.

That evening Mrs. Ford consulted the passenger list with a pencil, reading it with care to winnow out the mothers and daughters traveling together. The father might be present too, unobserved so far by Mrs. Ford. She marked several family groups with a question mark. There were no Burtons. Of course not. But the resemblance was so uncanny, she would have to find out who the woman was.

*   *   *

In the end it was easy.

The next day the sun shone brightly and the sea was calm. Mrs. Ford decided to climb higher in the ship than she had been hitherto and explore the sports deck in search of a quiet corner where she could sit in the sun. Stick hooked over her arm, a hand on the rail, she slowly ascended the companionway and walked along the deck to a spot where it widened out and some chairs were placed. In one sat the blonde girl. Beside her was an empty chair.

"Is this anyone's place?" Mrs. Ford inquired, and the girl, who had been gazing out to sea, turned with a slight start. A smile of great sweetness spread over her face and, confused, Mrs. Ford was again in a wood, long ago, with Michael.

"No—oh, please, let me help you," the girl said, and, springing up, she put a hand under Mrs. Ford's elbow to help her into the low chair. "They're difficult, aren't they? These chairs, I mean. Such a long way down."

"Yes," agreed Mrs. Ford, gasping slightly. "But getting up is harder."

"I know. We found it with my grandfather," the girl said. "But now he's got his own chair for the garden—it's higher, and he can manage."

"Your grandfather?" Mrs. Ford wanted the girl to talk while she caught her breath.

"He's lived with us since my grandmother died—before I was born," said the girl. "He's still quite spry, but a bit forgetful. He's a lamb."

"And are you like him?" She was, Mrs. Ford knew.

The girl laughed.

"Forgetful, you mean?" she said. "Maybe I am—Mummy always says I'm so clumsy and careless. But then, she's so terribly well organized herself. Granny was the same, Grandpa says. She always knew what to do and made instant decisions."

Roger had always known what to do and made quick, if not instant, decisions, Mrs. Ford reflected. "I dither a bit myself," she declared. "I miss my husband a great deal. He cared for me so."

"That must have been wonderful," said the girl, seeming quite unembarrassed by this confidence.

They sat there in the sunshine, gently chatting. The girl's mother was having her hair done, she said. They were cruising together—her mother had had severe bronchitis during the winter and it had seemed a good idea to seek the sun. Her father couldn't get away and so she had come instead. What girl would refuse a chance like this? Her mother had a great desire to see the Pyramids and that would be the high point of the trip for them.

"But you've traveled before?" Mrs. Ford asked. Her elder grandchildren, this child's generation, were always whizzing about the globe.

Mummy hadn't liked her going off just with friends, the girl said, but she *had* been to France to learn the language. There had been family holidays in Corsica, which she loved. They rented a villa. She had two brothers, both older than herself.

"What are their names?" asked Mrs. Ford, still feeling her way. She didn't know the girl's yet.

"Michael's the eldest—he's called after my grandfather," said the girl. "The other one's William, after Daddy."

Mrs. Ford's gently beating old heart began to thump unevenly. Should she say she had known a Michael, long ago? But the girl was going on, needing no prompting.

"Aren't names funny?" she said. "I'm glad I wasn't called after Mummy—her name's Phyllis, after her mother. It would be confusing to have two Phyllis Carters, wouldn't it?"

"I suppose it would," Mrs. Ford agreed, and now bells seemed to be ringing in her head, for her Michael's surname had been Carter.

"I'm called after someone else Grandfather knew," said the girl. "It's quite romantic, really. There was this nurse he met in the war—the first war, you remember."

"Yes, my dear, I do," said Mrs. Ford.

"She was very young and shy and kept being ticked off by this older, bossier nurse, Grandfather said. When he went back to France he wrote her lots of letters, but she never answered. Wasn't that sad? I'm named after her. Her name was Eleanor."

"Oh," said Mrs. Ford faintly, and her head spun. Letters?

"She must have married someone else or something," said the girl. "Or even died. All the letters were sent back to Grandfather. Mummy found them when she helped him clear up after Granny died, in her desk, locked up. She burned them without telling Grandfather. It would only have upset him."

"Yes, I suppose it would," said Mrs. Ford. There was just one fact that must be confirmed. "Your grandmother?" she asked.

"Grandfather married another nurse," said the girl. "Mummy's exactly like her, he says."

Mrs. Ford took it in. All those years ago Phyllis Burton had intercepted letters meant for her. Why? Because she wanted Michael for himself, or because she sought, as always, to despoil?

"And have you uncles and aunts?" she asked at last.

"No, there was only Mummy," the girl replied.

So Phyllis had managed just one child, and had died before this grandchild had been born, while Mrs. Ford, with two sons and two daughters, had survived into great age. And Michael had never forgotten, for this girl bore her name.

She could cope with no more today.

"What a nice little chat we've had," she said. "We'll be meeting again." She began to struggle up from her chair and the girl rose again to help her.

In the days that followed they talked more. Seeing them together, the mother would walk past, but if Eleanor was talking to any man among the passengers, or a ship's officer, the mother would break in upon them at once.

In Mrs. Ford's mind the generations grew confused and there were moments when she imagined it was this confident, domineering woman who had been so perfidious all those years ago, stealing letters meant for another, not this woman's long-dead mother. At night Mrs. Ford shed tears for the young girl that had been herself, waiting for letters that never came and in the end giving up.

But she'd had along, full, and happy life afterwards. And Michael hadn't persevered—hadn't tried to find her after the war.

Perhaps Phyllis had already made sure of him: she'd borne him just one child.

On deck, Mrs. Ford heard Eleanor being admonished.

"A ship's doctor won't do" came that dominant tone. "I've plans for you, and they don't include this sort of thing at all. It stops the instant you leave the ship, do you hear?"

Eleanor told Mrs. Ford about it later.

"He's a widower. His wife died in a car crash when she was pregnant," she said. "But it isn't just that. Mummy wants me to marry an earl, if she can find one, or at least some sort of tycoon, like Daddy."

"It's early days. You don't really know each other," said Mrs. Ford.

"I know, but he's only doing a short spell in the ship, then he's going into general practice. We could get better acquainted then, couldn't we?"

"Yes," agreed Mrs. Ford.

"And as for earls and tycoons—" Eleanor put scorn in her voice.

She'd learned typing and done a Cordon Bleu cooking course, Eleanor said. She'd wanted to be a nurse but Mummy hadn't approved. The girl seemed docile and subdued—too much so, Mrs. Ford thought.

Michael Carter, she remembered, had seemed to have plenty of money, though neither had thought about things like that when during that long-ago war they took their quiet walks and had tea in a cafe. Phyllis Burton might have destroyed the innocent budding romance simply because that was her way, but she wouldn't have married Michael unless he had been what was called, in those days, "a catch." She'd have made sure of the same for her daughter—and that daughter was repeating the pattern now.

"You're of age," Mrs. Ford said. "Make your own decisions."

Later the mother spoke to her. It was eerie, hearing that voice from the past urging her, since she had become friendly with Eleanor, to warn her against the doctor.

"But why?" Mrs. Ford said. "He seems such a nice young man."

"Think of her future," the girl's mother said. "She can do better than that."

"He'd look after her," Mrs. Ford said, and she knew that he would. The girl was timid and lacking in confidence; the doctor, experienced and quite a lot older, would make her feel safe, as she had felt with Roger. "It depends on what you think is important," she said, rather bravely for her, and Eleanor's mother soon left, quite annoyed.

Mrs. Ford smiled to herself and stitched on at her *gros point*. She'd help the young pair if she could. Nowadays, as she knew from her own family, people tried things out before making a proper commitment, and though such a system had, in her view, disadvantages, there were also points in its favor.

Mrs. Ford did not go to Cairo. The drive was a long one from Alexandria, and she'd been before—stayed with Roger at Mena House, in fact, years ago. She spent the day quietly in Alexandria. The doctor, she knew, had gone on the trip in case a passenger fell ill, as might easily happen. That evening he said that someone had fainted, but nothing more serious had occurred.

The next day was spent at sea, giving people a chance to recover from the most tiring expedition of the voyage. Among those sleeping in chairs on deck, Mrs. Ford saw Eleanor's mother. Her mouth was a little agape and her spectacles were still on her nose. In her hand she held an open book. Perhaps she was not as robust as she seemed, Mrs. Ford mused—her own mother, after all, the Phyllis of Mrs. Ford's youth, had not survived late middle age.

On the upper deck, Eleanor and the doctor were playing deck tennis. Mrs. Ford, seeing them, smiled to herself as she walked away. Youth was resilient.

Several days later the *Sphinx* anchored off Nauplia. The weather was fine, though a haze hung over the distant mountains and there was snow on the highest peaks, rare for this area. Mrs. Ford stood in line to disembark by the ship's launches with the other passengers going ashore. Stalwart ship's officers would easily help her aboard and she quite enjoyed feeling a firm grasp on her arm as she stepped over the gunwale into the boat.

A row of coaches waited on the quay. Mrs. Ford allowed herself to be directed into one. She would enjoy today, for while Mycenae, their first stop, was a dramatic, brooding place, holding an atmosphere redolent of tragedy, Epidaurus, in its perfect setting, was a total contrast. They drove past groves of orange trees laden with fruit. The almond trees were in bloom and the grass, which later in the year would be bleached by the heat of the sun, was a brilliant green.

The haze had lifted when the coach stopped at Epidaurus. Mrs. Ford debated whether to go straight to the stadium, which so few tours allowed time to visit and where it would be peaceful and cool, but in the end, walking among the pines and inhaling their scent, she decided to visit it again.

She walked past the group from her coach as, like docile children, they clustered around their guide and, sauntering on, using her stick, she turned up the track to the left of the theater where the ascent was easier than up the steep steps.

At the top she turned to the right and entered the vast semicircle of stone. She moved inwards a little and sat down, gazing about her, sighing with pleasure. Below stood her group; she had plenty of time to rest and enjoy her surroundings.

The sun was quite strong now and she sat thinking of very little except her present contentment. A guide below began the acoustic demonstration, scrabbling his feet in the dust, jingling keys, lighting a match. Mrs. Ford had seen it all before. Then her eye caught a flash of bright blue lower down—young Eleanor's sweater. She was almost at the bottom of the auditorium and with her was a tall young man easily discerned by Mrs. Ford's far-sighted eyes to be the ship's doctor. They were absorbed as much with each other as with the scenery, Mrs. Ford thought as she watched them together.

Then a voice behind her called loudly.

"Eleanor!" she heard. "Eleanor! Come here at once!"

Mrs. Ford reacted instinctively to the sound of her name and she turned. Her pulse was beating fast and she felt her nerves tighten with fear. Since her youth no one had talked to her in such a tone.

Down the steep steps of the aisle between the seats, Phyllis's daughter, whose name was also Phyllis, came boldly toward her, striding with purpose. Phyllis the malevolent, Phyllis the destroyer. Mrs. Ford's grip on her stick, which was resting across her knees, tightened as the lumbering figure in its sensible skirt and expensive jacket approached. Her pace did not slacken as she drew near. Mrs. Ford knew with a part of her mind that it was not she but her young namesake below who was the target of the imperious summons.

She acted spontaneously. She slid her walking stick out across the aisle, handle foremost, as Phyllis drew level, and by chance, not deliberate design, the hooked end caught round the woman's leg. Mrs. Ford tightened her grasp with both hands and hung on, but the stick was pulled from her grip as the hurrying woman stumbled and fell.

She didn't fall far—she was too bulky and the stairway too narrow—but she came to rest some little way below Mrs. Ford and lay quite still. No one noticed at first, for there were shouts and cries filling the air from tourists testing the amplification of the theater and attention was focused below.

Mrs. Ford's pulse had begun to steady by the time people began to gather around the body. Her stick lay at the side of the aisle. She retrieved it quite easily. She returned to her coach by the same way she had come, away from all the commotion, and was driven back to Nauplia where the ship waited at anchor.

There was talk in the coach.

"Some woman tripped and fell."

"It's dangerous. You'd think there'd be a rope."

"People should look where they're going."

"She must have been wearing unsuitable shoes."

The doctor was not at the table for dinner that night, and over the loudspeaker the captain announced that though sailing had been delayed this would not interfere with the rest of the timetable—the next port would be reached as planned.

Mrs. Ford's table companions related various versions of what had happened ashore to cause the delay. The woman, Eleanor's mother, had stumbled in the theater at Epidaurus and in falling had hit her head against a projecting stone, dying at once. Someone else thought she'd had a stroke or a heart attack and that this had caused her to fall, for she was a big woman and florid of face. The Greeks had taken over, since the accident had happened ashore, and the formalities were therefore their concern.

"Terrible for the daughter," someone remarked. "Such a shock."

"The father's flying out," someone else said.

Mrs. Ford ate her sole meunière. She had only wanted to stop Phyllis from interfering. Hadn't she?

Her son, meeting her at the airport some days later, found his mother looking well and rested. He knew about the accident—it had been reported in the newspapers.

"What a terrible thing to happen," he said. "It must have been most distressing. Poor woman."

"Well, she saw the Pyramids," Mrs. Ford replied.

What a heartless response, thought her son in surprise, and looked at his gentle mother, astonished.

ONCE UPON A TIME

by Amanda Cross

This was the only true story she had ever heard, Kate Fansler used to say, that properly began "once upon a time." Kate, who had never seen the beginning, said it was, nonetheless, as clear to her inner eye as any personal memory, sharp in all its detail, as immediate as sense itself.

The family to whom it happened was named Grant and they were in their summer home in New England. "The King was in the counting house, counting out his money; the Queen was in the parlor, eating bread and honey." That is, the father, as in this context we should call him, had gone into town for the papers; he had money invested and wanted to study the stock-market page. The mother, a college professor, was upstairs in her study, ostensibly writing an article for a conference on the uses of fantasy, in fact reading a novel by Thomas Hardy—which seemed, as she later said, sounding prophetic, to answer to her condition. The children were on the lawn playing a ragged and hilarious game of volleyball.

There were four of them, three boys and a girl, all twelve years of age. The girl and one of the boys were twins; the other two boys were school friends, come for the weekend. They, too, were twins, identical as opposed to their fraternal-twin hosts, and the badminton set had been their hostess gift. They had been invited for two weeks, as a favor to their parents, and because the resident twins were judged too self-reliant, and requiring outside stimulation. It had taken a whole day to put up the posts for the

net and another day to practice with the rackets and shuttlecocks.
The father had pointed out that they could play volleyball with
the same net, and had, the next afternoon, provided the ball.

There the four of them were, having both learned and invented
the game, playing at it furiously and with much shouting—the
girl was as good at it as the boys, and taller than the visiting
twins—when one of the visiting twins (they do not remain in this
story long enough to be named) shouted, "Look! It's a baby!"

And, as the four of them would remember the scene and tell
of it for the rest of their lives, a baby, wearing a diaper and shirt
and nothing else, came toddling toward them out of the bushes
that lined the property and across the lawn. The baby was about
a year and a half old and appeared to have learned to walk only
recently. It rocked toward them with that unsteady gait characteristic of babies and laughed, holding out its arms, probably for
balance but, as it seemed, reaching toward them. And, what
seemed most marvelous, it chortled in that wonderful way of babies, with little yelps of delight as it staggered toward them.

The volleyball players ran down the lawn toward the baby. An
adult, even the sort of twelve-year-old girl who played house and
dreamed of herself in a bridal gown, would have scooped up the
baby. These children simply stood one on each side of her—
which two took the baby's hands could never afterward be agreed
upon, perhaps they took turns—and slowly moved, midst coos
of encouragement, toward the house. The girl then ran ahead—
allowing a boy to take the baby hand she held, or so she insisted—to alert their mother. "Ma!" she called. "A baby walked
out of the bushes!"

The professor, reading of how Clym Yeobright's mother died,
returned to the New England summer afternoon with difficulty.
"What do you mean?" she is reported to have said rather crossly.
(The story had been retold so often that parts of it became "au-
thentic," as other parts continued to be debated.) She was
dragged by her daughter to the window—after having returned
her eyes to her book as though her daughter had merely said,
"An elephant with wings has landed on the lawn"—where she

witnessed the baby's progress toward the house, its hands being held by two attentive boys.

"Where did it come from?" she not unreasonably asked.

"Just out of the bushes," her daughter answered. The professor rushed downstairs and out onto the road. There was no sign of any car or person. Their house was at the end of a dirt road and any car or person on the road was clearly visible.

"Did you hear a car?" the professor asked. By this time she had reached the baby and held out her arms: the baby walked into them. The professor held and smelt a baby, and put its cheek next to hers, as she had not done for a decade—and then there had been two, which had (as she admitted only to herself and the mother of the visiting twins) doubled the work while halving those intense moments of a mother and baby alone in the entire world.

"We didn't hear anything," the children all said, jumping around her. "Of course we would have heard a car if there had been one." This was so obviously true, the professor argued no further. Someone must somehow have crept along the side of the road, set the baby toddling toward the children, and crept away.

"What did you think of when you saw the baby and heard that story?" the professor was often asked.

"I thought of Moses," she always answered. "And, of course, of Silas Marner."

This latter allusion turned out to be, on the whole, the more appropriate. The baby was a girl, as they discovered after the father, returning with his papers, had been immediately dispatched back to town for diapers and baby food. The mother, with three of the children, the fourth being left downstairs with the baby, searched the attic for a portable crib that had been retained from earlier years for the possible use of visiting young. When the father returned and they had changed and fed the baby, they all sat down at the table, the parents with a stiff drink, and discussed the matter.

"We could advertise," one of the children said. "Or put up a notice like they do with lost cats and dogs." Everyone laughed but, as the parents were quick to point out, no one had a better suggestion. And then the father looked at the professor and said: "Geraldine and Tom."

"Of course," the mother and the home twins said. "But," the children asked, "couldn't we keep her?"

"Our arms are full," the professor said happily. "Besides," she added, "if we'd wanted anyone else, we would have her by now. Our family is complete."

"Geraldine and Tom then," the home twins said, not really disagreeing with their mother. "But," the girl twin added, "she did seem to choose us."

"That's because we were playing on the lawn," her twin said. "It seems a good place where children are playing on the lawn."

"We'll have to tell that to Geraldine and Tom," the father said.

And that was where the "once upon a time" part of the story ended. The professor went away to call Geraldine and Tom, who immediately drove up from New York and looked at the baby as though she had indeed dropped from the skies. "It was *much* better than that," the children insisted. And they had to tell the story again, the first repeat of many. After that, it was courts and judges and social workers and the long, slow process of the law.

Geraldine and Tom, who might as well be known as the Rayleys, were friends of the Grants. Tom was a corporate lawyer who had made partner five years before, and was wildly successful and overworked. Geraldine ran an elegant clothing shop. Unlike those who discovered late in their thirties that they wanted a child, the Rayleys had always wanted one, but it had just never happened. Only lately, consulting doctors and learning that there was no evident reason for their failure, had they decided to adopt. Here they immediately ran into trouble: they were too old and they were of different religions, to mention only the major points emphasized by the adoption agencies. The other markets for babies they had not tried. Tom was one of those whom anything even touching upon the illegal or shady disgusted: he was a person of almost flaming rectitude and integrity, which, as the Grants used to point out to each other, was a pretty odd thing in a corporate lawyer, dearly as the Grants loved the Rayleys.

Geraldine and Tom's desire for a baby seemed to swell with the passing years—almost, the professor used to say, as a mother's body swells with the growing baby inside her. Afterward, many people were to remark how amazingly simple-minded the Grants had been. They had a baby who had toddled toward them out from the mountain laurel. They had friends who longed for a baby. What could be more logical than, pending discovery of the baby's provenance, bringing them all together? "But," people would say later, hearing the story, "the disappointment later for the Rayleys if the baby's mother had been found."

"It was all we could think to do," the professor would say when this point was made. "We all seemed to be acting as though we were in some fairy story; well, we were in a fairy story. And it did work out, so we did the right thing, Q.E.D."

For the Rayleys, after many years' experience of the law's delay, got to keep the baby. They adopted her legally, but even before that she was registered for the best school in New York, which Geraldine had attended. She spent her earliest years as a Rayley at an excellent nursery school. The baby, whom they named Caroline, remained as she had first appeared, a laughing, happy child. With adolescence she grew more serious and seemed oddly dissatisfied with her richly endowed life. Fortunately, her parents, as one might expect of a man of Tom's principles and a woman who endorsed them, were not advocates of material indulgence for children. Caroline was kept on a strict allowance and had to account for her evenings. Her parents were of a liberal persuasion, however, and despite all the horrors reported daily of adolescent extravagances, they and Caroline always got on. She went away to college and, eventually, to graduate school. In time, she became an assistant professor at a university in New York. That, of course, was where she met Kate Fansler.

It was, however, not Caroline but her father, Tom Rayley, who first talked to Kate at any length about that amazing scene on the lawn almost thirty years earlier. Caroline and Kate had become friendly, as happens now and then with full professors and much younger assistant professors. As Kate would often say, the friendship is not one of equals, nor can it pretend to be when one friend has such power, direct or indirect, over the destiny of another. All the same, they suited one another. Kate was reaching that difficult point in some lives when, growing older, one finds one's ideas and hopes more in accord with those of the young than of one's own contemporaries. Kate's peers seemed to grow more conservative and fearful as she grew more radical and daring. Not that Kate was then or ever of the stuff from which revolutionaries are made. Perhaps because of her fortunate life, her indifference—either because she had them or did not desire them—to many of the goods of life, she seemed not to barricade herself against disturbing ideas or changing ways. The same could not, surely, be said of Tom Rayley. He came to Kate in fear, though he could scarcely tell her of what. Fear came, he suggested, with his time of life.

"I've turned sixty," he said. "It humbles a man. For one thing," he added darkly, "the body starts falling apart. I've never had very much wrong with me, and all of a sudden I find I have to make a huge effort to hold on to my teeth, I've got a strange disease of which they know the name but not a cure, I've also acquired what they call degenerative arthritis, which turns out to be another term for old age, and when I got the laboratory report from my doctor, not only was my cholesterol up, but the lab had noted 'serum appears cloudy,' which didn't bother the doctor but sounded ominous to me. On top of all that, I'd rather Caroline didn't go off to live with her new-found mother or father in a community somewhere full of strange rites and a profound mistrust of life's conventions."

Kate and Tom Rayley had met when Caroline invited Kate home for dinner. Geraldine, like Tom, lived a life in which the strict control of emotion and the avoidance of untidiness, literal or psychological, were paramount. Highly intelligent, they were good conversationalists. Geraldine in particular offering amusing and revealing accounts of the international world of fashion and the Manhattan world of real estate, with which fashion, like everything else, was so intimately connected.

Tom seemed rather the sort who takes in information while giving out as little as possible. He was pleasant but, after the dinner, Kate realized she knew little or nothing about him. Only when she had been, to her astonishment, summoned to a private interview did Kate discover that Tom Rayley was an impressive man, just the sort one would think of as a senior partner in a corporate law firm. Kate wondered if his democratic convictions came from an open mind or his Southern boyhood at a time when all Southerners were democrats. Since Rayley had not turned Republican like so many of his sort, and had settled in New York, she gave him the benefit of the doubt: his was an open mind, fearful perhaps of aging and of loneliness, but not of those chimeras requiring for their alleviation—belief in nuclear weapons, separation of the races, and the strict domestication of women.

Kate was so astonished at his sudden frankness, helplessness, and revelations that she hardly knew what to say.

"What is this disease with a name but no cure?" she asked without really thinking.

"It's a rather personal male disease, apparently of no great significance, but calculated to detonate every hideous male fear ever recorded. It's called Peyroni's disease, but whether Peyroni had it, identified it, or dismissed it is unclear. The only problem once it is named, at least in my case, is that my liver responded in a regrettable way to the drug supposed to alleviate it. I can't imagine why we're discussing this."

"Because it made you fearful of Caroline's defection. I have to say," Kate went on, "that children seem to me notably unsatisfactory when it comes to the question of their parents. Between those who fantasize other parents and those who seek biological parents, it seems that no one is satisfied. Perhaps we ought to follow Plato's suggestion and have a world where biological parentage is neither known nor significant."

"I'm perfectly aware that my anxiety is irrational and illogical. As a lawyer, if not as a practical realist, how could I not be aware? I think that's why I wanted to talk with you. You, I sur-

mise, deal in stories like this. Caroline admires you and will probably speak to you about her 'original appearance' more intently
than she has spoken to anyone else. Also—and I hope you will
not desert me totally at this honesty—I did infer that as a sister
of the famous Fansler lawyers you would hardly be, shall we say,
a disruptive person."

"Not disruptive, but not soothing, either. I'm very unlike my
brothers in every possible way; perhaps you've heard that. And
if you're expressing some naive belief in genes, let me point out
the inefficacy of that attitude from an adoptive and loving parent."

"Oh, dear, yes," Tom Rayley said, in no way offended. "But
that's part of my fear, you see. How can I say it? That Caroline,
discovering something, one hardly knows what, will fall out of
our world and into some other world to me unspeakable. And
you, at least so far, while in another world, are not unspeakable.
I understand your language; I can even learn it."

Kate stared at him. "That is a remarkably intelligent thing to
say," she said. "I'm happy to talk with you, though Caroline is
my friend, and I shall certainly talk to her also: But I am bewildered: what can you possibly think I can do for you? Isn't this
all between you and your wife and Caroline, isn't it all about the
life you three have had together for all but a year and a half of
Caroline's existence?"

"You've heard the story then, the appearance from the bushes
of the laughing child?"

"Yes. I've heard it from Caroline. As she's heard it, and as it
has been disputed and refined over the years. But she and I have
not talked about it, not as you and I are talking now. It's an
amazing story certainly. Almost mythic."

"Exactly. It's myths I fear, you see. That's the whole point. I
don't mind a bereft mother or even father appearing after all these
years. I fear the power of the myth. I was wondering if you could
detect it: demythologize it. Isn't that what they do in literary criticism these days?"

"All I can do is talk to Caroline, which I do anyway. And to
you, if an intelligent question occurs to me. But where can this

lead except around in the same circles? Caroline isn't desperate for the truth, resting her whole identity and future life on some revelation. Your fears seem excessive."

"They are. They are the fears that come with the youth of senility, as another lawyer once described it. Will you just accept my trepidation as part of your agenda, one of those 'cases' you think about?"

"I can do that, certainly," Kate said, half amused, half fearful of his intensity, inadequately masked. "What of the mother of the twins, the one who was reading Hardy? Is she still alive?"

"Oh, yes—still a professor. And she's never moved an inch from the story, nor have her children. It's legend now. It's a truth beyond truth."

Kate had intended to mention the conversation with Caroline's father the next day, when she and Caroline walked home together, as was now their custom. They lived within a few blocks of one another but never, to their amusement, met except at the university. Those few blocks separated one New York City neighborhood from another. Caroline, however, mentioned the conversation first. Her father had called her the previous night to report upon the lunch he and Kate had shared.

"The general hope, I'm to gather, is that you'll come to dinner with the parents from time to time and head off the effects of any terrible revelation, or the lack of such a revelation, upon their daughter. I hope you don't feel unduly burdened. In the beginning, my appearance from the bushes seemed a good story—I don't know why it has become so fearsome."

"Stories of that sort do," Kate said. "Like the moment after an electricity failure, when the bright lights go on and the candles are scarcely visible, superfluous. Here we are, talking now about your amazing appearance, while before we used to chat on about everything, nothing outshining the rest."

"Do you mind?" Caroline asked.

"Partly. Partly I want to shout out that it doesn't matter how you were born or miraculously shone forth. What matters is that you have a blessed life and the chance for an interesting future.

But then I know that's nonsense. The question is, shall you be able eventually to forget the story, let it fade into the general history of things, or shall it keep, as they so wonderfully say in criticism today, foregrounding itself?"

"Certainly it will fade if it never changes, never gets any commentary added to it, never gets reinterpreted. Do you think you might be persuaded to go and see Henrietta Grant?"

"The mother of the twins—the one who was reading Hardy? What could I go to see her for? I could hardly request to hear the story again, as one might have asked a bard to recite the lines about Odysseus's meeting with Nausicaa. I mean, if she wants to keep telling it, why not tell it to someone who hasn't heard it before?"

"I don't think she tells it much, or likes to. Mostly others tell it now—her children, me, Mom and Dad. It's just that she's got to be the answer."

"The answer to where you came from?"

"Yes. She's the only one who could possibly know."

"Caroline, that's obviously untrue. Unless she was in two places at once, and nothing in the story allows one to believe that, the only person who can possibly know is the one who set you off toward the volleyball players from behind the bushes and then crept away. And at least with the needle in the haystack, you supposedly know what haystack you lost the needle in."

"You mean someone spotted that house, the children, the geography of the lawn, the dirt road, all of it, and just decided it was a good place to dump a baby."

"That's the likeliest explanation, surely."

"Perhaps. Except, Kate, I know I was a happy child and all that, but if someone the child knows puts her down, is she likely to go running, happily gurgling the while, toward complete strangers in a strange place? I mean, she couldn't have known the children, but mightn't she have known the place?"

"You're looking for a rational explanation, my dear. That is the great temptation with a story like this. As in the Gershwin song, where the Pharaoh's daughter is suspected of being the mother of Moses, the baby *she* found. Surely the whole point about marvelous happenings is that there isn't an explanation—anyway, not one that would satisfy a rationalist. I think that's why your father's so worried. He half hopes for a rational explanation, and half fears the lack of one: if you consider yourself miraculous, even miraculously adventurous for a baby, you become other worldly, part of legend, not simply his child."

"Does that mean I ought to look for a mundane answer or not?"

"Myself, I'd feel tempted to accept it just as it is, be glad you landed in that place, that your parents were there to claim you when called, that you were born at a later age than most in an improbable way. It all seems to me a kind of blessing, better than fairy godmothers around your cradle. But who am I to talk, having always known exactly where I came from, and regretting it the greater part of the time? There is, you see, the danger that you will waste your energies on the past and miss the present and the future. I think that's often a danger, and one worth risking only under the most extreme conditions—total despair or anxiety, for example. What can you learn from the past before you burst upon that volleyball game that's worth knowing? That's what I'd ask myself."

"There's always plain old curiosity."

"So there is. But maybe that's more my problem than yours. After all, I've made curiosity a kind of avocation. If you give me permission, I can promise to be curious enough for both of us."

"Does that mean you might try to discover something?"

"Probably not. It means that I'll go on wondering; you go on living."

"Should your curiosity ever lead to any answers, will you promise to tell me? No, don't protest," Caroline said as Kate started to speak. "Let's make it a bargain. I'll stop thinking about the whole scene, stop even telling it to new people I meet—I'll just say I'm adopted and let it go at that. I think you're right about the past entrenching itself in the present and future. But if I give up this wonderful question, you have, in turn, to promise to tell me if there ever is an answer. Agreed?"

Kate agreed, and with relief. The story was beginning to

frighten her in the hold it was getting on Caroline and Tom Rayley. She called Tom Rayley and told him of the bargain, urging him to forget myths and concentrate on his satisfactory daughter.

And there for a time the matter rested.

The resurrection of the myth was an outcome of Kate's meeting with Henrietta Grant. They found themselves together on a panel, both last-minute substitutes. Each, it later transpired, had agreed to fill in as a special favor, Henrietta to the remaining panelist, Kate to the man who had organized the panel in the first place. They were introduced five minutes before the panel began, each trying to remember where she had heard the other's name. Both thought of Caroline as the connection during the first paper, and nodded that recognition to one another as the man's words on the New Historicism in the Renaissance prepared the way for Henrietta on the New Historicism in French writing of the Eighteenth Century and for Kate on English writers of the Nineteenth.

"Shall we have a drink," Henrietta asked when they had answered the last of the questions and watched the audience disperse, "or do you feel duty-bound to remain for the next panel?"

"Neither duty-bound nor so inclined," Kate answered. "After all, we are substitutes—it's not as though we had signed on for the whole bit. And even if I had, the truth is I would like to have a drink with you."

They soon settled themselves in the bar of the hotel where the conference was being held. Kate felt she deserved a martini complete with olive.

"How is Caroline?" Henrietta asked. "I understand working with you has been a real opportunity. Not that I've seen her lately."

"I wouldn't call it an opportunity. We're friends, which is a good thing. The fact is," Kate added, as her martini and Henrietta's scotch arrived, "I never expected really to meet you, any more than I expected to come upon two sets of twelve-year-old twins playing volleyball. Or upon Huck and Jim on a raft, if it comes to that. Certain scenes live only in the imagination."

"The twins are not *that* much younger than you," Henrietta

laughed. "My twins, at least, have turned out rather well. I've lost track of the other two, so they remain always twelve in my mind. They moved away after that summer."

"I wonder if they tell the story of Caroline's arrival."

"I'm pretty sure they do. They got used to telling it that summer. It's not the sort of story you forget."

"It's all passed into legend by now. How does it feel to be part of a legend?"

"It was an amazing moment. I feel a kind of wonder about Caroline, as though, after that birth, as amazing and as charming in its way as that of Botticelli's Venus, she was bound to be a marvel, do something that would reverberate, become, in her own way, a myth."

"The birth of the hero, as Raglan and others have it, only this time a woman hero. More Moses than Effie *Silas Marner*. And of course the two sets of twins add a note—a kind of amazing circumstance."

"Not really," Henrietta laughed. "Think of the Bobbsey twins. Just a convenient circumstance." Henrietta looked for a moment down at her hands. "I do hope Caroline's stopped brooding about it. I worry about the Rayleys. I worry about her. Like those babies conceived *in vitro*: how can anything in life equal its first moment? I mean, can a life hold two miracles?"

"The whole point of heroic lives is that they do, isn't that so? The miraculous birth, therefore the awful and wonderful destiny. Not that I can imagine that for Caroline, who is such a sane person, which heroes rarely are."

"Male heroes," Henrietta said, and they went on to talk of other things.

But, the ice being broken, they met again from time to time, when Henrietta was in New York or Kate in Boston. And then one spring day Kate, finding herself at Williams College and remembering that Henrietta's country house, on whose lawn Caroline had appeared that long-ago afternoon, was nearby, telephoned on the chance that Henrietta might be there, might ask her to stop by.

"Your sense of geography is rather wonderful," Henrietta remarked. "I'm an hour at least away, and despite the careful directions I shall now give you you will get lost. Stop and telephone again when you realize you've made a wrong turn. And plan to spend the night if you come at all. You'll be far too late to drive anywhere today. I'm all alone, so there's plenty of room. I'll put you in the room where I was reading the day Caroline appeared."

Kate did get lost, did call again, did arrive as the day was darkening, the trees beginning to be outlined against the evening sky. Kate drove down the dirt road on which Henrietta's house stood; was shown the bushes that lined the property at its sides, and the lawn where the badminton net had been. Beyond the lawn was woods. The silence was amazing to Kate.

"Come in," Henrietta said. "We'll sit by the fire and lift a glass to Caroline."

"Has she been back here often?" Kate asked.

"Oddly not. The Rayleys visited with her once, but they wouldn't take their eyes off her. I think they feared she would wander off just as she had come, holding out her hands to someone else. It took them years to believe that Caroline was there to stay. They used to go into her room at night to be sure she hadn't vanished into thin air. Eventually Caroline became a real little girl who could be trusted out on her own. Fortunately, she was small when they got her, so she had time to grow into independence and they had time to accept it. The Rayleys are very sound people, which was a great relief."

"You knew that when you called them that day?"

"I knew them well, of course. But all I thought of that day was their longing for a child, and the child's need of a home. I felt, even though I'd just met Caroline, an urgency that she find the right home, not just be adopted by people I'd never heard of, however worthy."

Kate started to ask another question, but restrained herself. The time for questions had passed. The time for answers might come, but only Henrietta could decide that. They sat with their drinks in front of the fire and let the evening darken altogether before they turned on the lights and thought about dinner.

"I've a thick soup I made last night. It improves with age, like the best of us. Will that do? There's also homemade bread and decent wine."

"It sounds like the beginning of another fantasy," Kate said. "I don't get to the country much and rarely am offered home-made soup and bread. Mostly I subsist on nouvelle cuisine and fish, neither of which I especially like. When we're home, we eat omelettes or Chinese food, delivered by an intense young Oriental on a bicycle. This is a lovely change. Can we eat in front of the fire, looking like a scene from a made-for-television movie?"

"We are, I fear, insufficiently rustic."

But nothing else was insufficient. One of those times, Kate thought, when it is all just right and you never quite understand why, except that it was unplanned and in the highest degree un-likely ever to happen just that way again.

Dinner over, they sat sipping their coffee by the fire, dying because Henrietta hesitated to throw on another log—it would commit them to a delayed bedtime. Kate was beyond the most minor decision. It had been a long day, but she was in that odd state of fatigue past weariness. She simply sat. And Henrietta, having, it seemed, decided, threw a large log on the fire.

"I'd better tell you," she said, sitting forward and staring at the fire. "Someone, I suppose, should know. But if I tell you, it will end our friendship. I'll trust you, but I won't want to know you any more. Which is a pity—the world is not that full of intelligent friends."

Kate couldn't argue with the truth of that. "But if I say don't tell me, shall we go on being friends? Is it my decision?"

"Probably not," Henrietta said, sighing. "In telling you there was anything to tell, I've already crossed that bridge—I've already burned it."

"It's ironic," Kate said. "Like so much else. I guessed, of course—not what you would tell, but that there was something to tell. Once you knew that, we were destined to have only this one night by the fire."

"Truncated friendships are my fate," Henrietta said. "As you shall learn. There never is any turning back." Henrietta paused only a moment.

"It began with a young woman very like Caroline now, a graduate student. We became friends, as you have with Caroline. But it was, or seemed, a more perilous friendship then. Women didn't become close to one another; their eyes were always on the men. I was an associate professor, rather long in the tooth for that, but women didn't get promoted very rapidly in those days. We talked, this graduate student and I, about, oh, everything I seemed never to have talked about. Such talk became more ordinary later, with CR groups and all the rest. It's hard now to recall the loneliness of professional women in those years, the constant tension and anxiety of doing the wrong thing, of offending.

"You have to understand what a conservative woman I was then. If I felt any criticism of the academic world I had fought my way into, I never let it rise to consciousness, let alone expressed it. I just wanted to be accepted, to teach, to write. I like to tell myself it was simple. And my life was very full. There were the twins. There was my marriage—good then, better now, fine always; we've worked on it, examined our assumptions. But to understand this story you have to imagine yourself back then, back before Betty Friedan described the 'problem that has no name.'

"I asked my new friend to the country, alone, just as you are here tonight. The children stayed in Boston with their father—he was good about helping me to get away now and then, and they were all involved in Red Sox games and other things I could never pretend interest in. He thought it might be good for me to talk to someone—'girl talk,' he called it. None of us had any decent language for women friends." And Henrietta stopped and began to cry, not loudly, no noise at all. The tears fell silently. "Maybe you can guess the rest," she said.

Kate nodded. "She misunderstood, or you did. She made what used to be called a pass. Today I think they would say she came onto you. Were you terrified?"

"It isn't even right to call it a pass. It was a gesture of love. I can see that now. Then, I simply went rigid with terror. And that's what I felt: sheer, paralyzing terror. I knew nothing about women loving women, except that I feared it; we had been taught to fear it. My terror was obvious."

"And she ran away?"

"No. She didn't run. We went on with the evening—we'd arrived in late afternoon—we went on with dinner, we 'made conversation.' I never really understood the agony of that phrase until then. Somewhere in her diaries Woolf talks of beating up the waves of conversation. We did that. Nothing helped—not wine, not food. We said nothing that mattered. The next morning she was gone."

"Gone from graduate school, too?"

"Yes. I had no idea where she was or what had become of her. I tried, discreetly of course, to find out, but she seemed simply to have vanished—the way graduate students do vanish, from time to time. Sometimes they surface again, sometimes not. Once in a while—and this is what terrified me most—they kill themselves."

"But she went off and had an affair with a man."

"You seem to know the story. Is it as ordinary as all that?"

"Not a bit. One doesn't need to be a detective to guess the next step as you tell it. You've just kept it a secret so long."

"It was such a daring plot, you see. I didn't ever want to wreck the magic of that scene by telling anyone. It succeeded beyond my wildest hopes."

"You planned it."

"Of course. She was very clear about not wanting the baby, as she had been clear about having it. A rarely honest woman, for that time. She adored the child, but recognized her impatience, her lack of desire to be a mother, let alone a single mother. She had never told the father she was pregnant; she never told me who he was. I keep saying how different it all was in those days. You have to remember that.

"Caroline was a magic child—that made the plot easier. One of those children who are friendly, open, greet all the world with delight. I made excuses to visit the country house alone. It wasn't hard. I had work to do, and my husband knew the summer with the children here and guests was not an easy time for intense work. Caroline was brought here secretly, for a short time each day. I played with her. A game. I was in the house, Caroline was put down by the bushes, and she came toward the house to find me. It's simple, isn't it, when you know?"

"Did your husband know?" Kate asked.

"No. I was terribly tempted to tell him, but it was clear he would play his part better if he didn't know it was a part. His being off the scene was just chance; I didn't plan that."

Kate thought about it a while. "And your friend," she finally asked, "what became of her?"

"She died. In some freak accident. It was horrible. I heard only later, by chance. All the time she was here with the child, she never melted, never said anything meaningful beyond 'Help me' in the beginning, and, just before the end, 'Goodbye.' She crept off through the woods as Caroline moved toward the twins."

"Your plot worked more perfectly than most plots. Like magic."

"Just like magic. I didn't even know the Rayleys would be reached immediately that day or would come so soon. That afternoon's legend has always seemed to me to have some of the qualities of an Homeric hymn. But before and after the afternoon, that's the sorrow. We never made it up; she never forgave me."

Kate could find nothing to say except, "There's Caroline."

"Yes," Henrietta answered. "And she's your friend. Neither of you is my friend."

"That can always change," Kate said. "Maybe this time you'll find the words to change all that."

"Don't tell Caroline," Henrietta said. "Don't tell anyone."

"No," Kate said. "But I shall be breaking a promise to Caroline. I promised to tell her if there was ever an answer. Perhaps one day you'll let me keep that promise, or you'll keep it for me."

"Perhaps. But there are no parents for Caroline to find."

"There is a friendship between two women when that was rare enough. And there is the magic afternoon. That's more than most of us begin with."

Henrietta only shook her head. And after a time, she went to bed, leaving Kate by the fire. In the morning, before Kate left, Henrietta spoke cheerfully of other things. The sun was not yet bright on the lawn as Kate drove away.

SECONDHAND ROSE

by Joyce Christmas

Lady Margaret Priam became aware of the growing murmur outside the door that led into the stone-walled basement of the Upper East Side (and very upper class) church that had been donated for use by the annual charity sale of discarded luxury wearables of New York society. The pale-gray stone walls gave the big room a vaguely gothic feel, notwithstanding the thoroughly utilitarian fluorescent lights that marched across the low ceiling.

The sale was but minutes away. Ten, to be precise.

"We'll do so well today, all these *divine* designer frocks," Lucia Winchester said to Margaret. Lucia was one of the painfully thin sisterhood who lunched on meager salads at all the best places, but she was not as young as the deft plastic surgeon's knife and the expert hair colorist had attempted to make her. She must have known it, and very likely it troubled her greatly when she stood before the three-way mirror in the dressing room of her handsome Park Avenue apartment in full party-going regalia. Happily, the legs were still good.

"They *are* a bit out of date or we wouldn't have them," Lucia went on. Her hair was pulled back and fastened by one of those big black velvet bows. Terribly girlish; it didn't take a year away from her. "The furs alone! I know a *great* many women refuse to wear fur nowadays, but that's to our advantage. Look at those cast-off minks and foxes! Of course no one would donate a sable no matter how committed to animal . . . things. It would be like giving away the Mercedes!"

Her high-pitched, nervous laugh occurred without her opening her mouth.

"Just my little joke," Lucia said hastily, "but my *dear* Lady Margaret, when you think how much *we* paid for all these lovely things, it's almost a *sin*. Well, all for a good cause. There are even a few of my old things—old friends really—going off to help the less fortunate. Alvin says he'll get a nice deduction . . ." That laugh again. "You know how husbands are!"

Even Lucia Winchester had to pause for breath, but Lady Margaret was caught off guard by the sudden cessation of speech.

"It does look promising," Margaret said quickly, and saw that Lucia was surveying the portable pipe racks of gowns, dresses, jackets, knitwear, and coats with a look of narrow-eyed concentration, as though she were seeing many, many old friends about to be sent off to unspeakable fates in Queens or Brooklyn or even the Bronx. The ladies on Lucia's committee, however, did not seem troubled by the fate of the clothes as they busily arranged items on display tables and chattered animatedly.

Margaret really had no clear idea of what sort of people waited behind the mighty basement door prepared to pick over a great many size six frocks that might have appeared in the pages of *Vogue* or *Harper's Bazaar* two or three years ago. Other than the quality of the merchandise, however, she expected it would not be much different from the village jumble sales back home in her native England: one woman's unwearables were another's treasures.

"Some *exquisite* Kenny Lane costume jewelry, did you see it?" Lucia was saying. "And *wonderful* handbags. The men's clothes, too—shirts, ties, jackets, even evening wear. The lapels aren't quite *right* for this year, but the buyers will never notice."

What Margaret had mostly noticed was that she, a titled expatriate Brit living in New York on fairly modest means, could never have afforded the original retail prices of the donated goods. In fact, she would have loved the chance to pick through the racks *prior* to the sale, but Lucia had been adamant about not allowing her committee women to enjoy pre-sale privileges. Something about those substantial tax deductions allowed the contributors, or perhaps it was merely to keep the volunteers from engaging in indecorous struggles over a Valentino or a Lagerfeld outfit that was only the tiniest bit passé.

"And *dear* Lady Margaret . . ." The title rolled trippingly and unctuously from Lucia's tongue. Her rosy lips, which would have made Estee Lauder and the entire cosmetics department of Bloomingdale's proud, curved into a bright if insincere smile. ". . . we on the committee are so *honored* that you could find time to help us." She didn't quite curtsy. Margaret, in her mid-thirties, thought it unseemly to be fawned over by a woman twenty-five years her senior (but who might admit under torture to fifteen).

Margaret said, "I'm sure I'll have no trouble handling the cash-box, and it's really my privilege to assist . . ." She couldn't for the moment remember the charity she'd been roped into working for by her dear friend Dianne Stark. ". . . your wonderful organization."

Lucia Winchester wasn't listening. Her eyes, with their discreet application of liner, shadow, highlighter, and mascara, were darting nervously about the low-ceilinged basement. The committee ladies in their expensive suits and sweater sets were beginning to take up their posts at the tables set up about the room. Margaret had drawn cashier duty, and was near the exit where all would stop to pay for their selections.

Dianne Stark, looking well-put-together, as befitted a young Manhattan socialite with a rich husband, carried one more arm-load of dresses from the back room where the clothes were priced and hung them on a metal rack.

"Curtain up, almost," Dianne said as she joined Margaret and Lucia. "I have just put a modest price tag on one of my very own dresses. Paid a fortune for it, but Charlie hated it right from the start, so here it is."

Charles Stark and his much younger wife Dianne were shining

lights of marital happiness in society's often cruel and unhappy world—probably because Dianne was willing to surrender to charity a beloved frock her husband disliked.

"We do get the tax deduction," Dianne said, "but that scarcely makes up for donating a dress one bought at the designer's spring show in Paris only two years ago. Margaret darling, if you ever decide to marry that beau of yours, take my word. No dress is worth a household disruption. You can always quiver a lip and get a more acceptable one."

Lucia's smile was wan. "You're so witty, Dianne. Ah-*ha!* That . . . that *woman* has put the scarves and belts in the *wrong* place. I *told* her near the sweaters the accessories near the *sweaters*." Lucia flew across the room to the offending display, where a slim, attractive young woman with stunning red hair and pale, perfect skin was arranging and rearranging pretty little items on two card tables set together.

"I shouldn't have said that," Dianne said in a low voice. "I am ashamed. Poor Lucia's quivering lips don't carry much weight these days."

Margaret shook her head in ignorance.

"The Winchester marriage is in trouble. Everybody knows. Alvin Winchester has his trophy wife picked out—younger, prettier—who's waiting in the wings for poor Lucia to be offloaded into the limbo of dumped Park Avenue wives. You never keep up with the gossip."

"Oh . . ." Margaret felt a genuine pang of sympathy for the tiresome Lucia. "Do I know her?" Then she caught herself. Manhattan society gossip could indeed become addicting. "I shouldn't be asking." Yet, in spite of herself, she was curious.

Dianne lifted her chin in the direction of the counter where Lucia was briskly dragging the accessories tables to the spot where sweaters and blouses were piled, while the red-haired woman watched unsmilingly. "That's her. Verity Humble. Very brave of Lucia to have her on the committee, don't you think? As if nobody knew."

"Brave of Miss Humble to accept under the circumstances."

Margaret recognized Verity Humble. "I believe I saw her at a cocktail party last month. She was with some well-fed man three times her age. Oh! Would it have been the straying Mr. Winchester?"

Dianne nodded. "While Lucia was out in Arizona at Canyon Ranch getting slimmed and aerobicized. Look—everybody is watching them."

The committee ladies were, indeed, frozen in place, pretending not to notice that Lucia wore a bright, hate-filled smile as she fussed about with handfuls of scarves. Verity stood stonefaced behind the table.

"I hope," Margaret said softly, "there won't be any trouble."

Then the great wooden door opened, and a surge of women and a few men poured into the basement.

"No, no!" Lucia's voice rose shrilly above the chatter. "*All* bags and coats *must* be checked outside." She flew across the room and hustled a bewildered middle-aged woman in a trench coat with a large canvas shoulder bag back into the hall.

Dianne smiled cynically. "They steal, some of them. The nicest-looking people, too. Look, there's Benny Close. Do you know him? He does the costumes for an Off-Broadway theater company that Charlie and I support. Delightful man. He comes every year to pick up things for new productions."

Dianne waved to a broad, short man with a reddish face, a shock of white hair, and a tweedy jacket with leather elbow patches. He responded with a courtly bow and then elbowed an elderly woman neatly out of his way in order to go through a rack of evening gowns.

Lucia was back, breathing heavily from her encounter with the rumored Other Woman in her domestic upheaval as well as with the offending canvas bag. "Now remember, Lady Margaret. One of you takes the money and makes change, the other bags the goods and staples the bag. For the jewelry and small items, we do it in the European style. The volunteers give the customer a sales check, she pays you, you initial it, and Madame Customer hands the receipt back to receive her pretty little faux diamond pin. Got that?"

"Got it," Margaret said. The words didn't sound quite right in her English accent, but never mind.

"What is going on over there? They're throwing those lovely things around as if they were rags! Miss Humble really should be keeping them under control." Gravely incensed now, Lucia was off again, ostensibly to keep order, but perhaps to take this new opportunity to pour her wrath out on flame-haired Verity Humble.

"If you don't mind . . ." A dumpy young woman in a heavy turtleneck and jeans thrust a satin and chiffon evening dress at Margaret. "I want to pay for this."

The dress was priced at a hundred dollars—probably nine hundred or so less than it had cost brand new. It was not remotely the young woman's size, but who was Margaret to argue? She took her money and gave the dress to Dianne to wrap.

Dianne said, "Hello, Benny. Found something to tempt you?"

Benny beamed. "Have I ever, Dianne my pet. Just what one always hopes to find. Somebody has been exceedingly generous."

Benny held up a beautiful long black taffeta gown with a graceful, wide skirt, a deep V neckline, and a huge red silk rose at the waist. It was not a current fashion by any means, but Margaret recognized it as one of those classics that live forever. People in England didn't donate dresses like this one. If they had them, they trotted them out year after year.

"I caught a glimpse of one or two other things as well," Benny said, "but these women attack like sharks." He shrugged. "They never see the really good things, so I'll take my time."

"It's a gift you have, Benny," Dianne said, "being able to spot a designer from fifty paces. Who did this one?"

"You'd recognize the name," he said coyly. "One of those single-name fellows . . ."

"Can we keep that here behind the table for you?" Margaret asked. She rather wanted a look at the name on the label.

Benny shook his head. "Not this piece," he said, clutching the black dress to his chest. "Amazing what you find stuffed away in a corner among the secondhand lacy peignons and velvet dressing gowns." He shifted the gown to his arm, and looked questioningly at Margaret. "Lady Margaret Priam, is it? I thought I recognized you. And have seen your name in the social columns, of course."

As Margaret handed over change to a woman who was buying several blouses and an alligator bag—at a very reasonable price—she was aware that Benny Close was looking her up and down, taking in her short blond hair, rosy English complexion, her heavy silk blouse and nubby green wool skirt cinched at the waist with a supple leather belt.

"Dianne says nice things about you, Mr. Close," Margaret said. "I understand your talents are legendary."

"Then you must come along to our new production to see," he said. "We're doing *The Women*. Clare Boothe wrote it back in the thirties, but it's still so wonderfully bitchy and so timely still. I envision very very fancy dress. I have a Halston number and a Christian LaCroix you wouldn't believe, and now this. I'd love to find more sequins, and another true classic like this one. Ah, Lucia darling. You're the woman with a wardrobe to dream about. Such exquisite taste, and over so many years."

Lucia flushed beneath her well-contrived makeup. "Benny. I . . . see you're planning to contribute to our little charity with a purchase." She made a fluttery gesture toward the dress. "Wherever did you find that old thing? I don't remember seeing it on the racks."

"This old thing was stuffed in among the men's suits, and it will do for my second act. Isn't that little Verity Humble over there? Such a beauty."

Margaret tried to determine, in between making change and handing garments over to Dianne for bagging, whether there was anything malicious in Benny's voice or demeanor. He surely could not have spoken with perfect innocence, but his expression was cheerfully bland.

Lucia was another matter. If looks could kill was an understatement. Dianne caught Margaret's eye and winced.

Benny went on as if Lucia Winchester wasn't sincerely wishing him dead. "Yes, I do need more sparkle."

"I saw several things out there," Dianne said quickly. "Forty-pound beaded jackets and skimpy little sequined dresses—the sort of things you can only wear once because they're so noticeable, and people do remember, and then they think you can't afford . . ."

Margaret knew Dianne was not so insecure that she'd not dare to wear the same outfit twice to a gala. She must be trying to ease the tension Benny had created.

"I must see about straightening out those racks," Lucia said coldly. "These people have no sense of the niceties. Dianne, do see that the people in line are taken care of. We don't have time to waste on chatting with our friends." Lucia turned on her heel and plunged into the throng.

Benny looked after her with a strange, sad smile, and shook his head. "She was a real beauty once and now she's not giving up gracefully. Of course, she's never forgiven me for introducing Alvin to a lovely little actress a few years back who's gone on to do *quite* well in television. And of course, she never invites me to her little dinners and the like anymore."

The line at the cashbox was beginning to build. Apparently many of the customers at the sale were experts at combing the merchandise quickly and escaping fast with their goodies.

"Look at that!" Margaret exclaimed suddenly and rather too loudly.

A very tall woman in an elaborate frosted hairdo and really extreme makeup made a grand entrance. She wore impossibly high-heeled boots, tight jeans, and a shocking-pink satin blouse dripping with faux Chanel chains. The bargain hunters fell back at her progress.

Dianne looked up from folding a very nice cashmere sweater. "Oh, him," she said. "He shows up every year. He likes the finer things in life, wardrobe-wise."

The man—for indeed it was a man—headed for the dress racks.

Benny said, "That one has a better eye than even I do. I'd best get back, to my search before I lose out on all the good things."

The line at the cashbox was becoming impatient, so Margaret

and Dianne were forced to concentrate on totaling purchases, making change, and wrapping the goods. From time to time, Margaret caught glimpses of that mass of frosted hair above the racks of dresses and coats. Lucia seemed to have disappeared, although her arch foe Verity Humble bustled out of the back room with a new pile of belts, scarves, and handbags to replenish the accessories tables. Benny Close had accumulated a real armload now; he appeared to have discovered plenty of sparkle among the goods for sale.

"Won't someone please relieve us for lunch," Dianne muttered as noon approached, then said brightly to an older lady who had purchased a pair of barely worn Manilo Blahnik shoes, "I hope you enjoy them, ma'am, and thank you so very much." Dianne, having begun her adult life as a flight attendant, was very good with the public.

"I could use a sit down," Margaret said. The line had diminished considerably. "Handle the money for a moment, and let me see if I can't find Lucia to win a temporary reprieve from our post."

As Margaret made her way across the basement toward the back room where the donated clothes had been unpacked and priced, a terrific scream bounced off the low ceiling and the stone walls. The few customers froze, then slowly turned their heads in the direction of the scream. The chins of committee ladies behind the jewelry table dropped in a most unbecoming fashion.

Margaret kept moving forward, glancing between the pipe racks still laden with dresses, suits, and coats.

She reached the end of the room where the men's clothes were hanging. Between a rack of suits and another of sports jackets and casual shirts in designs no man she knew would consider for a second, she came upon a pale middle-aged woman clutching two neckties in one hand and the other to her mouth. She was staring down at the body of Benny Close surrounded by the fashion treasures he'd acquired. His normally reddish face was more or less purplish now and his open eyes stared blindly at the ceiling. There was something metal and gold around his neck.

The woman took her hand from her mouth and appeared to be on the brink of another scream.

"Don't!" Margaret said sharply.

The woman gulped and didn't.

Dianne came up behind Margaret. "Oh, Benny! Is he all right?"

"I think not," Margaret said. "Close the main door and keep everyone over there. Have someone call an ambulance—and the police, think."

"What *now?*" Lucia bustled out of the back room. Hysteria lay close to the surface. She stopped short when she saw Benny.

Margaret knelt beside him, but it was clear that he was dead, strangled by one of those pretty heavy chain belts that had become so widely popular that the upper crust felt the need to dispose of theirs and move on to new fashion horizons. She looked up to see all of the committee ladies, and the few customers, including the man in women's clothes, craning their necks to see the awful sight.

It must be rather like reality television to them, Margaret thought. "Please go away," she said aloud. Then she stood up and looked over the crowd, which appeared to have no intention of moving back. Red-haired Verity Humble, the keeper of the bags, scarves, and belts, was not among them.

"Go over there," she said in a commanding voice. They blinked, and they all moved.

"I was looking for a jacket in my husband's size," the woman who'd found Benny said, "and look what happens. They told me this sale was run by a nice class of women."

"Perhaps only in their own minds," Margaret said. She was staring at Benny surrounded by his selections. The red and yellow sequin design on the front of a rather elaborate gown sparkled in the overhead fluorescent lights.

Margaret didn't want to touch anything until the professionals arrived, and yet . . . She pushed the clothes gently with her toe, disarranging them as little as possible until she was satisfied.

"Lucia, we'd better wait with the others by the door for the ambulance and the police. They'll want to speak with you."

"Me? Why me?"

"You're the chairperson. Did you notice what's become of Verity Humble? She seems to have disappeared."

"Verity!" Lucia fastened on that quickly. "Of course! She took one of those belts and . . . there's a back door. Poor, poor Benny. He was such a nice man, one of the few theater people we ever invited to our home. How could she do this?" Lucia's makeup wasn't holding up well, and neither was she. "Verity is *not* a nice person. This just proves it."

"Mmmm," Margaret said noncommittally. She wondered if Verity's lack of niceness was more a matter of leaving a mess she didn't want to be involved in than creating the mess in the first place. Margaret took Lucia's elbow and guided her to the exit door near the cashier's table. The committee ladies withdrew to little whispering clumps, having seen enough of a dead man in the midst of all their former finery.

The frosted-haired person said in a husky voice, "Is one of you in charge?" He fastened on Margaret. "He had a lovely *robe de bal* I had my eye on, yellow and red sequins, but he got to it before I did. You think I could . . . ?"

"Sorry," Margaret said. "The sale is suspended."

Dianne said, "Sit down, Lucia. You look awful."

"It was a terrible shock," Lucia said mechanically. "Losing an old friend like that."

Dianne looked at Margaret, puzzled, and started to speak. Margaret motioned for her to keep silent. Dianne was going to protest that Benny was scarcely an old friend of Lucia's.

"It might make you feel better if you talked," Margaret said, then added casually, "I suppose we'll find it in the back room, Lucia. I do understand."

"I don't," Dianne murmured.

"Nor do I," Lucia said somewhat shrilly. "Send the police after that woman. I really have to put myself together. I must look a fright." She started to stand.

"You look fine," Margaret said untruthfully, "and you do understand me." It was tempting simply to allow Lucia to go off to fix her face and slip out the back way. "I know what you did."

Lucia gave up. "It was the most wonderful dress I ever owned, and naturally I own a great many superb things. Givenchy made it just for me nearly thirty years ago. He gave it to me with his own hands, practically. I was photographed in it by Norman Parkinson. It's a museum piece now. I was planning to leave it to the Metropolitan Museum's costume collection when I died." She looked up at Margaret, and the facade of proud society matron crumbled. She was merely an unhappy middle-aged woman on the brink of losing her husband and her gratifying social circumstances. "It's even in my will," she said. "Alvin kept nagging me to get rid of my clothes, clear out the closets—I do have really lovely big closets." She sniffed back a tear. "He wanted me to contribute things to the sale that I never wore. He didn't understand, but I thought if I did whatever he asked, he'd think twice about that—that—woman."

"So you donated it and then hid it away here. You planned to take it back, but Benny poked around and found it. Maybe he even recognized it as yours? Well, never mind that, but, Lucia, why did you bring it here at all? A friend could have kept it for you."

Lucia tried to speak, and then the big tears began to slip down her cheeks, severely damaging her makeup. "Alvin was there when I packed my dresses, he made a list for tax purposes, he was with me when our driver dropped me off here. How could you know what happened with Benny?"

"There was no black dress with a big red rose among the clothes he had with him when his body was found," Margaret said. "From what he said, he wouldn't give that dress up. Someone who wanted it badly would have had to kill him to take it from him."

What Margaret thought was: People will do amazing things to protect old friends.

SCARS

Kristine Kathryn Rusch

Her solace: those weekday afternoons before the school got out and the children invaded the pool. For the last two weeks, the weather had been fair. Sunlight streamed in the floor-to-ceiling windows on the north and south faces of the pool area, dappling the water with brilliant yellow light. Rena particularly liked the way the light filtered into the artificial blue depths below the surface. When she swam into such a patch, the water felt warmer, even though it couldn't be.

The pool was part of a rec center only four blocks from her new apartment, a fact that frustrated her more than the apartment itself. The apartment had three small windows facing south and east with barely enough room on the sills for her small collection of malingering plants. The counters were too low, the toilet too high, and the chrome bar in the shower always caught her in the back. More than anything, she hated the apartment's silence and hoped, at her six-month review, the shrink at the pain center would say she had recovered enough to care for a cat.

By contrast, the pool was never silent. Not even when she was underwater. She heard the rustle of the filters, the splashing of the other lap swimmers, and the rhythmic bubbles caused by her exhaled breath. When she surfaced, she heard voices and laughter, the radio on a rock-and-roll station she would never play, and the phone, constant and shrill against the echoey boom of the large room itself. She never paid attention to what happened on the decks. The fact that anything happened at all was enough for her.

Saturday, now, Saturday was different. She never went to the pool on Saturday, sayings its pleasures for the weekday, and for the pool attendants who were older. The teenagers who guarded the place on the weekends stared at her. They couldn't hide their revulsion. The adults were more skilled at concealing their shock.

But this Saturday her stereo's tuner went on the fritz, sliding past each station she tried to tune in. For a halfhour she got Christian broadcasting, mixing exhortations against sins of the flesh with some pretty good soft rock, and then that too faded into static. She had seen all the movies on television, and she had no interest in sports. Her neighbors across the street seemed to be out of town; their little girl and mongrel puppy had not been outside all day—an event Rena lived for—the vitality, joy, and love those two shared made her happy even while it made her ache.

She could no longer stand the silence. She grabbed her swim bag and let herself out the front door, promising herself that the stares would not bother her this time, would not ruin her solace.

She walked, as she always did, head down, wincing every time a car whooshed by. Cars still frightened her. It had taken her nearly a month to get enough nerve to take the bus. Before that, she had had Meals on Wheels and hoped that they never realized she wasn't really a shut-in.

The first hurdle came in the rec center. She stopped at the window and paid for her session. Disability, combined with the insurance and settlement money, left her more than enough to buy a membership, but she enjoyed being anonymous here. In her old life, she would have been greeted by name—she would have known everyone's name—but here she ignored the faces and personal histories as much as possible. The girl at the window was new, a recent survivor of the life-saving course who had that fresh-faced, bright-eyed athleticism so appealing in people under twenty-five.

She smiled when she saw Rena, an open, welcoming smile that

made Rena cringe. "Good thing you got here now," the girl said. "I was about to leave."

Rena glanced at the clock. Still a half hour before closing, but that late the desk attendants usually left money collection to the lifeguard. "I have time to swim, don't I?" she asked.

"Sure," the girl said. "In district or out?"

In response, Rena put a dollar and three quarters on the counter, signifying in district membership. It took a moment for her to get the last quarter out of her pocket; she was concentrating on that and so the girl's stare caught her off guard. The ribbed pink skin, the scars crisscrossing the back of her hand were the worst of her wounds; she had crisped both hands and most of her arms reaching into the burning car for Robbie.

The doctors were amazed that she had regained almost total use of them, but how did one tell that to an eighteen-year-old girl who had never left her hometown?

Rena didn't explain. She pushed open the door to the women's locker room and sighed when she heard voices in the shower. The hair dryer was running, and a woman was speaking baby talk in the changing area. A toilet flushed while Rena stood, indecisive. Did she go past the showers, past the perfect naked bodies, or around the concrete dividing wall directly into the changing area, past the full-length mirror?

She opted for the showers, noting that the women weren't perfect, their elderly bodies ringed with excess weight and tiny lumps of fatty tissue. They were talking to each other, oblivious to their nakedness, something she loved about women over fifty who had somehow learned to accept age with grace and not to mourn the loss of their youthful figures. She had talked to one of them once, a woman who had just had a pacemaker put in and who still wore a two-piece bathing suit despite a long vertical scar.

Six women stood in the changing area—apparently a class had let out—and one little girl who was standing on the bench, holding the handle of the suit wringer, volunteering to get the water out of everyone's suit. Rena kept her gaze averted and walked to the farthest corner. She set her bag on the wooden bench and undressed slowly, hoping no one watched.

She tried not to watch herself. In the space of an evening, she had lost her husband, her child, and the body she had grown up with. Somehow her face had been spared despite the intense, blistering heat when the gas can in the trunk ignited as she was pulling open the door to save an already dead Robbie. Now, every time she saw herself, that night came back in a blaze of orange against a moonlit sky—broken glass raining all around her; the smell of inky smoke, gasoline, and burning flesh as vivid as the moment it happened. Only the smell of chlorine diluted it. Only when she breathed into the water did she feel as if she were blowing black smoke out of her lungs forever.

With shaking hands she pulled out her neon—green one-piece suit. The color was hideous, but at least it wasn't black or red or yellow or any mixture of those three. She slipped it on, then wrapped herself in her towel, hiding in its fluffy warmth. She could feel the gazes upon her, but she pretended she didn't care.

She walked past the women with what dignity she could and headed into the pool area. This late in the day most of the swimmers were gone. Only the middle lane was taken by a man Rena had never seen before. The lifeguard—a tall, reedy girl-woman—stood feet apart and life stick clutched against her stomach. She watched the swimmer intently as if she could control each breath he took.

Rena hung up her towel, took a kickboard off the stack, and climbed in the shallow end. The water was cold, and she realized with a shock that she had forgotten to take the required shower. She shot a quick glance at the lifeguard, as if she were going to get kicked out of the pool for failing to follow the rules, but the lifeguard didn't seem to notice.

The man finished his lap, surfaced, and shook the water off his face like a shaggy dog. Rena slipped into the water, hiding her body. He smiled at her and she smiled back, glad he couldn't see how she really looked. His hair was long and dark; it matched the long dark hair on the rest of his body. He put both hands on the side of the pool and levered himself out.

She left her kickboard on the side, then slid underwater completely and pushed off cater-corner for the deep end. She loved the pool when it was empty. She felt almost normal then. Her doctor was so proud of her: when he first saw her after she had moved here, he thought she would never regain full use of her body again. But he had recommended the swimming, saying that non-weight-bearing exercise would stretch her scars gradually and, combined with physical therapy, might give her a normal range of movement. After spending the first week in terror of revealing her body, she finally went to the pool and remembered her love for the water. It was that love, not any dedication to health, that gave her what little freedom she had now.

The laps felt easy; she had found a rhythm. She kept her count, eyes open. A child had left a tiny ring on the bottom, and she was half tempted to dive for it, or maybe catch it with her hand. As she made her flip turn and headed for the deep end, she began planning her move. She glanced at the lifeguard, saw her talking to a slender man—a boy really—as tall as the guard herself. Not the right time then. She was still insecure enough that she wanted the lifeguard's eyes on her when she tried something new.

On the sixtieth lap, she heard a whoop echo over the music. Disappointment ran through her. School was out, and the children would take over for rec swim. Then she remembered: no school. It was Saturday. The pool would close soon. The call was probably the lifeguard warning her to get out.

But she only had ten more laps to go. If the lifeguard wanted her out, she would have to touch her to get her attention. Rena swam as fast and as hard as she could. The push felt good. In water, at least, her body obeyed her.

When she was finished, she pulled off her goggles and squinted at the clock. The pool should have closed fifteen minutes before. The lifeguard was going to be mad at her. She sighed. She probably should have paid attention to that call.

She climbed out of the pool, the water dripping off her body, and grabbed her kickboard. The air, which had seemed warm when she got in, now had a chill. Someone had left the door to the Jacuzzi open. She peered through, but no one sat outside. The Jacuzzi was silent. She went back in and headed for the pile of kickboards.

Rena didn't see the blood until she stepped in it. It was warm and thick, not cool and thin like pool water. She set her kickboard on the pile and swallowed—hard—thinking perhaps she was having one of her nightmares in the daylight. But no. The body was real. The lifeguard lay flat on her back, left hand in the water, eyes open and unseeing, blood draining from one long slash across her throat.

It took the police five minutes to arrive. While she waited, Rena huddled by the phone in the pool office. She shivered in the cool air. She had retained enough presence mind to touch nothing—she hadn't even taken her towel off its peg. Each second felt like an hour. She stared at the clock, concentrating on the movement of the hands, forcing herself to think of nothing but that.

Her psychologist would have been proud of her: no screaming fits, no flashbacks, no posttraumatic shock. She had stayed calm. She wasn't letting herself think about what had happened while she was happily doing her laps.

The sound of a car's wheels crunching gravel in the parking lot frayed her nerves even more. She stiffened, barely allowing herself to breathe. Outside the engine shuddered to a halt. Car doors opened and released a burst of static from the police radio. Then the first door slammed, followed quickly by the other.

She should have gotten up, but she half expected them to die in the parking lot. As if the murderer were still out there, waiting, not attacking her because she was invisible to him. But footsteps rang on the tile floor, the sound echoing over the now-calm water.

"Hello?"

The sound made her jump even though she expected it. She tried to answer, found her voice stuck in her throat. She swallowed, then managed, "Over here."

As the footsteps approached, she gripped the plastic seat of the stool. The policeman who peered in was redheaded, freckled, and young. No, not young, boyish. But his eyes had a maturity that she recognized. He was in his thirties, as she was, only time had improved his features instead of ruining them.

His gaze was flat as he took her in. She cringed even more, not used to such scrutiny but unwilling to look away. He grabbed her towel from the peg and tossed it at her.

"You look cold," he said.

She wrapped the towel around herself and nodded. The terry-cloth was plush, warm, and soft against her skin. She had very little feeling in her hands and arms, but the rest of her scars, left by a hundred pieces of broken glass, had nerve endings intact.

"She's—by the lifeguard station," Rena said.

"I know." His voice was gentle. "My partner's with her."

Rena let out the air she had been holding. She could feel the terror nibbling at her edges, threatening to overwhelm her.

"Did you see what happened?" he asked.

She shook her head, swallowed. "I was swimming." Then heard how odd that sounded. Swimming while a woman died.

"And you saw nothing?"

She shifted under the towel. A tingling formed inside her, energy building up. "I heard a yell. I thought she wanted me to get out of the pool. I—" she looked away. "I wanted to finish my laps."

He leaned against the door, his thumbs hooked on the pockets of his jeans. He wasn't wearing a uniform; she hadn't noticed until that moment. His blue chambray shirt and faded denim gave her a degree of comfort. "Were you the only one in the pool?"

"There was a man in the dressing room, I think. He had just got out. And . . ." She frowned, an image she couldn't quite reach flitting through her mind. "Someone. I thought I saw someone. But I don't remember."

Two more cars pulled up. At the sound of their engines the shakiness she had kept inside moved out. Her entire body trembled.

"You need to get dressed," he said.

She glanced at the locker room door. "Don't you need to look for evidence?"

His smile was rueful. "You watch a lot of crime shows."

She shrugged.

"I'll take you home. You can change there. Then we'll need you at the station to make a statement."

She bit her lower lip to keep her teeth from chattering. It took all of her strength to force out the words. "Am I under arrest?"

"Not right now," he said.

Rena had never had a guest in her apartment. For the first time she saw it through someone else's eyes. The obsessive neatness of a single person's life, the coffee table with one book overturned to the correct page, the television remote next to the only dented spot on the couch, the absence of knickknacks, crocheted pillows, photographs—anything that would have made a house a home. She had had a home with Dennis and Robbie; she couldn't bear to be in it after they were gone.

"I'll just be a minute," she said.

She fled the living room without looking over her shoulder for the detective's reaction. In the car he had told her his name, Joel Bellin, as if they were meeting on the street instead of over a dead body. She was the one who had insisted on "detective." She didn't want to forget his words. "Not right now" meant that she would be charged later. And she didn't want to be too comfortable with the man who charged her.

The bedroom door had no lock, but the bathroom's did. She grabbed a shirt and a pair of jeans and set them on the laundry hamper. She was so cold and shaken that she couldn't forgo the shower. Still she had to check the lock twice before she felt safe enough to take off her suit.

The water warmed her and made the trembling stop. She got dressed quickly, and except for her wet hair curling around her shoulders and the faint scent of chlorine, she felt as if she had never been to the pool. It took a minute for her fingers to grab the bathroom lock, but when she did, she let herself out.

He was still in the living room where she had left him. He stood in front of her only bookshelf, scanning the titles. There was a bit of her in the house after all. Shelf after shelf of historical novels and science fiction. Books that took her away from here, but never even pretended to unite men and women or even to examine families.

He stared at her for a moment, taking in the clothes, and then he said, "You know I'm going to ask about it eventually. You may as well tell me."

The directness was new. No one had been as blunt before. She felt heat in her cheeks. "Car accident," she said.

"You alone in the car?"

She shook her head.

"Anyone else survive?" he asked.

Orange against the black of the night, the gagging stench of smoke. Her eyes watered, remembering.

"I'm sorry," he said, and the words sounded sincere.

"It was years ago." She picked up her purse, gripping the strap carefully, and slung it over her shoulder.

"Not that many," he said.

She met his gaze. "Enough," she said, ending the conversation.

Even the police station looked clean in this town. She would have thought it safe if not for the bulletproof glass over every window. Bellin led her through the back tunnels, painted white to hide the concrete architects had thought so important in the late sixties. The air had a processed smell, lacking only the stale odor of cigarette smoke to make it feel like the office building she used to work in when she lived in the Midwest. But this was the West. No one smoked in public here.

Voices echoed down the hallway first, mixed with ringing phones and the blare of a radio. She straightened, bracing herself, and Bellin glanced at her, then looked away. She hated the way he saw everything yet said nothing. Either he should comment or stop looking.

He pushed open the double doors, and suddenly she was enveloped in the cacophony. The conversations didn't stop when she entered. People sitting on desks, behind desks, interviewing other people, some in uniform, some not. Two women stood by the coffee machine stirring Sweet'n Low into steaming chipped mugs. A man, feet propped on his desk, phone cradled between his shoulder and ear, looked at her face, then her hands, then at Bellin, apparently realizing that her injuries were not current, not today's problem.

"This the suspect?" a woman whose voice had the rich, deep timbre of a natural contralto asked.

Rena jumped. Suspect. She hadn't expected it so soon.

Bellin took her elbow, sliding his hand under her forearm, and braced her palm. Her curved fingers, their deep scars, the pink skin, flared like neon in the room. She couldn't look up at the woman who spoke.

"How much range of movement you got, honey?" the woman asked.

Rena tried to grab Bellin's forefinger, wincing as the skin pulled. She could make a tight fist, but it was work. She could move her fingers out of the fist easily, but she couldn't straighten the fingers at all.

"You're right," the woman said. "No way. Not holding and stabbing at the same time."

Finally Rena brought her head up. The woman was short and stocky, but her heaviness was in her muscular shoulders, her powerful arms. Her skin was the color of good coffee, and her dark hair hung straight over her ears.

"I'd like to take a statement from you," the woman said.

"Am I a suspect?" Rena asked. She would find a lawyer if she had to. She could afford it. The money sat in four different accounts, untouched. Blood money. Some actuary's estimate of the price of human lives.

"No," Bellin said. He let go of her arm, and it fell to her side, still warm from his touch. "I'll drive you back when you're done."

"Thanks," she said, but he had already turned away, picking up papers from a cluttered desk between them. She felt bereft without him; she had been using him as a lifeline since he appeared at the pool.

"I'm Detective McCary," the woman said. "Must have been pretty frightening, coming out of that pool."

"I didn't see her at first," Rena said.

McCary led her into a small room with no windows. The concrete hadn't been painted here, and the room had a chill that felt as if it would never go away. Metal folding chairs surrounded a

Formica table with a tape recorder built into the top. McCary produced a cassette from her pocket. "You mind if I record?"

Rena shook her head. She stated her name and address as McCary asked her to do, then retold the story, detail by detail.

"And you saw no one?" McCary asked.

Rena frowned. That tantalizing sensation at the corner of her memory had returned. No one? "I saw—someone." Almost. She almost had him. "It was so brief. I was doing laps, not thinking about it." She bit her lower lip, ashamed of the next admission. "I work so hard now at ignoring people. Like maybe they won't see me if I don't see them."

"Because of the hands?" McCary asked.

Rena swallowed. "The whole body. All but my face."

"But people don't see that. And your face is striking. Model pretty."

Rena closed her eyes against the words. Dennis's words, "model pretty," as if she could have been something other than a secretary, a wife, a mother.

"Sorry," McCary said. "Didn't mean to upset you."

"The whole thing is upsetting, isn't it?" Rena said as she opened her eyes and shivered. Her hair wasn't quite dry yet, and the chill was sinking in.

Then—suddenly—the memory came: a slender man, a boy really, with a teenager's thinness, talking to her, gesturing. Rena had seen him before. In the Jacuzzi outside. He had come out of swim team practice to look at her, his eyes dark and cold as he stared. He had mumbled something under his breath, something she had to work hard at not hearing, before going inside and laughing with his friends.

"He was young. I saw him once before. I think he's on the swim team."

"Can you identify him?"

That face, long bones, not fully grown yet. An uneven beard and lips too full for a boy. And those eyes.

She nodded.

"Good," McCary said. "We'll get the entire team in for a line-up."

Rena heard the dismissal. She reached out, almost touched McCary's hand, then stopped before she could bring herself to do so. McCary watched, brows furrowed.

"The girl," Rena said. "Who was she?"

"I thought you knew," McCary said. "You been going to the pool for months."

"Not on Saturday," Rena said.

"Ah," McCary said, and she appeared to make a mental note, as if the information went into a file somewhere in her head. "She was the head cheerleader at the high school. Her father works at the university. Her mother is one of those charity wives."

"Her name?" Rena's tone was insistent, but she kept her head bowed, submissive, so she wouldn't seem too demanding. She just thought it proper that she should know who the girl was who had died on such a beautiful afternoon.

"Candace Walker." McCary smiled, and there was sadness around her eyes. "She hated to be called Candy. I always got the feeling she was waiting to be on her own so she could change her name."

"You knew her, then," Rena said.

"She went to school with my daughter. They had the same homeroom." And more, McCary's tone said. But Rena wasn't going to press. It really wasn't her business, this relationship between high school girls, now over forever.

"It must be hard for you," Rena said.

McCary studied her for a moment. "Death is always hard," she said.

Bellin drove her home. His insistence. She tried to take the bus, but he had objected. "You need to be gentle with yourself," he had said.

They didn't talk all the way across town. The radio interrupted the silence with occasional bursts of static. When he pulled up to her apartment, he stopped the car slowly. She fumbled with the latch, and for the second time that day, he touched her. He put a hand on her shoulder.

She didn't want to think about how long it had been since

someone had touched her voluntarily, with no medical purpose in mind.

"He saw you, you know," Bellin said.

She nodded, unable to look at him.

"Does he know who you are?"

"No." Her voice sounded soft, even to her.

"Does he know where you live?"

"No."

"Can he find out?"

Slowly she brought her head up, tilting her chin as her mother had once taught her for a different arrogance altogether. An arrogance that was designed for a more flirtatious age, where women had fewer rights and so had to use their attitudes to scare men away. "I'm not the kind of woman people remember."

"You're precisely the kind of person he would remember."

"But he thinks I'm beneath contempt."

"You've spoken to him?"

"Once." She flushed. The boy's words fluttered at the edge of her consciousness. If she concentrated, she would be able to hear them.

She had blocked the words for a reason. She pushed them away.

"And?"

"He doesn't believe I'm human."

The sentence made her flinch. It was only one of several things he had said, the only one she would allow herself to remember.

Bellin brought his hand up again, then clenched his fist as if uncertain about how to treat her. But he didn't say "I'm sorry," nor did he back down. "Is your name on file at the rec center?"

"I'm not a member. I always pay in cash. I prefer it if people don't know who I am." She spoke in a rush, with an anger she hadn't realized she was holding until that moment. All this stress. A girl was dead—murdered—and Rena wanted no part of it. She wanted to hide in her apartment, to find a book and disappear in someone else's world—forever.

He reached into his pocket and pulled out a card. Then he

grabbed a pen off the dash, scrawled on the back of the card, and handed it to her. "My home phone. I want you to call me if there's trouble."

"I'll call 911," she said.

"Take it anyway."

And because she could think of no way to argue, she did. Then she tugged on the door handle and pushed the heavy door open. She was glad the neighbors weren't home. What would they think, seeing the scarred woman getting out of a police car?

After she got out, she nodded to him, not sure what to say. Gratitude was inappropriate—gratitude for what? taking her away from her world?—and goodbyes seemed trite. So she said nothing. As she pushed the car door closed, he raised his hand in a half wave. She nodded, then turned her back, hurrying to the apartment because she knew he wouldn't leave until she was safely inside.

But when she got inside, she almost went back and asked him to join her. Instead she leaned on the door and scanned the apartment for changes. Nothing was out of place. The empty feeling was a familiar one. She had felt it each night since she had moved to Oregon, a painful reminder that she had no one to come home to, no one to talk with, no one who cared. If she allowed it, the feeling would turn into a full-blown panic of the kind she hadn't experienced since the Midwest, in those awful days when she had finally been released from the hospital, when the attorneys and the doctors and the insurance agents somehow thought she could live in the same house where her husband had laughed and her child had played and she had been happy for much too-brief a time.

In the middle of the night, she awoke in pitch blackness, her bed warm and her feet still cold. Her heart was pounding. She had dreamed that the boy/man was with her. He told her she wasn't worth killing, that she wasn't worth noticing at all, that people like her didn't really exist. In his left hand, he held a glass shard—tinted glass, the kind that came from car windows—and he brought it slowly, lovingly, to her face. When its point touched the fold of skin beneath her left eye, she screamed and forced herself awake.

With a shaking hand, she turned on the lamp by the bedside. She touched her face, feeling its smoothness, the only comfort she had. The room was silent. Only the hum of the refrigerator to remind her of civilization. She got out of bed and staggered into the bathroom, the stiffness in her joints making her realize how deep the panic went. She flicked on the light and peered into the mirror. Nothing marred her cheek. No scars on her face, but the hands that touched her skin were unfamiliar to her. In her dreams, her hands were unmarked, as smooth as her face.

The panic welled, like a bubble: if he wanted to find her, he could. Everyone would remember her—the scarred lady. He would wait outside her window and then let himself in, carrying a knife—a glass shard—big orange flames against the night sky.

She found herself standing over her jeans, clutching Bellin's card in her hands. She stared at his scrawl—he crossed his sevens in the European method—and slowly set the card back down. *If there's trouble*, he had said. But nightmares weren't trouble. They were expected, especially after someone had witnessed a murder.

The Sunday morning paper had Candace Walker's high school graduation photograph on page one. Rena unrolled the paper on her kitchen table and pressed the sides down while staring at the dead girl's face. Her fingers brushed the side of the plate, sticky with honey. The scent of her half-eaten English muffin mingled with the aroma of the Coffee Corner's French Roast special. But her appetite was gone.

For a minute Rena stared at the photo. It was a graduation picture. The photographer had given Candace a sensual grace she hadn't had at the pool. The soft lighting and the scooped neckline of the dress made her look as if she were about to be kissed instead of photographed for a yearbook.

Rena ran her fingers along the neckline. The ink felt soft,

smeary, and left her fingertips black. She took a deep breath and read, studying each line, looking for her name.

But the police had been careful. The article focused on the murder and the discovery of the body but did not mention any witnesses. A few of the things Rena had told them were reported to the paper by a police spokesperson, but none of the important details was present. No mention of Rena or the boy or the cause of death. But an entire paragraph devoted to the rec center's being closed until further notice.

She sighed and absently picked up her coffee mug. It slid through her fingers, catching on her thumb and spilling on Candace's photograph. Rena blotted it with her napkin, apologizing to Candace under her breath. Then realized it didn't matter at all.

The shrill cry of the phone made her freeze. Her breath knotted in her throat. The cry came again—not muffled as it was when she heard the neighbor's phone—but clear and pure. Hers. Who would call her on a Sunday? The only calls she got were from salespeople and the clinic reminding her of her appointments.

Carefully she set her coffee mug down and walked into the living room. The phone was on the end table near the spot on the couch. She pressed the speaker button to answer. It was always easier than picking up the handset.

"Yes?" She sounded vulnerable. A woman alone. She suspected all her callers knew that just from the tone of her voice.

"Rena? It's Joel Bellin."

The detective. She pressed a hand over her heart. She had recognized his voice the moment he had spoken her name. "Yes?" she said again.

He cleared his throat. "We, ah, we've rounded up the members of the swim team and will have a lineup this afternoon. I'd like to bring you in to look at them, if you don't mind."

The boy's eyes hard and cold, filled with something more than contempt. Something like hate. She had assumed it was because she was damaged. Perhaps it had been something else. "No, I don't mind," she said, but the fear came back, beating against her stomach like the wings of a trapped bird.

"I'll be there in an hour," he said.

"I'll be here," she said, and hit the button, severing the connection.

She stood over the phone for the longest time, wishing she could leave the apartment, go anywhere. Swim. But she wouldn't be able to go to the rec center now. Maybe never again. She had never revisited the site of the accident, sometimes going blocks out of her way to avoid it, finally moving halfway across the country to escape it. She certainly couldn't return to the site of the murder.

She went back into the kitchen and picked up her mug. Candace Walker's hopeful face, wrinkled from the spilled coffee, haunted her. Almost unwillingly, she read the girl's biography. Short, dry facts: good student who planned to attend the University of Oregon in the fall, survived by her parents, grandparents, and a younger brother. The obituary was longer than Robbie's had been—what does a reporter say about a five-year-old boy? He hadn't been to school yet. He had learned to walk at eight months, to read by the age of three. Accomplishments, but not the kind that made a resume. He had laughed a lot, and his hugs were fierce. He had had a little boy smell of sunshine and peanut butter.

She was gripping the mug so tightly the scars on her hand pulled. Odd she had never mourned Dennis the way she mourned Robbie, even though she had loved her husband dearly. But he had lived, and he had told her more than once that he did not fear death.

But her son. Her son. He had been her hope. Her future. Her immortality. A bundle of smiles and tears and wonder. Newspaper articles never captured the essence of someone's being. What happened to Robbie's joy and Candace's strength? And who would remember them when their loved ones were gone?

The damp concrete smell permeated the observation room. Four chairs were lined up behind the one-way mirror, and through it was a room little wider than a hallway where, for the last half hour, men and boys had paraded in front of her, holding numbers to their chests as if they were prizes in a raffle.

Bellin sat beside her, so close she could feel the warmth of his arm next to hers. McCary stood behind them, hands on her hips, frowning at the scene below. The room was cold; the air-conditioning on high. Rena wished she had coffee, tea, something hot to keep her hands warm.

None of the people in the lineup bore more than a casual resemblance to the boy she had seen. All were tall, thin, and athletic. All had dark hair and narrow features. But none of them had the eyes or the cruel cut to the lip. After the third group, she found herself questioning her own memory. She closed her eyes for a moment, and his image rose again in her mind, and she knew she had not seen him. She asked them to continue.

Finally the room below was empty. Bellin sighed and leaned back. "That's it," he said.

"That's it?" she repeated, knowing it sounded stupid but unable to help herself. She had thought it would be so easy. "Was that the entire swim team?"

"Plus," he said.

"Maybe he was just someone associated with the team," associated with the team," McCary said.

Rena shook her head. Of that she was certain. "They don't allow anyone but the swim team in the pool area during practice. Even when people show up early for a meet, they have to stay in the bleachers." They had to have missed someone. Had to.

"We used the coach's year roster and asked him to add names to it if he had to. He didn't. This is the team," Bellin said.

"Are you sure the boy was on the team?" McCary asked.

"I don't know." Rena pressed her hands to her forehead. "He was there one afternoon when the team was there. He wouldn't have been in the pool area if he wasn't on the team."

"But you were," Bellin said.

She shook her head. "I was in the Jacuzzi. They let people stay in the Jacuzzi all day."

"He was there, then," Bellin said, more to McCary than to Rena. "Someone else is bound to remember him."

A headache had built behind Rena's eyes. She wanted the boy

caught. She wanted to go back to the pool, to her quiet, dull life. "Are they protecting him?"

"I don't know," Bellin said.

"I should have brought Sasha's yearbook," McCary said. "Do you mind if I bring it by tonight?"

Rena smiled weakly. "I have nothing better to do."

Rena made a pot of coffee and paced nervously, straightening as she moved. She found it more difficult to have an expected guest than an unexpected guest. She had spent the last half hour wondering what McCary would think of the apartment.

Her stereo still didn't work properly so the only music came from the clock radio she kept in the kitchen, but the music sounded so tinny she shut it off. She almost turned on the television before she realized that any sound would be intrusive.

The kitchen smelled of French Roast and chocolate chip cookies. She hadn't baked since Robbie died. The pain shrink would probably say it was good that she was reverting to old habits, but she wasn't so sure. She would rather have had a swim at the rec center, followed by an evening alone with a book. Anything but this.

At the hum of a car pulling up, she froze. Then the car door slammed, and she hovered near her front door like a girl about to meet a blind date. When the bell rang, she had to count to ten before opening the door so she wouldn't seem too eager.

Detective Bellin stood before her, his white shirt open at the collar, his hair loose and curling around his forehead, the yearbook held casually against his thigh. "Detective McCary couldn't make it," he said. "Problems at home."

Rena swallowed back an odd disappointment. She liked McCary, hoped they would be able to talk about more than murder over the coffee and cookies she had made. "Nothing serious, I hope," she said.

He shrugged. "Her daughter hasn't been doing too well since the murder. It doesn't help to have a mom who is a cop."

"I should think it would," Rena said. "Protection and all."

"Who protects a cop's family," he asked, "while the cop is protecting the city?"

She had no answer to that except to stand away from the door and let him in. He wore a different pair of faded jeans with cowboy boots peeking out beneath. His hair was still damp on the ends. He had been home to change before he came to see her.

"Smells good in here," he said.

"I made some cookies. Chocolate chip. You want some?"

"And coffee," he said. "The good stuff." He smiled, and it wiped away all the lines, the hurts, the age, hidden in his face. For the first time she noticed him as a handsome man, and the realization made her step away.

"I have cups out in the kitchen. I figured we could sit at the table—"

"Good idea." He waited for her to lead him there, even though he knew the way. She went immediately to the counter to remove the plastic wrap covering the cookies. Her hands were shaking so badly she could hardly get it off, but he didn't offer to help and for that she was grateful. She didn't want to seem weak in front of him. She didn't want to seem weak in front of anyone.

"You didn't have to come out here," she said. "I could have gone to the station."

"I know."

She crinkled the plastic wrap and tossed it in the garbage under the sink. Then she leaned against the counter, unable to look at him.

"You don't have to take care of me," she said.

She wasn't sure how she wanted him to answer. A quick denial would have confirmed her suspicions, and no one answered an accusation like hers with the truth. His silence, though, was unexpected.

The clatter of mugs on the Formica was the only sound in the room. She gripped the handle of the coffeepot firmly, hoping her hand wouldn't slip and make her regret her words. The coffee poured smoothly, its rich steam coating her face. She took his mug to him, cradling it in both hands, and set it gently before him.

"Is that what you think I'm doing?" he said, putting her back on the defensive.

She put the sugar and cream in front of him, then returned to the counter for the cookies. The fragile plate felt awkward in her hands, but she didn't drop it. She set it down carefully and got her own mug before joining him.

Without saying a word, she grabbed the yearbook from the chair he had placed it on and put it beside her mug. The yearbook was covered in pale-blue leather with the school's emblem and name embossed in gold. The effect was a washed-out, clearly unprofessional choice of some hapless yearbook staff. The scent of new leather and fresh ink mixed with the coffee. She opened it to the index, found the page with the swim team, and stared at the picture.

She had seen all those faces. Young boys with their scrawny bodies, looking defiantly at the camera. They wore red briefs as swimsuits, a color that made most of them appear even more pale and sickly. All the boys had been scattered through the afternoon's lineup. She read the caption underneath and realized that the whole team was in the shot. How odd. She really had thought she understood the rules about pool attendance.

"Not there?" Bellin asked her.

"He's not in the official photograph," she said.

She studied the others on the page: the boys hovering over the pool, a boy in goggles with his head shaved coming out of the water, a series of slightly arched bodies caught in the opening dive. He wasn't in any of them.

She closed the book and started over, looking at the whole thing page by page, trying to ignore the loopy, unformed writing of McCary's daughter's friends, the banal sentiments that the girl probably treasured. She stopped only when she saw Candace Walker's signature at the end of a long page of writing covering several school photos.

To the First Runner Up: Got to work a little harder, friend. Don't want to go through life always a bridesmaid. Seri-

ously, thanks for covering. Couldn't've done it without you.
Too bad you're not going to State. I can use the competition.
—Candace

"Charming, huh?" Bellin said.

Rena nodded. She remembered that bitchy friendliness that wasn't really friendly at all. She had probably participated in it willingly when she had been in high school, and she still saw it at the pool among the girls' swim team. "What does she mean by covering?"

"I don't know," Bellin said, "and neither does McCary. Her daughter says it has to do with missing cheerleading practice, but McCary's not sure. She's working on it."

"Anyone thought to get Candace's yearbook?" Rena asked.

He smiled and took a cookie off the plate, as if her suggestion pleased him. "No," he said and took a bite, making a production out of enjoying that first small taste. She ignored him and went back to the book.

Nothing for pages. She thought it odd that all yearbooks looked the same. The fashions changed, but the faces never did. It was almost as if she were looking at pictures of her friends in 1990's garb. About twenty pages from the end, she stopped and frowned at a photograph in the corner of the girls' swim team page. Bellin had gotten up to get himself another mug of coffee. She took the moment of privacy to stare at the face, eyes burning at her as they had that afternoon in the Jacuzzi.

"That's him," she said, and pointed. She wouldn't put her finger on the page. To touch his photograph seemed too personal and closer than she ever wanted to get to him again.

Bellin stood behind her, his head just above her shoulder, his hands spread on the table around her, as if he were protecting her back while staring at the picture. "Different color trunks," he said.

And he was right. The boy, unnamed in the caption, was standing beside the diving board, talking with someone hidden by the metal rails. His trunks were blue and fit so snugly that she could see the bulge outlined by the light. A girl, the only person credited in the photo, was doing a cannonball off the high board, her hair streaming above her head.

"Another team?" she asked.

"Could be," he said. "At least we know what he looks like now." He patted her on the shoulder. "We'll find him."

"Good." His words took a tension she didn't even know she carried out of her body. She glanced at him, then returned her attention to the book, determined to see if the boy appeared in the last few pages. He did not.

When she finished, she slid the yearbook back to him. "What else do you need from me? Do you want me to testify?"

"Later." He had returned to his chair, leaving her back cold. His hands were wrapped around his steaming coffee mug, and most of the cookies were gone from the plate. "Another lineup, though. You are planning to stay in town?"

His question had been routine, not intrusive. She made herself speak lightly. "Have nowhere else to go."

He nodded, then his gaze met hers. He studied her for a moment, his eyes moving as they took in her face. Finally he said, "I don't think you need taking care of, you know. I think you're one of the strongest women I've ever met." Then he grinned as if to take the intimacy from his words. He grabbed another cookie and waved it at her. "Thanks for dinner."

"That's dinner?" she asked, but he was already in the living room and pretending he didn't hear. She took the yearbook to him and watched as he let himself out. The drama was over. The diversion in a life of sameness was gone. She was now a woman cursed with another nightmare, and a vague sense of loss.

Rena knew she was dreaming because she still had a sense of her body, curled on its left side, warm and snug in her queen-size bed. But part of the warmth came from the Jacuzzi outside the swimming pool at the rec center, the swirling water caressing her tired limbs. In the dream, it was February—cold, drizzly February, her favorite time in the hot water. She sat with her back to the pool, and lifted her face to the rain, her body warm and her head cool. Only there did she really feel alive.

She didn't hear the door, but the splash made her look up. A boy, teenage thin with corded muscles running along his arms and his chest, had dropped a black practice brick into the hot tub. His dark eyes glittered as he looked at her, his full lips twisted into a smirk.

Think anyone wants to look at you, bitch?

The words reverberated in her head. She felt the warm bed and willed herself to open her eyes. But she couldn't. She had to hear this, to remember, to see if he had given her a clue.

I should really cut your face to match so you never go out in public. Freaks like you are too ugly to live.

He left the hot tub, turned his back as he headed for the glass door. She put her feet on the brick and thought of picking it up, or hurling it at him, and then he stopped as if he had read her mind.

Don't ever show your deformed self around me again, bitch. You got that?

She didn't move. Her entire body was trembling, but she didn't move. He pulled open the door, letting out the sound of a splash and the roar of the crowd. Then the door closed, leaving her in silence with the memory of his words.

The rain streamed down her face, at once hot and cold, fresh and salty. She sat out there until she grew light-headed from the heat. Then she grabbed her towel, and walked around the building to enter from the front so she wouldn't see him, wouldn't hear his deep voice ever again.

But it echoed in her dreams. Her dreams. This time she struggled and surfaced, her breath catching in her throat. If he had hated her so much, why hadn't he hurt her? He had threatened to cut her.

The darkness seemed to carry his face. Slender, menacing, it formed and re-formed on the ceiling, against the windows, over the nightstand. With a shaking hand, she turned on the light and basked in its warm glow. Her bedroom, done in neutrals, the off-white walls unadorned, seemed reassuringly familiar. He was only a dream, but the dream was as close as sleep.

She got up and went into the kitchen, her feet cold on the tile floor. The kitchen still smelled faintly of cookies and coffee, reassuring smells, morning smells, family smells. She sank in her chair and put her face in her scarred hands. Her life would never be normal. She had to accept that, had to accept accidents that destroyed everything she loved and viciousness that tainted places where she felt safe.

A dream image passed before her closed eyelids, a cheering crowd. She brought her head up. There had been a meet that day. He didn't belong to the local team. He had been part of the visiting team, hence the different trunks. And if she tried, she could probably remember the day, and find out who he really was.

Excitement rose in her chest, and she had to pace to keep from feeling overwhelmed. February gray—an early meet, before Valentine's Day because the roses on the back fence which had bloomed on Valentine's Day weren't even budding yet.

Two weeks of newspapers. Something to do. If she found nothing, she wouldn't contact Bellin or waste his time. But if she found something . . .

If she found something, she might be able to show that young punk that even freaks had a right to live.

The public library was a single story red brick building that took up less than half a city block. Branch libraries in the Midwest were double the size of this town's only library. She had always dismissed it, thinking a place this tiny wasn't worth her time. Since she had extra money and nothing to spend it on, she bought books at the local chain stores where the turnover was so great no one had a chance to remember her.

When she walked through the door, therefore, she was unprepared for the smell of processed air, dust, and old books. A wave of nostalgia crashed over her, quicker than she could stop, and for a moment Robbie's hand was in her own and Robbie's voice rose over the din, asking for the story lady. Her own rose with his, shushing him, reminding him that libraries were quiet places.

She had to lean against the hardcover fiction shelf (A—Ca) to catch her breath, half wishing the ghostly presence would remain, half wishing she would never hear from him again. The loneliness she felt after his visits was almost more than she could bear.

But she had a mission, a purpose, for the first time in months. She swallowed hard and made herself stand, going forward when all she wanted to do was run.

No one had noticed her. Even though it was a Monday afternoon, the library was full. Adults filled the chairs at the tables, browsed the shelves, stood in line in front of the desk. Two women briskly stamped books and then ran them through the demagnetizing machine, while one elderly woman assigned library cards. Rena pushed her hair off her face. She asked the elderly woman where the microfilm was, and had to follow a wrinkled finger to the far back corner.

The card catalogue had been replaced, probably to save space, and patrons were lined up to use the only computer terminal. She passed the stacks of phone books and current magazines and entered a tiny, musty room that smelled of oil and dust. Four microfilm machines sat in the corner. One had a hand-lettered sign that read OUT OF ORDER.

She looked in the drawer for the local paper and found that her memory served: the first half of the year was already on film, which made sense in a library this small. She wound the brittle film through the old-fashioned machine, wondering why no one had bothered to computerize this, and turned the knob until she reached the sports section for the first part of February.

It didn't take her long to find the meet. The paper had it all, a list of the students who worked on the meet in the small announcement on Thursday, and local coverage on Friday. A photograph accompanied Friday's story, and she caught a glimpse of his blurry back, made recognizable by the fact that he was heading out the glass doors to the Jacuzzi. To harass her.

He was from Seavy Village, a coastal town just north of Florence. The team's members were listed; only one lost his race, by a mere two-tenths of a second. The loser's name was John Garnsey.

Two-tenths of a second. It all made a sad, pathetic kind of sense to her now. She put the heel of her hand against her eyes and closed them. Two-tenths of a second. The time it took to skip the median and crash into oncoming traffic. The time it took to say "I'm sorry" to the only survivor, burned, covered in glass, and unable to cry because there was no fluid left in her body. The time it took to smell bourbon on the breath.

She gave a shaky little sigh and went outside. The air was cool and the sun hidden behind a cloud. The bus wasn't due for fifteen minutes. She leaned against the bus stand and wished she could think of nothing.

Rena explained it to Bellin on the phone while she sat on her comfortable couch, the receiver cradled between her shoulder and ear. She had called him because she could not face him. Her voice remained calm, but her body shook as she told him her theory.

It seemed both obvious and hideous now. Candace Walker had run the timer on John Garnsey's race. She had clocked him two-tenths of a second shy. And in his righteous self-centeredness, he had believed that she erred. For he couldn't believe he would fail. Someone else had to be to blame.

The loss must have cost him something. Reputation. The respect of his teammates. Something. Enough to cause him to come back and check the lifeguard board. Enough to make him return a third time and kill her, not caring that Rena was in the pool because Rena wasn't human.

She choked out the last phrase, the part about not being human, and then said nothing. The silence echoed in the phone lines, and for a moment she thought Bellin didn't believe her. Then he said, "Excellent work. I'll tell McCary, and we'll contact the authorities in Seavy Village."

His praise shook her more than the crime did. She clasped her hands tightly together, running her thumbs along her scars to keep herself focused.

"Detective?" she said, her voice calm again. "I'd like to see him when you bring him in."

"You will," Bellin said. "We'll need to do another lineup."

They put him in the third set of men and boys, second from the end. Rena sat in the hard plastic chair and leaned toward the one-way glass, clutching the neck of her sweater with one hand, the edge of the chair with the other.

John Garnsey appeared to be staring right at her. He wore a Beastie Boys T-shirt and tight bluejeans and held his number just above his belt buckle as if he was ashamed to hold it.

Think anyone wants to look at you, bitch?

She took a deep breath to wipe the sound of his voice from her memory. As she did, she saw him in a quick, sideways, chlorine-filled glance, gesturing as he argued with Candace Walker on the last afternoon of her life.

"That's him," she said. "Number two."

"You sure?" Bellin asked, his tone cautious.

She turned, wondering why he doubted her. Both he and McCary were watching her, their expressions flat and unreadable. She glanced back at the boy. She held his life in her hands, as she had once held Robbie's. Only she had grabbed Robbie too late.

Freaks like you are too ugly to live.

She shivered. Once. The air-conditioning was too high. Even the sweater she had brought to compensate didn't help. "That's him," she said again. "I'm sure."

Beside her, Bellin exhaled. "Looks like we got a case," he said to McCary.

She nodded, then reached forward and squeezed Rena's hand. "Good work," she whispered. "I'll take care of this," she said to Bellin, and left the observation booth.

Rena was shaking. Her fingernails had turned blue. "Tell me," she said, still staring at the boy's face, "that he dated her. Tell me that she two-timed him or that she beat up his sister."

Bellin put his hands on his knees as if he were bracing himself to speak. "He had never lost a race before." His words were soft. "At least not in high school. Lost once in junior high and came charging out of the water at the timer, but the coach held him back. He was smaller then."

The car was hot, hot, too hot as she reached for Robbie. His eyes were open, his mouth filled with blood. Dennis was still in the driver's seat, twisted toward the back as, in the last moment of his life, he, too, tried to save his son. Rena took a quick gasp of burning air, a sharp "hah!" as her heart snapped—

From below, Garnsey stared at the wall as if he saw her, as if he knew she was accusing him.

"Does he know what he did? Does he understand?"

And as the paramedics pulled her away from the fireball, the glass rain, she saw a form lurch toward her in the red-gold light. His suit was silk and rumpled, his hair mussed where he had run his hand through it. "I'm sorry, lady," he said, the bourbon on his breath so strong she nearly gagged. "But you shoulda steered outa the way . . ."

"People like him," Bellin said, "don't believe anyone else exists."

She put her hand over her heart as if she could ease the ache. Her palm was warm, but not warm enough. Never warm enough.

"We'll need you to testify," Bellin said.

Then she looked at him, really looked at him. The fluorescent light took the youth from his face and accented the tiny white scars on his chin and cheeks. The crow's-feet near his eyes were deep, and the area around his mouth showed that he would be wearing sorrow lines as he grew older.

"I'll testify," she said. She could be strong for that.

One by one, the men filed out of the room below. Garnsey had an athlete's gait, a confidence that belied the emptiness beneath it. She didn't understand it. If she could face a drunken man who had slaughtered her family, if she could live every day alone with only scars and memories, then how could that boy kill over the loss of a single race? "How do you face the world every day, knowing that there are people like that boy in it?"

Bellin stood and placed his hand on her shoulder. She could see his face reflected in the glass, a wavery ghost over an empty room. "It's hard," he said. "But I find my hope when I meet people like you."

The warmth of his hand had penetrated her sweater, like a small, hot sun sending its heat to damaged places within. She leaned her unscarred cheek against his work-roughened knuckles.

Time to start taking risks again, to step out of the shadow of a lurching, drunken man in a rumpled silk suit.

"I owe you a real dinner, detective," she said.

"Joel," he said, reminding her of the warmth he had shown that first afternoon warmth that she hadn't realized until now had saved her.

"Joel," she said, and smiled.

THE MAN KALI VISITED

by Janice Law

I am at the inquest and a sallow-faced man with short hair and a blue striped suit is warning me to tell the truth, the whole truth, and nothing but the truth and asking me to state my name and occupation. I am stumbling over my words and forgetting American idioms and remembering irrelevant slang from Bombay because I am feeling hopelessly and irredeemably foreign. Not only is the "truth" in this matter slippery and elusive, but the court does not seem ready for the "whole truth"; and "nothing but the truth" may be impossible.

"My name is Neena Dasgupta and I am office manager and secretary to the publisher of *Skin* magazine." *Skin* magazine runs photographs of pretty women with no clothes on and stories about sexy women by young men of minimal talent and maximal imagination. Its publisher, Mr. A, was my employer and my salvation. Thanks to *Skin* magazine, I went from being the discarded wife of an ambitious graduate student to an independent woman on a good salary.

"Will you tell the court where you were on the afternoon of September 9, 1993?"

"I was at the office of *Skin* magazine until five-thirty P.M." Very nice offices, too. I helped with the design. Modern and airy but with interesting colors, cinnabar, ochre, deep pink, and turquoise; colors of the subcontinent, colors for moments of nostalgia and reflection.

"Can you describe that afternoon for the court?"

"It was a most ordinary afternoon. We were laying out pages for the November issue, and I personally was getting Mr. A's schedule organized for the next few weeks."

What this means is planning everything for him, paying the bills, answering his correspondence, dealing with the lawyers, two ex-wives, his elderly mother, and his neurotic Doberman's veterinarian. Although insufficiently appreciated by the puritanical American public, my poor Mr. A was a creative person. He wanted to distill sex into pictures and to distill women into beauty. Perhaps those were wrong desires, yet from my point of view, they seemed quite traditional. Our temple sculptors have been turning naked men and women into images for centuries. But in this new and different climate, it is natural for people to keep their clothing on. And so instead of grottoes and temples full of beautiful sculptures and paintings, we have *Skin* magazine which pays me, as I have mentioned, very well to be keeping Mr. A's schedule straight and seeing that his printers are paid and checking that all models are old enough or are accompanied with permission forms signed by their mothers.

" 'Mr. A' is Mr. James Rembrandt Addison?"

"That is correct."

"And Mr. Addison was in the office that afternoon?"

This is, for anyone who knew Mr. A, a foolish question. Where else would he be? *Skin* magazine was life as he was wanting to live it, where all women are beautiful and sympathetic, all men are attractive and successful, and the dull stretches and sharp edges of life are covered by a mist of desire. This was childish, of course, but we are all as childish as we can manage. What is sad is that we cannot contrive to be children forever, not even in fantasy.

That is what I have learned from this matter, but I do not think the judge wishes to hear my ideas. He is an elderly man with a red face and white hair. I am thinking that he has grown old listening and judging, which must be a so tiring life. I am guessing that he will not want complications in the simple case of a fatal heart attack.

That is definitely how Mr. A died. No "foul play" of the or-

dinary sort. He was completely alone, I am sure. Of course I
would willingly have stayed with him and supported him in the
face of immaterial, as of material, threat, but he would not permit
that. To let me stay would have been to acknowledge the situation, the implications, the dangers, all of which were complicated,
elusive, and unusual.

I decide not to attempt this part of "the truth." Instead, I say,
"He went out jogging at one as usual and he had a reservation
for lunch at one forty-five at La Caricole. He returned at two
forty-five and worked on slides and picture selection until five.
Mr. A always had the final say on pictures."

"The office closes at five?"

"Yes, but Mr. A often worked later and I sometimes stayed
late, too, if there was a shoot scheduled."

"Why was that?"

"Mr. A, Mr. Addison, was always very proper."

There is laughter in the court and the judge is displeased. You
are seeing here an illustration of my point: the"whole truth" is
not required because it is not welcome. But Mr. A, who took
sexy photos and published soft porn, never told a dirty joke, fon-
dled a model, or made raunchy remarks. He could be very sweet,
and all his sexual energy was going into his pictures. Which were
always of a perfect woman in a perfect situation. Which were
pictures. Only. If you are understanding my point.

"Please go on, Ms. Dasgupta."

But I must be careful. I am tending to drift off into the realm
of "whole truth," which is dangerous. I must stick to "nothing
but the truth," which I like because it tells what I must leave out
without committing me to exactly what must be put in. "Some
of our younger models have been known to lie about their ages,"
I say. "Mr. Addison always felt it important in uncertain cases
to have an older woman in the studio."

"Yourself."

"Yes. All the other staff are very young and neither Toby nor
Mark, the assistant photographers, would have been quite suitable." Most unsuitable, in fact. When I am at a shoot, I wear my
large gold earrings and drape a scarf over my head and carry a

clipboard and see that they sign everything in sight: permissions, waivers, statement of age, contract, model's agreement, et cetera, et cetera. We have never had any trouble.

"And what time did you leave on the evening of the ninth?"

"I wanted to finish up some correspondence, and I was still working at ten to six when Mr. A asked me to leave."

"He asked you to leave?"

"He said there was no need for me to stay." Of course, I had been intending to stay; the correspondence was just an excuse. I believed that she was coming and I was afraid for him. But that, too, is an unpalatable "whole truth." For Mr. A, too. Or perhaps it was just too late for him. Maybe it was too late from the first day, the first day she arrived at the office.

"And what sort of mood was he in?"

"He was looking forward to shooting a favorite model. I think he said she was scheduled for six-thirty."

"Do you know who she was?"

Now here is a difficulty, a case where the "whole truth" and "nothing but the truth" are in conflict. "Nothing but the truth" is obviously safest, and I hear myself say, "I believe it was to be Ms. Kal."

"You believe?"

"That was the name written in his calendar, yes."

"The mysterious Ms. Maria Kal. The Ms. Kal with no known address."

The judge is again displeased. He feels that it is unbusinesslike that we have no address for her. I could explain that manifestations rarely have addresses in the modern sense, although they may have localities. Indeed they may have localities. Ms. Kal's, I think, is around our business. I think she was attracted. And why should that be surprising? For millenniums we have tried to attract spiritual forces: flowers, incense, sacrifices, dances, songs, prayers, rituals spiritual and sexual. We call the forces and sometimes they come. But they do not leave an address; they do not present Social Security cards or sign waivers or fill out W-2 forms. They come, like Ms. Kal, invoked but unbidden, and in surprising form.

It was late, I remember. Six P.M. or maybe six-thirty. The July issue had just been sent to the press, and Mr. A had been working, working at the last minute as he always does, checking this, changing that, driving the retouchers mad with his demands for perfection. And I am, of course, reassuring him and calming them and closing doors when tempers are getting high and talking to the printer and being, as Mr. A is always telling me, indispensable. So we are at six-fifteen P.M., say, on that June evening, the evening of the solstice, the longest day, the shortest night, a significant day with the warm breezes, the perfect sky. Toby and Mark have gone home; Lydia has made the last coffee of the afternoon; the building's cleaners are running vacuums and polishers in the halls. I am tidying up and getting my purse ready to go when there is a knocking at the locked office door.

I am thinking to ignore it and then it comes again and, such ill luck!, I open the door. There is Ms. Kal as I saw her: a handsome woman of indeterminate age. Older by ten years than our models, though how old I can't say. Perfect skin, wonderful figure, magnificent hair, but mature eyes. Our models tend to be perfect but half formed, all the better to take on the suggestions of the photographer, to be the receptacle of fantasy and desire. In contrast, Ms. Kal was mentally fully formed, her intellect aged and bottled in bond like the premium whisky that advertises in *Skin*. Thirty? Maybe, though forty was not out of the question. Way, way too old and yet impressive! Perfect in her own way, splendid black hair, pale caramel skin, green eyes: a northern princess carrying the blood of warriors and maharajahs or the most wonderful nautch dancer ever imagined.

She would see Mr. A. I am explaining that he is so busy, so tired, that our models are booked so far in advance and only through certain reputable and famous agencies. And she is smiling, smiling without showing her teeth, which I know will be sharp, and making little impatient gestures like a fine horse, and walking toward Mr. A's office and, before I can stop her, putting her head in and calling him out. I am hoping, hoping, he will send her on her way. But instead, he makes a little sound as if he's just sucked in his breath—and hers with it. "Come in," he says. "Come in. I've been waiting for you." I am feeling very cold because this is not true in the business sense: no appointment, no phone calls, no letters, no contacts. So he can only mean that she is the one he has been waiting to shoot; she is the one who is looking exactly right with no retouching; she is desire and sex and woman all distilled and perfect.

"You have no address for this woman?" the judge asks again.

"Alas, no. I did not wish to interrupt their first conversation, and she was never on the books."

She came, she went. Always late, always at the last second, always on the spur of the moment. A curious and vivid phrase, that and so right for her. Mr. A would prepare to work late, to shoot her picture into the wee hours, to work till dawn in the darkroom—and then to sulk all day the next day because he had failed. There was always something wrong with the film, with the light with the always so mysterious inner workings of the camera. Despite an obsessive, heartbreaking persistence, Mr. A never did succeed in getting a usable picture of the absolutely unique Ms. Kal.

"But she did come to the office more than once?"

"I only saw her once. It was my understanding she came several times." This, I am thinking, is safe to say. And quite true.

The judge shakes his head. He is still trying to make sense of a senseless situation. "I have a description given by Mr. Toby Bell one of the assistant photographers on the magazine. He has testified that he saw Ms. Kal one night when he returned to pick up a camera which he had left on his desk. He describes her, if you remember, Ms. Dasgupta, as slim, blonde, extremely pretty, and about seventeen years old."

"That is not the woman I saw. And Mr. A, as I have explained would not have been photographing a young woman of 'about seventeen' alone in the studio at night."

"On the other hand, your co-worker, Penny Rohmer, may have seen her leaving the offices. Ms. Rohmer describes a fashionably dressed African-American with very short hair."

"I do not remember any such model."

The judge is not pleased with my memory. As the keeper of

the calendar, I should be more accurate, more precise. I should have the full name and address for Ms. Kal and a consistent description of her. I shrug and draw my scarf around my shoulders. I am not venturing into the "whole truth." I have my green card but not my final papers. I am a "resident alien" who must be mature and logical, not a tabloid-crazed citizen who can safely spot Elvis or go joyriding with Martians.

"Now, on the night in question, did you see Ms. Kal—or whoever the model was—arrive?"

"No, I did not. Though I knew she was coming, though I feared the consequences. Mr. A's ambition had become an obsession. He was dropping all his other work, even neglecting his true and only love, the magazine; he was forgetting the joys of fantasy and letting Mark and Toby shoot the November photo spreads. A great mistake, I was reckoning. They lacked Mr. A's so fatal imagination; they lacked his style and flair. But he could think of nothing else but Ms. Kal. Would she return? Could he succeed? Her photos would be the crown of his career, the artistic summit of his ambitions, absolutely unprecedented and, of course, worth a fortune. Meanwhile, I was telling him that she was bad luck, a dangerous woman, a manifestation to be avoided at all costs. Poor Mr. A was alternately laughing at me and drinking bourbon straight out of the bottle in his darkroom.

"All right, Ms. Dasgupta, will you tell the court what happened when you arrived at the office the next morning."

I feel the tears in my eyes and begin to shake. I was truly very fond of Mr. A, and I am still uncertain whether I am under Ms. Kal's sentence or protection.

"The witness," the judge says, "can have a minute to compose herself." When I am composed, we go on.

"Just take it slowly, please, Ms. Dasgupta. What time did you arrive at *Skin* magazine?"

"About eight-forty. It depends on which bus I catch. Sometimes I am as early as eight-thirty and sometimes it is almost nine o'clock. I go in and do a little work and then I am opening the office at nine for the others." I could explain a good deal about the office routine, and I would like to do so. I could tell how I open up the shades on the west side and close the blinds on the east. How Lydia starts the coffee machine that wheezes and groans so that Toby and Mark are making rude remarks. How I turn on my desk radio to the classical station and listen to Monteverdi or Bach, so soothing, so regular. Instead, I must tell about seeing the red light above the darkroom door.

"This was unusual?"

"The red light is only on when someone is working in the darkroom. Mr. A worked at night but rarely until nine in the morning. And Toby and Mark did not have keys." But I was not thinking about Toby and Mark, I was thinking terrible thoughts and remembering terrible memories of the ignorant old village festivals for the goddess with their rivulets of blood and the smoking corpses of headless goats. The goddess of the dawn feeds on blood; the patroness of sex bears our death.

"Please continue," the judge says.

I am surprised to be in the big square courtroom with the so white walls, the green tinged lights, the brown seats. I had been in the office, our pretty airy office with the colors of the subcontinent, ochre, cinnabar, turquoise, and pink, knocking on the door of the darkroom, calling, imploring, begging, then warning that I must be opening the door, the sacred darkroom door never to be opened when its red light is on. I turn the knob, push the door, and blood-colored light washes over darkness. I see the shape on the floor and fumble for the switch and then, in an instant, I am seeing and understanding everything. Poor Mr. A, my benefactor, employer, and friend, is lying on the floor, his tongue out, his face a hideous mask of fear and horror, his bodily fluids mingling with puddles of developer and fix. I put my hand on his chest and touch his wrist and his jugular vein, but Mr. A has already been transformed, swept away on the great wheel of earthly illusion. Perhaps he is even now being reborn in Bombay or Brooklyn, screaming into life with all his old sorrows and pleasures forgotten.

I stand in the darkroom, knowing I must be calling the police and 911 and preparing to tell "the truth," "the whole truth," and "nothing but the truth." But first I am having a look around.

There are strips of film, developed film, hanging up against the light, and I can make out images of a nude woman of extraordinary beauty, images which were waiting, I think, only for me and which are fading now with unnatural rapidity, fading and twisting, and going back into the chaos of all things before "truth" and "whole truth" and "nothing but the truth" got separated and distinguished from lies and untruth and indeterminacy.

On the floor lies a single print, the first, perhaps, of the negatives Mr. A had been developing, the print that would have crowned his career and made his fortune. I pick it up carefully because it has lain in the water and chemicals and is creased and stained. I turn it over and even though I am expecting the worst, I am frightened. The voluptuous Ms. Kal had been transformed into the dark goddess with her long red tongue, her necklace of skulls, her girdle of human hands, her black and terrible body, at once the womb and tomb for every thing living now and in the future, through every incarnation.

In the windowless courtroom, I tell the judge "nothing but the truth": how I found Mr. A, how I screamed, how I ran out to call 911.

"Now, Ms. Dasgupta, I know this is difficult for you, but these next questions are very important. Were there any photographs?"

I am so glad he has asked me something I can answer honestly. There was *one* photograph, which now resides wrapped in a piece of fine silk under a garland of flowers in my bedroom. The photo I managed to secrete out of the office under the noses of the so busy crime scene technicians, investigating officers, coroner, and photographer. But there were other *photographs* and I am pleased to say, "Oh, yes. There were photographs of Everly Chique for the November issue. They were hanging up to dry and some of her slides were still on the light table."

"Ms. Chique is employed by Hot Stuff Videos, Inc., I believe."

"Ms. Chique has extensive video credits, yes. She is scheduled to appear in our Skin Flicks feature for November."

"According to the office records, these photos were taken on September sixth and seventh. Is that correct?"

"That is correct. Toby was shooting those. He is still learning, but Ms. Chique is very experienced with photo sessions."

"Now I want to be clear about this. There were no other photographs, negatives, roles of film, in the darkroom?"

"Oh, yes, sir. As I am sure the police have been reporting. Some blank negatives, some torn-up papers. Nothing usable, alas, and all the time poor Mr. A lying dead on the floor."

"The police on the scene described him as lying in a pool of liquid with several flat plastic pans around him. How does that fit with your recollection?"

"It is fitting perfectly. He had obviously been working developing something. Perhaps he was discarding the results. Perhaps there was a flaw in the film. I am thinking a roll of film had not come out."

"Did you remove anything at all from the darkroom, Ms. Dasgupta?"

"No, I did not." Now I am lying. You see how treacherously one slips from a decent approximation of the truth to outright lies? But what should I say? That I removed the photograph that killed Mr. A, a now fading but still dangerous representation of the goddess whom I know as Kali and whom Mr. A knew as Ms. Kal? That would be the "whole truth," but what good would it do us? I am thinking "nothing but the truth" with one exception is what I will be sticking with.

"And did you take anything into the darkroom, Ms. Dasgupta?"

"Some flowers. For the dead." It is appropriate to be ending with truth and a lie. Or with a truth that is not the "whole truth." They understand flowers for the dead. That is very appropriate and how often have I been sending expensive flowers to the funeral service of this person or that for Mr. A. But they might not comprehend flowers for the cruel goddess, who may be lonely in this cold and alien land, who may yet visit me.

Now the judge is rebuking me for tampering with the crime scene, though my actions were understandable and, he believes, innocent. I sense it will be all right. I will keep my green card; I will get my final papers. I must be, I think now, under the protection of the goddess, for he is saying, "Thank you, Ms. Dasgupta. That will be all," and I am stepping down from the witness stand.

L.S. SMOOT MEMORIAL LIBRARY

3 1150 1001 2822 8

F   Women of mystery
Wom   III

WITHDRAWN

L. E. SMOOT MEMORIAL LIBRARY
KING GEORGE, VA. 22485

GAYLORD R

L. E. SMOOT MEMORIAL LIBRARY
KING GEORGE, VA. 22485